Worse Than Dead

Cal Brett

Copyright © 2019 Cal Brett
All rights reserved.
ISBN: 978-1-7347226-0-4

DEDICATION

For my grandmother, Eunice, who told us the scary stories and inspired us to believe in things that go bump in the night.

COVER ART
Kim May-Ohara

ACKNOWLEDGEMENTS

Many thanks to my family and friends who inspired, supported, critiqued, nagged and even those who told me it could not be done. To my beta readers and editors, I am eternally grateful.

Special thanks to the writers who inspired me with their work and honored me (the new kid on the block) with their support:

- **Ryan C. Thomas** – author of Hissers, The Summer I Died, Born to Bleed, Bugboy and many other books that will terrify and enthrall.

- **Tyler Barrett** – author of the What Remains series. Barrett has a great spin on zompocalypse fiction that will keep you on the edge of your seat.

If you enjoy **Worse Than Dead,** I encourage you to pick up any of their books, available at Amazon of course, for a good scare!

Contents

CHAPTER 1 1
CHAPTER 2 9
CHAPTER 3 19
CHAPTER 4 28
CHAPTER 5 35
CHAPTER 6 42
CHAPTER 7 52
CHAPTER 8 63
CHAPTER 9 73
CHAPTER 10 83
CHAPTER 11 94
CHAPTER 12 98
CHAPTER 13 109
CHAPTER 14 120
CHAPTER 15 130
CHAPTER 16 140
CHAPTER 17 148
CHAPTER 18 157
CHAPTER 19 168
CHAPTER 20 181
CHAPTER 21 192
CHAPTER 22 201
CHAPTER 23 212
CHAPTER 24 224
CHAPTER 25 234
CHAPTER 26 241
CHAPTER 27 249
CHAPTER 28 258
CHAPTER 29 265
CHAPTER 30 271
CHAPTER 31 283

Zombies weren't the worst thing about the apocalypse. As with the entirety of human civilization, people held that distinction. When the ravenous undead hordes rose up and ate their way through the best of human kind, they only left two types of people in their wake; the frightened, starving, skittish folk who scampered through the ruins, and the brutal takers who preyed on them. In some ways they were symbiotic. The meek were too scared to rise up and the strong coveted their power and violence such that they would not stoop to build anything more than what they had. There was no tomorrow. Only the day. Only the moment. Because in the world after the end of the great age, fortunes could and often did, change in an instant.

Chapter 1

It happened so fast Robbie didn't feel the pain of the punch until he was on the ground. The unexpected blow to his jaw sent him reeling. He bounced off the wall and fell to the hard floor with a flailing thump. An involuntary gasp escaped him as his lungs pushed the air out of his chest, leaving him breathless. Then the kicking started and loud grunts rattled out of him with each booted blow to his ribs, until he lay curled in the corner, in shock and pain, unable to move.

"God damn you make a lot of noise Robbie." Trent growled down at the beaten boy. "You need to shut up unless you want those dead fuckers coming up here for dinner."

"What the hell…?" Robbie groaned through swelling lips. He turned his head to look at the older man, standing nearby, flushed and out of breath from the exertion. "Why…?" he gasped weakly.

"Why?!" Trent chortled. "I've been hanging out with you two for weeks and you're still keeping all your stuff to yourself. That's why, dumb ass. Didn't offer to share. Not that I'd share, but that would have been polite. I need to know where you keep your supplies. I can't spend another day skulking around with you two pathetic losers. You're going to give me what I need... then, we can start to enjoy ourselves, or I can enjoy myself. You two..." He pointed "not so much."

Robbie took a shallow painful breath and was able to look beyond Trent to see Kelly on her knees beside him. He had his right hand tightly gripped in her hair and was holding her down facing the floor. She struggled against him, but he held her firmly.

"You fucker," she mewled flailing her arms at him, "leave us alone!"

"Oh don't worry, bitch," Trent replied looking down at her, "we will get some alone time soon. Now quit fighting or I'll beat the fuck out of you and cut up your little boyfriend."

"Damn it!" Kelly seethed angrily and lowered her arms in fuming submission.

"That's better, now we can get on with things," Trent gloated still catching his breath. Like a puppeteer, he used his fingers in her hair to raise her face towards Robbie.

"Oww!" she shrieked and Robbie caught the fright and anger on her voice.

"Quiet now." Trent chided. "Quiet... Let's not invite the stinkers up to our party. Now, let's all calm down and try to have some fun... wouldn't you like to have some fun?"

Trent made her head nod as if she were agreeing with him. She struggled ineffectually against him until he kicked her hard in her ribs. The wind was knocked from her and she collapsed onto her knees gasping.

"That's a good girl." Trent said looking back and forth between Kelly and Robbie, trying to determine if there was any fight left in them. Deciding there was none, he used his left hand to slide off his back-pack and pull out a large knife. "Remember this? It's my BFK. My 'Big Fucking Knife'. Don't fuck with me and I won't have to use it on you. Got it?!"

Robbie and Kelly both nodded. They had seen the knife before. It was Trent's primary tool and weapon. It was a heavy thing almost as big as a machete and he used it for everything from hacking up zombies, to breaking into houses, to cutting open cans of food. They both knew it was sharp and he was good at wielding it. Neither wanted to test him at the moment.

Trent shoved the knife into a sheath on the back of his belt and dug back into the pack. "Now see, I have something special for both of you," he said as he wrapped a thick, leather collar around Kelly's neck and tightened it up to fit snugly against her throat. Kelly's eyes widened as she felt the rough leather press against the skin of her neck.

He dug around in the pack again and came out with a chain which he attached to a loop on the back of the collar. There was a click as he snapped it into place. The chain looked like one that might be used to tether a large dog. Thick and strong, with small bells, it jingled lightly as Trent used it to pull Kelly backwards towards the wall across from Robbie. She coughed and pulled at the collar as her knees dragged across the floor.

The room they were in was once the fifth-floor utility room of a downtown office building. A narrow window provided a good view of the street below and enough light to see during the day. The glass was tinted so they could see out but no one, and no thing, could see in. The walls were lined with steel pipes running from the concrete floor up through the metal skeleton of a long gone dropped ceiling. The pipes, which once ran water and electricity to keep the building alive back when it was filled with busy 9 to 5 staff, now were simply cold, solid metal tubes.

Trent wrapped Kelly's chain high up on one of the heavy pipes and secured it with a padlock. She sat down and leaned back against the cool metal with an angry grunt, her eyes glared up at the lock that bound her in place. Trent admonished her to "stay" while he walked over to Robbie and locked him similarly to a pipe on the adjacent wall. The man who, until moments ago, they had thought to be a friend stepped back to admire his work.

Although still in pain from his beating, Robbie pushed himself up. He leaned back against the pipe and stared out through his long, dark bangs as he caught his breath. The ringing in his head began to subside and he was able to take stock of their situation. Kelly sat directly across from him but well out of reach. Trent was closer, between them, but still too far away to attempt a counterattack. He thought of his weapons but realized they were in his backpack which Trent had taken from him at some point.

Robbie felt like an idiot. They had only known Trent a few weeks, but they had begun to trust him. They had run into him while scavenging and hit it off. He had helped them clear a few houses of the dead, with that BFK of his, and having a third set of eyes and arms had proven helpful several times. These days it wasn't a good idea to trust people too quickly, but he seemed ok. He didn't complain about sharing what they found together and didn't push them on their supplies or where they were living. It had only been yesterday when they had shown him their hideout in the office building.

Robbie had spotted Trent staring at Kelly a few times, but love was rare in the apocalypse and if those two hit it off he wasn't going to get in the way. She had been his big brother's wife, but they hadn't seen Roy in over two years. Kelly did a pretty good job taking care of herself, him too since Roy went missing. So, if Trent stuck around for her it didn't seem like it would be a bad thing. But here it was... A bad thing.

"Ok," Trent said looking at Kelly with a wry smile, "you know what comes next."

Kelly shook her head and said, "Fuck you Trent!"

"Not yet, sweetie," Trent replied. "First, go ahead and strip down to your skivvies."

"Come on Trent," Robbie said angrily, "leave her alone!"

Trent looked over at Robbie and laughed, waving the knife at him. "Oh you thought I just meant her? No, no, no. You too, Bro. Strip out of those clothes. I better see some skin from you all in the next few minutes or I'll have to start cutting on someone."

"What the hell man?!" Robbie cried. "Why are you doing this!?"

"I said..." Trent kicked Robbie in the chest again, driving his big boot down hard into his ribs. "Take 'em off!"

"Robbie!" Kelly screamed.

"See, there you go, getting noisy again Kelly." Trent said turning to her, "I hope you don't bring the dead heads up here looking for a snack. Cause you guys are all tied up and it would just be a zombie buffet for them."

Trent moved as if to kick Robbie again, but Kelly stopped him "Wait! Ok. Ok. Don't hurt him."

"That's better," Trent said and stepped back from Robbie.

"It's ok Robbie," Kelly said, starting to fumble with the buttons on her jacket, "do what he says, and he won't hurt us. Right, Trent?"

"Yea, that's right." Trent replied with a snort. "Don't worry, Robbie. I ain't no pervert. I just figure you're less likely to run off or try anything stupid in your boxer shorts. Just don't try any hero shit and you'll be fine."

Neither Kelly nor Robbie believed him but there wasn't anything they could do about it at that moment. As distasteful as a stripping for this jerk would be, it wasn't the worst thing that could happen, Kelly thought. At least it might keep them alive long enough to figure out a way to escape from this lunatic. She saw Trent watching her and made a point not to look at him as she stretched up to pull down the coat's inner zipper. She remembered reading somewhere that it helped if you could personalize yourself with an attacker, but Trent had been hanging around for a month and probably knew them as well as anyone could. If he hadn't developed any sympathies for them by then it was doubtful anything she did in the next few minutes would change his mind.

She pulled the heavy, green Army jacket off her shoulders and drew her arms from its thick sleeves. It was late spring and the days were getting warmer but they never went outside without being fully covered. The long sleeve, red T-shirt she had on underneath was dark with sweat and stains. They seldom got fully undressed or changed clothes anymore. They lived, slept, and wore what they had until it was too damaged or they came across something better. She slid the jacket down behind her and used its bulk as a pillow against the hard metal pipe.

Kelly looked up at Trent who leaned against the windowsill, watching them. When his eyes met hers, he flashed a crooked smile and waved his knife at her. "Pick it up cupcake. No dawdling, I've got plans for later. You too, Robbie. Quit fucking around."

Kelly leaned forward as much as her restraints allowed and started unlacing her boots. It took a few minutes to get them untied and she had to tug forcefully to pull them off. She had been wearing them for weeks and it felt like the heavy leather hiking boots had molded to her feet. Her thick socks were slick with sweat and dirt and the smell made her pull her head back. Holding her boot at arm's length she got a whiff of her armpits too and winced at the harshness of her own body odor.

"Ugh!" Kelly scowled at the smell as she began pulling down her socks. "I don't suppose you're going to wash these clothes for us?"

"I said, shut up!" Trent charged quickly at her and slapped her hard across the face, "Shut up and strip off!"

The slap sent Kelly tumbling over with a muffled cry. Robbie lunged forward but the collar caught him. Trent spun around and pointed his knife at the younger man.

"I told you no hero shit!" Trent growled while waving his knife. "Now get to it or next time I swear, somebody loses a finger. I'm looking at you, Rob!"

"Ok, ok…" Kelly sobbed "I'm sorry. Please don't hurt us. I was only trying to…"

"Trying to buy some time?!" Trent raged back to her. "Trying to get me off guard?! Hoping I'll give you a chance to take my head off?!"

"No, no…," Kelly said her face still stinging, "I was…"

"Enough talk!" Trent growled. "Now get on with it or I start cutting things off you and I damn sure will leave some marks so you remember that shit! You too, fuck-head!" He shouted at Robbie as he walked back to the window and looked down at the street. "Shit, I think all this yelling has got them stirred up out there. I sure hope they don't figure out we're up here and come looking for lunch."

Robbie kneeled down at the end of his tether with his attention entirely on Kelly who lay curled up on the floor across from him. In spite of the older man's warnings he was not worried about the zombies getting in. The first floor of the building was a pharmacy and medical supply store with brick walls and narrow windows well above eye level. That's why they had chosen this place. Kelly and he had pulled down the metal security doors to cover the glass on the front entrance. The back door was reinforced steel and he knew it was securely locked. Even if they got in they would need to get through another locked door in the back leading to a short hallway with some elevators and stairs. They had blocked all that off from the inside.

The only practical way in was by climbing up onto a dumpster in the alley and jumping up to the fire escape ladder. All that took way more agility than any zombie could manage, any zombie they had seen anyway. A few years ago, nobody had ever seen dead people come back to life, go berserk and start killing the living. Who knew what would happen next. Anything was possible.

His eyes met Kelly's as she sat back up. A red blotch marked the spot on her cheek where she had been hit. She looked at him and mouthed "I'm ok," but she was clearly shaken. Her hands quaked as she reached back down and continued removing her heavy socks. She nodded for him to continue as well.

Robbie sighed angrily but sat up and began pulling his jacket off, sliding it to the floor behind him. Leaning back onto the cool metal pipe he started unlacing his boots. With each move his ribs screamed and he could feel the bruises yanking at the nerves under his skin. He slowed his movements and did his best not to groan each time the pain flashed through him.

Half-way through the laces he had to sit back and take a breath. Looking down at himself for the first time in a while it occurred to him that their 'survival workout' had replaced the extra weight he had always carried with a more taught and muscular frame. 'Not that the extra muscle helped today,' he thought as he went back to work on loosening his boots.

When Kelly had her socks off she paused and realized the next step would be humiliating. She would need to remove her pants. She was wearing shorts underneath but taking away the protective covering of her long pants would leave her exposed in a way she did not want to be, with this asshole Trent. She decided to bite the bullet and just pull them off.

She kicked off her heavy green safari pants causing the memory of when she first put them on to pop into her head. They were a lucky find in the stock room of a home and garden store they had looted the previous fall. 'That means,' she thought, 'I've been wearing them for about six months.'

She liked them because they had plenty of pockets and were tough on the outside and soft on the inside. She looked at them crumpled at her feet and immediately missed their warmth as she felt the cool air of the room creep up over her legs.

Looking down at herself for the first time in a while, she noticed that her legs were more toned and muscular than she remembered. The extra cushion that used to adorn her hips and bottom was gone and her muscles were visible through the taught skin over her thighs and calves. There were even taught, rope-like muscles stretching down her arms. Trading an easy life for one where every day required feats of extraordinary strength to survive had resulted in a gymnast like body.

'Wonderful,' she mused internally, 'it only took the end of the world to get into the best shape of my life and everyone else is too dead to appreciate it.'

She also saw the cuts and bruises that she had known were there but hadn't actually seen. Each purple spot marked a hard collision with something. Most often done in an effort to outpace the ferocious dead.

'Too many dark rooms and dark corridors,' she thought. 'Too much running over uneven and debris scattered ground. Too much scaling old elevator shafts, climbing through windows and swinging from fire escapes.'

"Nice stems." Trent ogled her as he paced impatiently between his two captives.

Kelly rolled her eyes.

Trent was about to say something else but a rattle from out in the street caught his attention. "Keep going, sweetheart," he ordered as he turned to walk back to the window. He stepped over her outstretched legs as he went and Kelly briefly considered leaping up and biting into him. She dismissed it almost as quickly, realizing that while it might be gratifying it would probably only make things worse.

'Worse?' She thought. 'How could it get any worse? I suppose he could be feeding us to the hungry hordes out there. Something to look forward to, then.' Her dark sense of humor bubbled up. 'At least Trent seemed well enough distracted by whatever was going on outside that he wasn't standing there leering at her anymore.'

Chapter 2

The dead weren't fast, but they never stopped coming and, in numbers, could easily trap you or worse. They had found people, or what was left of them, trapped in basements, second floor apartments and other places with thick walls. Their bodies starved and emaciated. They avoided the undead but suffered an equally horrible death of dehydration and starvation. Trapped, they died slowly as the creatures pawed at the walls around them so that their safe havens had also became their tombs.

Kelly's shorts may have been purple… or pink at one time. She couldn't remember. The color had faded and what remained was a greasy looking grey color. Some printed flowers were still barely visible on the waist band, and the swish logo still stood out on the side but the fabric was thin and torn in several places.

Looking past the shorts she was also reminded that she had not shaved in ages. Thick fields of hair ran down her legs like grasslands over the Serengeti. She noticed the ink from her socks had left dark stains on her feet that made it look like they might also be covered in fur.

'Great,' she thought, 'I look like a damn werewolf and smell like a bear, maybe Trent will be grossed out and leave me alone.'

She considered fighting him if he tried anything frisky, but her face still throbbed from where he had hit her and she wondered how much good it would do. She didn't even want to think about what he might do to Robbie if she resisted him. 'He might do those things anyway,' she fretted, 'but maybe we can buy some time to think of something.'

Kelly looked over at Robbie as he worked at his jeans. Although he still acted like a boy sometimes, she realized he had grown into a man over the last two years. The chubby boy of 16 was gone and replaced by a man whose body had been chiseled and tortured by the same harsh conditions of her own survival. She felt a kind of sadness for him since there were no girls around for him to keep company with. They occasionally met other living people, but it was rare and not usually friendly. Everyone was out for themselves these days.

She looked away at the shadows in the hallway and tried to think of a way to escape but nothing practical came to her. She knew she would have to wait for an opportunity.

'Something would happen,' she thought, 'something had to happen.'

They had escaped death, and un-death, so many times over the last few years she wouldn't let it end like this. She closed her eyes and escaped into herself trying to think of a way out of this mess.

Robbie had seen Kelly start to undress but quickly looked away before she could catch him and assume he was ogling her. He made an effort not to look in her direction as he worked on his own clothing. He had a lot of respect for her and didn't want things to get weird by making her think he was a perv. He also held out hope that his big brother, Roy would return one day. Soon, he hoped.

'Right now would be good, Roy,' he thought, 'burst in the door guns blazing and take out that asshole Trent. But his older brother did not appear in the doorway and it seemed that the cavalry was not coming that day. Robbie kicked off his jeans and sat back against the wall.

He looked over at Trent, who was still gazing intently down at the street, and wondered if there was time to try to unhook the collar. He slowly reached up to his neck and followed the leather around to the back where it was attached. The connection seemed to be held by some sort of clasp but he couldn't find the release mechanism. He frantically felt around but the movement caused the chain to rattle.

Trent turned around with a suspicious glare that turned into an evil smile. "Ok my little cupcakes is everybody comfortable?" He sang out while inspecting their efforts. He looked Kelly up and down then said. "Well done, good job. Now for part two. Lie down on your stomachs and put your hands behind your backs."

Trent took his time tying them up. Robbie tried to struggle at first but a few kicks from the older man put an end to that. When it was done, Robbie was stretched out under an overhead pipe with his arms above him. His feet were linked together with handcuffs and there were other straps or ropes he couldn't see binding it all together so that his mobility was limited. He kept wondering where the hell Trent found all the ropes. He had just kept pulling them out of his backpack.

Kelly was pulled up and tied similarly across from Robbie. Having not shaved or showered in ages, he figured he must look like a cave man.

Worse Than Dead

For the last two years, Kelly had been a combination of mother, big sister and teacher for Robbie. He was only 16 when Roy went out to scavenge for supplies one day. Ordinarily they would only go out together, but Robbie had twisted his ankle the previous day and was still recovering. Kelly was less adventurous back then and Roy had insisted he could move faster alone. It was supposed to be a quick run to a storage shed they had discovered containing supplies for a local convenience store. It was only a few blocks from their hide out and zombie presence was low so they figured he would be able to get there and back in a few hours. That afternoon when Roy had not returned they started to grow worried. They sat up all that night waiting and the next day they set out looking for him.

With Kelly's help, Robbie had limped all over the area but found no sign of Roy. When they reached the storage locker, the door hung open. They took this as a sign which probably meant he had to leave it quickly without relocking it. Unfortunately, he left no clues as to where he went next.

They were searching an old gas station when a mob of undead began shambling after them. It took two hours to lose them and another few hours zigzagging their way back to their hide out. They arrived, exhausted, after sunset. Kelly had been sure that Roy would be there waiting for them when they returned. She was crestfallen when they found the loft apartment dark, undisturbed and as empty as it had been when they left it.

In the last two years, he had grown up a lot and Robbie still looked at Kelly, not as a woman but, as his brother's wife. He saw himself as her protector until Roy returned. It angered him to be hanging there unable to stop whatever Trent planned to do with them. Maybe he should have let Trent beat him to death. That may have been better than whatever he had planned. But, he knew he couldn't do that. He decided he wouldn't give up and leave Kelly alone with that miscreant. He wouldn't give up. They had been through too much. He knew he had to wait for his chance.

After Trent was done securing them, he circled a few times inspecting his work. He occasionally swooped in to re-tie or change the configuration of a knot, until he seemed satisfied. "Well yes," he finally said with a salacious smile, "I think that will do."

Kelly's eyes went wide when he walked behind her and spanked her bottom.

"God damn!" he exclaimed with delight. "Your ass is fine, Kelly. Do you do Pilates or something? I do not know how Robbie there kept from jumping on this. How did you do it, Robbie? Are you gay or something?" He laughed as he groped her. "Holy crap you don't know what you are missing. I am going to have some fun with you, Princess."

Kelly felt her face turn red with anger and embarrassment at their predicament. Making it worse was that Robbie was strapped just a few feet away. She struggled but the ropes burned and cut into her skin until she was frustrated and exhausted. She let her body relax so that she hung in the restraints and turned to stare down at the floor. She had no idea what Robbie must be thinking but she couldn't bear looking at him while they hung there defenseless.

"Now relax, Sweetie." Trent instructed as he released her. "We will have plenty of time to play later. Don't get all excited."

All Kelly could think about was that she was going to kill this asshole the first chance she got.

"Ok, you two, I need to step out for a little while. I guess I don't need to muzzle you, right? I don't suppose you are going to be yelling for help or anything." Trent stepped over and looked out the window before turning and walking out of the room. "Relax," he said over his shoulder as he left.

Robbie listened as Trent's footsteps receded down the hall. Then he heard the click of the stairwell door being opened followed by the swish and light thump as it closed. They had oiled the door to reduce the noise but in the quiet of the building, Robbie could hear it well enough. He could even hear the light echo of his footsteps going down the stairs.

13

When he was fairly certain Trent was gone, he tried again to free himself but after a few minutes he gave up, exhausted, and just hung there. Every time he pulled against the ropes in one spot, they seemed to tighten up somewhere else. Nor could he reach any knots or other connectors he could loosen. He wasn't giving up but he was getting scared. He looked over at Kelly's slumped body. She did not return his gaze but he could see that she was crying. Her head shook and trails of tears ran down her cheeks and dripped down onto the floor.

"It's ok, Kelly," Robbie growled. "Were going to get out of this. It may suck for a while but we will survive and we will think of a way to get out. And when we do, we will fuck that motherfucker up!"

Kelly responded with a sniffle but did not look up.

Time is a relative concept. The two of them hung there silently as the shadows in the room got longer and the hot afternoon faded into the warm evening. There was nothing either could think to say. Their muscles ached and extremities tingled. There was no getting comfortable hanging in the ropes. Shifting their weight from one area simply caused the circulation to restrict in another. The pain grew until it felt as if the entirety of their bodies was cramping. All they could do is hang as if they were trapped in giant spider webs just waiting for the creature to return to suck out their insides.

They were exhausted by the time they heard the sound of someone climbing back up the stairs. The sun had set behind the horizon leaving their little room in darkness. They felt terror at the thought of their tormentor's return but also relief that he might loosen the ropes and let them collapse to the ground. Or kill them. That thought ran through both of their minds and in some way they both welcomed it over the continued pain of hanging in the ropes.

They heard the stairwell door open and a beam of light flashed down the hall. This was followed by the sound of boots approaching. The light shined in the room blinding Robbie who for a moment prayed it was someone other than Trent. But then they heard the voice.

"Well I see you decided to stay for the party." Trent said as he ambled back in the room plunking down several gym bags. He then wandered around the room placing and lighting candles he pulled from the bags. "There," he said, turning off the flashlight and admiring the flickering glow. "Now we have some ambiance."

"I bet you all are feeling pretty sore about now, yea?" Trent asked but didn't seem to care about an answer. He pulled some items from his bag that looked like more ropes and chains in the candlelight. "Don't worry. I'll be taking you down now so you can get some circulation flowing. How about ladies first? You wouldn't mind that would you, Rob? Would you like that, Kelly?"

There was a moment of quiet as he seemed to wait for her answer. "What's that? I didn't hear you. Do you want to be let down or not?""

"Yes," Kelly finally said weakly.

"Yes?" Trent queried. "Yes what? What's the magic word?"

"Please," Kelly croaked, "yes, please."

"See there we go," he praised and began working on the ropes behind her, "all we need is to show some respect and understand the rules. You see, Trent makes the rules. Trent holds all the cards, so if you do as I say, we all get along happily. You break the rules, well that won't end well for you all. Understand?"

"Yes," Kelly gasped as her arms and upper body were loosened and lowered. She fell to her knees and rested her head on the floor with a groan. "Oh Jesus," she moaned as the blood flow returned to her limbs in a rush of pain.

She looked up when she heard the thump of Robbie being dropped to the floor nearby. She saw him kneeling with his own head on the ground in front of him and empathized with the relief and pain he must be feeling as the blood still returned to her own limbs.

Robbie looked up and met Kelly's eyes from across the room. They both winced in frustration at their situation. Although they didn't speak, they conveyed an understanding to one another of the anticipated assault to come, and their powerlessness to stop it.

Trent pulled at Robbie's leash and led him on his knees back to the wall where he quickly secured him. "There you go Robbie. Best seat in the house. Just sit there and relax for a bit."

Robbie looked over at Kelly kneeling on the floor and quickly looked away. He sat back against the pipes and breathed deeply as feeling continued to painfully push the numbness from his limbs.

"Comfy?" Trent asked.

"Water?" Robbie replied. "Can we please have some water?"

"Well now," Trent answered, "since you were so polite and I'm in a good mood, I don't see why not." He walked over to the stacked boxes of water they kept in the room and pulled off two bottles. He rummaged through a bag and found a plastic dog bowl and tossed it down next to Robbie. Pouring one bottle into the bowl he said, "Sorry buddy, I don't think I can untie your hands just yet but enjoy."

"What about Kelly?" Robbie asked.

"Don't you worry about her," Trent said walking over to the bound woman who glared at him. "Hey now, don't look at me like that little lady. I'm going to treat you real nice." He unscrewed the lid of the second bottle and tipped it to her lips.

Kelly's thirst overrode her desire to tell Trent where to shove it and she began to drink. After chugging half the bottle, she felt better and pushed it away. Letting the cool liquid run down her throat.

"There now," Trent declared with his hands raised as if in surrender, "everybody had enough? Are we ready to get down to business?"

"Business?" Kelly, newly hydrated, felt emboldened and fired back. "What do you want Trent?"

Kneeling in front of her he said, "I just want what everyone in the apocalypse wants Kelly."

"And what is that," she spit back.

"Your supplies of course," Trent said calmly, "your food, water, weapons, fuel, that kind of stuff."

"Fuck you!" She spit.

"Maybe later," he smiled, "but first you're 'gonna tell me where you keep your stuff."

"We aren't telling you anything," Robbie growled angrily.

"Now, see" Trent said. "That's the kind of attitude I thought we had moved beyond. Look. You're going to tell me, so let's just skip all the theatrics and the kicking and screaming and cuts and bleeding. Ok?"

"Trent," Kelly sighed, "we can't tell you about what we don't have. We're living day-to-day just like you. You see what we have right here."

"Bullshit!" Trent yelled. "I've heard you talking about taking things to the 'storage site'. Now you tell me where that is, or I will have to get rough. Is that clear? This is your last warning."

"We really don't…" Kelly began but Trent punched her, spinning her sideways on the floor. She saw stars and suddenly felt like she was falling into a vast empty abyss. She felt her body pulled down into a swirling pool of spinning lights.

"Noooo!" Robbie screamed, pulling against his collar.

"Damn, you've got a hard head, Kelly!" Trent said as he shook out the hand he used to hit her. "I told you I wasn't messing around."

The older man unhooked Kelly's leash and easily lifted her limp body over his shoulder. He turned angrily to Robbie. "Now, you're 'gonna see what happens, dumbass!"

"Put her down," Robbie shouted. "Leave her alone!"

"Shut the fuck up!" Trent snarled as he strode from the room.

"Bring her back you sick asshole!" Robbie frantically cursed after them. "Leave her alone! Just leave her alone!"

Robbie thrashed and pulled against the ropes until he grew exhausted. His mind raced for a way to escape but he came up empty. Afterward, he sat alone in the flickering candlelight sobbing. His physical and emotional trauma merged into a dark agony that burned through him. He could only stare blankly into the dark corners of the room feeling broken and completely drained.

As the hours went on, Robbie found himself on a plateau. His agony reached its zenith and, while it did not fall, it began to feel like a constant. After a time, it didn't so much as become bearable as he began to accept it. He began to be able to move and think within it, in spite of it. The pain was there regardless, so he decided that he would work through it. As his soccer coach had always told him and his team-mates, "No pain, no gain!"

Robbie snickered at how stupid this sounded. The giggle caused his lungs to hurt so he just lay there, still and quiet. Waiting. At some point he slid into darkness and either slept or simply vanished into a place with no light or sound.

When the sun came up the next morning, he was still alone. In the dawning light, he pulled up his shirt to see dark purple bruising over his skin from Trent's beating. When he moved, even slightly, it hurt. Since it was also painful to lie still, he shuffled about in his small space to transfer the ache from one place to another.

He was shifting from side to side. Sitting on one cold butt cheek then the other when he heard a door open. It didn't sound like the stairwell door but he couldn't be sure. For a moment he worried that the dead may have found a way in, but the echo of footsteps coming down the hall was steady and confident. These were the heavy, booted paces of someone moving with purpose. Unlike the ravenous pasty creatures in the street who seemed to wander aimlessly without any direction until they found prey.

Trent entered the room with Kelly over his shoulder, wrapped in a blanket. He plopped her down on the spot where he had taken her and re-connected her to the tether. Robbie could tell she was alive, but her face was pale and she had a distant look in her eyes. She didn't say anything, just sat there staring.

Trent pulled a bottle of water from one of his packs and filled Robbie's dog bowl. "There you go sport!" He chuckled.

Robbie said nothing.

"Wooo! I need to go talk to a man about a horse," Trent announced. Then he started back out the door and laughed, "Keep an eye on her for me will you, Rob?!"

After he was gone, Kelly began to sob "I'm sorry Robbie, so sorry…"
There was a long pause followed by Robbie speaking in a calm and subdued voice, "It's ok Kelly. We're going to get through this. We may both have to do… things, but we are going to get through it. We're going to survive. We just have to be strong."
She felt relief hearing his words with no judgement or admonition and suddenly felt physically and emotionally exhausted. "Ok, thank you," She said quietly. Then she lay there staring at the ceiling until sleep took her and she faded off into troubling dreams and nightmares.

Chapter 3

Days crawled by slowly while Trent took out his aggressions and whims on his two captives. It hadn't taken long for him to beat out the location of their main food supply. He beat them again when he found out that it was in the basement of the same building they were in. It angered him that it had been so close all along and he had not found it himself. Especially given that it was logical to keep the supplies close by, in the cold underground of the building's storage rooms.
He made Robbie go with him when he went to check it out, just to be sure they weren't trying to trick him into walking into a den of trapped undead down in the dark. Robbie, still tied, shivered in the corner as Trent went through their stacks of canned food and bottled water. Their tormentor opened a few cans of fruit and ate them in front of the younger man just to be cruel.

Worse Than Dead

After the fight was out of him, Kelly watched as Robbie sank into a depressed haze. He stared blankly at the walls and only spoke when she asked him yes-or-no questions. In spite of the abuses she suffered, Kelly felt like the best way to keep them both alive was to engage with Trent, to talk to him and make sure he thought of them as people. Maybe even people he wanted to keep around… even if only for entertainment.

She laughed at his jokes and agreed with his tirades against the idiots out in the world. When he looked out the window and angrily accused the crowds of undead below of getting what they deserved, she would nod and say he was right.

To her surprise, this had been effective if only to the degree that they were still alive and the beatings and torture had lessened. She had also been able to convince him that they didn't need to be tied up so completely all the time and he had reduced their bonds to only what was needed to keep them in place. Catering to his huge ego also paid off in that he would occasionally do things for them. Weird things, but at least not angry, deadly things.

"Wake up, buttercups!" Trent called out cheerily when he returned to the utility room late one afternoon.

Robbie had been dozing and startled awake at the noise. He winced as pain shot through his limbs. His muscles and bones ached from lying on the cold floor. Kelly turned from watching the sky through the tinted window to see that Trent carried two buckets full of water. He set them down sloppily on the floor and began digging things out of his backpack.

"You are not going to believe this," the older man said excitedly, as he set the buckets up on small metal frames. He then produced small cans of Sterno and slid them into the gap underneath. He lit the gelled heating oil and stood back proudly from the flame and exclaimed, "Ta dah!"

"That's great, Trent!" Kelly said with practiced enthusiasm on her face but internally worried about what he was up to, "What do you have in mind?"

Both Kelly and Rob's hearts jerked when Trent withdrew a large pair of scissors. He held them up and snapped them open and closed.

"Snip, snip!" He said with glee.

"I don't understand," Kelly stammered. "What is that for? What are you going to do?"

Trent didn't answer but instead, giddily slid a plastic chair over and indicated she should move off the floor and into the seat.

Kelly hesitantly cooperated, moving nervously into the chair. "You're kind of freaking me out Trent. What's going on?"

"You'll see," he said. "Don't worry, you're going to like this."

She sat rigid, as he moved one of the buckets behind her and began using a cup to ladle warm water over her hair. The water ran down her face and splashed onto the concrete floor. She squinted as the warm liquid washed over her eyes. It burned, but she feared closing them fully without knowing what he was up to.

Adding to her confusion, a fragrant floral scent hit her nose as she felt the older man begin massaging something into her hair.

"I hope you don't mind," Trent said from behind her, "I picked 'Island Flowers' but if you have a favorite just tell me and I'll keep an eye out the next time I'm at the salon."

Kelly remained quiet and still as Trent washed and conditioned her hair. Then her heart skipped a beat as she heard the metallic snip snip of the scissors.

"Your split ends are out of control, girl," Trent sing-songed as he pulled and cut her long, tangled locks. When he was done, he washed it again and toweled it dry.

Kelly wasn't sure how to react to the spa treatment. Trent was clearly psychotic, but he had put a lot of work into the haircut. The towel even smelled clean.

"There we go," Trent said. "Fresh and clean as the morning dew. Now let's see how we look."

"Ok," Kelly stammered.

"Bet you would never have guessed I owned a chain of hair salons before all this," Trent said as he unhooked the leash and clicked a longer chain from the wall into place on her collar. "I mean how many straight male stylists are there, right?"

"I don't know. I guess I never noticed." She lied, "But I never would have guessed. How did I get to be so special?"

"I just miss working in the shop sometimes," Trent said as he helped her to her feet. She turned and he pointed her to a full-length mirror he had placed against the wall. "I really liked doing hair back in the day and I was damned good at it. Aren't you lucky I found you?"

"Yea," Kelly said unsure. "Yes, so lucky."

"What do you think?" He said with a smile.

Kelly stared at herself. She was surprised to see that her hair was nicely shaped with an intentional mussy look. Running her fingers through it she noticed that the grease and dirt she had become accustomed to was gone. Replaced with clean feeling locks that came down to her shoulders. The smell and tingle of the shampoo was strange after so long without any kind of bath.

"Sorry I don't have a blow dryer to do it properly," Trent said, "but we got a good effect with the towel don't you think?"

"Y…Yes" she answered still in shock over her transformation, "Its beautiful."

Trent's personality was indeed, unlike anyone she had ever encountered at a salon; gay or straight. But, she wondered, how anyone would know who was crazy and who wasn't, in the old world. Back then, they would have to hide it, in public anyway. These days, it might actually help with survival to be a raving psycho who is unafraid to lie, steal, hurt or kill to get what they want. She recalled reading a study in her college psychology class that found one percent of people are psychopaths and four percent are sociopaths.

After giving her a few minutes to admire his handiwork in the mirror Trent strapped her back into the chair and announced he had some errands to run. He gathered up his salon tools and was gone as suddenly as he arrived.

She looked over at Robbie, who sat on the floor leaning against the pipes.

"What the fuck was that?" Robbie said when he was sure Trent was out of earshot.

"I don't know." Kelly replied. "Add that to the list of crazy shit to think about in this world."

"Yea." Robbie answered. "Your hair looks nice though."

"Shut up," Kelly snapped.

She sat there thinking back through all the bad things she had done in her life. The times she had talked back to her mother, not left tips for waiters, or taken someone for granted. She had once kissed another boy when she and Roy had just started dating. It was a thing she felt very guilty about afterward. But, she could not come up with enough bad karma to justify the universe putting them in the path of a violent, socio-psychopath madman like Trent.

She lost track of the time, being tied up in the small room, and sometimes Trent would come in angry and lock them in the janitor's closet for long periods. It was dark there and she didn't know if hours or days had passed. Trent used her mostly but found ways to humiliate and abuse Robbie as well.

Most mornings they would wake to Trent rattling their chains. "Wake up, bitches! Let's go!" He would say. "Get up off your asses! It stinks in here. We're going to the roof."

The flat area on the top of the building was partially covered by rusting air conditioning equipment and other old world mechanical workings. A few areas were open in between all the equipment and from there they could see most of downtown as well as the rolling tree-covered hills in the distance. For a short time, they could breathe the fresh air and enjoy the sun on their skin. Even the small pebbles set in the tar covering the rooftop felt nice against their feet after the cold dirty concrete down below.

Trent would follow them out and tug them over to the corner they had turned into their toilet. They had attached a long wide plank that hung out over one of the building's low walls. The plank had several holes in it so they could sit and do their business. Below was a narrow ally that had a large storm drain in the middle. They had felt pretty clever months before, when they had set up the arrangement. It seemed the safest and most sanitary option they had. The smell from the alley could waft up to the roof at times but eventually it would rain and everything would wash into the drain.

The alley below was partially fenced at either end so that the undead could get in or out but not easily. Sometimes a group of them would get stuck there and just amble back and forth until something outside became interesting enough that they pushed their way back through the loosely hanging chain link. Their activities on the roof often caused such crowds to gather in the alley, frantically clawing at the walls to get to the human meat far above, only to be rewarded by a stream of urine or human excrement in which, Kelly and Robbie had noted, they did not seem interested.

The low wall had heavy, metal brackets that may have been used to attach cable, at some point in the past, and Trent used them to tie Robbie and Kelly to each end of the board.

"Do your business and clean up good, I aint wiping anybody's ass." Trent said one morning as he walked away towards a connecting wall. He lit a cigarette and looked out over the city. Then he propped his foot up onto the low wall and gazed down at the main street. It was crowded with the shuffling forms of the dead. He chuckled at the former denizens of the city now doomed to wander around aimlessly until their bones turned to dust. 'That's probably not much different than what you idiots were doing before,' he mused.

He sat down on the wall and looked back at his two captives and wondered how long it would be before he had to kill them. It was tempting to keep Kelly, but he could never trust her. He was only keeping Robbie alive as leverage with her. He knew they would do whatever he said as long as he could threaten the other. But he wasn't stupid, he knew they would take the first opportunity to kill him. Maybe not kill, he smiled, they were still weak in that way. Keeping their humanity and all.

He also knew they were smart so they would think of something eventually. They might not have the guts to kill him, but they would try to take him out and he couldn't wait around forever wondering when, or how, that would happen. Also, there was the matter of food. The longer they were alive the longer he had to share the limited supplies with them. The way he had it figured they had about 3 months' worth of rations for three people. Nine months if it was just him.

He looked over and saw Kelly with her back to him. 'One good thing about this zombie apocalypse' he decided 'there aint no fat chicks. Not many chicks at all,' he complained to himself, 'but the ones who survived were all doing daily zombie p90x classes.'

He recalled a group he had discovered a few years back. They were holed up in their basement living on bottled water and canned fruits and vegetables. He'd been in the house looking for food when he saw the basement door was boarded up. He remembered breaking it in and looking down at the four faces staring up at him. One man and three women. They didn't even have any weapons. 'Idiots,' Trent thought.

All he had to do was show them his BFK and they agreed to do whatever he wanted, he snickered. "Morons."

He had tied them all up and strangled the guy right away, while the women screamed. Then he started working his way through them. He did every sadistic thing he could think of before ending their lives. 'The trouble,' he thought with a smirk, 'is that everything gets boring after a while.'

He killed two of the women and just for fun, left the last one tied up in the dark. He laughed at her muffled pleas as he had closed the door to the basement and left her there with the rotting bodies.

He decided he would keep Kelly and Robbie alive for a little while longer. At least until he got bored.

And so it went. He did what he pleased with them. Twice a day he would walk them upstairs to use the restroom. Sometimes, if he was lazy, he would just walk them down to the janitor's closet and let them pee in the drain intended for washing out mops and mixing paint. When Trent was away, the two captives sat quietly wondering if it was worse if he came back, or got killed out in the world and left them tied there to die.

Occasionally Trent would get into a spa mood. He would come in with the buckets of hot water. Then he would pull out his scissors and razors, and give her a haircut. During these sessions he was almost a different person. He seemed sincere and caring and talked to them about places he had been and things he had seen. They welcomed this bit of news since, other than trips to the roof, they were largely confined to their little utility room.

It was on one of these "good" days that Kelly convinced Trent to let Robbie bathe in the leftover soap and water. As he was finishing up, Trent handed Kelly a bottle of shampoo and told her to wash the young man's hair and beard. When she was done Trent stepped over behind Robbie, who was tied to a chair, and began running his hands through his hair.

"You have good roots, Robbie," he said. "You just need some shaping."

With that, Trent retrieved his bag and pulled out several pairs of scissors and his straight razor. They held their breath as Trent had a habit of going from nice to evil very quickly. Robbie and Kelly stared at each other as Trent grabbed Robbie by the hair and brought up his scissor. Each time Trent brought the sharp tools, Kelly feared he would stab Robbie in the neck. But he began cutting and shaving until Robbie's face began to appear from under his long bangs.

When he was done, Robbie had gone from cave man to movie star. Kelly noted that with his shaggy beard gone he looked more like a bad boy celebrity than her little brother in law. His muscular frame, square jaw and dark wavy hair would make any Hollywood actor jealous. His green eyes glittered in a way that reminded her of Roy and she smiled at him in approval.

"Oh my god, Trent," Kelly poured on the praise hoping to keep him in a good mood, "he looks wonderful. You did such a good job."

"Thanks," Trent said as he carefully put away his tools. "I just wish I had a hair dryer. I could have done amazing things."

When he was done putting things away he said, "I'm glad you like it. How about you, Rob?"

"It's great," the young man acted pleased and added nervously, "never even got a cut this good back in the day."

"Damn right you didn't," Trent said. "That's a $500 cut back in my salon."

Later, when Trent had gone, Kelly began whispering. "Robbie," she called to him quietly, "one day we are getting the fuck out of here. Just me and you. Do not give up on me, understand?! We are not giving up. Neither one of us."

"Yea I know," Robbie said, his face barely visible in the moonlight. He did not sound convinced.

Chapter 4

A few days later, when they emerged onto the roof for their regular ministrations, they were greeted by a hot summer sun hanging over a light blue sky. A few small white clouds floated in the distance making the view seem more like a painting than real life. 'A perfect day, but for the zombie apocalypse and being a madman's captive slave,' Kelly thought.

Trent announced that they were all getting pale and needed some sun so they would lay out on the roof for a while. He had Kelly spread out some large towels over the rooftop gravel.

"Lie down," Trent ordered as he pulled his shirt over his head, leaving him in cut off shorts and his old army boots. Stretching out his thick, muscular arms he took in a deep breath and posed there for a moment, as if to soak up the sun. He then tucked his big knife into its sheath in the back of his waistband and looked over at Robbie, who stood near the edge.

"You 'gonna jump?" Trent said with a sneer that made it sound like he expected him to do it.

"Not today," Robbie replied only half sarcastically. He sat down on the low wall and looked out at the skyline. Trent had not secured him to anything but he was bound at the hands and feet so he didn't have many options for escape. Except the one his captor had suggested. Robbie looked down at the sidewalk again and seriously thought about it.

Eight floors was a long way to fall. 'It might even kill me,' Robbie thought. 'Probably not though,' he reasoned, given his luck recently he would most likely survive just long enough to be torn apart by the throng of cannibalistic pedestrians gathered below. They glared up at him desperately moaning their pleas for him to leap into their outstretched arms. 'No thanks,' he said to himself. Death didn't bother him but things hadn't gotten so bad that he wanted to experience being eaten alive on his way there.

Trent was wearing sunglasses so Robbie couldn't see his eyes but he was sure he was keeping a close watch on him. If only Kelly could get her leash free she might be able to get it around his neck and strangle him, he considered. But running the idea through in his head he realized Trent would easily overpower her and probably give them both a beating for their trouble. Maybe worse.

Trent was glaring at Robbie from behind his shades. He had deliberately not tied the teen to anything. He was hoping he would make a move. He could see the gears turning in the boy's head. He could tell by the way he kept glancing over at them that he was plotting something or at least thinking very hard about it. Trent wanted him to try.

If the boy came at him, he could kill him and that would be self-defense. Kelly would not like it but it would be better than just killing him outright. Without Robbie, he would be the only human around to keep her alive.

'In time,' he told himself, 'she'd get used to it and forget about Robbie and that long dead husband of hers, altogether. She'll be my personal possession and plaything. Then I'll have to kill her, of course, because that would be boring. But breaking them is such a thrill.'

The low roof wall was rough and hot on Robbie's bottom so he stood and rubbed his cheeks. Since he spent long hours every day tied to a chair he made the most of the short periods when he was able to stand. Stretching his muscles as much as possible in the cuffs, he made an effort to go slowly. He knew any sudden movements might antagonize Trent.

Trent watched Robbie rise up and begin flexing. 'Here we go,' he thought, 'the little fucker is going to make a move. Perfect.'

But Robbie didn't. He just stood there looking out over the city as he extended his arms and legs. This pissed Trent off. He wanted the kid to make his move. After a few minutes he decided to make it happen. Standing up he walked towards Robbie while drawing his big knife. Robbie saw him coming and tensed, afraid Trent planned to stab him. Kelly sat up, her eyes wide, with the same thought. She was about to shout when Trent stepped up to Robbie.

"Give me your hands," he said.

Robbie slowly raised his hands which were bound with plastic flex cuffs.

Trent ran the knife up and cut the cuffs off. "There you go man. Relax a little."

"Thanks," Robbie said warily as he rubbed his wrists. He was thinking of grabbing Trent's neck but he still had the big knife out. That would be a short fight, he thought. Trent slid the knife back into the sheath in his back waistband and stepped away.

Robbie breathed a sigh of relief but suddenly Trent lunged back punching him in the gut while yelling, "What the hell, Rob!"

Caught off guard, Robbie doubled over from the blow. Stunned and confused, he threw his arms out and tried to push back against the larger man who had grabbed him by the waist and was jerking him back and forth shouting, "Back off Rob! Don't do it!"

It was a show, Robbie realized, as he desperately grappled with the bigger man. Trent was trying to make it look like Robbie was attacking him. From behind, Kelly would only see Trent's back and Robbie's flailing arms. He didn't have time to consider whether she would believe it. It didn't matter. He was losing his footing and it was clear what Trent intended.

With the ankle cuffs on, his stance was unstable. He tried to throw his weight forward, to keep from going over the wall, but Trent pummeled him with his fists and pushed him back until he felt himself losing his balance. He felt his upper body going over backward. The whole struggle had happened in a blur, as if time had speeded up, but suddenly everything slowed down as his equilibrium shifted. He watched his arms fully extended and his hands grasping at air in front of him. He was tumbling back over the edge of the wall into open space.

As he went over he caught a glimpse of Kelly, in wide eyed panic, rising up screaming from the towel. Then she was gone and the world was upside down. The sky was under his feet as his legs scraped past the lip of the wall, following him as he raced backwards towards the ground. In that hair of a second he was angry, but resigned, to a headlong crash into the cement below.

Kelly watched in horror as Robbie disappeared off the side of the building. She rose to her feet in a rage and charged at Trent shouting "NO!"

Trent turned just in time to brace himself for her assault. He bent his knees, just like back when he played high school football, and absorbed her attempt to tackle him. She was stronger than he expected though and her forward motion pushed him back hard onto the edge of the wall. She wrapped herself around his waist punching at him with everything she had.

"Easy gal! He attacked me," he tried to say, but her adrenaline laced punches knocked the wind from him. She was like a whirlwind of angry spinning fists. He felt his lips and nose sting as she bloodied them. Everywhere he tried to grab her resulted in a strike from another direction until finally he had had enough. He stopped trying to restrain her and punched her hard in the ribs. At first this did not register and he had to repeat the blows, harder and harder until she crumpled at his feet in tears.

Kelly lay in a heap at Trent's feet and looked up to see him drawing his fist back again. She didn't care. She didn't care if he threw her off the roof or beat her to death right there. She had lost the will to go on. She screamed "No! No! No! You fucker! Nooo!"

She glared up at him through tears and sweat and snot running from her nose and prepared for the beating he was about to deliver. Then she caught a glimpse something suddenly moving behind him like a shadow. An arm wrapped around his chest and pulled him over the wall. Trent's torso swung backwards and vanished but somehow his legs clung to the lip of the wall. It was impossible, they were eight floors up, but someone had grabbed Trent from behind and was pulling him over the wall. In spite of the surprise of the attack, Trent managed to lock his strong legs to keep from falling all the way off. Kelly had no idea what was going on but she didn't wait. She stood up and punched Trent in the balls as hard as she could.

Trent screamed and lost the grip with his legs sending him plummeting down the side of the building. Kelly raced to the edge and was shocked to see saw Robbie hanging upside down just below the lip of the wall.

"Oh my god!" she shouted, "Robbie!? How?"

"Please help me," Robbie muttered breathlessly as he sat up and reached out to her.

"Yes, yes, oh my god! Robbie!?" She grabbed his hands and helped pull him back onto the roof. As she hoisted him up she realized the cuffs on his ankles had become snagged on one of the metal cleats mounted along the outside wall. It must have happened just after he went over, stopping his fall and, enabling him to sit up and grab Trent from behind. She hugged him as he rolled back over the edge.

"Oh god," she cried, "I thought you were gone!"

"Me too," he winced while rubbing his head, "I may have a concussion and I think...."

"Aaaaagh!" An angry howl blasting up from below cut him off. Trent's voice bellowed out like the war cry of a mad berserker, "Motherfuckers!"

They both looked back over the edge and, to their shock, saw Trent standing on top of a pile of squirming bodies. He must have landed on them, breaking his fall, and the force of his impact knocking everything down around him. Somehow he had survived and had time to jump to his feet. Using his heavy boots he stomped on those wriggling beneath him while swinging his blade and fists at the others advancing towards him. He was outnumbered but fighting back with mad ferocity.

They watched in shock as he pummeled, punched or sliced everything that got near him and seemed to be holding them off. He glanced up at them and they could see his eyes blazing with anger.

"When I get back up there!" he shouted up to them as he stepped off the pile shouting as he attacked, "You motherfuckers!" slice, "will!" punch, "pay!" kick. Somehow he began to make a hole through the front ranks of the undead. Grey and desiccated body parts were flying as chunks of grey flesh and dried blood spewed into the air around him.

Kelly and Robbie looked on in horror as their tormentor began to plow through the crowd! Their eyes grew wide in fear as they watched him bash his way towards the fire escape. Trent's will was strong but his progress began to slow as more and more of the hungry creatures pressed in around him. From above, it looked like every zombie in the neighborhood had been attracted by his enraged yelling. They were streaming towards the sounds like sharks drawn to bloodied water. They crowded in behind him as he moved away from the wall until he was fully encircled by their clawing biting mass.

For a few more steps Trent pushed through them, hacking them down and knocking them out of his way but then the weight of the tide turned against him. A grey face got through and latched its teeth onto his shoulder. Several others must have grabbed his legs from below. For a few steps he dragged them, but then others got through and clamped down with their teeth and claws. He may have somehow been ignoring the pain of having his flesh ripped and torn but their weight became overwhelming. He bellowed out an angry string of curses and launched himself forward in a desperate attempt to push through. But it was like diving into a large wave. The zombies surged over him and he disappeared beneath them.

The dead leaped on top of him to make the world's bloodiest rugby scrum. In a flash, Trent's body was covered and all they could see was the pile of writhing creatures that had taken him down. The volume of Trent's yelling was replaced by the low-pitched moaning and scratching of the dead.

"That's it," Kelly whispered hopefully, more to herself than to Robbie. "He can't survive…"

She was interrupted by a familiar growl that was at first muffled, but then suddenly burst out into a loud howl. Trent, impossibly, thrust himself up and erupted from the pile of creatures on top of him. The biting things fell away, pulling bloody strips of flesh with them, as he came up punching and began stomping forward again over their prone bodies.

Kelly gasped in fear and shock. She could see he was being ripped to pieces. Chunks had been torn from his arms and legs and the skin on his back was nearly ripped completely off. He was covered in his own still pumping blood. Yet, somehow, he had gotten back up and was still coming, still enraged and swinging, unwilling to accept his fate. He charged forward for several yards before they took him down again. The tide simply rose up and pulled him down as if dragging him to hell.

Robbie and Kelly watched the scrum pitch and bow as Trent continued to fight from underneath. It looked as if he were trying to crawl forward with the mass of undead on top of him and literally eating his body away from around him. He dragged them like a football receiver hell bent on reaching the end zone with the entire opposing team piled on his back.

The scrum pushed a few more yards before suddenly collapsing leaving only the monsters moving above. Trent did not emerge again but Kelly and Robbie continued to stare down in disbelief at the writhing mass.

Finally, Robbie clambered up. "Come on," he said holding out his hand. "Let's go."

Kelly seemed uncertain and gave Robbie a frightened look.

"He's not getting up again Kelly." Robbie said looking down at the buffet of horror below. "He can't hurt us anymore."

Kelly took his hand and stood but didn't look away from the street. She said, "I just can't believe it. It happened so fast. I was starting to think it would never end."

Chapter 5

Kelly woke with a start from a dream where Trent was holding her down while stabbing her with his knife. She knew it was a dream but she felt real pain, like Trent's knife was still in her, burning and twisting. She was crumpled into a tight ball with her hands holding her abdomen. As she came more fully awake she slowed her breathing and made her body relax until the pain dissipated. She straightened out on the couch and wiped tears from her eyes as she pushed the nightmare further out of her head.
	She looked around at the break room they had set up in when they came down from the roof. The sun was not yet up but the moon provided enough light through the blinds to see that their tormentor had not returned. The room was quiet and still. Robbie lay curled and snoring in blankets on a couch across from her. They had spent the last few days in exhausted sleep, rising only to drink, eat and relieve themselves.
	Still feeling the ghost of pain in her guts, Kelly quietly sat up and decided a walk might help her stretch out and feel better. The loose sweats she was wearing had tangled up while she slept so she pulled them back into place and stood. She liked to be alone in the peaceful, cool of the mornings so she wrapped her blanket over her shoulders and silently padded out of the room.
	The glow of the sun woke Robbie. He rubbed the sleep from his eyes and yawned as he gathered his bearings. Sitting up groggily he noticed his sister in law was not in her spot on the couch across from his. He dropped a leg onto the floor to balance himself and stood up slowly. The morning sun was just above the horizon and narrow shafts of soft orange light were beginning to ease over the walls.
Robbie stared at the old coffee pot in the corner and wished it could still offer up some of its magical black liquid. He missed getting Starbucks on the way to school in the mornings. With a sigh he adjusted the loose t-shirt and shorts he was wearing and peeked out into the hallway. It was empty.

"Kelly?" He called out quietly. A quick check of the other offices on that floor revealed that she was not there so he padded up to the roof. "Kelly?" He said in a whisper as he stepped out into the open air. The roof was wet from the evening dew and a cool breeze bit at him as he scanned the area for her. She wasn't there so he returned to the stairs and began checking each floor as he went down.

When he arrived at the fifth floor, he saw her standing there with her blanket wrapped around her old sweatpants and t-shirt. She leaned on the door frame looking into the utility room that had been their prison and torture chamber.

"Hey," he said softly as he walked to her.

"Hey." She replied looking over her shoulder at him.

"You ok?" He asked.

"I can't stay here anymore," she said.

"Yea," he answered, "let's get upstairs. We don't have to come down here…"

"No." She said, "I can't stay in this building anymore. I need to move. After what happened, everything is a reminder. I wake up afraid that Trent will be standing there."

"That asshole is gone, Kelly." Robbie said, "He's never going to hurt anyone again."

She turned and grabbed him in a tight hug and began to cry, "I know but I feel like part of him is still here. I want to go someplace where I don't think of him every time I turn a corner."

"Ok," Robbie said stroking her hair, "we don't have to stay here. We can go anywhere we want. We can go up to my folk's cabin in the mountains. Remember we talked about that a while back? I was thinking, if Roy is still alive, and couldn't find us… that might be where he went. Roy might be there."

Kelly thought about it for a moment and said, "It's a good idea but the mountains are a long way off. It would be a risky trip, and we don't even know what condition the cabin is in these days. I'd hate to get all the way up there and find out the roof had caved in. I think we need someplace closer."

"Ok," Robbie said. "Do you have any ideas?"

"Yes," she replied. "Do you remember that brick building on the river? The one they had just finished renovating?"

"I think so," Robbie answered, trying to remember.

"We tried to beak into the lobby there early on, when Roy was still with us," she said sniffling.

"Oh yea," he recalled, "the tall building with the big, wooden, doors inside?"

"Right," she said approvingly, "we hid in the entryway for a while but couldn't get the interior doors open so we kept moving. Well… those doors are probably still shut so I bet nobody else has been in there either. I think if we could get in there now it would make a great place to hole up. And those Condos looked really nice. We can get a view of the river."

"But, what if Roy is at the cabin?" Robbie asked.

"If he's still alive, he could be anywhere Robbie," Kelly said sadly. "We can't be wandering the earth, risking ourselves, looking for him under every rock. Besides, the last time he saw us, we were in the city. You know Roy as well as I do. If he is alive, he would never leave Fort Garcon without us, he will be looking for us here in town. And we need to stay here so when that time comes, we can find each other. Ok?"

"Yea, I suppose," Robbie seemed persuaded. "The river is just a few miles away but it will take us a while to move all our supplies over there."

"We don't need to move everything," she answered, "we can keep this place as a safe house, just in case."

"Ok," Robbie said, "sounds like you've thought it through already. When do you want to start?"

"The zombies on the street should clear out in a few more days if we stay quiet," Kelly said thoughtfully, "then we can go scout out the new place. It shouldn't be long."

Although they had decided to go, they remained trapped by the whims of the undead in the streets below. Hours on the hot roof dragged while they waited, and wished, for the crowds to find entertainment elsewhere. Two long days later, as the afternoon ebbed, Robbie glared down impatiently at the throngs of hungry undead still encircling the building. Kelly boiled water on a grill nearby.

"You want beef or chicken noodles today?" She unenthusiastically pointed to the plastic wrapped packages stacked nearby.

"I don't think I can eat any more Ramen noodles," he replied exasperated. "I can't believe how quiet it has been. We need a distraction to draw them away."

"Something will happen," Kelly said walking up beside him, "all we need is a good wind to knock over a billboard or something and these things will be off chasing it."

"I hope so, or we will never get out of here." Robbie said, "Damn. It's like Trent cursed us."

"Don't say that asshole's name," Kelly spat.

"I've got an idea," Robbie pointed. "See that big metal street sign about four blocks up? It's just barely hanging there. If I can get down there and knock it loose that will start a stampede to the north and we can get out of here."

"No Robbie." Kelly rolled her eyes at him, "first you would never get past them. There's too many down there. Second, even if you did get by, then you would have to get all the way up there without any of them seeing you, and third, banging that sign would be like ringing a dinner bell. They would come after you and you know how hard they are to lose."

"I could do it." Robbie said with confidence. "Look, I could jump to that building there. It's less than 10 feet away and its one floor lower than us. Then all I'd have to do is follow the roof tops to the corner and…"

"And what happens when you jump over there and break your ankle, or even sprain it?!" Kelly admonished, "These buildings are old and haven't been maintained Robbie. What if you jump and go right through the roof? If you got hurt you'd be trapped over there and I'd be over here and there's nothing I could do for you. That's assuming you could make the jump?! What if you missed?!"

"Kelly," Robbie whined. "We can't just wait here until we starve. You know those things will wander around down there unless something draws them away. We have to do something, and I know I could…"

"No!" Kelly said, and paused, seeing his disappointment, "Ok, maybe you could, but it's a big risk that we don't need to take just yet. We have plenty of water and food. Look, I want to get out of here just as bad as you but I don't want either of us to get hurt or killed in the process."

"But!"

"No Robbie," she scolded him with her eyes, and stalked back to the grille.

"Ok," he acquiesced and started angrily throwing rocks down the street. Unable get them far, or loud, enough to have any influence on the flesh eating herd churning around beneath them he slumped down against the low wall and fumed.

At night, the roof was not as hot as the halls and offices below so they spent their evenings sitting there, staring out at the silhouettes of the dark buildings around them. They couldn't see the ocean but they could track the clouds and storms rolling in, and along, the coast a few miles away. A storm on the beach usually meant a cool salty breeze for their perch downtown. They looked forward to seeing the dark purple clouds, whose bellies flashed with lightning in the distance.

Kelly was finishing up a can of peaches when a noise caught her attention. The silence of the world was so great without the cacophony of civilization that she often marveled at how small sounds travelled and stood out in this new world. Something sounded like rolling waves crashing on a shore far away. It was just a whisper at first so she froze to verify that she had actually heard something new. The drawn out rumbling grew louder and more distinct, echoing through the tall buildings downtown.

She knew the sound but hadn't heard it in so long it took a moment to get her head around it. Her memory scrambled to verify what she knew by instinct to be the growl of an engine and the gravelly hum of tires rolling over pavement; a car. Maybe more than one. As it grew closer it grew louder and she heard the throaty rasp of a diesel.

"Robbie!" She called out. "Do you hear that?!"

Robbie climbed upstairs and looked into the distance where she was pointing. "Hear what?"

"Cars," she said, "more than one. I think there is a diesel. Maybe a big truck."

They both ran to the edge so they could see down the boulevard that ran like a straight line through downtown. Whoever it was, they seemed to be driving back and forth through the city streets. The sound came from one direction and then seemed to turn and go back the way they came. At last they caught a glimpse of the source of the noise. Several vehicles drove through an intersection, almost too far away to see, and were quickly gone again into the maze of city streets.

"What the hell are they doing?" Robbie asked, "Who drives around a city at night making all that noise?"

"It doesn't matter," Kelly said with a smile. "It may be exactly what we need. Look."

The zombies on the street below had taken notice and clusters of them were starting to break away from the vortex. Larger groups began to break off as the sounds grew louder until there was finally a stampede of stumbling lurching bodies moving away towards the engines. The creatures filled the streets like a surging tide hemmed in by the walls of the buildings.

"There!" Robbie shouted while indicating three vehicles that had emerged into an intersection about six blocks away. At the lead was a large, red Ford F-350 with exhaust pipes pointing up behind the cab, behind that were two trucks, one blue and one white, which would have also been considered large if not for the hulking F-350 they followed. The trucks paused at the intersection and they heard indistinct shouting as the occupants seemed to be conferring on which way to go next.

They seemed, for a few moments, unaware of the tidal wave of ghouls that charged forward hoping to sink their teeth into the rare human flesh that had appeared in front of them. When the horde burst from the shadows of the buildings, they were just over a block away from the trucks. A loud cry went up as the people in the caravan seemed to spot the creatures at the same instant. There was yelling and some scrambling as figures rushed back to their vehicles. The big diesel roared to life as the driver stepped on the gas and spun the wheel away from the onslaught. The other trucks followed, the last of which was nearly swallowed up by the crowds of undead converging on the intersection from three sides. They heard the pop, pop, pop as someone fired a gun at the creatures to cover their retreat.

Kelly and Robbie listened as the trucks roared away with the stumbling, stinking herd in pursuit.

"I don't know who you are," Robbie shouted at the trucks, "but thank you!"

"Shhhh," Kelly cautioned. "Quiet down, Robbie, we don't want to give those things a reason for turning around."

Robbie laughed and jumped down from the wall, giddy in the moment. "This is what we've been waiting for."

"Yes," Kelly responded with a beaming smile, "yes, it is. Let's check our bug-out bags. We can probably get out of here in the morning."

Chapter 6

The sun had not yet broken the horizon when Robbie and Kelly excitedly made their way down to the second floor. The open window looked out onto the bottom platform of the fire escape. They had both woken early in anticipation of release from the offices that had kept them safe but trapped for so long. One benefit to the long wait had been that they were able to wash and dry their clothes. They each wore their full kit with backpacks full of essentials and blunt weapons strapped to their sides. Robbie carried a machete while Kelly wielded what had once been a shovel handle, that she called her "bow staff." They looked down and waited for the night's shadows to slowly pull away from the streets below.

"Should we go while there are still some shadows where we can hide?" Robbie asked.

"No, wait." Kelly whispered. "Let's not get stupid now. We need to be able to see everything that's down there waiting for us."

The smell had met them on the way down and gotten worse as they came closer to the ground. They both wrapped t-shirts around their faces to help block the stench and keep any particles out of their mouths and noses. They didn't know if that mattered but it seemed like a reasonable precaution.

As the sun rose it revealed a layer of pinkish gray sludge coating the street. Kelly wrinkled her nose as she realized it was the debris of the dead. The things had been circling the building for weeks. Any that had fallen would have been trampled under the feet of the others and eventually worn down into a mash that resembled lumpy apple sauce. The walls on the surrounding buildings also had a dark buildup of dirt and grime from the press of bodies grinding themselves against them. It looked like flood waters had risen and receded leaving a thick gruesome stain behind.

"Ok, let's go," Kelly nudged Robbie, "but don't touch anything down there. It's covered in zombie sludge."

Robbie scrambled down the ladder as quietly as possible and scanned the area as Kelly came down behind him. They both paused a moment, listening for anything that may have been attracted to the rustle of their descent. When nothing happened they set out in the direction of the river which was fortunately in the opposite direction the herd had gone the night before. They moved carefully but quickly to get away from the area and the stench.

The number of abandoned and crashed vehicles that filled the narrow city streets made progress like moving slowly through a maze. Travel was made more difficult by the many blind spots and dark cavities in the crumpled cars. Some cars had bodies still strapped into their seatbelts. Many were truly dead while others were re-animated but dormant, just waiting for a meal to walk within range. From experience they knew the dead could also lurch out unexpectedly from under cars and the many gaps between the wrecks.

There were occasions in the past when they had simply bounded over the hoods of cars huddled together in tightly packed rows. That method worked well for moving fast but made lots of noise and attracted unwanted attention. Instead, and despite the rising heat and the noxious smell, they threaded their way slowly and methodically, through the city and its traffic. Moving slowly was safer but the heat sapped their energy. They could feel their fluids sweating out and soaking into their heavy clothing. By the time the sun rose into the middle of the sky they had only progressed a mile or so from where they started. They both knew they would soon need to find a way to get out of the streets and into the shade.

Kelly made a hushed clicking sound. Robbie looked back and she pointed ahead to a lifeless body hanging out of a car window. Unsure whether the thing was a threat, and not wanting to risk stirring it, they backed up several vehicles and crawled under a truck. The few seconds beneath the undercarriage of the truck was a blessing and curse. The brief moment in the shade was appreciated but the feeling of being trapped in the tight space outweighed any desire to stay there.

Emerging on the other side of the truck, Robbie spotted an empty storefront with a faded sign that read "Great Location! Commercial property for rent. Contact H. Ellison Realty." He helped Kelly up and led the way through the broken storefront window and into the shade inside. A quick glance around revealed only a few broken chairs and empty wire display stands laid out on the concrete floor. He could see from the dust built up that no one and nothing had been through there in a long time. It also gave them good visibility of the street. Robbie crept to the back and peered into the darkness of an office or store room. He couldn't see anything in the gloom but he made a low whistle knowing that if there were any undead inside they would respond.

"Nothing," he whispered after a long moment of quiet.

"Ugh," Kelly sighed as they relaxed slightly and pulled water bottles from their packs. "That stench is up my nose."

"I know," Robbie said in a hushed tone, "I almost hurled."

They poured the warm water over their faces and sloshed it in their mouths to wash out the wretched odor.

"Well, we are out of the frying pan," Robbie said as he squatted down against the back wall.

Kelly grunted her assent as she knelt next to him. "Let's not rest long. I don't like being out here in the open."

"I don't know," Robbie replied, "it's nice not to be cooped inside anymore. Besides, I think all the stinkers around here must have taken off after that gang with the red truck."

"Umm," Kelly nodded, her mouth full of water. Swallowing she said, "I hope you're right. I don't know. I'm feeling nervous."

"It is a little freaky being at street level again," Robbie said. "We just need to get used to it, you know. We're a little rusty down here but it won't be long before we get re-acclimated."

"Maybe you're right," Kelly stood up shoving her water back into her pack. "Let's get moving. It's not much further to the river."

Robbie stood and they walked towards the front of the store, but froze as they heard the sound of a bottle clink, clink, clinking as it rolled across the concrete just outside. They both saw the bottle at the same time as it shot by the front of the shop. Whoever, or whatever, had kicked it was very close. They had no time to run without being spotted so they both instinctively slid over and flattened themselves against the wall. They hoped that whatever it was went by without looking into the shop. The plate glass window was tinted, but most of it was gone so that it would only take a sideways glance to see them. They stood absolutely still and listened to the approaching footsteps.

Three tattered figures appeared just outside the shop window. They shambled along the sidewalk in the direction from which Kelly and Robbie had just come. Fortunately, they walked on by, seemingly focused on the noise of the bottle they had inadvertently kicked down the street. Robbie could tell by the way they twitched that they were in the alert state that the things went into when they were agitated or in pursuit of prey. It didn't take much to get them worked up and any sound or motion could set them off. To Kelly and Robbie's relief, when the trio reached the spot where the bottle had stopped rolling they continued on in the same direction; bumping along through the twisted tangle of cars.

Kelly and Robbie had both been holding their breath and exhaled quietly as the creatures continued walking away. The sense of relief was short lived as movement across the street caught their eyes. A group of four figures staggered along the far sidewalk. The panel truck Kelly and Robbie had just crawled under sat with its bumper crashed up against the shop across the street. It was quick math to figure out that when the ghouls got to it they would be turned and routed directly towards the store where Robbie and Kelly were hiding.

Robbie turned to Kelly and motioned with his eyes towards the back of the shop. She nodded and they slowly turned and quietly stepped towards the doorway leading to the back of the store. They stopped at the opening and peered into the dark room beyond. They did not like walking through dark, unexplored areas but didn't have much choice in the matter at the moment. If the things spotted them in the shop it would get ugly and they only had seconds to get out of sight.

Kelly stepped over the threshold and was almost instantly swallowed up by the shadows. She prayed that the back of the store was as empty as the sales floor. Robbie ducked just inside the doorway behind her, keeping an eye out for anything that might have already locked onto them.

Kelly ran her hand along the wall as she slowly moved forward and tried to adjust her eyes to the dark. Her fingers ran over papers attached to the drywall with thumbtacks. She imagined dried out OSHA posters, work schedules and sales reports. Things that scavengers wouldn't be interested in taking. A shelf with, what felt like binders, led her to a wall. She felt a large metal box that might be some sort of control panel, a fire extinguisher and then spotted a small point of light ahead. Getting closer she realized it was a narrow window that had some sort of cover over it. As she grew closer, she could see light pushing through its eroded corners.

She prayed Robbie could follow along the wall behind her. They had walked through enough dark buildings to have developed a system. It helped them not get lost and to find each other if separated. Always go to the left, always keep a hand on the wall, always move slowly and measure each step. Some of these old buildings had holes in the floors or they were rotting out and unable to handle the weight. Many had crap hanging from the ceilings and they all had debris like chairs and office equipment strewn about. Of course they had broken the rules many times when running from mobs of undead, but it came in handy when they needed to move quietly.

Her hands found something she thought might be a door. It had a long rectangular bar that felt like an emergency release lever across it so it likely lead out of this space if not out of the building. As she was about to signal for Robbie, she heard a loud thunk behind her and the sound of something solid hitting the ground. The things had found them. Back before the end, the sound would have been swallowed up by the city's background noise.

In the post-apocalyptic quiet of the afternoon, however, the sound of a machete cleaving into a skull, and the body collapsing to the concrete floor, made the little store an echo chamber. The noise reverberated out, breaking the silence of the empty street like a drum corps hitting the opening notes in a parade.

"More coming...," Robbie rasped quietly but with urgency, "is there a way out?"

"There's a door." She said shoving on the emergency bar and wincing at the loud squeak it made as it slid in its long unused track. She heard the lock disengage but the door didn't move. "Working on it." She turned and put her back against it and pushed with her legs.

Whack! She heard Robbie strike down another zombie and it hit the ground with a heavy thud. She heaved with all her might and felt the door give but something seemed to push back against it. Not zombies, she thought, something heavy leaning against it.

"There's something blocking it from outside." She grunted. "Can you help?"

She could see Robbie's silhouette just outside the doorway and the shadows of the creatures lurching toward him and knew the answer.

"No," he said and lashed out at another undead cranium. "I can hold them here for a few minutes but if I move, we're fucked."

Worse Than Dead

She heaved against the door and felt whatever was on the other side give just a little. The door slid open a few inches and she could see the gloom of an interior hallway through the crack. The high walls were unfinished drywall so she knew it was likely a back access for the retail shops in the building. She shoved again and something slid down clattering loudly on the other side of the door. The crack opened wide enough that she could press her boot against the door frame for better leverage.

If she had more time she would be more careful, more worried about what might be waiting in the gloomy hallway, but she could see Robbie swinging non-stop and knew they had to get through quickly. She could hear his breathing getting heavy and knew he couldn't keep it up much longer. They would deal with the other side when they got there.

She let the door press back against her and she quickly counted "1, 2, 3…" before shoving with everything she had. She felt the strain from her calves to her thighs while sweat poured down her face from the exertion. She heard the cracking of wood and slowly something behind her began to give. Gradually the gap widened, 4 inches, 6 inches, finally to about a foot. Kelly didn't wait any longer, she held the door with her hip while she unstrapped her backpack and slung it through.

"Any luck back there!?" Robbie shouted, no longer concerned about the noise.

"Throw me your pack!" Kelly called back.

Robbie snatched the pack from his shoulders and threw it towards the sound of her voice. He couldn't stop swinging for long. A line of undead were now surging through the front of the store. Robbie kicked over a display to slow them down and keep them from flanking him. Luckily they were spread out and he was able to stop them at the office doorway but his arms and shoulders were straining. His muscles burned from the work out and he knew he couldn't keep up the defense. It took a considerable effort to sink a hatchet into a skull, even an old rotted one, and quickly pull it back out. He knew he only had a few more swings before he would miss, or glance off or get the blade stuck. Then what?

Kelly shoved Robbie's pack through the opening and shouted, "Come on!"

Robbie kicked hard at the two lumbering creatures in front of him sending them back into the arms of the three that followed. The group went down in a gnashing, flailing heap while Robbie spun and ran towards the back of the office, praying that Kelly had found a way out.

Kelly wedged herself in the door to keep it open and as Robbie neared, she pushed through. The door started to close but Robbie hit it as hard as he could and jammed himself into the opening. It was a tight fit. Almost too tight. He had to slow down to push himself through the narrow space. The creatures were right behind him and he could see their empty eyes and snapping jaws in the dim light. He pressed for all he was worth.

Half of him was in the hallway and half was in the office. One of the things grabbed his right arm while Kelly grabbed his left. Robbie was certain the next sensation would be that of teeth biting into him when he suddenly broke free and tumbled into the hall. Kelly scrambled around and slammed her foot against the door to close it before bracing herself against it.

She saw that a stack of bed frames, still wrapped in plastic, had been leaning on the door but had slid down, giving them just enough room to escape. The door began to vibrate as dead hands began slapping at it from inside.

"It won't be long before one of them hits that exit bar," Kelly said holding the door shut while Robbie got to his feet. "Push those bed frames back up against it."

Robbie scrambled up and shoved the frames against the door. Then he braced one against the opposite wall of the narrow hall to keep them in place. "That won't hold long but might buy us a few minutes," he gasped.

"Then we better get moving," Kelly said as they both strapped their bags back on.

Along the hallway every 20 or so feet, in both directions, was a doorway similar to the one from which they had just emerged. Several of the doors, shops that must have faced the street, had small windows which let in narrow shafts of light that reflected on the pale drywall. The glow was just enough to see that the hallway was littered with furniture and items from the stores. Pointing towards the darker end of the hall, Kelly said, "This way leads away from the street. Maybe we can find a way to the other side of the building."

"Ok," Robbie snapped the last of his pack's straps in place and motioned for her to go ahead. "Watch your step. This place is a major fire hazard. I hope the Fire Marshal doesn't see this shit."

"Shh," Kelly hushed as she started down the hall.

As they walked away the sound of their pursuers groans and slapping echoed through the hall behind them. Their movement was slow but methodical as they made their way through the dusty junk and debris. Several times they had to stop and help each other over precariously stacked desks and chairs. They had seen this before. It was a sign of the last desperate struggle of some person or group. Furniture was stacked at choke points to hold back the undead long enough to retreat a little further. There were no bodies here and the dust was thick so whoever it was had either escaped or gotten up and wandered away a long time ago.

They followed the hall through several turns as it continued along behind the building's retail space. Finally they reached an intersection where three halls came together in front of a wide service door. There was no window on the door but they guessed that it must lead into a public area of the building. Kelly quietly approached and leaned her ear close to the door. Robbie raised his eyebrow in an unspoken question of whether she heard anything. She shook her head, 'no.'

Robbie looked back down the hallways coming into the intersection. They were dark. Being off the main street, those shops didn't have the natural light shining in. He looked back at Kelly and used two fingers to point at the door and shrugged, another silent question. 'Go through?'

Just then there was a click and clatter from the direction they had come. A door had opened somewhere behind them. Maybe not the door they had come through, but somewhere back there the creatures had found their way into the service hallway. The echoes of their shuffling feet scraping over concrete and their bodies impacting and dragging along the walls reverberated through the empty air. They both knew it wouldn't be long before the animated corpses were tripping over the collected debris and discarded furniture scattered in the hall. They were far enough away to escape but the noise would raise the curiosity of any other undead who might be lurking in the area. They needed to go quickly.

"Crap!" Kelly whispered, raised her axe handle and pushed open the door. She held it open for a moment, just long enough to be sure there was nothing waiting immediately on the other side, before stepping through. Robbie followed her with his hatchet ready.

They stepped into a short hallway. On the left and right were cavernous openings, which smelled of earth and mold, marking entrances to what were once public restrooms. A large plastic garbage can sat near a set of water fountains. Robbie grabbed it and slid it over in front of the double doors they had come through. Kelly gave him a questioning look.

"It won't stop them," Robbie whispered, "but we might hear them when they come through."

Kelly accepted the explanation with a nod and they stepped to the mouth of the hall. Beyond, there was a large atrium and food court. Light streamed in from above through the clouded tiles of an ornate raised glass ceiling. Aside from a few overturned chairs and a layer of mold on the floor, the area was surprisingly undisturbed. Rows of small fast food counters surrounded the court. Their brightly colored facades were faded but still recognizable. They scanned for movement or human figures but saw none. Anything could be hiding in the dark recesses of the restaurants but that didn't pose an immediate threat.

"I think that's the main entrance down there." Kelly said pointing to the right. Down some stairs was a long row of glass doors, a small gap and then another set of doors leading out onto the street.

"The security gates are down," Robbie indicated the metal lattice that stretched down over the doors on the far side.

There was a clang and a crash somewhere in the corridor behind them.

"No way to get them up in time." He said looking back.

"I think that takes us back to the main street anyway. Back where we started," Kelly opined. "If we cut through the mall there has to be a back entrance or parking garage we can get out through."

"Ok let's go," Robbie agreed as another crash sounded behind them, "we can't stay here."

Chapter 7

Keeping low they ran through the food court and out into the central concourse of the mall. Huge decorative planters filled with lush, fake grasses and trees gave them cover but also might hide other things. In the center of the concourse, a bank of rusted escalators lead to a second level. Robbie glanced up but didn't see any movement there either. He hoped there weren't any jumpers upstairs.

"There," Kelly pointed. At the far end of the hall, just in front of a big box department store, a light was shining in from the side. That has to be one of the exits. Let's go."

They moved quickly down the wide hallway, trying to step quietly while keeping low and watching the corners. The corridor was about 100 yards long and lined with the famous brands and stores that had filled up so much of their lives back in the day. Each had large plate glass windows that once displayed the latest styles and products.

The windows were now clouded with dust and mold making it hard to see beyond the signs hanging against them. In many, there were unmoving human shaped figures that seemed to be standing sentry over the long-closed shops. They hoped those were mannequins but kept their movement to the middle of the hallway just in case.

As they neared the end, they heard a thump and rattle that could only be the plastic trash can tumbling to the floor. Immediately after that, they heard the slapping and moaning that signaled the arrival of a large group of flesh eaters.

They reached the entrance to the retail store and turned left to follow the light into the side hall. Ahead they spotted another row of large glass doors and beyond that, the ground floor of a parking garage. They sped to the doors and skidded to a halt just in front of them.

"Shit!" Robbie cursed. Here too, the security gates were down. The metal bars were thin and they hadn't seen them until they got close. The gates rattled as Robbie pulled on them but they were locked tight.

"Stop!" Kelly whispered loudly. "They'll hear you. We're going to be trapped."

They turned and ran back to the main hall. Down by the escalators they could see movement as figures began shambling out of the food court

They looked around frantically for another exit but found that all the doors were locked and all the stores had their security shutters down.

"God damn!" Robbie said under his breath. "What fucking Mall Cop sticks around to lock everything up during a zombie, fucking, apocalypse?"

"We have to go back to the escalators," Kelly said out of breath. "Maybe there is another way out upstairs. But, we have to go now before there are too many to get by."

"Go," was all Robbie said as they sprinted back towards the growing crowd of undead shoppers.

In moments, they were back at the intersection in front of the escalators, dodging through a few dozen tattered undead figures. The creatures seemed to be lost. Their faces had the vacant look of someone who has entered a room but forgotten what they came for, until Robbie and Kelly dashed into their midst. This seemed to give them renewed purpose and they suddenly began to jerk about to follow the tasty morsels suddenly almost in arms reach. The morsels didn't slow though, they ran ahead, pushing and shoving the zombies out of their way before they could react.

Kelly was in front and bolted up the unmoving escalator, choosing the one on the right out of old habit. Right behind her, Robbie glanced over at the food court as they ascended and saw that it was filling up fast. A collective groan rumbled through the horde as a thousand dead eyes turned to watch their dinner disappearing upstairs. Less than an instant later the groan turned to a roar as the creatures bared their teeth and began a stampede towards them.

The pair reached the top and sprinted straight along the upper level. Robbie was thankful to find that this floor seemed as deserted as the previous with nothing but clouded shop windows along their path. Looking down over the railing, he saw that many of the zombies had stayed on the first floor and were following them from below. They shambled along with their arms outstretched as if begging their prey to jump down to them. He would have laughed except, looking back, he noticed that an equal number had managed to maneuver up the escalator and were spilling onto the landing behind them.

Their hearts raced as they reached the hallway leading to another exit.

"Dammit!" Kelly spat as they again skidded to a halt. A van had rammed into the gate effectively blocking the way.

Robbie dropped to his knees hoping to see a way under the van but the gate was tangled up tightly in its undercarriage. In his mind he did the math and realized they might be able to get it undone if they had time. But, looking back down the hall he realized they didn't have that luxury.

Kelly frantically pulled at the doors leading off the hallway but they all seemed to be locked tight. Like Robbie, she considered, just for a second, that they might be able to work a door open but she came to the same conclusion. No time! Undead figures shuffled towards them less than 30 yards away. They would be fighting for their lives in less than a minute and given the size of this group she knew it would be a losing battle.

She pulled out her bow staff and set her feet. She knew they would die but at least they would go down fighting. She decided if this was the end, she did not want to be cornered so she began walking intently towards the creatures. She intended to greet them and introduce them to the business end of her stick.

Two approached her and went down with heavy cracks to the head. Behind them were three more and behind them at least a hundred. Kelly started swinging. She was so focused she almost didn't hear Robbie calling her from behind.

"Kelly!" Robbie called. "Over here! Come back! What the hell are you doing?! Get up here!"

She glanced back to see Robbie scaling one of the large columns that ran all the way up to support the glass ceiling. It was made with interwoven crossbars that she had assumed to be decorative. In an instant she dropped back, darted to the column, grabbed the highest rung she could reach and began climbing for her life. The throng of hungry zombies slammed into the column right behind her. Swinging their arms at her feet, they desperately grabbed after her as she pulled herself up and out of range. They howled in starving frustration as the thing they wanted to eat got away.

"Oh shit," Kelly gasped as she caught her breath at the top. "That was too close."

"You ok?" Robbie asked.

"Yea," she sighed breathing heavily. "Just another day almost getting eaten by zombies."

"It's not over yet," Robbie said, apologetically nodding behind her.

Kelly swung her head around half expecting to see the undead swinging after them through the rafters like monkeys. Instead, she saw that there was a lattice of girder trusses stretching out from each of the columns that held up the frames for the rooftop windows.

"Oh…" she said letting out her breath as she realized what was next.

"See that ledge over there above the store fronts?" Robbie asked. "We'll have to go across hand to hand but once we get there we can break one those windows and climb out onto the roof. There has to be a service ladder or some way down from there."

"Yea," Kelly tried to sound confident but her uncertainty was clear. It was a long way to hand over hand and although she knew she was stronger than ever, she wasn't sure she had the upper body strength to make it.

"You can do it," Robbie said encouragingly. "It's only what? 20 feet to the ledge? Easy day."

"The only easy day was yesterday," Kelly answered trying to reassure herself as she rested her head against the cool metal of the column.

"Come on, Kel," Robbie said, "we can't go down, and we can't stay here. We can do this."

"I know," she said, "I just hate it. I'm starting to think we shouldn't have killed Trent. At least we would be alive and safe."

"You know that's not true!" Robbie exclaimed. "You know he was going to kill us as soon as he got tired of us. Now stop talking shit and let's get across that beam!"

Robbie scrambled around to Kelly and reached up to grab the truss. "I'll go first. After I'm across, you follow. Ok?"

"Got it," Kelly replied looking down at the surge of snapping ghouls that surrounded the column and seemed to fill up every inch of space below. She didn't like the idea of climbing across the ironwork but didn't see any other options.

Robbie grabbed the bar with both hands and pulled hard to test it. The ironwork didn't budge so he lifted his weight off the column and slowly let himself hang freely over the hungry crowd below. He immediately felt the strain on his fingers and palms. He was strong but not used to holding all of his weight in this way. A shot of panic ran through him but he knew there was no way down and no other way to escape so he swung himself forward, grabbed the truss further out and began making his way across as quickly and carefully as possible.

By the time he reached half way, his fingers were burning from the strain of his weight. Each time he released the bar with one hand, he felt the other sliding and was just barely able to grab the next length. One slip and his body would pull loose and send him spiraling into the hungry mob below. The pads under his fingers were on fire as he wrapped them again and again around the rough iron truss. He swore there was some sort of grease on the bars causing his skin to slip and slide.

The other side seemed suddenly too far away and he began to fear that it might be out of reach. The muscles in his fingers were going numb and beginning to ignore his commands to hold on. He could barely get his hands to grip in time and he felt gravity pulling at him as if it had him by the ankles. Running out of options he used everything he had left to swing up and grab the bar between his knees. He quickly wrapped his arms through the bars to free up his hands and gasped in relief as he felt the weight shift.

"Robbie!" Kelly shouted. "Are you ok?!"

"Yea," he panted as he clinched and unclenched his fingers trying to get blood flowing through them again. The skin was torn and blood was beginning to trickle through the lines of his skin. He doubted they would be able to grip the bar again. He could feel his weight pulling at the grip of his knees and the bar beginning to eat into his elbows. He knew he couldn't stay in that position long.

Robbie hung his head back and looked straight down at the ghouls waiting below to feast on him. Then he glanced over and estimated the ledge to be about five feet away. It seemed such a short distance but he questioned whether he could make it. He decided the longer he hung there the worse it would get. He knew he had to move, and fast, before his muscles were too sore to go any further. Using his elbows and knees as clamps, he began crabbing along the piping towards the ledge and tall side windows. He closed his eyes and ignored the pain until his foot hit the outer wall. Then, although dizzy and exhausted from hanging upside down, he swung up and grabbed the cross beam. His bloody hand nearly slipped and it felt as if the beam were white hot but he held long enough to swing himself up and over. He slid down and slumped onto the metal shelf, shaking his hands to run cool air over the torn blisters.

He heard Kelly the first few times she tried calling to him but could only respond with a raspy moan of pain.

"Hey!" She shouted. "Move out of the way. I'm coming over!"

This brought Robbie back to his senses and he called back, "No! Don't! You won't make it."

For a moment it seemed as if she didn't understand, but he held up his hands to show her the blood and blisters.

"It's too far," he said, "and the bar has got some kind of grease on it."

She paused and looked down at the crowds gathered at the base of her column. "What then?" She asked.

"Give me a minute," Robbie replied. "I'll go down to the other end of the mall on the ledge. I'll make a bunch of noise so they follow me. When it clears out you climb down and back up on this side. See?" He pointed, "There's another column that comes up on this side in the corner of the building over there. When you get up just follow the ledge this way and we can meet in the middle."

Kelly thought for a second but didn't see any alternative. "Yea, ok" she said. "Be careful."

"You too," Robbie said as he crawled to his feet and began to creeping along the ledge. It was only about 3 feet wide and divided by regular support beams and struts which made movement slow but much easier than hanging upside down from an iron bar over a sea of zombies. "Come on you fuckers!" he yelled.

The stumbling corpses below took notice and began to follow him like a tide that had rushed in one way and now crashed back over itself going the other. There were a lot of them, Robbie noted. They were bunched up like Black Friday, after Christmas and going out of business sales all fell on the same day. He could feel the floors and walls vibrate as the mass moved together. Once a large group of them got moving in one direction the others were drawn in by the noise and motion.

'Pack animals in life and death.' Robbie thought, while he threaded his way through the ceiling structures.

Kelly shifted around to the back side of the support beam so that she was exposed to fewer undead who might be looking up. From this side, it was only those further below on the first floor who could see her. That was ok. They were far enough away that they weren't a threat. 'Unless I fell,' she thought, but she pushed that idea out of her head. She peeked around to watch the horde on the second level turn and begin to follow Robbie as he moved down the hall. He yelled and clanged his knife on the metal supports to keep their attention. Most of them followed, some looking up at him hungrily while others shuffled along following the mob, unable to raise their heads due to various gruesome injuries.

Within a few minutes, the mob had mostly cleared out down below. There were just three that she could see, still near the base of the column. Two stood motionless with their jaws open and staring off into space like shoppers trying to remember where they had parked. They were about ten feet apart from each other and Kelly estimated the nearer of the two to be five feet or so from the bottom of the column. The third had no legs and was dragging itself slowly along the tiles further away. There was notably no trail of oozing gore following behind the thing which told Kelly it had been dead and crawling that way for quite a while.

Kelly looked up and saw the mob of undead following Robbie across the walkway over the food court and decided her chances were as good as they would get. She scrambled down the outside of the column, used the railing as a step and jumped down onto the floor. The nearest creature spun towards her at the sound of her feet hitting the ground. But, it was slow and Kelly was able to bring her stick around to crush its skull. It collapsed into a heap with the other one coming her way in a drunken stumble. She dodged it and used its momentum to heave it over the balcony and down into the throngs below. She paused and leaned on the railing to watch it fall. There was a loud thud, which echoed through the empty building, as it crashed into the crowd below.

Kelly looked back down the hall and saw that the noise had captured the attention of the trailing end of the herd following Robbie. Several had started to break off and come back. 'Time to go,' Kelly thought and turned to run towards the column along the wall. To her shock something was tangled around her feet and her forward motion spun her towards the ground. The fall happened fast and she hit the ground hard, seeing stars for a second. When she opened her eyes her head was on the floor looking down the hall. She could see the undead crowding her way and, still in a foggy panic, she pumped her legs to clear whatever had caused her to trip. Then she realized what it was.

The damned legless one had hold of her boot. The fall had propelled her slightly ahead of it but the thing, it looked like it may have been a woman once, had a death grip on her shoe and was using it to pull herself up. Her mouth gaped open in a wide, hungry snarl revealing ragged teeth set in blackened gums. Kelly instinctively kicked at its face, knocking it back, but having no effect on its grip.

"Shit!" Kelly growled in anger and fear as she noticed the mob getting closer. Realizing she had little time, she flipped over and began crawling towards the column against the outside wall. The legless creature dragged along behind her but did not loosen its grip. Seeing the live, human prey moving in front of them caused the tangle of undead to surge forward. Kelly noted they were closing the distance quickly and she turned her crawling into a panicked kicking scramble across the cold tile floor. The last few feet she was able to stand and pull the creature behind her like a ball and chain.

When she reached the column the tide of snarling people eaters was just 15 feet behind her. Grabbing the decorative lattice of trusses she began scaling up in an adrenaline fueled route. She strained to quickly pull herself out of reach, hand over hand, too frightened to look back or down. She felt the vibrations of the undead crashing into the column as they all tried to be the first to sink their teeth into their fleeing prey. Just as she thought she might be out of arm's reach, she was suddenly jerked to a stop so hard that she almost lost her grip.

"Aaaah!" Kelly screamed as she fought to keep her hands firmly on the ironwork. She was able to get one foot onto a bar and try to push herself up but her other leg was being held and pulled down. Glancing over her shoulder she saw that the legless woman was still latched onto her and the creatures below had grabbed onto her. They were unwittingly using her as leverage to drag their dinner back into their grips. Their arms flailed and Kelly looked out into the sea of undead faces glaring at her, willing her to drop down and join them.

Instead she shouted, "NO!" and began pulling herself up with all her strength kicking hard at the ghoul wrapped around her ankle. 'How could these things be so strong?' she wondered as sweat began pouring down her brow.

She kicked and kicked until suddenly she felt the weight come off her leg. Looking down she saw that the thing's arms had come off and the torso tumbled back down into the throng. She watched as the half woman was swallowed up and disappeared under the crowd, likely to be crushed beneath their feet.

"Bitch!" Kelly yelled down as she kicked off the dangling arms and began to scramble up away from the horde of hungry mouths. Her hands and fingers burned as she reached the ledge at the top but she pulled herself over and lay back to catch her breath.

"You alright?" Robbie called from the other side of a tangle of support beams.

"I don't know." Kelly answered with a sigh, looking down at her foot expecting to see the hands still there, holding on. The tight grip of the legless woman were gone but had been replaced by a searing pain. "My ankle," she cried.

"Bite?!" Robbie said with alarm.

"No…" Kelly groaned in pain. "Twisted, I think. That bitch grabbed my foot. I must have turned it wrong trying to get away."

"Ok, wait there." Robbie said. "I'll bust out this window and come around to you."

Kelly leaned back on the ledge stared down at the ravenous mob. Her heart raced, her arms ached, her ankle pounded and suddenly her chest heaved and tears welled up in her eyes. The salty water seemed to boil up uncontrollably from inside and pour down her face as she began to shake and cry. Her vision blurred and the things below seemed to melt together like an impressionist painting as her teardrops rained down on them. She was barely aware of the sound of breaking glass near or of Robbie pulling her from the ledge and out onto the roof.

Chapter 8

Robbie helped her into the shade of a huge sign for a long-gone department store and leaned her against its base. She sat there hunched over as her tears and adrenaline drained to be replaced with exhaustion and sore muscles. Robbie sat with her for a while then decided to give her some privacy by exploring the roof while she rested.

When he came back, she was stretching and massaging her ankle hoping the pain would subside. It wasn't swelling, she observed with some relief, but it hurt like hell anyway.

"It will be dark in a few hours," Robbie said kneeling next to her. "I think we can still make it to the river if we stick to the roof tops. It's a little further from up here but safer than trying to get across from street level. Do you think you are up to it?"

"Yes," Kelly sighed and looked around, "I don't want to stay up here tonight."

"That's the spirit," Robbie said offering her a drink from his canteen. "How's the ankle?"

"Hurts like a bitch," she winced.

"It's maybe a mile that way," Robbie pointed at the roofline of the buildings nearby.

"More like three miles if we stay on the rooftops," Kelly growled.

"Maybe, but it's safer up here and it's mostly flat." Robbie replied. "These buildings are close together so we should be able to move across without too much jumping or climbing. There's a row of old warehouses as we get closer to the water."

"Ok," Kelly said holding out her hand. "Help me up."

Robbie lifted her and pulled her arm around his neck for support. "Come on, let's get out of here. I always hated malls."

Kelly looked back at the window they had broken to get out.

"Forget something?" Robbie said.

"No," she replied, "just a little paranoid I guess."

"I don't think they can climb," Robbie laughed, "not yet anyway. And the good news is, there is only one way out of that mall so that's a few hundred we don't have to worry about running into on the street any time soon."

She nodded in agreement and they moved out across the rooftop. It was slow going even though the buildings were connected in many places and only inches apart in others. There were drops and climbs and uneven surfaces mixed with rocks and crumbling concrete. Kelly's ankle held her back while Robbie's blistered hands made his grip unsure. They had to stop often to rest, but as the sun was setting, they had gone far enough that they could see the river.

"Look," Robbie indicated as Kelly limped up behind him. "You can see the water right through there."

Kelly held her hand up to shade her eyes. The buildings closer to the water were taller, blocking much of the view, but she could see the glittering surface of the Apalachicola River in the distance between them. "I think we went too far," she said, "the Century Bridge seems closer than it should be. "

"Yea," Robbie answered. "We had to go upriver some, to the north-west, so we could cross over without going down to street level."

"Why didn't you tell me that?" Kelly asked annoyed.

"Didn't think it would matter," said Robbie. "Even if there aren't many dead on the streets, we're in no shape to run or fight very well."

"I guess," Kelly sighed in agreement. The ache in her ankle had stretched up her leg and her other hip and knee were getting sore from compensating as she limped along. "I'm not going to be able to go much further," she winced. "How long do you think we have?"

"Not far," Robbie replied pointing along a row of warehouses that stretched out ahead of them. "We just follow the roofs down to the wharf area over there. See? We should be able to climb down there and then work our way along the waterfront up to the condominium."

"It will be dark by then," Kelly pointed out.

"Yes," Robbie agreed. "We will have to play it by ear when we get to the wharf. If it looks clear, we'll go down. If not, we will have to find a spot to hole up for the night."

Kelly gave him a look he recognized as her not liking what he was saying.

"On the bright side," he smiled, "it looks like these are all old warehouses so there should be plenty of zombie free places to sleep tonight if we need."

"What makes you think that?" Kelly asked.

"These are all wide open, multi floor brick buildings built in the 1900s," Robbie reasoned. "Nothing's getting in, and with all these big broken windows and wide-open storage lofts, anything inside would surely have fallen out by now."

Kelly gave him another look but didn't have the energy to argue with him about his poor logic. The pain in her legs and back was growing while they stood there talking. It wasn't much better when they were moving but at least the hiking and climbing gave her something else to concentrate on. "Ok, let's go," she said.

Robbie turned and climbed over the ledge onto the first of the warehouses. Unlike the office buildings, these had roofs with a slight pitch. They were also covered in layers of green moss and undergrowth that sprang from years of built up sediment. Medium sized bushes and trees had sprouted from the crevices making it like walking through a thicket on a hillside. Kelly watched him wind away through the calf-high grass and briars as she struggled over the low wall dividing the two roof tops.

Ordinarily, they would worry about walking through such undergrowth, especially as the shadows lengthened and it became difficult to see what lay below. The dead could be lying still and dormant just below the grassy stalks. But, they were tired and their muscles ached and, while they remained wary, they both assumed the likelihood of any living dead skulking in the grass on a rooftop was small. As the thought ran through her head, Kelly eased herself down onto the mossy surface and looked over for Robbie.

She saw his silhouette nearly at the far side of the roof and began limping after him. Catching his shadow scrambling over the next wall, she started to shout after him to wait for her, but it was all she could do to push forward with all her joints on fire and back aching as if it were in a vice. She knew she would have to stop and rest again soon.

She limped on but her progress was further slowed by the uneven surface of the ground. The dirt piled in awkward ways and the lumps of grass and thorns made it so that she had to pause with each step to ensure she had a solid surface to place her feet. She miss-stepped a few times, pain shot up her leg and she nearly lost her balance. Each step seemed more difficult and she began to fear that if she fell into this lumpy grass she would not be able to get up again.

By the time she reached the low wall separating the next warehouse the sun had set. A thin ribbon of red marked the spot on the horizon where the star ducked behind the earth in the western sky. Kelly leaned on the concrete barrier to rest and take the weight off of her ankle.

Crunching of footsteps drew her attention to a figure approaching in the darkness.

"Is that you Robbie?" she called out.

"Yea," Robbie replied.

"Where the hell have you been," she complained. "I can barely walk. You can't just leave me like that."

"Sorry," he replied, "I went ahead to find a way down."

"Well don't just take off like that," Kelly whispered angrily, "at least let me know where you are going."

"Yea," Robbie said sheepishly, "I will. Sorry."

"Did you?" Kelly asked.

"Did I what?" he answered.

"Find a way down?!" She glared at him.

"Oh... yea," Robbie stuttered. "Only two more buildings to go and there is a fire escape we can take to the ground. Looks like a few blocks to the water front. Then we can make our way back to the condo."

"Are there any of them down there?" Kelly asked absently rubbing her foot.

"It was getting dark," Robbie replied, "but I only saw a few. If we are quiet I think we can slip past them."

"Ugh." Kelly sighed in pain. "Look, I don't think I can go much further tonight. I can hardly walk. We need to find a safe place to hide until morning. Hopefully, it will be better by then."

"Ok," Robbie replied, "I thought about that. We are in the Farmers Market area. There are offices in these buildings we can hide in. Come over here and look down."

Robbie led her to the edge where there was enough moonlight to reveal the warehouse entrances down below. A large, refrigerated truck with "Baldwin Produce" and a cornucopia logo painted on the side was backed into the nearest bay. Old crates were stacked nearby with similar markings. Whatever produce was in them was obviously long gone.

"See those steps down there and that doorway?" Robbie pointed. "Those are where the offices are for the warehouses. That's where they keep the money and do the books so they are walled off from everything else. The doors are metal and the walls are stone and brick. We just need to find one that is open and slip in without being noticed."

"How do you know all that?" Kelly asked.

"Roy and I worked down here one summer, about two blocks over, a fish supply place." Robbie replied, "We were supposed to load trucks and stuff but when they figured out we could read and do basic math, they moved us into the office. Most of the guys out here working the docks are not the brightest bulbs, you know. The lady in the office, Ms. Julie, was the owner's girlfriend so she didn't really care if a couple of high school kids did the books as long as she didn't have to."

"Yea, ok." Kelly stopped him from going further. She was exhausted from the pain jolting through her body and felt her energy reserves ebbing. "Look, it's going to take me a while to get to the fire escape and it's just a waste of time for you to help me…"

"C'mon," Robbie said encouragingly. "You can do it."

"No," she hushed him. "Listen. I can do it but it's going to take me a while, so you scout ahead. Find us a spot to crash. I'll wait by the ladder on the roof until you come back. Alright?"

Robbie nodded his understanding.

"Go on then," she waived him away but followed up with a, "be careful," that was equal parts worried, warning and threat.

67

"I will," he whispered back as he climbed over the low wall onto the roof of the last warehouse.

Kelly took a deep breath to steal herself and began to slowly limp after him. It only took a few agonizing seconds to climb over the wall but when she got her footing and looked up again, she could make out Robbie's dark shape already half way across the overgrown expanse. She looked at the ground and had just begun to take a cautious step forward when she heard a loud crack! Her head jerked up as she heard a crash, a muffled shout, and the sound of breaking glass. She couldn't see anything in the darkness but the echo of heavy objects and debris thumping to the ground instantly confirmed that he had fallen through.

"Robbie!" She screamed, the need to remain quiet suddenly forgotten. She fell to her knees and scrambled forward through the brush, dragging her bad foot and ignoring the thorns and sharp blades of grass slicing into her hands. She followed the echoing waterfall sound of loose dirt and sand pouring down into space. She felt her way forward in the darkness until she came to a rectangular section that was darker than everything else. She plunged her hand down into the gap and felt only nothingness and the cloud of thin particles of dust kicked up by the collapse. "Robbie?!" she rasped in a loud whisper down into the hole and paused for a reply. None came.

"Oh fuck, fuck, fuck!" she cried in a hoarse whisper, "Robbie?! Robbie?!"

Somewhere, not far away, she heard moans and the familiar scraping and dragging of preternatural feet attracted by the noise. Kelly scrambled back and dug into her back pack for her small pen light, then rolled over and pointed it down into the darkness. Before clicking it on she said a quiet prayer that the things had not already found him. Then she pushed the button and stared into the abyss expecting the worst.

At first the cloud of dirt and dust reflected her light and she couldn't see anything. But, after a moment, her eyes adjusted and she began to make out shapes on the floor far below. A tangled, weaving jungle of stalks and vines grew up towards her. Whatever had been in there before had taken root so that the entire warehouse was laid with a fetid carpet of stalks and plants. She almost could not see beyond it but as the dust settled she caught the outline of a figure laying still just outside the rows, near the brick wall of the warehouse.

Kelly quickly scanned around to see if any of the creatures were approaching through the thick stalks. She saw none but her beam of light was narrow and barely made a dent in the darkness of the huge building. She could hear them coming closer but they seemed to be outside the walls. Not in the warehouse yet, but close enough to be very concerned. She had to get down there before those things found Robbie. She had to drag him someplace safe. It would be hard but, even if he were dead, she would not let them have him.

Kelly leaned into the hole and ran her light along the inside wall. There were some ledges and metal girders supporting the ceiling. She cursed. On any other day she could likely shimmy over and down but with her ankle sprain and overall state of pained exhaustion she doubted she could do it. And if she fell, she told herself, that wouldn't do either of them any good. She looked around for other options.

Spotting something at the edge of her light, she ran it back and saw in the center of the warehouse, an enclosed safety ladder running up to the roof. It looked like it was probably old and rusted before the zombie apocalypse, but it was a better option than trying to 'spiderman' her way down the inner wall. "Hold on Robbie," she said with a grunt as she pushed herself up and crawled towards the spine of the rooftop. Once there she quickly located the metal cage intended as a repair access. Beneath it was a heavy looking hatch.

Kelly heaved on the hatch but it wouldn't budge. *Rusted shut*, she thought, and breathing hard from the exertion, sank over her knees. *I'm not giving up*, she said to herself panting as her body begged her to lie down and quit. *I'm just thinking.*

She wondered if she could climb down and try to get in through a door or window at the ground level. But, the undead were outside the building now. She could hear them moaning and scraping along the loading areas, banging into things. The clamor would bring more. If she were at full strength she might be able to do it or lead them away and loop back around. But not now. Tears of frustration began welling up in her eyes.

"Nooo," she wailed under her breath as she grabbed the hatch and began shaking it with all she had hoping to loosen it. On her second try she felt a lever between the hatch and the rooftop. She pushed at it until it shifted in an arc and she heard something click inside. Grabbing the hatch again she pulled hard and though it resisted it slowly began to rise. Her back and shoulders protested at the effort but she finally got it all the way open.

Grabbing her small flashlight again, she shone it down onto the brown flaking steps of the ladder below. "Oh thank god," she gasped and climbed down the hole.

Inside the warehouse she could still hear the moans of the dead but their sounds were muffled by the thick walls and heavy carpet of plant life below. She did a slow careful hop down the rungs to keep the weight off her injured ankle. The steel ladder groaned as it begrudgingly fulfilled its long forgotten purpose but it held her weight as she descended. As she neared the ground she scanned the canopy of tall plants for movement, and seeing none she let herself down through their tangled branches and leafy stalks.

When she reached the ground it felt like creeping into a tunnel. The closeness of the growth around her gave her the creeps and it didn't help that she was unable to see more than a few feet ahead through the dense foliage. She felt like she was in a haunted house where anything could jump out at any second. It was quiet, which she told herself was good, but couldn't shake the feeling that the silence made it scarier. She knew if the undead were already inside they would be making plenty of noise but that didn't help slow her heartbeat.

She noted that the packed earth where she stood was actually a pathway a few feet wide. On either side, railroad ties had been laid to create plotted garden beds. She began to limp through the channel between the raised beds. Robbie was over to her right somewhere and she hoped that the path would let her turn in that direction soon. She didn't think she had the energy to cut through the thick leafy stalks or fight her way through whatever grew inside them.

The agitated howls of the things outside crept in but the thick walls of the old warehouse made them seem far away. Frustratingly, her own footsteps and breathing echoed loudly in her ears as she pushed through the fetid passageway. She moved slowly and stopped every few feet to listen and hope nothing was closing in on her. She tried to slow her breathing and relax the heartbeat that was banging in her ears. But, all she could hear was herself and the plant life brushing against her as she limped painfully onward.

Emerging at an intersection she sighed with relief that there was a path going in the direction where she hoped Robbie still lay. She turned and pushed on hoping it was the right direction. In the undergrowth she suddenly feared she may have lost her way and had to fight back panic that she might have gotten lost in the thick vegetation.

A spider web wrapped over her face and she began to flail at it as she lurched forward. Suddenly finding herself in a more open area she flung at the web until she could see again. She still felt the silky strings against her skin but she readied in case something more deadly waited nearby. The darkness did nothing to ease her fears but nothing lurched out from its depths.

The cool brick wall of the old warehouse rose up in front of her and she placed her hand against its cool surface to steady herself. The path was slightly wider here. She began stumbling along the wall until her little light caught a figure laying prone just ahead. She rushed to him praying that she was not too late.

Flipping Robbie over, she shook him and put her head to his chest. She sighed with relief when she heard a heartbeat and breathing. "Thank god," she whispered and began to beg, "Robbie! Robbie! Wake up honey. We gotta move. We can't stay here. Come on."

Robbie lay still in the dirt as she held him.

"Ok, Ok, I got you," Kelly said as she grabbed him by the lapel of his jacket. "I'm going to get us some place safe. Just hold on." She pulled and fire lit up her ankle causing her to drop him again. Covering her mouth to stifle a scream, she knelt face down in the dirt until it became bearable again.

Catching her breath, she looked around hoping to see an office or some other enclosed structure but with her pen light she could not see further than a dozen feet through the outstretched branches of the overgrown gardens. She knew she didn't have the strength to drag him around in the dark and she would not leave him again. She had no idea how long it would be before the undead found their way inside. All these old buildings had started to fall apart and there was bound to be an open door or collapsed wall somewhere.

Finally, tears of exhaustion and fear running down her face, she looked up at the jungle of thick stalks inside the raised garden and had an idea. It was a last resort but that's all she had left. She put Robbie's head in her lap, grabbed him under his arms and began scooting backwards while pushing with her good foot. She pulled him over the hump and into the thick brush. Pressing down the stalks and vines with her back and butt she dragged him until they were all the way inside and completely engulfed within the deep brush.

She checked him again to ensure he was still breathing. When she was sure he was still alive she lay down next to him and rested her arm over him so she could feel his heart beat. She lay there, too tired and in too much pain to do anything else.

"Come on Robbie," she whispered more to herself than him, "make it until morning. Can't do anything tonight with those things outside. I'll think of something in the morning and you'll be ok. You're going to be ok. I'm going to lie here with you and keep watch. I'm going to stay up all night and make sure those things don't find us."

She lay back in the lumpy soil and stared up at the lines of the dark stalks stretching out above her. It was quiet except for the grumbles of the creatures stumbling around on the other side of the wall. Her breathing slowed as she tried to relax, the ache in her back eased a bit while pain in her ankle thumped like a drum in her ears. The steady beat reminded her of a song her dad used to play when he worked in the garage. It was called 'The Heart of Rock and Roll or something,' she thought, and it began to play in her memory.

Chapter 9

Kelly used to love playing in the garage when her dad was out there working on his old car. At first she just went there to hide from her mom, so she wouldn't have to clean her room, but found she liked spending time with her dad. The smell of grease and leather would fill the air while he tinkered and polished. He taught her how to do an oil change and fix a flat tire, which hadn't been that useful, but it did build up her confidence.

She lay there on the cold concrete, trying to loosen a rusted bolt under the wheel well when her dad shined his shop light at her and said, "Uh oh, I hear your mom, I think it's time for you to go clean your room."

"Can you stall her I'm almost done?" Kelly asked looking up at her dad who was wiping his hands on an old greasy rag. With the glare of the light in her eyes she could only see his blurry outline. He looked very young, like he did when she was a little girl, which struck her as odd but it was hard to see with the bright light aimed at her face. "And can you turn off that light!"

"I don't think so," he replied as he walked towards the door to the garage. She hoped he would talk to her mom but the next sound she heard was her mother's voice and it didn't sound happy.

"Oh come on Mom," she pouted, "I can clean my room tomorrow."

"Do not fucking move you sons of bitches!" came the reply.

'Not Mom!' She jerked awake and through the glare of light she could make out two figures standing in the pathway near their feet. Her mind scrambled to put it all together while her hands instinctively searched for her bow staff.

"I said," the voice shouted, "do not fucking move or we will unload this goddam buckshot into your ass, man!"

Still shaking from the shock of being suddenly awakened, but realizing that if they were talking they were not the undead, Kelly help up her hands palms out to show she held no weapons. Squinting to see through the sleep crud that had built up in her eyes, she began to get a better picture of who was yelling at her. Two elderly women stood there holding the largest guns she had ever seen.

One of the women, using both hands to level a giant silver revolver, was thin as a rail with long grey hair flowing down her back. She wore a tie dye sun dress, which draped over pale white, freckle covered skin. The other woman was larger, with dark brown skin. She had a double barrel shotgun pressed against her shoulder and pointed right at them. She wore a blue print dress that looked like something her grandmother might have worn shopping back when the world was normal.

Kelly looked at the huge shotgun. Fortunately, the woman did not look nervous or scared and Kelly hoped that meant she wouldn't accidentally pull the trigger. If it went off at this range it would blow them to pieces.

"What are you all doing in here?" the black woman asked sternly.

"Yea! What the fuck are you assholes doing in our garden, man?" the thin white woman asked.

"I'm sorry," Kelly answered hesitatingly, "we were crossing the roof and fell through. My friend fell through."

The thin woman looked up at the hole. "Well fuck me! Another goddamn hole in the roof. Just what we fucking need, man."

"Ease up, Sunshine," the black woman said never taking her eyes off of Kelly. "You say you were crossing the roof. Where were you going?"

"We were trying to get to one of the condominiums over on the water," Kelly answered, "but I hurt my ankle on the way. After he fell I, I couldn't move him and those things were out there so we hid here. I'm really sorry. We didn't know this place was yours. We just needed a safe spot to spend the night."

"Is he ok?" the woman pointed with the shotgun at the motionless Robbie.

"I don't know," Kelly answered honestly. "He's breathing but the fall knocked him out. I couldn't get him to wake up."

"Is he bit?!" The white woman said waving the pistol at the boy.

"No" Kelly answered. "He just fell hard. He must have hit his head or something. Look, we can just go and we won't bother you anymore. He will be fine I'm sure."

"He doesn't look like he's about to get up and walk any time soon," the woman with the shotgun said, "and you say you hurt your ankle? Can you walk?"

"Don't worry about us," Kelly said nervously, "we will be ok. We've gotten through worse than this."

"I'll bet you have," the big woman's face acknowledged the tough times everyone had been through since the fall. "Throw those backpacks over here."

Kelly didn't want to lose their gear but hoped maybe these old ladies would just Robbie them and let them go. She didn't have much choice in any case so she tossed the bags out onto the path.

"Sunshine," the woman said, "why don't you take a look and see what's in those bags?"

The thin woman knelt down and began going through their things. She grumbled as she pulled the cans of soup and dried foods out. "God damn, do you know how much sodium is in this crap? All these preservatives will kill you faster than those Undies, man."

Finally she looked up at her companion and said, "Nothing but shit food and standard survival gear."

"Ok," the black woman said. "Who are you?"

"I'm Kelly," she answered, "and this is Robbie. We were living downtown but we thought life might be better over on the river. So, we were moving. We didn't know there was anyone else out here, really."

"What did you do before?" the lady glared at her.

"I was a student, at the state college," Kelly continued, "working on my Masters in Fine Arts."

"And?"

"And?" Kelly asked puzzled, "...and I worked at Applebee's on the weekends, and taught art classes at the Senior Center on Wednesday nights. We, my husband and I, were saving to buy some land out of town where we could build a house, and..."

"Alright, that's enough," the woman pushed. "You and your husband there been on your own this whole time?"

"No," Kelly stammered, "I mean, he's not my husband."

The black woman lifted an eyebrow.

"He's my brother in law," Kelly quickly added.

The two older women shared a questioning glance and looked back at her.

Kelly got the feeling they didn't believe her. "But, there were more of us at first. One by one things happened, you know, some people just left to go find their families and never came back. Others, well, the zombies were everywhere in the beginning. We lost people. Friends. Good friends."

"What happened to your husband?" the thin woman asked.

"He..." Kelly started. Her eyes had started to well up. "He went out for supplies about two years ago. We haven't seen him since. We've looked but..."

The two older ladies stared at her.

"Look," Kelly sobbed, "we can go. We don't want to be any trouble."

"Ok honey," the black woman said lowering her shotgun. "Why don't you come out of the corn and let Sunshine take a look at your ankle?"

Kelly hesitatingly crawled from the thick stalks which she now realized were corn. She kept her hands up and when she was out, she leaned back against the stacked railroad tie that made up the container wall. Looking up she saw light beaming in from the ceiling and realized it was not a regular roof at all. It was the glass roof of a green house. There were large areas where the glass was dark because of the growth on the top but, even then, pinholes of light broke through.

"Oooh!" Kelly groaned as she stretched out her leg. "No wonder he broke through. We didn't know it was glass. It was so dark."

"Yes," the black woman said. "We have been meaning to clean it off but we aren't as spry as we used to be."

"Hold still," the woman called Sunshine said as she looked at Kelly's ankle. "Oh, that is swelled up pretty bad, man. We totally need to get your foot out of this boot."

"Are you a doctor?" Kelly asked.

"Yes," Sunshine smiled, "not the MD kind... but I know a little about anatomy. Wait right here." she said as she stood. "I need to take a look at your friend."

Kelly couldn't move even if she wanted. She noticed the woman with the shotgun had stepped back. The gun was pointed down but the lady remained alert and clearly wasn't taking any chances.

"Can I ask your name?" Kelly said looking up at her.

"Beatrice Baldwin," the black woman said. "And my hippie friend is Sunshine Baldwin. No family relation. We just happen to have the same last name"

"That's a pretty big coincidence," Kelly nodded, "especially now a days."

"We knew each other before," Beatrice replied. "This is our place."

"Oh?" Kelly asked, "The greenhouse is yours?"

"Well," Beatrice shifted, "everything for a few blocks actually belongs to us. Not that it matters now."

"Baldwin Produce?" Kelly said as it suddenly came to her, "Oh yea, you are Baldwin Produce! I've seen the trucks."

"If you've eaten in any restaurant within three states you've probably had our fresh vegetables," Sunshine said as she climbed back out of the corn.

"I see," Kelly nodded and motioned with her thumb over her shoulder at Robbie. "How is he?"

"I'll tell you straight, man," Sunshine said. "He's out cold. Could be a concussion or bad internal head injury and coma. Without a brain scan or something there is no way to know what it is or how long it could last."

Kelly's shoulders slumped and she felt like she might cry again.

"On the bright side," Sunshine continued, "he is breathing, there are no major injuries visible, he isn't bleeding out, and most importantly he isn't bitten. Nothing looks or feels broken and there's no major swelling. Just a few cuts and bruises really. He could wake up any minute."

"Oh," Kelly sighed, "you say you're not a medical doctor?"

"No," Sunshine said, "but I do have a Masters in Biology, a PhD in Science Education and was a tenured Professor in the Science and Biology faculty at Taylor-Whitehouse University for 25 years. Plus I'm certified in CPR and first aid by the Red Cross. So, I know a little about how the human body works. Is that good enough for you?"

"Yes," Kelly said quickly. "Sorry, we just haven't seen anyone in a long time. Thank you for looking at us. So what do we do? Do you want us to leave?"

Beatrice glanced over at Sunshine with a raised eyebrow. The thin woman wrinkled her own eyebrows and looked back at her. Kelly could tell they were in some sort of silent conference with one another but wasn't sure what the outcome would be. After a few seconds they both nodded and looked down at her.

Finally Beatrice spoke, "It doesn't look like you could get very far with that foot and your boy there isn't going anywhere either. You can stay here for a few days if you like. Hopefully your boy wakes up soon. If not…well, I don't know. Let's see how things progress."

"Oh!" Kelly sputtered. "Thank you! We won't be any trouble and we can help out with the work if you like…"

"Don't get too excited," Sunshine cut in. "We don't know you so we aren't exactly inviting you into our house, dig? You and the boy…"

"…Robbie" Kelly said.

"Yea, Robbie," Sunshine continued. "You two will have to stay down in the warehouse storage room. It's a little dusty but you can clean it up so it's not too bad. There's a pull out couch and a sofa down there. More important, it's safe. Nothing can get in and as long as you don't start banging on the walls the things outside shouldn't hear you. Dig?"

"Yes," Kelly said enthusiastically, I… dig. It's fine. We won't be any trouble I promise. You don't even have to feed us. I'll take care of Robbie until he wakes up and we can eat what we brought with us."

"Oh hell no," Sunshine winced, "we're not going to let you eat that crap. That shit will clog up your arteries! We have plenty of fresh food. You'll eat healthy while you are under our roof."

"Easy there, Sunshine," Beatrice interjected. "They may want to eat their own food. Let's not be forcing anyone to do anything."

"It's ok," Kelly beamed up at them, "we would love to have something fresh. We haven't had anything fresh since… well, I don't know how long."

"Alright, we will see, but first things," Beatrice said. "Let's get you two out of the greenhouse and up to the office."

"Probably need a wagon for the boy," Sunshine said and then yelled, "Maurice!"

Beatrice looked at her friend and rolled her eyes. "Sunny, Maurice has been gone for almost a year."

"Oh yea, man," Sunshine replied as a look of sadness swept over her face. "Damn, I'm getting forgetful in my old age. I really miss him."

"Me too," said Beatrice, "why don't you go get one of the wagons while I talk some more to our new friends?"

"Yea, yea, will do," Sunshine said before loping away through the stalks.

"She really is a PhD and a very smart lady," Beatrice said conspiratorially as she watched her go, "but age takes its toll on all of us in its own way."

"It's ok," Kelly replied as she rubbed her ankle. "This whole thing has made everyone lose their mind a little."

Beatrice smiled and after a short pause asked. "So you were an art student? What about him?"

"He was in high school," Kelly looked back over her shoulder at Robbie who lay on his back in the corn. "When it all went down, my husband Roy was able to rescue him and a bunch of his friends from the school. They went looking for their parents but... weren't able to find them."

"How did you survive?" Beatrice asked.

"We found a house boat up at Moonlight Warf, so when they got back, we were able to shove off and anchor out in the river just in time to watch the city go absolutely crazy. We didn't know if those things could swim so we kept our heads down and tried to stay quiet."

"How long were you on the boat?" Beatrice asked.

"About a month," Kelly looked down at her knees, "it wasn't a great boat to begin with and it started to leak being out in the main part of the river. It was pretty old for all the rocking and rolling and extra weight. There were a bunch of us on board with all the kids. We ran out of food and water in a few days and started making runs to other boats for supplies. When the boats ran out of stuff we started going along the pier, to the little shops."

"That's when we started losing people." She went on as she massaged her ankle. I don't know what happened to most of them. They may have been killed by those things, or whatever. Part of me hopes they just ran off and never came back."

"I'm sorry," Beatrice sympathized. "What happened to the boat?"

"The boat. Yea." Kelly continued with a sigh. "One night, something big hit us. Roy said it was probably a tree, but we didn't know. After that, the boat started listing and we knew we had to get off. Long story short, we got ashore and most of us were able to get to an office building we were able to lock down. We've moved around some since then but that's our story in a nutshell."

They both looked over at the sound of a squeaky wheel rolling towards them from the front of the greenhouse.

"Have you been here since the beginning?" Kelly asked.

"Before the beginning," Beatrice answered. "We built this company up from a small stand at the farmer's market. We bought our first warehouse 30 years ago and now, or at the end, we were the second largest produce supplier in the region."

"Why did you stay?" Kelly asked.

"When it all went down we couldn't evacuate, we just couldn't," Sunshine added as she pushed through the overgrown stalks of corn, pulling a large red wagon. "The green houses needed to be tended 24/7. If we left, it would all die, man. We just couldn't. We had our hearts in the soil, man."

"Back then they were saying it would all be over in a few weeks," Beatrice said. "The walls here are thick, the windows are high. We had plenty of fresh food and our own well for water. We figured we could ride it out and be ready to start distribution as soon as the roads were open again. We knew people would need our food when they came back."

"That shit didn't happen," Sunshine said with a cackle.

Beatrice lifted an eyebrow and nodded her head in agreement. Then she looked over at the figure laid out among the stalks and said, "C'mon and let's see if we can't get your boy loaded up and moved someplace that's not on top of my corn."

After some struggle, the three of them were able to get him loaded onto the large wagon and head back to the main entrance of the warehouse. A large enclosed breezeway separated the growing yard from the main entrance. Kelly thought it may have originally been used to back trucks into the greenhouse. The width, and small offices along the sides, gave it the look of a stable. Luckily, two huge wooden doors sealed off the street entrance. She noted that there was no light coming through so they were probably reinforced and sealed from the outside.

Kelly soon found herself on an old lounge chair next to Robbie who was laid out on a pull out sofa in what the two older ladies called "the basement." The room was small with concrete walls and a narrow window at eye level. The window had bars and was covered except for a small area that let a little light in from the street. Their hosts had also lit a few candles to provide additional light. Aside from being a cluttered, and a little dusty, the room wasn't bad, Kelly decided. Not the Ritz, but much nicer than many of the places she had slept over the last few years.

She really didn't like that they were locked in. Sunshine had apologized but stated the obvious, that they didn't know them and couldn't have them wandering around unsupervised. Kelly was in no position to argue and just prayed that the two ladies weren't actually crazy witches looking for human sacrifices, or barking mad cannibals. She doubted the latter since there was plenty of food around. She had seen more fresh vegetables in the greenhouse than she had seen in several years, and heard Sunshine mention that she had to go calm the pigs.

'Pigs!' Kelly imagined the luxury of fresh pork and bacon. If these ladies were half what they seemed, they would need to find a way to start trading with them as soon as they got settled again. She had to find out what they might want or need. To her, it seemed they had everything already, but there had to be something. She stretched out her injured ankle and tried to relax while she considered what that might be.

Chapter 10

There was a click in the lock and Sunshine appeared with a tray of steaming food. It smelled delicious, causing Kelly to cast aside thoughts that it might be poisoned or drugged, and dug right in. There was no pork, but there was fresh bread, vegetable stew and some sort of tea that she thought must be mint.

"How is it?" Sunshine asked as she watched Kelly stuff cornbread in her mouth.

"Delicious!" Kelly muttered with her cheeks full. "Thank you. I, we, haven't eaten like this in quite a while."

"I'm glad you like it," Sunshine said. "That crap food you've been eating will kill you same as the Undies."

"Undies?" Kelly asked between slurps of stew.

"Ha! Yea man," Sunshine laughed. "Before the TV stations went out there was this idiot preacher who kept talking about the undead walking the earth in the end times. I guess his church had their own broadcast tower somewhere around here because it was the only thing on after everything else went dark. He was broadcasting like 24/7 for a while and had his whole flock gathered inside. One of the ladies that was a regular kept calling the undead – 'undies' so we picked it up as a joke."

A shadow fell over her face before she went on. "Of course, the undies, the dead, got in eventually... They left the cameras running as the damn things tore them apart."

There was a long pause.

"But, we still call them Undies," Sunshine finally snorted. "Sorry to be such a downer at dinner, man."

"It's ok," Kelly replied, "thank you for the food. It's delicious and I don't know how to repay you."

"No need missy, eat up, heal up and carry on. It's all we can ask." The older woman smiled and looked over at Robbie. "Any changes there?"

"No," Kelly sighed.

"He'll be fine," Sunshine said patting her on the knee. "I'm sorry we don't have any ice for your ankle."

"It's ok, I'll just keep it up for a while," Kelly nodded at her propped up foot.

"I'll be back later to pick up the tray and I'll bring some blankets. It gets chilly down here at night. Anything else you need?"

"No, we have more than enough," Kelly replied, "thank you."

The older woman left and Kelly heard the lock click in the door again. She leaned back in the chair and looked over at Robbie on the couch. He was so still she couldn't even tell if he was breathing. After a few minutes, this bothered her enough that she got up to check on him. Limping over, she placed the back of her hand in front of his nose and was relieved to feel warm air gently stroking her skin.

She sighed, stood up and looked around the small room. It was jammed with boxes, old furniture and, never to be used again, office equipment. Some of the angular plastic and metal machines looked like they were probably out dated long before the undies showed up. Spotting a glimmer of wood and silver against one wall she hobbled over to investigate. Behind several boxes of printer paper was hidden an aging dressing table and mirror.

After a few minutes struggling to move the boxes without putting any weight on her foot she also uncovered an aged bench. The green fabric on the seat shimmered through the dust and looked as if it was quite nice at one time. The old desk was chipped and worn with the remnants of what looked like a painted floral pattern on its sides. Kelly recognized the splotches & stains on its surface as fingernail polish and other spilled make up. Kelly ran her fingers over the scalloped carvings running along its edges and around the tall mirror.

The glass in the mirror had taken on the appearance of mercury, cracking and surrounded by gold and black scales. Her reflection looked back at her as if it were on the other side of a looking glass, in a different time and place. She found an old napkin and wiped away the dust.

She wondered if one of the Baldwins might have used this for getting ready for dates back in their younger days. She imagined them sitting there doing their hair and nails. Getting dressed to go out, back in a time when nobody had to worry about the undead stalking their every move.

Looking at herself in the mirror she saw that her face had taken on a harder look than she recalled. Her eyes had a seriousness about them and the lines of her cheeks seemed more severe. Gone were the soft features and girlish dimples she recalled from the last time, years ago, when she had sat at a dressing table.

She wondered if she also saw sadness, but determined that wasn't it. After a few minutes it came to her. It was the empty look she remembered seeing in pictures of people living in combat zones and places where they were starving and without hope. She realized that's how she felt inside. Empty.

She tried to think of the last time she had had any real hope. Every day since Roy vanished had been about survival. Life was lived minute to minute with no time to think about things getting better in the future. She felt like her soul had gone to the bottom of a dark place and forgotten how to find its way back out into the sun. She tried to remember who she was before, but even that seemed impossibly long ago.

'I'm not that girl anymore,' she thought, 'but I'm not going to be a frightened animal who runs and hides for the rest of my life either.'

"Rob," she whispered to his reflection on the couch. "We are getting up and out when you are better. We're going to make a life. Get well, Rob because we are not going to just survive, we are going to live... And I can't do it without you."

Kelly limped back to the lounge chair and closed her eyes.

Robbie chased his older brother Roy through the thick mist. They moved across the rooftops in a slow jog, dodging rusted air conditioner units and tufts of growth that had sprouted from the dirt on the softening platform. It was dark but they had been this way before, so he felt safe following along their previous route. The moss and undergrowth absorbed the sound of their footsteps which lessened concerns that anything in the streets below might hear and follow their movements. Ahead he could see Roy's silhouette as he reached the ladder mounted to the side of the warehouse.

"Roy, wait!" Robbie called as he watched his brother swing around onto the steel rungs.

Roy paused and signaled for Robbie to hurry up. He then started to descend.

"Wait!" Robbie called again as Roy began to disappear downward. Robbie increased his pace and bounded over a small bush as he aimed toward the ladder.

He cleared the bush easily and still had his eyes on the ladder when his left foot touched down on the soft earth. His foot sank deep into the thick sediment and he felt himself stumbling forward. He brought his other foot down heavily to keep from sinking deeper into the muck. But, rather than help with his balance, this caused a loud crash and he felt himself falling. He knew immediately that he must have sunk through a weak spot in the roof and reached out his arms to stop from going down further.

"Roy!" he shouted loudly as he felt himself sinking. When his hands met the earth, rather than stopping him, they sank right through as if it were an empty crust. The surface flashed by and something hit him hard in the head. He found himself in darkness with flashes of light glittering around him as he seemed to rocket through space. As his body spun, he caught a glimpse of the floor in the moonlight. It was a long way down, a really, long way down and his heart lurched as the surface came at him like a fly swatter.

Robbie thought he would die when he hit but he saw the moment of impact, heard the slap of his body meeting the ground, felt the pain as if he were being punched everywhere at once, and choked as the air was forced out of his lungs. He even felt himself bounce back up as his body jerked from the assault. Then falling again, as tendrils of agony bolted through his head and neck. Only this time, he fell into a dark pool where the pressure squeezed out the last of his air and prevented him from drawing in another breath. In those milliseconds of dark, airless, descent he braced for the next impact.

In Kelly's dream, Trent was again stabbing her in the belly. She could only stand there as he worked the knife in and out of her. He had that cruel smile on his face as he drove the blade all the way in to its hilt, and back out again. Somehow, she knew it was a dream but was unable to move, or run away. The wound burned with pain as blood gushed from her stomach, spraying all over Trent's hand and splattering droplets up onto his face.

"How do you like that?" He asked cruelly.

"It hurts," she said to him, matter of fact, as if it weren't obvious.

Trent just laughed, enjoying her torment. He stepped back to admire his work and howled like a wolf. Using the bloody knife, he pointed at her and began telling her something, but his words were swallowed up by the dream. She strained harder to hear him, but didn't understand.

Until he shouted, "Roy!"

Kelly jerked awake just in time to see Robbie lurch up from the couch across from her, mewling with the most inhuman moan she had ever heard! She leapt up onto the back of her lounge chair and grabbed her heavy bow staff. Frightened by his sudden reanimation, she drew the staff back and prepared to crush Robbie's skull.

The room was lit by a few candles and she watched intently as he jerked and floundered in the shadows of the couch. Her heart sank and her eyes began to tear as she realized what was likely to happen. Her mind ran through the scenario; he would stop twitching, only to turn and look at her with dead eyes. Then he would lurch up at her with hate and malice and when he got close she would bash in his head.

'What would I tell the old ladies,' she wondered, and quickly decided 'the truth'. Surely they would believe that he had died and come back. He wasn't doing well. He had been out for almost two days. They had only been able to drip small amounts of water into his mouth. That's probably why they had locked them in there, she reasoned, so when he came back he couldn't get out.

"Oh crap, Robbie," She whispered almost in tears, "I'm sorry, I'm sorry."

Robbie flopped back on the couch and groaned. But he didn't move and made no effort to rise up again. Kelly stared suspiciously, the zombies usually woke up hungry and pissed off.

"Robbie?" She stage whispered across at him with her staff still ready to swing.

"Uggh!" came the reply but there was no additional movement, no attempt to rise again from the couch. He just lay there.

The way he was sunken into the old cushions and draped in shadow, Kelly couldn't tell if he was still breathing, or not. After a few moments of silence Kelly slinked down off the chair and set her foot on the ground as softly and quietly as possible. The recliner seemed to sigh in relief as she brought her other foot down and removed her full weight from its arms. She looked over at Robbie to see if he, or it, had noticed the sound. His body didn't move, so she took a tentative step towards him. As she eased forward she kept her staff up, ready to swing, and concentrated on closing the gap between them with the stealth of a ninja. When she was within the length of her staff she stretched it out and jabbed him in the ribs then quickly jerked back, ready to strike out.

Looking for any sign of movement, she was ready for him to leap up and come ferociously scrambling after her. But there was nothing, so she leaned over and jabbed him again.

"Ow!" Robbie croaked.

Kelly's eyebrows went up. "Robbie?"

"Whaaat?" He said in a breathy, pained voice.

"Oh my god! Robbie, is that you?" She blurted, not quite ready to believe it.

"Yes," he responded, "please stop poking me. It really hurts."

"Oh, thank god," Kelly stammered in relief. All of the tension drained out of her and she dropped the staff down to her side before scrambling over to him. "Are you ok? I mean, how do you feel?"

"Hurts," Robbie spoke the single word with a stutter.

"Where?" She asked, "where hurts?"

"Everywhere," he answered.

"Ok, ok. Just a sec," Kelly said as she bounded over to the door and started knocking on its solid wood frame. "Ms. Sunshine! Ms. Beatrice! Come quick! He's awake! Robbie is awake!"

When she scrambled back to Robbie's side he turned his head and she could see his eyes were normal, not the milky white of the undead.

"Where?" he groaned.

"It's ok," she answered and in her excitement at his being alive the story came spilling out uncontrolled. "We're safe. We're with these two ladies. They call themselves the Baldwin Sisters, except they really aren't sisters because one is black and one is white. They ran a produce company but now they don't but they are still here and they've sealed the place up. One is a doctor, I think they both might be doctors, but not the doctor, doctor kind. I mean not medical doctor, like PhD doctor. And they grow their own food. And the walls are really thick. And we're ok for now…"

Kelly realized she was rambling and wrapped Robbie in a hug before tearfully stammering. "I'm so glad you're not dead!"

"Me too," Robbie gasped, "but please, you're crushing me and it really hurts."

"Oh, sorry, sorry!" She said letting him go and rising up to sit on her knees next to him.

Robbie noticed she had tears running down her cheeks juxtaposed by a huge smile. "So, I didn't catch all of that, but I think you said we are safe and something about fresh vegetables?"

Just then, the lock outside clicked and the door swung open. The two Baldwin women stepped down into the basement.

"So, you decided to join us in the world of the living?" Beatrice asked.

"Yes," Robbie replied, "although, I'm not sure if I had much choice in the matter. Are you the…the…Baldwin sisters Kelly was telling me about?"

"That's us," Beatrice said walking over to put a large hand on Robbie's forehead. "How do you feel?"

"Like I got run over by a train," Robbie grunted.

"Well that can happen when you take a three story fall, man," Sunshine said. "You're lucky you landed on soft plowed dirt or you might not have made it."

Robbie groaned in pain and said, "I don't feel lucky."

"Well, you are." Beatrice consoled him. "Very lucky to be alive. Can you wiggle your toes? How about your fingers?"

When Robbie had performed these feats, she proclaimed that he would be fine. "You are going to be sore for a week or so. You might have a broken rib or two. Nothing we can do about that except wrap you up and keep you still until they heal up."

"Ok," he said. "Do you think I could get some water?"

"I'll get it," Sunshine announced and shuffled back out the door.

Two weeks later, he was able to sit up and help with simple chores. The "sisters" started bringing him large baskets filled with long green beans. He learned quickly how to get the little round peas from their shells by manually separating them. After doing what his hosts called "shucking" peas for the first few hours, he looked down and saw he had about half a bucket of the little green orbs. He was thinking whoever did this task, of which he was previously oblivious, before the end of civilization, had his full respect. Before then, it had never occurred to him how the little round peas got from the farm and into the cans where he usually found them.

"Hey Robbie," Kelly walked in carrying a wicker basket, "how are you doing?"

"Ugh!" He replied. "Not so good if that's another basket of peas to shuck."

"Sorry, Bro," she laughed setting them at his feet. "We have to earn our keep, and at least you aren't out in the greenhouse picking them. My back is killing me."

"How is it out there?" Robbie asked.

"It's hard work," Kelly replied.

"I meant," Robbie waived his hands, "out there. In the big world."

"Oh," Kelly said, "About the same I think. I've only been out a few times since we got here. The walls are pretty thick here so you can hardly even hear what's going on outside. Why?"

"I'd just like to get moving again as soon as we can," he said.

"Look Robbie, it's bad out there. It's been bad out there and it's going to stay bad out there." She said, sitting down on the coffee table across from him. "The Sisters really have the right idea."

"I don't think I could stay locked inside like this all the time," Robbie winced as he shifted.

"I mean," she continued, "doing our own farming is the only way to survive. There are only so many old grocery stores left to raid and the sisters just told me all that stuff expires soon anyway. Even the canned stuff. We can't stay here forever, and I doubt they would even let us. But, it's time we stopped thinking day to day and start thinking long term."

"I thought we were thinking long term," Robbie answered, "…moving to this new building?"

"That's just another place to crash." She looked at him sympathetically. "Yes, maybe it's safer than before, maybe it's nicer than before, but it's not going to help us stay fed. We're going to have to figure out how to stop scavenging and start providing for ourselves."

"I don't think I'm cut out to be a farmer," Robbie sighed.

"Are you cut out to be a starver?" She fired back sarcastically. "Because that's what we're going to be if we don't start growing our own food."

She looked at him for some sort of response, but he just stared at her quizzically. "What's gotten into you?"

"Look," she said moving closer so that their knees nearly touched, "we've been on the run since this thing started. Even back in mid-town, before that dickhead Trent, we were just living day to day. Sleeping in old blankets and eating whatever we could find. I'm tired of that. We need to find a place we can call home and try to live again."

"What have we been doing?" Robbie asked.

"We've been surviving," Kelly said with a hint of sadness. "We've been running and hiding and scrounging and surviving. We need more than that or what's the point?"

"What about the zombies?" He shook his head. "How can we have a normal life with those things out there?"

"Those things aren't going anywhere, as far as I can tell, so we just have to learn to live with them." Kelly replied, "It's the new normal. They are nasty and evil but, we are smarter and faster than they are. All we have to do is stay away from them and keep them away from us. Look, nobody is coming to save us. Remember when we used to talk about how all we had to do was hide out until the police got everything back under control? And then we would say if we can just survive until the Army gets here? Then everything would be fine?"

"Yea," Robbie sighed.

"Well the police are all dead and the Army isn't coming. Nobody is coming to help us. And we have to…" she paused and her eyes misted up "we have to accept that Roy isn't coming back either. He's gone just like everyone else. We have to do this ourselves."

"We don't know that about Roy," Robbie argued.

"Look," Kelly said, "I'm not giving up on Roy either. I'm just saying we don't know where he is or when we might find him and we can't sit around waiting. We have to act as if we are on our own and if… when, we find him, so much the better, right?"

Robbie sighed. "Sounds like you have been thinking about this. What do you have in mind?"

"The condo we were scouting has a landscaped courtyard around the pool area that sits about 10 feet above street level," She said. "There's a high concrete wall around it. We could pull up the palm trees and decorative stuff and plant vegetables. Maybe even get some chickens and pigs."

"Animals make a lot of noise," Robbie countered.

"Fine," she said, "no animals…yet. But there is enough room we could plant a large garden in the courtyard. And it's only a mile or so from here so we could set up a trade system."

"I suppose it makes more sense than running all the time," Robbie looked into her pleading eyes and knew he would do whatever she wanted. Finally he nodded and asked, "When?"

"Soon!" Kelly leaned in close and looked into his eyes. "You keep healing. As soon as you are up to traveling we will move over there. The sisters have been teaching me how to do basic gardening and said they would give us some seeds and clippings to get started."

She leaned in and wrapped him in a hug as she kissed him on the cheek. He blushed at feeling her warmth and soft curves pressing against him. He hugged her back and for a moment he wished she would stay there in his arms but she quickly stood up and turned to go. As she walked away he kept his face down hoping she wouldn't notice the redness.

"I'll just keep shucking these peas then," he joked as he watched her walk to the door. She seemed to have more sway to her walk than usual.

"Yep," she said over her shoulder but stopped and turned at the threshold. "We'll be out here in the garden if you need anything." Then she blew him a kiss and walked away.

Robbie sat there a little stunned. She had never looked into his eyes like that. Never hugged him like that. Never blown him a kiss like that. Never shown any interest in him in THAT way. His heart raced and he was at once confused, aroused, and conflicted. He shook his head and told himself he was just imagining things, just pent up since there were no other young women around. He tried to put it out of his mind and focus on the peas but was only minimally successful.

Chapter 11

When Robbie couldn't bear remaining on the couch any longer, and griped about it enough that Sunshine wrapped his ribs, he started to get up and move around again. Under the Baldwins' watchful eyes, he was soon shuffling about and working on getting stronger. At first, he only walked around inside the green houses but once he had mastered that, he went outside and maneuvered through the industrial area. The area was fenced in and only open on the front side so there were few of the undead to deal with. Robbie mostly avoided them but he was gradually confident enough to confront and end some of the slower ones.

He began to rise early to practice carrying his pack, swinging his machete, and moving quickly. His fall made him especially careful of where he stepped and at first he found it difficult to focus on the ground while also being aware of what was going on around him. He gradually got better at doing both until he felt more confident in his ability to travel through more hostile areas.

One morning he walked out of the greenhouse where he found Kelly and the Baldwins having breakfast at a small card table.

"Good morning, ladies," Robbie said as he dropped his pack and pulled up a chair to the table.

"Good morning," they all replied.

Beatrice took a plate and spooned some scrambled eggs onto a slice of toast then slid it over to Robbie as he sat. "We've been talking about your problem," she said.

"My problem?" Robbie asked.

"Your problem" she pointed at both he and Kelly, indicating she meant the two of them.

"Oh?" Robbie said, "...and what is that?"

Kelly looked at the older two women conspiratorially and said. "We've been talking about the best way to get over to our building."

"Oh that," Robbie replied, "I've been thinking about that too. From the roof I've been watching several groups of the undead but they are mostly out in the streets in front of the warehouses. I was thinking we might be able to slip down behind the warehouses and work our way along the waterfront. The building is only a few miles away and near the water so we could..."

The three ladies looked at each other and Beatrice spoke. "Well, we discussed that but unfortunately the waterfront is broken up into different piers and docks. Most of the docks are fenced off with heavy gauge fencing topped with razor wire or have steel buildings that run out over the water. It would probably take days just cutting through and moving from lot to lot."

"What about a boat?" Robbie asked with a mouth full of eggs. "We could find a boat and row down with the tide."

"It's an industrial ship yard man," Sunshine said. "Can you pilot a container ship? There aren't any rowboats down there."

"Ok." Robbie said realizing they had already figured it out. "So what is the plan?"

"We think," Kelly began, "that if we can create a small distraction up the main road a bit, this will draw all the undies away so you and I can slip out. After that, we can make our way east down to Riverside Avenue. Riverside runs along the water between downtown and the shops on the boardwalk. From there we can find a spot to climb over the wall and get into the building."

"A small distraction?" Robbie asked. "How are we going to do that?"

Beatrice answered, "Sunshine and I will slip over to the other side of the warehouses. There is a little store over there that sold wind chimes. We hang one up on the gate and jingle it a few times. It's just loud enough to capture the interest of the undies nearby and when they move, any others within sight will follow along. You hide out on the roof and when you see them wander away you climb down and head east."

"Ok, but," Robbie said, "once they start moving how will you get away and back here?"

"We cleared out the warehouses over there back when Jose was still with us." Beatrice explained, "They are all locked up and zombie free. We thought maybe we would come back and turn them into more greenhouses at some point. We can just make our way back through the warehouses and cut across back here when the coast is clear."

"But," Robbie countered, "what if they see you?"

"We ain't as slow as we look, man!" Sunshine cackled, "'sides it's only maybe 50 yards between Hinson's back door and our front door. We can make it and once we are inside it won't matter. They can't get through these walls."

"Well I guess so," Robbie said unsure, "when would we go?"

"Soon," Kelly said, "maybe tomorrow if you are up for it."

"I'm fine," Robbie assured then looked at the Baldwins, "are you ladies ready?"

"We will be tomorrow," Beatrice answered nodding to Sunshine.

"Well then, thanks for everything. Really," Robbie said. "We really appreciate it."

"Don't mention it," Beatrice smiled, "it's been nice having some company for a while."

"But you know what they say about company and fish!" Sunshine laughed and they all joined her.

"Seriously," Kelly added, "you saved us and we wouldn't be here without you, so if you ever need anything just let us know. We need to work out a way to signal each other."

"How about we plan to meet here once a month to catch up on gossip and trade vegetables?" Sunshine offered.

"Sounds good," Robbie and Kelly agreed.

"I guess that means we'll need to find a calendar," Robbie added.

"Yes, you will," Beatrice said. "Let's finish breakfast and we can start getting ready."

Robbie had trouble sleeping that night and lay on the couch staring up at the ceiling. He had studied the old route map that the Baldwins had posted near their loading dock and was confident he knew the way and a few alternates. So much had changed and there were so many variables, he worried about what they would find once they set out. Streets could be blocked and unpassable. Zombies could be lurking around every corner.

He and Kelly had braved and survived these things for the last few years, but now he felt somehow different. Like he had something to look forward to. In the past he felt as if Kelly was taking care of him. Now he felt like he needed to watch out for her.

Robbie heard the Baldwins in their kitchen before dawn and began to smell breakfast cooking. Kelly, who had been sleeping on the floor, sat up and stretched.

"Let's go get some eggs," she said sniffing the air, "I don't think they are going to serve us in bed."

Chapter 12

By the time sun came up the next morning, Robbie was fully kitted up and peeking out onto the main street in front of the warehouses. Kelly was a block behind, keeping an eye on their rear. Robbie could see the backs of the trailing end of the neighborhood zombies as they lurched away north towards the tinkling sounds of wind chimes. He hoped the Baldwin ladies could get away before the ravenous group arrived.

He scanned the road for any stragglers, but saw none ahead in the direction they were headed. He took longer than he may have in the past, wanting to be sure, before they stepped out of hiding. They had been safe and, he hoped hadn't grown soft, over the last few weeks. He didn't want that to lead to any stupid mistakes. But, other than the chimes, the road was quiet, so he motioned Kelly forward.

Kelly moved up next to him, took a quick look around, stepped carefully out onto the sidewalk and began walking in a low crouch. Robbie scanned up the windows in the buildings across the street looking for any movement or shadows that might mean trouble. Seeing nothing, he turned to watch as Kelly moved out to the curb and followed it east, away from the direction they had sent the mob of undead. As she approached abandoned cars, she made a wide arc around them, careful not to move back too close to the building.

In the early days of the outbreak, they learned the hard way that the undead didn't mind flinging themselves through upper windows to land on their prey below. They had lost friends to this kind of attack. That continued to be an issue, but as structures aged, they had the additional problem of actual pieces of the buildings falling off. Even a small chunk of concrete falling from a skyscraper could crush a skull. A sheet of glass falling from several floors up could slice a person in half or cut them up badly if they were too close to the exploding shards.

Kelly's eyes moved left and right as she patrolled forward. She made a quick inspection inside, between and under the dusty parked vehicles as she moved slowly down the street. Most of the shop windows were covered in a film of dust and mold at street level but she made an effort to look for shadows and listen for movement as she made her way along. Approaching the large entrance of what had been a chain clothing store, she paused under the awning. Two of the big double doors had been crushed inward and two others hung open, their glass in tiny fragments all over the once trendy tile entry way.

She peered into the dimly lit store and saw several figures standing in the gloom. She waited and watched, but they did not move.

'Mannequins?' She asked herself. The figures remained still. She picked up a small square of glass and tossed it down the store's main aisle. It made a small tap, tap as it rattled along the tile. The noise didn't carry far but would perhaps peak the curiosity of any undead within earshot. None of the figures moved. 'Mannequins,' she decided. 'Probably mannequins,' she reassured herself as she stepped out around the glass and continued to the corner.

Robbie stepped out of hiding when he saw Kelly go around the store front and moved quickly to meet her on the sidewalk. Reaching the corner where she crouched, he slowed and made eye contact. Kelly signaled to move on. All clear so far. Robbie hustled to the other side of the street and began slowly clearing the way as Kelly had done before.

They took turns leap frogging past each other as they made their way down the street. Each scouted ahead while the other covered their rear. It was a technique they had developed for patrolling that provided some security from both the dead and the living. If the one in front ran into any living people, the other could try to move unseen and provide backup if needed. If they ran into the undead, the scout would try to lead them away while the other could either hide or attack from behind.

They were several blocks into their journey before they spotted their first undead. The remains of a cab driver, who sat forever strapped into the front seat of his car. His pasty skeletal hands slapped at the raised window as they quickly maneuvered past. Their second encounter was a woman who must have spotted them from a condominium across the street. They didn't notice her until they heard the window shatter high above and saw her plummet to the pavement with a loud slap, followed by the clatter of pieces of glass and metal as they followed her down.

"Go!" Robbie shouted before the echo of the creature's plunge had subsided. "Every damn thing within a mile will be coming this way now."

They sprinted ahead half a block before a lanky creature stepped out of a store front and right into their path. Robbie barely had time to turn his shoulder into it as they collided, but fortunately, the thing, mostly skin and bones, was hammered back onto the sidewalk. Robbie leaped over it before it could recover and kept running.

"You ok?" Kelly asked as they ran.

"Yea." Robbie said. "Think he got the worst of it."

"Good," Kelly replied, taking a glance back to see the thing struggling to get back up. She also noticed that several dozen had emerged from the shops they had just run past and now seemed locked onto their trail. "More coming. We need to get off the street."

"It's two blocks to our turn," Robbie panted, "can you make it?"

"Yes," She gasped, "You?"

Robbie didn't answer, just kept running. Kelly stayed with him but knew they couldn't keep up the pace much longer. She realized they had no idea what was beyond the turn. She started looking around for a way to climb up into one of the buildings but didn't see anything. They would need to go inside somewhere to find a staircase. Going inside had its own dangers.

They dodged several more undead who stumbled from doorways in search of whatever was causing the commotion. Kelly noted that the crowd behind them was growing. Most were shambling slowly but a small group were moving faster than the others and making it harder for her and Robbie to duck out of sight and lose them.

"Turn up here on Canal Street," Robbie pointed.

Robbie turned onto the road sloping to the river just ahead of Kelly but quickly adjusted back and continued straight across the intersection. A second later, Kelly saw why and followed him back along the sidewalk.

At the bottom of the hill, a crowd of undead milled in the low spot where the road turned and ran along the river. They had seen it before. The creatures followed the path of least resistance downward until there was no further to go. Then, they just stood around until something motivated them to go back up the hill. Even if they did not see Robbie and Kelly race by, they would certainly notice the pack of dead shambling along in their wake. That would be enough to get the creatures curious and moving.

"Next street!" Robbie said gasping.

Two blocks later, they noticed that the street seemed to be rising away from the river.

"Crap!" Kelly panted. The pounding was causing her ankle to ache again. "We can't keep running. We have to find a place to cut through!"

"Up here," Robbie grunted and motioned to a falafel shop with a steel door. The door was closed but its windows were set at about chest height and they were all broken out. "This way," he called out as he leapt up and pulled himself over into the shop.

Kelly, having little choice, flung herself in right behind him.

They quickly gained their footing on the inside and prepared for anything that might come at them. Luckily, nothing did. They ducked behind the counter as the faster of the zombies reached the front of shop.

"Stay down," Kelly whispered, not sure if the things could see into the shop. "Is the front door locked?"

Robbie took a quick peek around his side of the counter. "I don't know but the closed sign is up and the shade is drawn," he said quietly.

"Ok, ok," Kelly sat down with her backpack against the counter while she tried to quietly catch her breath.

They could hear the zombies outside the shop but couldn't tell if they were gathering or walking passed. It was loud as the things crunched through broken glass and debris while muttering their growling, moaning sounds.

They sat still and waited for the creatures to start their banging on the door and walls but, after an eternity, the noise started to die down and it gradually grew quiet again.

Robbie waited ten more minutes before he risked another look. Quickly pulling back he turned to look at Kelly. "Clear," he whispered through clenched teeth. His injured ribs burned from the exertion.

Kelly pulled herself onto her knees and crawled to the edge to get a look for herself. She couldn't see much through the small area of safety glass in the metal door but there were no decrepit heads visible through the broken shop front windows. She could still smell them on the wind but not as strong as before. She nodded to the back of the shop.

"Wait here, I'll look around," she said as she crept towards a swinging door she guessed was the kitchen.

Pulling her small solar powered flashlight from her belt she shined it under the door. There was about an inch of clearance but all she could see were the greasy reddish floor tiles and the bottoms of some shelves. More importantly the light did not cause anything to react on the other side.

"I think it's ok," she said, reaching up to put her hand against the door. "Ready?"

Robbie nodded and she softly rapped her fingernails on the door's Formica façade. It made a click, click, clicking sound that didn't carry far but would likely cause anything undead on the inside to reveal itself. After a moment of silence, she lightly pushed at the door to see if the hinges would squeak when it moved. They did, but not much, Robbie and Kelly both froze and listened to see if anything outside might have heard. They listened for a few beats to the sound of the breeze thumbing through the old flyers and other papers that littered the street. When nothing more menacing seemed likely, they nodded to each other in agreement to go ahead.

Kelly rose up into a crouch with her hand still holding the door ajar. Robbie braced himself while she pushed open the door, which produced a high-pitched whine, until it was all the way open. Kelly held her light up and stepped inside. The room was small and had been used as an office and storage space. Boxes of plastic forks and plates sat deteriorating on rusting metal shelves. "It's ok," she said.

Robbie leaned in, took a look around, and moved a trash can up to keep the door propped open. "Is there another way out?" He asked.

"Two doors in the back," Kelly answered as she shined her light around, "keep an eye on the front and I'll check it out."

Robbie eased back over to keep an eye on the outside.

Shining the light on the door at the back of the shop, Kelly saw that it was mostly blocked by brooms, mop buckets and cleaning supplies. There was also a row of wire shelves, stocked with precariously leaning boxes, pushed up against its edge.

Kelly turned and took in the other door. It was narrow and covered in novelty calendars depicting colorful scenes of dark skinned people frolicking on beautiful exotic beaches. The fanciful writing looked Arabic so she had no idea where those places might be. 'Far away,' she thought, 'in places that aren't there anymore.' But then she amended her thought, 'the places are still there. But, the people are gone.' She wondered if she would ever see such a sandy beach again.

"Psst," Robbie interrupted, from the front of the shop. "What are you doing?"

"Just looking around," she answered. "Everything ok out there?"

"So far," he said.

Kelly tapped on the narrow door, and waited for any response. When none came, she reached out and turned the door handle slowly. When she heard the lock disengage, she pulled the door slowly open. To her relief, nothing leapt out at her. Shining her light inside, she saw that it was a small bathroom.

A body, the really dead kind, sat slumped back on the toilet. The apron wearing figure had been there so long he had dried out completely, so there was almost no smell. On the grimy yellowed wall behind its head was a brown halo where its brains had blown out.

"Eew", she whispered.

Finding bodies didn't shock her. She had come across similar scenes so often in the last few years that it was almost a relief that they were completely dead and not a danger. The gun lay on the floor near the dead man. She reached down and picked it up. Several bullets were still visible in the chambers. She didn't know much about guns, but it looked like it would probably need some work before being safe to fire. Still, she knew enough to find the safety button and click it into place, just in case. She stepped back and closed the door, leaving the shawarma cook alone in his tomb.

"Can we go out that way?" Robbie asked.

"No," Kelly said. Keeping her voice low. "Too much crap against the door. Something would fall and since we don't know what's on the other side, it's not worth it. I think we go out the front and back track towards the cut off down to the river. Most of those things will have followed the crowd and gone right by us."

"Yea," Robbie answered, then noticed the gun in her hand, "hey, what's that?"

"Gun," she answered, "found it on a dead guy back there."

"Can I see it?" Robbie asked.

Kelly handed it to him. "Be careful. It's loaded but I don't know if it still works. Last thing we need is a gunshot to ring the dinner bell."

Robbie turned the gun around in his hands. "Safety is on."

"I know," she replied taking it back from him. "Let's put it away before anything happens. We can work on it later when we are safe."

Kelly wedged the gun into her back pack and edged around the counter towards the front window. "Come on, looks like the coast is clear." She crawled up onto the small counter against the window. She lay there on her stomach for a moment to look up and down the street, then she dropped down onto the sidewalk.

When Robbie heard the crunch of her feet hitting the ground, he followed her over and dropped into a crouch with his back against the wall. Once he got his balance, he saw Kelly had her back against a car parked at the curb. She motioned behind her to let Robbie know there was something, probably undead, on the other side of the street. She made a chopping sign with her hand pointing down the hill indicating that they should get moving. Then she indicated they should leapfrog like they had before. Robbie wondered why they hadn't decided what they were going to do before they rolled out onto the sidewalk but it was too late to worry about that. He nodded for her to go ahead.

Hunched over and with her head down, Kelly began a quick walk back towards Canal Street. Robbie watched her until she reached the corner, then hurried to catch up. When he approached he tapped her shoulder and she motioned for him to go ahead. He dashed across the gap between the buildings and past the storefronts they had sprinted passed less than an hour earlier. Along the way, he tried to keep his vision swiveling between the stores on his left, the maze of traffic on his right and the sidewalk ahead.

It occurred to him that they sometimes went a full day like this. Moving silently through the streets without talking. Just motioning to each other with their hands and faces to indicate what they were doing next. There was some comfort in the routine of it and that they had worked together for so long that they didn't need to say anything. Both knew what the other meant, even without words. It was easiest to get lost in the work, be totally focused on the moment and forget about the big picture.

Kelly passed Robbie at the next corner. As they approached Canal Street, she spotted a few undead stumbling down the road, making their way in between the cars. She signaled Robbie and they hunkered behind a van until the threat passed.

At the top of the street, Robbie peeked around and noted that the large crowd of creatures at the bottom had shrunk to just two emaciated figures who looked as if they may not have had the strength to walk back up the steep hill. Kelly raised her shoulders as a question and he answered by holding up two fingers. Then he indicated they should continue down the hill and ran his hand in front of his throat to indicate they should kill them. Kelly nodded and they stepped around the corner.

Robbie pulled his machete from its sheath and Kelly began spinning her bow staff as they walked down the slope. The two creatures saw them coming and began slouching towards them. Robbie moved quickly and met the first in the middle of the street, chopping into its skull and sending it to the hard asphalt. Kelly danced around next to the other and swung her staff hard into its ear. The impact of the stick made a loud thwack and caused the thing's head to spin around to face the opposite direction. Its body continued forward however causing Kelly to step back, spin her staff and bring it down hard on the things head. It collapsed to the ground in a pile and Kelly watched it for a moment to be sure it didn't get back up.

"She didn't see that coming," Robbie said with a grin.

Kelly raised an eyebrow at his bad joke.

"You see," Robbie said with a straight face," because her face was backwards she couldn't see…"

Kelly rolled her eyes. "Yes."

"Because she wasn't looking…" Robbie continued to rib her.

"I get it. Shut up. Let's go," she shook her head.

They turned left and walked down the middle of the road along the docks. To the left, a modern stone wall rose up, creating a level platform for the buildings up on Riverside to look out over the river. To their right were the rows of old waterfront warehouses that had been turned into trendy night clubs and shopping piers before the dead rose. Beyond the warehouses was the dark rolling river. A few large boats could be seen between the piers, long ago sunk in the shallows and resting just below the surface.

They walked slowly and side by side rather than leap frogging as they usually did. There were too many alleys and alcoves along the way for that tactic to be effective. Unlike the streets in the city above, the two lane road here had few cars blocking the way. There were several panel trucks backed up into docking bays and a few vehicles slowly rusting in the narrow metered parking along the sidewalk. Although covered in mud and mold, they were undamaged, unlike most other vehicles in the city that had been caught up in the panic to escape or the later battles and fires that had raged in the days right after the end. These looked as if they may had been left by drivers who walked away and never returned.

"Thursday morning," Kelly whispered.

"What?" Robbie asked.

"It was a Thursday morning when it all started." Kelly replied pointing at the cars.

"Was it?" Robbie said looking left and right. "I don't remember."

"These cars were probably parked here Wednesday night by people who worked down here." Kelly explained, "…but they never came back. Those trucks were the early morning deliveries."

"Hmm," Robbie said disinterestedly. To him they were just obstacles and potential hiding places for the undead. "How much further do you think?"

Kelly looked ahead along the row of buildings. "About two blocks I think."

They moved around several downed palms that would have once served as decorative trees on the sidewalks. A gentle, salty, breeze blew in from the river shuffling their brown fronds.

"Contact," Robbie said quietly as he nodded ahead toward two scruffy figures slowly shambling in their direction. He motioned for them to move over to the wall and crouched low as they moved ahead. There wasn't much to hide behind but they got as far from the things as they could while assessing the threat.

"How many?" Kelly asked.

"I only saw two," Robbie whispered back.

"Ok, let's take them out," Kelly said as she got a clearer view of the creatures and became more confident that they weren't the vanguard of a larger group. "I don't want them following us while we try to find a way inside."

She rose up and strode towards the things with Robbie close behind her. They became more excited as Robbie and Kelly approached. Their previous, slow lumbering pace, transformed into a lurching, snarling attack. Kelly caught the first one at the knee with her staff and used its momentum to send it face first onto the asphalt with a slap. Of course, this didn't seem to faze it and it began immediately crawling toward her. Before it could get far, Kelly brought the heavy end of the stick down on its head and crushed its skull. She looked up to see that Robbie had dispatched the other one.

"More." Robbie said pointing down to a bend in the road about 100 yards away. A crowd of a dozen or so shuffled into view.

"It's ok," Kelly said huskily and started walking quickly back towards the wall. "We're here."

Chapter 13

Robbie followed Kelly into a narrow driveway built into the wall. He guessed it was wide enough to fit two trucks. The sides of the driveway were made of thick concrete streaked with rubber, paint and scratches left by the many vehicles that had scratched along its surface in the days when there were daily deliveries. At the entrance, a tall chain link gate had a sign hung that read – 'Riverside Condominiums Loading and Unloading Only.' He made a brief attempt at closing the gate behind them but realized it was on a chain connected to an electrical box. The rusty chain gave barely an inch and made a loud grinding sound as he pushed against it.

"Leave it!" Kelly whispered.

Robbie gave a quick glance down the road and noticed the approaching zombies were still about 50 yards away but definitely locked onto them. He let go of the gate and ran to catch up with Kelly.

He found her at the end of the alley climbing up onto a loading dock. A rolling metal garage door was closed to about a foot off the ground. It had been stopped from fully closing by a body laying over the threshold. A pair of legs wearing dirty blue jeans and work boots stuck out onto the dock. While Kelly peered underneath, Robbie walked over to a smaller standard size steel door nearby.

"Is it unlocked?" Kelly asked as she tried to shine her light into the darkness without getting too close.

"There's no handle," Robbie replied looking at a nearby keypad. "Looks like it was operated by this, but without power there's no way to unlock it from this side."

Robbie glanced over to another steel door down at the end of a short alley just off the dock's steps. He quickly determined it was too far away and not worth the risk. If it was locked, they would be trapped in the alley with nowhere to go.

"I guess we have to go this way then," Kelly sighed. She still couldn't see anything in the darkness under the garage door.

109

Robbie looked back down the alley and saw that the leading edge of the undead had reached the gate. "Yep, we got about 30 seconds to get through."

As the throng of creatures began lurching towards them, Kelly and Robbie dropped their backpacks and shoved them through the narrow opening. They took it as a good sign that nothing inside immediately pounced.

"Go!" Robbie said, "I'll hold them off."

Kelly didn't hesitate. She pushed her fighting stick through, lay flat on her back and began squeezing under head first. She held the flashlight out in front of her and kicked with her feet, ready to start fighting on the other side. It was a tight fit and she struggled to get her chest and hips through the narrow gap.

There was a set of steps at one end of the dock. Robbie moved to the other side hoping to keep the approaching mob from noticing the easy way up. The deck platform was about four feet above the driveway. Robbie knew this wouldn't hold them long, but hoped it might slow them enough for him to get into the loading bay. As they bunched up against the dock, he began stabbing down into any that tried to crawl up onto the platform.

After stabbing at several, he realized the crowd was reaching critical mass and would soon start spilling over the platform. He glanced back and saw Kelly's feet finally disappear inside leaving marks in the dirt where she had struggled. Three of the creatures suddenly lurched onto the platform. Robbie took two out, but as he did, others followed them up and the third was rising to its feet. Further down the crowd had gotten large enough that the ones at the far end had discovered the steps.

"Shit!" Robbie shouted pushing several shamblers back off the dock and into the crowd, "Kelly can you get that gate up?! I don't have time to crawl under!"

As he continued to fight, he noticed the body with the boots suddenly pulled back and disappear into the garage. There was a clanging of chains on the inside and he backed up, preparing to roll under the gate. "Kelly!" he called as he hacked down two more. "Cutting it close out here!"

He heard the garage door begin to move behind him but as he got ready to throw himself under, rather than rising, it slammed shut. "Dammit, Kelly," he shouted banging on the metal and lashing out at several more hungry monsters. "Not funny!"

The crowd on the platform was growing and Robbie realized he had nowhere to go. With his back literally against a wall, he began hacking and kicking at the mob closing in around him. A man in torn mechanics overalls attacked and Robbie caught it in the chest with his boot. Using the garage door for leverage he hammered out as hard as he could causing it to stumble backwards and trip over the waitress climbing onto the platform behind him. The mechanic did a flip worthy of a Hollywood stuntman, knocking several others from the deck and slapping back into the sea of grey faces surging into the loading area. A dozen or so went down under their weight but not enough to slow the surge.

Robbie's safe space was slowly closing in and bodies were piling up in an arc around him. He realized the wall of bodies wasn't helping, as those behind tripped and fell over them causing him to fight both the walking and the crawling.

He heard a click to his right and suddenly the side door, with the keypad, swung open. It knocked several creatures down as Kelly pressed out hard into their ranks. "C'mon!" She yelled and started hammering the crowd from the open doorway.

Robbie had to push and chop as he cleared his way to her but jumped through the door just as the excited monsters crushed into the space behind him. Kelly stepped back into the bay as one of the things lunged in and latched its teeth onto her arm. She screamed realizing she had no time to get him off, she grabbed its head and pulled it with her through the opening. The door slammed as its feet were pulled through, leaving the rest of the mob clamoring outside the metal door.

Robbie had seen Kelly pull the thing with her into the room but as soon as the door closed they were left in complete darkness. He leapt back and grabbed at where he had last seen the biter's shoulders but missed and only arrived in time to hear the sound of two bodies landing, struggling on the concrete floor. With only the sound of the thing's growling and Kelly's cursing to guide him, Robbie dropped to his knees and began grasping for where he thought the creature's feet might be. After several misses, he finally grabbed what felt like a tattered pair of running shoes and worked his way up to a slick and shredded pair of jeans filled by bony legs.

"Get the fuck off me!" Kelly roared and Robbie could hear her pounding the thing, most likely in the face. Apparently it wasn't letting go, so Robbie grabbed it by the waist and rolled, hoping to leverage it off of her. The body came with him and as soon as Robbie rolled on top he jumped up to put his knees on its emaciated chest. He grabbed its arms and held them down while also keeping his head back hoping the thing couldn't get close enough to bite his face off. It didn't move. It didn't fight at all. It just lay there. Dead?

He could hear Kelly gasping and cursing as she seemed to scramble away.

"Kelly?" Robbie called. He didn't dare move to go find her. The thing seemed dead but he did not want to let it go and lose it in the total darkness. He listened intently for anything else that might be in the bay with them but his heart was pounding and the zombies were banging on the garage door so loudly that it was impossible to hear anything else. He called out again, "Kelly?"

"Just a sec," she answered from the darkness.

Suddenly a small light came on illuminating a narrow shaft in the room. The light shined around and found Robbie. "Ugh!" he groaned and shut his eyes to the bright light.

"Get off that thing and come help me find the head," Kelly said.

Robbie opened his eyes and saw that he was holding down a headless corpse. "Ew!" he jumped backward off of it and quickly rose to his feet.

"Careful," Kelly said shining the light around, "when you pulled it away the head came off. I hit it pretty hard and I don't know where it went."

"Ok," Robbie gasped and followed her light beam as she searched the floor.

"There!" Kelly pointed the beam at a grotesque grey head laying in the corner of the loading bay. Its single cloudy eye glared at the light while its teeth snapped as they approached.

Robbie stabbed it with his machete and it ceased moving. They both leaned on their knees and breathed hard as they recovered from the fight.

"You ok?" Robbie finally gasped.

Kelly shined the light on the sleeve of her jacket. The leather was torn in several places but the teeth didn't go through. "I think so," she said in relief. "Going to be a hell of a bruise though. Goddam thing had a bitch of a grip."

"What took you so long to open the door?" Robbie finally asked.

In answer, Kelly shined the little light around the room showing three other bodies lying in the dust. "One, two, three," she counted. "Sorry, I had to take care of them first."

"Yea ok," Robbie said accepting her explanation but still not happy at being left outside. Then he turned and indicated the rumbling sound of hundreds of hands banging on the metal garage. "You think those doors will hold?"

"Probably," Kelly answered uncertainly. "But, let's not hang around to find out."

They grabbed their bags from the floor and followed Kelly's light to a set of swinging double doors at the back of the loading bay. The doors looked like they might have been installed not long before the fall. They were still covered in plastic and with protective cardboard taped over them. There was a lock near the top of the door but the bolt was not thrown. Kelly gently pushed at the left door which eased quietly open. She shined her light in and saw an empty hallway leading to another set of large doors flanked by two service elevators.

They slipped inside and, after ensuring there were no undead, Robbie turned back and clicked the bolt into place. The hall was marked with the scratches, smudges and stains of having been used extensively during construction. The floors were concrete and the walls were covered only by unpainted drywall. A stack of materials and tools lay off to the side as if waiting for the construction workers to arrive and start building again.

They checked that the elevators were closed and then approached the large door beyond. There was a narrow gap underneath and Kelly knelt down to look through.

"Stairwell," she said, "I think. Looks clear."

"Let's go then," Robbie said stepping forward. "Hold the light up. I'll open the door."

Kelly stepped back and shined the light at the door as Robbie pulled it open. They found themselves at the base of a concrete stairwell that looked like it might go all the way to the top of the building. The stairs were wide framed by metal handrails and, like the previous hallway, it looked as if it had seen intensive use as a way to transport construction materials.

"Can you hear anything up there?" Kelly asked looking up the center of the stairwell.

"No," Robbie replied peering up, "can't hear anything over that banging at the loading dock."

"Well, I don't suppose we can go back," Kelly finally said and started up the stairs.

They went up two flights before they came to another door. A sign on the wall nearby read "1".

"Lobby?" Robbie asked.

"Probably," Kelly answered.

"Shall we give it a try?" he continued.

"Might as well," she said.

Through the door, they found themselves in an unfinished room. Light poured through several large windows that looked out over the main street downtown. The skeletal framework of a metal dropped ceiling hung above them but with no tiles in place, the pipes and wires of the building's inner workings were clearly visible. Kelly clicked off her light and they walked over to look out the windows.

They were about 10 feet above the street but they both stepped back when they noticed several undead stumbling along down below. Even though they were probably safe there was no reason to rile them up. Kelly nodded towards another set of doors and they walked back in that direction.

Although dusty and scratched on this side, the doors were large and ornate, indicating that the area beyond was likely the lobby or a public space. Kelly knelt and peered underneath.

"Carpet," she whispered. "Can't see anything but with all that racket out back, I'm pretty sure anything in here would have come running already."

The pounding seemed like a distant rattle from where they were but it would be enough to raise the interest of any creatures within earshot.

"Open it up then," Robbie nodded at the door and stepped back, assuming a batter's stance with his machete.

Kelly turned the knob and pulled the door inward. When nothing leapt in at them, they moved ahead and found themselves in a short hallway of narrow cubicles. Kelly did a quick check of the shadowed offices with her flashlight. Personal items and coffee cups still sat on the desks. A large chart marked "Sales Goals" was taped up in one area. Another brightly colored poster listed the names of salespeople followed by glittering stars showing how successful they were at selling units.

Having cleared the area, they moved up to look out into the larger room. It looked like the main lobby, a wide open area with windows looking down onto the street. The room was laid out in the forced fashion that only a professional decorator would choose. Dusty but expensive looking furniture, artwork and knick-knacks were laid out as if being posed for a photo in a magazine. A wide intricate stairwell went down a floor towards the street but was blocked at the bottom by a row of heavy folding wooden panels. At the top of the stairs was a desk and a podium which Kelly guessed was intended for the concierge.

Aside from a layer of dust, the lobby seemed largely undisturbed by the collapse of civilization. Stacks of brochures and floorplans were neatly lined up along the desk, ready for handing out to potential buyers. On the back wall hung a giant print of an architect's depiction of what the building would look like on a beautiful clear day, with the words 'Opening this Summer' blazoned across the top.

Robbie picked up one of the brochures, flipped it open and began to read in an announcer's voice. "The Riverside is a modern building built with green materials and sustainable systems. Residents will breathe easy while living in an environmentally friendly location in the heart of downtown. Enjoy the lower utility costs that come from our solar array and natural rooftop insulation. Our green rooftop helps our neighbors by reducing the building's UHI effect. Blah, blah, blah, well I'm glad to know we have less UHI. Whatever that was."

Kelly laughed, stepped behind the podium, and eyed a brass bell sitting on top.

Robbie saw her gaze and said, "Don't."

She stuck her tongue out at him and said, "I wasn't gonna…"

Robbie raised an eyebrow at her. "What's that?" he asked as he dropped the brochure back on the desk and walked over to a bank of elevators. A poster leaned against a sign board with an arrow inviting investors to 'Visit our Model Units on the Top Floor.'

"Should we take a look?" Robbie asked.

"It's a bit opulent," Kelly replied unscrewing a bottle of water from her pack. "It may be out of our price range."

"I'm sure we can swing it," Robbie answered, "I know a guy at the bank."

She smiled, took a long swig and walked over. Looking up at the numbers over the elevators she said. "I don't know, it's quite a hike."

"It's what we came for isn't it?" he said.

"I suppose." She replied, drained the water bottle and slid it back into her pack for refill later.

"Well, I don't want to jinx it," Robbie said, "but, nobody was living here and the building has been closed up since before the outbreak so there can't be many undead in here, right?"

"Yea, but like you said, don't jinx it." Kelly replied pointing at a door beyond the elevators. "There's the main stairwell. It will be dark in a few hours and I really don't feel like trying to clear every floor today. If we can get to the top without any trouble we can barricade the stairwells and clear the rest tomorrow. How does that sound?"

"Peachy," said Robbie as he stepping over to a door marked 'STAIRS.' "Ready?"

Kelly pulled up her stick as he put his hand on the door latch. Seeing her in position he pulled it open and stepped back. The door swung silently in an arc until it reached the wall where it bounced off of a rubber stop with a thud. Robbie stopped it with a booted foot as it began its return. The inside landing of the stairwell was empty and they both breathed in relief.

Where the other stairwell had been all utilitarian, this one was clearly meant for guests. The richly colored carpet from the lobby continued inside and the handrails had a brass shine to them.

Robbie stuck his head in the door. The shaft had the stale smell of a place long locked away from fresh air. To his left, the stairwell wrapped around and continued downward into darkness. In front of him they coiled upward with narrow shafts of light drifting in through thin windows, on each landing. No movement or sound caught his attention, so he stepped in and made room for Kelly to come through behind him.

"Windows," Robbie said pointing up.
"I see," said Kelly.

They paused for a moment and listened. They hadn't made much noise but the sound of the door opening and thumping against the wall would have drawn any undead nearby. None presented themselves and Robbie started upward. Kelly let the door close completely behind them before she followed. It was on a hydraulic swing and she admired how it quietly slipped into its frame with just a click as the latch fell into place. At the first landing they peered through the narrow window and saw that it overlooked the bay.

"Nice view," Robbie said and moved on.

Kelly paused a moment longer before following him. They were only a few floors up but she could see the rooftops of the restaurants and clubs along Water Street. Beyond, she could see the small waves of the river as they bobbed along and a few of the wrecks that were close to the surface. Gulls drifted overhead in the afternoon light, occasionally diving into the water for a meal. It almost looked peaceful.

"Kelly," Robbie whispered back to her from the next landing and she hurried to catch up.

Near the door on this landing was a pad for digital keys and a brass sign that read 'Fitness Center' and 'Meeting Rooms'.

When Kelly reached him, Robbie continued upward. They moved carefully but slowly, checking that each door was fully closed by pressing lightly against it and stopping frequently to listen. At the eighth floor, they were getting winded but feeling confident. The stairwell offered no surprises until they reached the 10th floor.

As Robbie rounded the corner at eleven and looked up to the next landing, he stopped suddenly. Kelly was several steps behind and seeing him freeze, she came to a quick halt as well. She raised her eyebrow in a question when he looked back at her. He nodded up the stairs and mouthed the words, "door, open"

Kelly quietly stepped up so she could see the landing. A bucket sat on the floor holding the door open but nothing else seemed out of place. Robbie inched up along the wall until he reached the side of the door frame. Kelly wanted to tell him to be careful but she knew better than to make any noise until they found out what was on the 10th floor. She pursed her lips, well aware that Robbie knew how to handle himself, having now grown up doing this sort of thing.

She watched as he kneeled down, to present a low profile, and eased around to look inside. When he didn't jump immediately back, she felt a small amount of relief. He then stood and stepped into the door to get a better view. He still said nothing and had not signaled for her to come up, so she waited.

Finally, he waved her on and stepped aside so she could look for herself. The floor was unfinished, with exposed drywall along a hallway. Scaffolds, cans of paint and boxes of materials created obstacles they couldn't see around. While many of the rooms had no doors, which let light into the hall, most were covered in plastic sheeting so they could not see into the individual rooms.

On the bright side, nothing moved, they heard no unusual sounds and while the area did look a little chaotic, it was not a mess. Tools and supplies were neatly stacked along the hallway, patiently waiting for the tradesmen's return. A broom and half full dust pan even rested against one of the walls.

"I think its ok," Robbie whispered from behind her. "If there were undead in here they would have knocked that broom over by now. Look. There aren't even any marks in the dust on the floor."

Kelly saw all this and agreed.

"Do you want to check it out?" Robbie asked.

"No," Kelly said feeling tired. "Let's close the door and keep going up. Anything in there can wait until tomorrow."

"Ok," Robbie agreed and picked up the handle to the bucket against the door. He indicated to Kelly to step back as he lifted the bucket out of the way and held onto the door to ensure it closed gently and quietly. He needn't have worried. The hydraulic arm, though long unused, performed as designed bringing the portal back to its frame with a gentle click.

They waited a moment, listening, praying that the slight noise wouldn't bring anything that might be wandering the building looking for dinner down on them. When a minute had passed without any ill omens, they turned and began climbing the stairs again. They continued cautiously and slowly, but the next floors presented no additional challenges as they made steady progress.

Chapter 14

When they finally arrived at the top floor, they pushed off their exhaustion and looked at each other excitedly.

"We made it," Robbie said.

"It's not locked is it?!" Kelly squeaked when she saw the digital keypad and speaker next to the door.

"Shouldn't be," Robbie whispered. "It's against fire codes to lock stairwells. That was probably some sort of security alarm."

"Oh," she sighed, "wait, how do you know that?"

"My Uncle James was a fireman," Robbie said. "He had some great stories."

"Oh yea," she recalled and leaned her ear against the door to listen.

"Anything?" Robbie asked.

She shook her head, put her finger tips to the rich brown stained wood and tapped several times. Robbie stood ready in case something decided to suddenly crash out into the stairwell. For long moments nothing happened. Robbie glanced back down the stairs to ensure nothing was coming up behind them, but saw nothing.

Finally, Kelly stepped back, "I don't hear anything. How about, I'll pitch and you swing?"

This was code that she would open the door, while she stood ready to take off the head of anything that might launch out at them. She stepped up and grabbed the handle.

"Ready?" she nodded and he counted, "One... Two...Three" and pulled on the door. It came open an inch or two but then slammed shut again as if someone had jerked it from the other side. The door thumped loudly as it pounded against the rubber grommets of its frame sending a drum like sound echoing throughout the stairwell.

"Shit!" Kelly gasped and her heart began to race.

Robbie quickly checked back down the shaft, expecting to see all the doors below burst open spilling hungry undead into the stairwell in search of the source of the noise. The echo rumbled off the concrete walls for long seconds like a thunderstorm passing through a canyon. He waited, but heard no sounds of doors or footsteps from below. "What happened?!" he finally asked glancing back at Kelly.

"I don't know," Kelly answered. "I lost my grip I think, but, it felt like it pulled away from me."

"Pressure," Robbie said.

"What?" Kelly asked.

"Could be a pressure difference between the stairwell and the hallway." Robbie answered, still keeping a concerned watch down the stairs. "If it's sealed up tight."

"Ok," Kelly said. "Try again?"

"Yes," Robbie said quickly, "we need to get out of this stairwell and barricade this floor. No telling what might be down below and come looking for us."

"Get ready," Kelly responded, "we still have to clear this floor and whatever is behind this door."

"Go!" was all Robbie said and turned back to face the doorway.

Kelly grabbed the handle more tightly this time and gave it a strong tug. A whoosh of air rushed out and enveloped them in a cloud that smelled of mold and wood and dust. Robbie stepped up to take on anything that appeared. Kelly stepped back and blinked to clear her eyes, but nothing emerged from the dark and dusty hallway.

Kelly tapped on her flashlight and they peered in to see a long, straight hall with another door on the far side. A patterned burgundy carpet ran along the floor with rich matching wallpaper. Antique looking brass light fixtures were spaced evenly along the way underneath a tall ceiling capped with mahogany stained woodwork and trim. Dusty spider webs stretched across the space but they looked abandoned as if even the spiders too had left this place.

"Swanky," Robbie said, "looks like the Haunted Mansion at Disney."

"Yea," Kelly agreed still shining her light around. "There's nothing in the hallway. Let's get inside and close this door before anything comes looking for us."

They eased inside and Robbie used his leg to keep the door from slamming shut again. As the gap narrowed, air began rushing through more quickly and the door tried to pull closed in the vacuum. Holding his foot against the base, he eased it shut until the sound of the rushing wind abruptly stopped. In the silence, they both stood and listened for anything that might have followed them up the steps or be approaching from down the hall.

"It's damn dark in here," Robbie said finally. "Can you see anything?"

"There are some signs up here," Kelly said pointing with the small light.

They approached the first, a standee which had a similar design as the one downstairs. An arrow pointed to a closed door and read 'Magnolia Floorplan.' As they moved down the hall they found each of the doors had a similar sign nearby with the model names and a small map of the floorplan inside. When they reached the center of the hall they found the bank of elevators surrounded by tall mirrors, several couches and an antique looking dresser. The top of the dresser was covered with more stacks of brochures. A sign read 'all models open.'

"Creepy." Robbie whispered. "Let's clear the hallway first. Make sure all the doors are closed. Then we can start on the end and clear them one at a time."

"Good idea," Kelly agreed.

They moved carefully but it only took a few minutes to confirm that all the doors were closed. They took a moment to inspect a door with a glass pane that turned out to be a small tile covered room with a trash drop. At the end of the hall, they listened at the doorway they assumed to be another stairwell but heard nothing.

"Don't open it." Kelly said in a hush.

"Don't worry I'm not," Robbie replied quietly. "Ready to start with the apartments?"

She nodded.

"May as well start here," Robbie said indicating the one nearest the stairwell.

"I've got to pee," Kelly said shining her light on the door.

Robbie guffawed as he put his hand on the door knob. "Well hold it a little longer. I think these suites have balconies looking out over the river."

Kelly just braced herself in front of the door and raised her staff in readiness. Robbie waited a beat, then turned the latch and pushed the door open. The room was lit by windows facing the river and the blue afternoon light spread out over the fully furnished model. Using one of the brochures as a guide they entered and it only took 20 minutes or so to confirm there were no undead present. They propped the door open to help light up the hallway and moved on to the next.

As they went, they found that each unit had been staged in a different but very luxurious style. Each one looked, and was equipped, as if it were ready to appear in an episode of one of the high fashion living shows on HGTV. Aside from the dust and spider webs of course.

As they queued outside the door of what the sign described as the Valencia floor plan, Robbie read from the glossy brochure, "…this is their largest and most deluxe model. Ready?"

"I've got to pee," Kelly replied.

"You've been saying that for an hour," Robbie sighed.

"I keep forgetting," Kelly said.

"Can you hold it a little longer?" Robbie asked, wondering how anyone could "forget" that they had to pee.

"Sure." Kelly confirmed.

Robbie pushed open the door revealing a short hallway leading into a larger living area. The room was well lit, as all the others had been, with large windows looking out over the river. Robbie stepped over the threshold, glanced around and listened but heard only his own breathing. Looking back at Kelly he said. "How do you forget to…"

"Look out!" Kelly shouted as a thin figure lurched from around the corner ahead of them and charged at Robbie. It lunged with its mouth wide and teeth exposed. Robbie was unprepared and off balance, so even with its small frame, it crashed into him with enough force to knock him off his feet. He was just able to raise an elbow up to block its snarling jaws from snapping onto his face as he went down. Once on the ground, the thing began clawing and flailing as it tried to tear into him. He kicked and squirmed in a panic as he struggled to fight it off.

The two bodies were entwined and squirming frantically on the floor making the thing an impossible target. Kelly couldn't swing without hitting Robbie so she jumped behind them, grabbed under its arms and heaved it as hard as she could down the hall. Perhaps it was the adrenaline, or maybe the thing was just skin and bones, but it flew at least 10 feet. It tumbled and rolled to a stop, but instantly spun around and began scampering back towards them. This time Kelly was ready, as it charged, she raised her staff and hit it in the head as hard as she could.

Kelly saw that it had been a woman with brown hair, as its skull twisted around nearly backwards from the blow. The force spun it around but, with the ferocity of a wild dog, it swung back around and came at them sideways. She braced to hit the thing again but suddenly Robbie was there cleaving in its head with his machete.

"Bitch!" he yelled as sank his blade down with a dull thunk. The ferocity instantly vanished from its face and the zombie fell directly to the floor.

Worse Than Dead

They both stepped back from the dead woman and began scanning in all directions for others. They listened but could only hear one another's heavy breathing. Kelly realized her hands were shaking as she tried to keep aware of everything around her all at once. Seconds ticked by and they waited for the sound of hands pounding on doors as the undead awoke all around them. But none came.

"Shit!" Robbie said finally. "What the fuck?!"

"Dammit, Robbie," Kelly said as she turned back to the open room. "Pay attention! You damn near got us both killed!"

Robbie turned to face her. "Yea, crap, I'm sorry," he said, obviously shaken. "Everything was so quiet I lost my focus."

"Robbie," she said, staring at him intently. "What is that?" She pointed at his head. Robbie put his hand to the side of his face and came away with red liquid streaming down his palm.

"Did she scratch you?!" Kelly cried and stepped toward him.

"No," he stepped back from her, "no…I…I'm fine. I hit my head on the door when she tackled me."

"Are you sure?" Kelly stammered and stepped toward him again. "Let me see it."

This time he let her get close. "Yes." Robbie said wiping at the blood. "She didn't bite me. I hit it on the door."

"Come inside and let's take a closer look," Kelly pulled his arm towards the apartment. "There's not enough light out here."

"We need to clear this place first," Robbie said with a hand to his head. "We don't need any other surprises."

As soon as they had cleared the rest of the rooms, Kelly shut the front door and ordered Robbie to, "Sit down! We need to get you patched up. You're bleeding all over."

Robbie flopped down onto the couch and let Kelly disinfect and bandage his cut with her first aid kit.

"It doesn't look like a bite," she said.

"It's not," Robbie countered offended, "I told you I hit it on the door.

"I know what you said," Kelly countered, "but she could have scratched you, I don't know. It happened so fast."

"I'm ok," Robbie said holding the side of his head.

"I believe you," she tried to say calmly but, couldn't hide her concern. "Look, I think we've had enough excitement for one day. Let's button up here for the night and we can finish clearing this floor tomorrow?"

"Good idea," Robbie agreed leaning back onto the couch cushions. He looked over at the sliding glass door leading to the balcony and noticed it was smeared with finger marks and zombie sludge, as if the undead woman had been standing there clawing at it. The glass was smudged and stained up to the height of where the creature's hands would reach. "Hey, look at that."

"What?" Kelly said as she repacked the medical kit.

"The door is all smudged up," Robbie pointed, "like she really wanted to get out onto the porch."

"Probably got locked in here and that was the only source of movement," Kelly opined as she glanced over.

Robbie stood and walked towards the door but stopped. The wooden flooring in front of the door was as stained and bloody as the glass. "Looks like she must have just paced back and forth in front right here. Notice everything else in the room is clean?"

Kelly snorted, "You think she's been standing there at that window for all these years?"

"That's what it looks like." Robbie guessed.

"I guess it's possible," Kelly said joining him. "Those things don't seem to recognize doorways unless they are following something. If there was no noise in the hall this may have been the only source of entertainment."

"Yea," Robbie agreed. "Welcome to your sucky afterlife. Stuck in a high rise condo forever."

"Probably better than being outside," Kelly opined. "At least she had a nice view and the birds weren't trying to eat her eyeballs."

"Ew," he said, "I guess the zombie afterlife sucks no matter where you end up."

"True," she agreed walking back to their packs and pulling out an energy bar. "Are you hungry?"

"Not anymore," Robbie replied but made his way back towards the kitchen. A long granite counter top separated the galley kitchen from the large living room. He walked in and began checking the cabinets. "Check it out. Cardboard food."

Kelly joined him and laughed that the cabinets were stocked with cardboard facades of food boxes. The refrigerator was the same, even including a large box with an image of a cooked turkey. The end of the island had two bar stools on each side and was decorated as a breakfast area. She pulled out one of the chairs to sit down and noticed that underneath the island were a pair of dark blue women's heels and two purses pushed neatly up against the cabinet's base. She picked up one of the shoes and looked it over.

"She had good taste in shoes," Kelly said as Robbie continued to rifle through the cabinets. "These are Jimmy Choo."

"Jimmy who?" Robbie looked up confused.

"Jimmy Choo." Kelly said with a sigh. "Very expensive back in the day."

"Oh," Robbie said disinterestedly and returned to exploring the drawers.

Then Kelly stopped and looked back down "Two purses…"

"Is that another type of shoe?" Robbie asked.

"No." Kelly continued. "There are two purses. That means there were two women here."

"Not in here," Robbie said. "We checked already. Maybe the other one left before it started?"

Kelly picked up both bags and started rifling through them. "Definitely two women."

"How can you tell," Robbie asked.

"Different types of make-up…" she answered as she looked through the contents of the bags, "different types of jewelry, two wallets, two sets of keys. Nice rides." She held up the two key fobs. "One is a BMW and the other is a Range Rover."

"Um, that's not a good sign," Robbie said. "If her car is still here then she is still here somewhere. Maybe in one of the other units."

"She may have run out when her friend turned," Kelly guessed. "She couldn't get back in so may have tried to get home another way."

"That would be hard without her wallet," Robbie said. "She wouldn't have gotten far on foot. Especially without her shoes. Not that day."

"Yes, but if she took off in a panic she might not have thought of that until it was too late," Kelly conjectured. She pulled the wallets out and lay them on the counter top beside each other. Both were high end brand names. One was a grey alligator style. The other was caramel brown and she could smell the leather. Opening them up she found two driver's licenses with the smiling faces of two women who could have come off the covers of fashion magazines. It was hard to comprehend how one of them could have been the wild haired cave woman who attacked them in the hall.

"Maria Isabella Cortez," Kelly said reading the ID information next to the picture of a woman with jet black hair and rich tan skin that strongly suggested a Hispanic background. "Twenty six years old, five feet five inches tall, requires corrective lenses and an organ donor."

"And, Taylor Michelle Fuller," she said looking at the other ID. The woman had blonde hair and blue eyes with the high cheek bones and pale skin Kelly thought might be from Germanic genes. "Thirty two years old, five feet six inches tall and lives at 532 Bayside Drive."

"Bayside Drive," Robbie chimed from across the room. "Swanky part of town. Over by the Yacht Club, right?"

"Yep," Kelly affirmed.

"I wonder what they were doing up here?" Robbie asked. "The outbreak hit overnight and by morning the city was in chaos. Who goes condo shopping before sunrise?"

"Ah," Kelly answered as she held up a card pulled from one of the wallets. "They were with the realty company selling the building." Looking at the card she read, "Maria Cortez – Senior Vice President for Sales – Riverside Condominiums, Inc. I bet they got here early to set up for the day's potential buyers. One of them got bit on the way in and turned after she got here. The shit hit the fan and the other one hauled ass."

"Sounds plausible." Robbie said. "Well, I hope her friend got out ok but let's not take any chances. I don't want to risk her busting in on us in the middle of the night. Help me move this dresser against the front door."

"I have to pee," Kelly said.

"Will you go take care of that already?!" Robbie said exasperated.

"I think I will," Kelly hopped up from her stool and walked purposefully to the bathroom. Under the cabinet, she found an unopened roll of toilet paper and strode back out holding it up like a trophy. "Behold! Mana from heaven!"

"Good for you," Robbie said still struggling to shove the chest across the floor.

Kelly stopped and frowned at the thick layers of grime, blood and zombie slobber coated over the glass door and handle. She walked back to the kitchen and looked under the sink. "Voila!" she said pulling out a full bottle of Lysol cleaner, a container of Clorox wipes and a box of yellow kitchen gloves. She then marched back to the door and gave the area a thorough scrubbing. When she was done she opened the door, stepped out onto the balcony and flung the used gloves and wipes off into the air.

"Litter bug," Robbie called out as he watched her from inside.

Kelly gave him the finger and took a look around. The balcony was about five feet wide and stretched nearly the entire length of the apartment. Each condo on this level had a similar terrace with a narrow gap between them. As this was the top floor, the only thing above them was the roof. She glanced up and verified nothing looked like it might fall. Outside several patio lounges, chairs and tables had been staged while all the cushions had been piled together against the railing. Kelly took it all in before strolling to the far end.

Chapter 15

There was a time not so long ago, when she would never dream of relieving herself over the edge a fancy condo balcony in the hip part of downtown, but those days were in the past. She pulled one of the fancy teak chairs over for balance, climbed up onto the railing and wrangled her pants down. Hanging her bottom over the outside, she checked the wind direction and let loose. After holding it for so long, it was pure bliss and she sighed with relief.

She sat there and enjoyed the view. This high up, much of the destruction was not so obvious and she could almost imagine it was just a nice normal day before the end of the world. In the distance to the north, the iron girders of Century Bridge stretched out across the river. Its wide lanes connected Fort Garcon to the beaches further west, and the state capitol to the east. The setting sun sent a golden glow over the river, shining in the windows of the buildings on either side. She saw groups of figures moving along the sidewalks in the distance and imagined them to be regular people out shopping rather than the undead, that they most assuredly were. To the south, the city gradually gave way to commercial wharfs and piers before returning to long and winding stretches of green as the river ran down to the Gulf.

She finished up, hopped down and was reattaching her belt when she spotted something odd among the piles of cushions. Kelly clicked her belt in place, grabbed her staff and stepped closer. A black high heeled shoe seemed to be wedged between the cushions. Kelly used her staff to move the top cushion and reveal the rest of the shoe; a boot actually. She slowly shoved the other pieces out of the way until her suspicions were confirmed.

"Hey Robbie!" She called, "I think I figured out what happened to Taylor Fuller."

"Oh?" Robbie queried as he walked to the door and saw the body, the fully dead kind, laying among the faded cushions. "Oh."

"Yea," Kelly said. "Out here the whole damn time."

"Man that would be a fucked up situation," Robbie said looking back at the bloody streaks along the inside of the glass. "Your friend turns into a zombie and chases you out here. But there's no way down and you can't get back in. She was trapped. I think I would just jump and got it over with."

"Maybe she was waiting for someone," Kelly said, "…thought she could wait it out for help to come."

"But from up here she could see the whole thing go down," Robbie countered. "When the sun came up she would have a bird's eye view of the whole nightmare unfolding."

"Some people don't quit easy," Kelly said looking down at the drawn and emaciated corpse. "She probably piled the cushions on herself to keep warm."

"Smart." Robbie said sadly. "Too bad help wasn't coming."

"Yea." Kelly replied.

"How do you know it's Taylor?" Robbie asked. "Can't for sure," Kelly said but nodded to the corpse's matted blonde hair. "Taylor had blonde hair in her driver's license photo. The one in the hall had dark hair, right?"

"I think so," answered Robbie. "I wasn't paying close attention to that while she was trying to bite my face off."

"How long do you think it would take to die from dehydration and exposure out here?" Kelly asked, and then answered herself. "Three days without water and your body starts to shut down. A week or two maybe? Laying out here with no cover, getting weaker, hoping for a break, praying your homicidal friend inside forgets about you and wanders off, hoping somebody shows up to save you. But nobody does."

"Well," Robbie interrupted Kelly's morbid narrative, "she's at peace now, right? Why don't you come back inside? We'll bury them tomorrow."

Kelly had started to sweat and felt her stomach getting queasy. It wasn't the corpse. She had seen thousands of those. It was as if she could feel this woman's final moments of loneliness and despair in her heart. The ache reached down into her intestines. Before she knew it, she was leaning over the railing puking down the side of the building.

"You ok?" Robbie came over to her when she started heaving.

Kelly nodded. "Yea, sorry, just got a little overwhelmed."

"C'mon." Robbie rested his hand on her back and noticed she felt warm. "Why don't you come in and lie down. Let me help you."

"I can do it myself. I'm ok," Kelly said as she stepped back from the rail and made her way back inside. She lay down on the couch feeling suddenly drained and tired. Robbie grabbed a canteen of water from his pack and handed it to her. She drank it deeply. "Don't ever leave me like that Robbie. Ok? Promise?"

"Sure Kelly," Robbie said kneeling beside her. "I won't. Where would I go?"

"I know, right?" She said and smiled. "I'm really tired all of a sudden. Would it be ok if I just lay here for a bit?"

"Yea, no problem," Robbie answered. "I've almost got the place buttoned up. The sun is setting. We can't do anything productive until morning anyway. Just lie here and relax."

Robbie checked that the front door was locked with the dresser firmly braced against it. He then walked through the house, re-checking in all the closets and under all the beds until he was confident there was nothing that would go bump in the night. As late afternoon shadows fell, he pulled the heavy blackout curtain so that it covered most of the wide windows.

"Don't close it all the way," Kelly requested as he got close to the open sliding door. "Let's leave a little open for the view and to keep some air flow."

"Yea, ok," Robbie agreed and stepped out onto the balcony to look down at the river front as the last light bounced along its empty streets. "Hey, hear that?"

"What?" Kelly asked.

"Exactly," Robbie said. "Nothing. The loading dock where we came in is below us. I can't see it but I don't hear the pounding any more. The undies must have wandered off."

"Or they got in and are making their way up here after us," Kelly groaned.

"Thanks, Suzie Sunshine," Robbie shot back. "Well, we're safe in here at least for tonight."

He said this as he looked over at the exposed and decrepit body of the blonde realtor laying on the deck. He contemplated just dumping her over the railing but then decided, after all she had been through, she deserved better. He went back in and found a sheet in one of the closets to cover her. Then he piled the cushions back on top to hold it in place. 'Not very dignified,' he thought, 'but maybe it will be ok until morning.'

They stole fancy blankets from the bedrooms and stretched out on the long couches in the living room. Kelly fell asleep almost immediately. Robbie lay in the dark listening to the sounds of the building. A few times he got up to check that the doors and windows remained locked. Looking out over the river he admired the sparkle of moonlight on the water. At night the city almost disappeared and just became dark boxy silhouettes against the darker sky. He considered staying up and on watch, but the silence of the night finally convinced him to close his eyes and he was quickly asleep.

Early the next morning, Kelly's insides began to roil, waking her suddenly from sleep. She jumped from the couch and dashed out to the balcony just in time to puke her guts up again. Leaning on the railing, she gasped as her stomach jerked and churned through several rounds of spasms. Just as she thought she might be through it; another bout would twist through her body until she could only spit bile out into the morning air.

When the sickness had finally passed, she shook and gulped lungsful of fresh air as her body recollected itself. Leaning her head on the cool railing felt good against her hot skin. She spent minutes appreciating that simple pleasure while staring down at her bare feet on the balcony's concrete floor. Glancing over, she saw that several of the outdoor cushions had fallen over, exposing strands of the dead realtor's blonde hair. It flitted in the morning breeze. Kelly thought she might get sick again but somehow the sight of the corpse did not trouble her this time.

"Sorry about that." Kelly whispered, feeling guilty that she had somehow disturbed the dead woman's resting place.

She wandered back inside and found Robbie, still stretched out, sleeping on the couch. Moving to the kitchen she grabbed a bottle of water from their stash and washed her mouth out. Spitting into the sink, she tried to recall where they had put the bag with the toothpaste. Before she could remember, a narrow shaft of sunlight broke through the curtains and into her eyes.

"Ow." She stepped back from the blinding ray. It drew a line down the wall of cabinets behind her. Rubbing her eyes, she turned and absently opened the nearest cabinet marked by the light. It was empty, but the rising sun had begun pushing the shadows from the dusty shelves. She started going through the cupboards to see if they had missed anything in their hasty initial search.

Behind one of the carboard displays she found an ornate wooden coffee and tea caddy with an assortment of individually packaged "gourmet" brews. Behind it were several unopened boxes of coffee, tea and "fancy" single serve snack cookies. She opened one of the boxes and the smell of fresh tea washed over her and flooded her senses. She couldn't believe it. It had been so long since she had had a cup of tea, she felt her eyes start to well up at the thought of it. Before she knew it, tears were rolling down her cheeks and she leaned on the kitchen counter sobbing.

"Are you ok!?" Robbie suddenly appeared at her side. "What happened?"

"I'm fine," she sobbed. "Stupid. It's just…I'm sorry. I never thought I'd have tea again."

"Oh…" Robbie said uncertainly. "You're crying about tea?"

"Yes," Kelly stood, wiped her eyes and sniffed. "Do you think we could start a fire and boil some water? I'd really like a cup."

Robbie wasn't sure if the fireplace worked so he went out and got a small fire going in the grill on the balcony. He was surprised to find that the fancy looking tea pot on the stove wasn't just an ornament, but a sturdy and practical device. He boiled the water and Kelly made them tea. They opened the curtains and spent that first morning sampling the dark mixtures from the condo's collection of fine china cups. As the sun rise over the river, Kelly's heart swelled, and she felt for the first time as if they had found a safe place t call home.

The next few days were spent clearing the rest of the building. As they walked through the vacant rooms, they became more and more convinced that it must have been locked up tight before the fall, with just the two realtors inside. They found that only construction on the upper floors and lower public areas had been completed. The condos on the very top floor were staged with furniture and decorated as if the editors of some style magazine might drop in for an inspection. The lower floors were fully decorated to impress potential buyers. While the middle floors were mostly stark open spaces of concrete, drywall and metal studs.

Robbie pointed out the locations where the construction crews had left their tools, materials and equipment; expecting to return the next day. "I suppose it's a good thing we will never have to go far in search of a ladder or a hammer."

"True," Kelly agreed and pointed to the end of a hall, where several rooms had been roughly boxed in with sheets of drywall. "Did you see that?"

"What?" Robbie asked, looking up from the tools.

"I thought I saw something move." Kelly whispered.

The two instinctively raised their weapons and stiffened. Kelly nodded ahead and they carefully slipped down the hall towards the room. It had no door and sunlight shined through its window creating a rectangle of light on the opposite wall. When they were close Kelly tapped her staff on the concrete floor. The sound was enough to attract the interest of any undead creatures nearby, but none appeared.

After a moment, Robbie slipped ahead and peeked into the room. "Shit!" He said as he jumped back.

"What?!" Kelly hefted her staff and prepared to fight. "What is it?!"

"Bees!" Robbie cried stepping backwards away from the doorway.

"Bees?" Kelly lowered her staff, confused.

"Yea," Robbie went on with a shudder, "bees, hornets, wasps, I don't know."

Kelly raised an eyebrow. "Bees. Really?"

"Look." Robbie pointed.

Kelly walked up to the doorway. Sure enough, in the far corner near the window, a section of drywall was missing, creating a narrow gap between metal framing. She could see rows of yellow hexagonal comb just inside. A cloud of small yellow and black insects buzzed around the combs. Groups of them whisked busily in and out of the room through a triangle shaped section that had broken from the window. The room was alive with their activity as they bounced around in the sunlight. She realized she must have seen their shadows reflected on the outside wall.

"Bees, right?" Robbie asked remaining a few feet back.

"Honeybees I think." Kelly said.

"Like, honey, honeybees?" Robbie asked.

"Yes." Kelly answered. "Honey, honeybees. We might be able to collect honey. I bet the Baldwins would trade for that."

"Yea, maybe" Robbie said, "but how do we get it without getting stung all to hell?"

"I don't know," Kelly said thoughtfully, "we might have to make a trip to the public library to find out."

"That big old spooky building downtown?" Robbie whined.

"Robbie Bruce." Kelly chided. "You don't mind fighting the undead but you're afraid of going to the library?"

"I'm not afraid," Robbie replied. "It's just a big old building. No telling what's in there."

Kelly snickered as she started to walk away. "C'mon Shaggy lets finish clearing the building before Mr. Smithers shows up in a monster suit."

"Ok." Robbie hurried past the room with the bees to catch up with her. "If I'm shaggy, are you Velma or Daphne?"

"I'm always hanging out with you so I must be Scooby," Kelly laughed.

The next day they buried the two realtors in a Japanese style meditation garden just off the pool deck. Kelly reasoned that the area was respectful of the dead women and had too many rocks to be useful for any gardening she and Robbie might later do. They marked the graves with stakes and since neither could think of any prayers, they stood there silently for a few moments.

"I've been thinking." Robbie said finally, leaning on the shovel with sweat dripping down his face.

"About what?" Kelly said, stepping under a palm tree to get out of the sun.

"About Roy."

"Oh?"

"I'm thinking that once we get settled in here," Rob said. "I'd like to go out and spend a few days looking for him."

"Robbie..." Kelly sighed.

"You could stay here." He explained. "I can do it by myself."

She looked at him doubtfully, with raised eyebrows.

"No, really." He went on. "We have been on the run since the day he disappeared. We've never really been able to do a real search. I don't think I can let it go until I know we have done everything we can to find him."

"Robbie." She said again, forcing herself to sound calm. "I miss him too. Every day. I want him back, but it's been... years. If he was still out there. Still alive. Don't you think we would know by now? And if he's not alive? Then, what?"

"That's just it," Rob countered. "I want to know either way, and I don't think he would give up on us."

"I wish and pray for him every day," Kelly argued, "but even if he is still alive, we have no idea where he is. We can't just go wandering around out there. You know that. It's too dangerous with those things."

"I can handle myself," Robbie said. "Those creatures are slow, and I know how to keep away from them."

She squinted from the sun, even in the shade. "It's not just the undead and you know it! Fort Garcon is falling apart around us. You get out there and hurt yourself! Fall through a roof, slice yourself open on some broken glass, twist an ankle, get trapped in a flooded basement, and then what?"

He looked at the ground.

"Look." She went on. "We aren't giving up. If he is out there, and alive, we will find him, or he will find us. We just can't keep risking our lives for it. We have to think of ourselves first now, ok?"

"I guess." He nodded and kicked at the ground in frustration. "I just…"

"Robbie," she blurted, "I need you right now, ok? I can't risk losing you. Not now! You're not going out there on your own and that's final!"

"Kelly," Robbie continued. "I keep dreaming about him being out there. I think if I don't at least go looking for him it'll drive me crazy."

"I can't talk about this right now, ok. It's too hot out here." Kelly wiped the sweat from her forehead with the back of her hand. "Can we not do this, right now?"

"C'mon Kelly," Robbie pushed.

"Not now!" She began to walk towards the doorway and stumbled as the blood seemed to rush from her head.

Robbie dropped the shovel and grabbed her arm.

"I need to go back inside," she said. "This heat is making me dizzy."

"You've been sick a lot lately." Robbie said. "Are you ok?"

"Yes." Kelly blurted. "I'm fine. This heat. Its just a too much. Can you help me upstairs?"

They had decided to stay in the large "La Valencia" model, with 1237 written in fancy brass numbers on the door, as it was the most spacious and well apportioned. With all the other doors on the floor propped open, they had their choice of bedrooms and décor, but more importantly, they could keep an eye on everything. With one side of the building facing the river and the other facing downtown, they had great views in all directions. All they had to do was keep a low profile so nothing on the streets below got interested enough to come up and visit.

It took another week to explore most of the building. Some areas were locked off and a few of the lower levels just seemed too dark and foreboding so they chose to put that off. On the roof, rather than the rocks and tar they encountered on most buildings, they found that this one really was "green." The entire roof top was a garden of tall grass. Around the edges, arranged like awnings were arrays of solar panels.

"Well I'll be damned," Robbie said. "I guess we need to go check out some books on solar panels."

"And gardening. Is your library card up to date?" Kelly called back as she dug in the dirt. She found that it went down several inches before hitting something hard that felt like concrete. Pulling at it she found several layers of some sort of netting holding the dirt in place and giving the grass roots something to hold onto.

"Can we grow food up here?" Robbie asked as he inspected an electrical panel on the end of the solar array. A big switch was turned to "ON" and padlocked in place. Stickers on the box warned of danger and high voltage.

"Not sure," Kelly replied. "It's not very deep. I don't think it's intended for anything other than this grass but there is a lot of silt built up over the years. We might try some tomatoes. The Baldwins said they would give us some seeds."

"Cool," Robbie said as he followed the cables from the solar panels over to where they ran down the full length of the building. He looked over, he called back, "The batteries for the solar panels must be in the basement."

"Great," Kelly said sifting the dirt through her fingers. "More dark and spooky places to explore."

"Yea but imagine if we can get the power on?!" Robbie said excitedly. "Hot showers!"

"That would be nice," she agreed, "but don't get your hopes up."

"Umm," Robbie considered. "True."

Kelly wiped the dirt from her hands and looked out across the city scape. "Before we worry about that we need to make a run back to the other building and pick up the rest of the supplies and food."

Chapter 16

Three days later, they dropped their packs full of the last of their supplies onto the floor and collapsed onto the couch in their condo.

"Holy crap that was close," Robbie said propping his muddy boots up onto the glass coffee table. "I thought that fat one was going to…"

"Get your dirty feet off the furniture!" Kelly admonished him while slapping his leg.

"Jeesh!" Robbie said lowering his feet. "Since when do you care about furniture?"

"We've got a really nice place here Robbie," she said. "I just want to take care of it. I'd think you would too. I mean we might be here a while."

"Yea, I guess." Robbie agreed reluctantly. He had learned in the last few years not to get too attached to a place. To him it was a safe place to sleep for the moment. He had had to rush out of too many others in the middle of the night, and the middle of the afternoon, and early in the morning and all hours of the day and night. It was against his experience to get start thinking of anything as permanent. Others they had traveled with had done that and it caused them to hesitate when it was time to get out. It caused them to get dead, and as images of those times and people flashed through his head Robbie knew he didn't want any of that. "What's the big deal? There's a table exactly like this in every other unit on this floor here if we need another."

"Yes," Kelly sighed. "But this one is here now and we should take care of it. As a matter of fact we need to take our boots off. We're tracking mud all over the carpet."

Robbie raised his eyebrow and gave her a look that said – 'have you lost your mind?'

As she unstrapped her boot laces, Kelly glared at him as only a women can. "Take your boots off! We're going to take care of this place! It's going to be our home. Ok?!"

It wasn't a question. It was a statement, with no alternatives or argument.

"Ok, Kel," Robbie raised his hands in surrender and then reached down to take off his boots. "I just don't think it's a good idea to get too attached, you know? That hasn't worked well for us in the past."

"I understand" she growled, "but this place is different. We've never been in a place like this. We're going to make it safe. It's going to be safe here. It's going to be our home."

"Yes, dear," Robbie said sarcastically.

"Don't you 'yes dear' me, Robert Bruce!" Kelly said sternly then stood and took her boots to the front door where she dropped them. She then stormed away into the back hallway towards the master bedroom.

"Jeesh," Robbie said under his breath as he watched her stalk away. They had had fights before but never out of the blue like that, and never over anything like this, that he considered so stupid. He finished taking off his boots and looked around for someplace to put them that wouldn't draw more of Kelly's ire. He finally decided the back patio would work best and set them down outside the sliding glass door.

Grabbing his bag, he went into the guest bedroom and changed into a pair of loose shorts and a t-shirt. It felt odd being so casually dressed after years of sleeping in his tactical clothes, ready to fight or bolt in an instant. But they felt safe in the condo and had begun to let their guard down once they had locked everything up for the night. The condominiums outer doors were secure, the stairwells were closed, and the traps they had set up would alert them of anything got inside, long before it found them.

Unsure what to do next, Robbie walked out and sat down on the sofa again, feeling like a scolded puppy who has been punished but doesn't know why. He tried to enjoy being alone but found himself worrying about what Kelly was doing. His eyes stared at a large clock on the wall. The hands had stopped at 6:45 and the second hand hung straight down, and still, but he imagined it ticking the seconds away. Once he had imagined it, the ticking sound seemed stuck in his head. Finally, the anticipation got to him and he rose to go check on her.

Robbie found Kelly curled up in the middle of the king size bed in the master bedroom. Her eyes were red from tears.

"You ok, Kel?" He asked quietly as he sat on the edge of the bed.

"Yes," she sniffed. "I'm sorry. I'm just tired and feeling overwhelmed. I'm sorry I snapped at you."

"I understand," Robbie said softly. "It's been a tough few weeks…years."

She smiled, "I really think this is a good place. That we can make it here. I want you to want to stay. I don't want you to leave me. I couldn't take it."

"I'm not going anywhere," Robbie said reassuringly. "Where would I go?"

"Just don't, ok?" Kelly asked.

"Don't worry." Robbie patted her knee. "You're stuck with me."

She smiled up at him. "Thanks."

"Hey," Robbie said. "Why don't you relax? I'll go get some dinner started and we can have a nice quiet evening looking out at the stars. How does that sound?"

"Sounds lovely," she sniffled and took hold of his hand.

They sat there quietly for a few moments without saying anything.

"Ok," Robbie finally said pulling away and standing up. "Those MRE's aren't going to heat themselves up. Do you want the spaghetti or the chicken and rice?"

Kelly thought for a moment about the boxed military rations they had found in the back of a National Guard truck a few months prior. While each MRE offered a different entrée they were all fairly bland in flavor. "Surprise me," she finally said.

"You got it," Robbie called back as he walked down the hall towards the kitchen. He felt better knowing that Kelly was no longer angry with him. The meals only required a little water poured into a self-heating pouch. After he got them going, he propped the entrees up against some large decorative candles. He then made two place settings, and even laid out the little forks, knives and napkins for two. Then he opened a package of powdered drink mix and, using the fancy glass from the pantry, made two drinks. The bright green mixture didn't look anything like wine but he figured that would be ok.

A few minutes later Kelly walked out. "Well this is nice," she complimented him.

"Thanks," Robbie stuttered as she walked towards him.

Kelly had shed her gear and changed into a long black t shirt with the name of an old metal band on the front and a pair of cotton shorts. "Nice," she said, admiring his place settings and the steaming food.

"…Are you feeling better?" he finally asked.

"Yes," she said sitting next to him, bringing her feet and knees up onto the couch. After a moment looked over and locked eyes with him. "I've been thinking, and I've come to some hard realizations."

"You have?" he asked.

"Yes," she replied seriously. "We've been running around with our lives on hold for the last few years."

"Well the undead walking the streets will do that," Robbie smirked trying to lighten her mood.

"The undead are just an obstacle," she replied. "We have learned how to deal with them and now they are only a problem if we do something stupid."

"Or twist an ankle while scavenging," Robbie interjected.

Kelly smiled but raised an eyebrow. "You're missing the point. What I've realized, and come to accept, is that it's just us now. We're alone. Nobody is coming to rescue us."

"You're just realizing that now?" Robbie asked as he pulled at a sealed packet of crackers.

"What I mean, dummy, is that…look…" She paused, "Roy isn't coming back."

Robbie stopped and stared at her. While he didn't worry about Roy as often as he used to it was always in the back of his head that he would come back one day. He couldn't imagine Roy as dead, or becoming one of those things, so he had a kind of fantasy that his older brother had gotten injured or hit in the head and then gotten lost. Robbie and Kelly had moved around a lot since Roy went missing, so he imagined him out there wandering the streets looking for them.

Robbie had never thought of it logically, but subconsciously, he half expected to come around a corner one day and bump into Roy coming the other way. His brother was resilient like that. Always the smart one, the tough one, the captain of the soccer team. He couldn't imagine Roy dead, or worse, just running away.

"I mean it, Robbie," she said as she put her hand on his knee, "I'm sorry. Nobody hates the idea more than I do…did. But, it's reality. He isn't coming back. And…I think I've finally come to terms with it. It's hard to say but I'm finally over him. I mean, I'll always love him, but he's gone and I've got to, we… have got to, move on."

"What do you mean?" Robbie asked more seriously.

"I mean," she whispered and moved closed to him, "it's just you and me now. I've been waiting for a dead man and I have a very alive man right next to me."

She leaned in and wrapped him in a hug. He hugged her back, not wanting to misinterpret her intentions, but feeling her warm body against his started something in his libido. His could hear blood starting to speed up, pumping faster through his heart and other places. It was so loud in his ears he wondered if Kelly could hear it too. He felt as if he had a jet engine revving up inside his body and he wasn't sure he would be able to slow it down. It made him nervous and confused as he sat there fighting to stay still and just hold her.

He thought the engine might shake him apart from the inside as she curled herself further into his embrace. Unable to resist further, he almost instinctively leaned in and kissed her full on the lips. To his surprise and elation, she pressed her lips back against his and they fell into a long deep kiss. He pulled her as close as he could, feeling as if he never wanted the moment to end. They ground their bodies' tightly together breathing heavily with excitement.

When Kelly suddenly pulled back and looked into his eyes, Robbie thought he saw doubt on her face and he immediately felt like he may have got it wrong. Taken her beyond where she wanted to go.

"I'm sorry" he stuttered apologetically, knowing she could likely feel his heartbeat quicken between them "I got carried away…"

"It's ok," she whispered, staying close and cuddled up against him.

"Um." he gasped. "What are we doing?"

"This," she said with mischievous grin as she kissed him again.

"Oh?" Robbie groaned.

"You like that?" Kelly asked.

"Oh yea," Robbie said, not caring at the moment who it was seducing him.

They made love on the big couch. Living in fear and surviving in the moment had repressed any thoughts of physical attraction these last few years. But now it exploded between them and their pent-up desires made up for their inexperience and lack of practice. It was desperate and fast.

Afterward Kelly lay on top of him, looking into his eyes and seeing his total exhilaration mixed with unease.

"Sorry," he panted. "I didn't mean to…"

She stopped him with a kiss. "It's ok," she said. "I liked it."

"Really?" He gasped.

"Yes," and she kissed him again. She kept her body pressed to his. Knowing it was likely the first time for him being with a woman. She wanted, needed, it to be good for him so she encouraged him as he caressed her. This was not the lusty 'can't keep us apart' sex she and Roy had shared but she found herself enjoying being touched and desired after so long. In a few minutes Robbie was ready to go again, and they made love eagerly amongst the soft cushions.

Afterward, Kelly lay enveloped in Robbie's arms with her head resting on his chest listening to his breathing become rhythmic as he fell into sleep. She had not climaxed but that wasn't important to her. He had, several times, and that is what she needed. To ensure that he would stay with her in spite of what was already growing inside her. There was no reason for him to know it wasn't his. She needed him to stay to help her get through the pregnancy and then to keep them all alive afterward. She didn't think he would leave them but she couldn't take that chance. Not now.

They spent much of the next day in each other's arms. It was as if he wanted to make up for all the times they had spent living with each other but off limits when it came to intimacy. Kelly relaxed and let herself enjoy the attention.

As the sun rose on the second day, Robbie woke to find her in the kitchen wearing one of the fancy white terrycloth robes from their closet. The robes were embroidered with the burgundy logo of the Riverside Condominiums. She stood boiling water over a can of Sterno.

"Good morning sunshine," Kelly said with a smile.

"Good morning to you," he replied.

"Coffee or tea?" she indicated he had his choice.

"Coffee please," he replied.

"I'm not that good with coffee," Kelly warned him as she prepared the cup, "but I found a French Press in the cabinet. Maybe you can figure out how to use it." She slid him the steaming liquid as he sat down at the granite counter across from her.

"We need to get out and do some scavenging today," she said pointing her cup out the window to the city beyond.

Robbie pouted, sticking out his lower lip. "Darn I was hoping we could do the same as yesterday."

Kelly raised an eyebrow. "I'm all worn out from yesterday thank you very much. I need some rest and we are running low on some things, so I need you to put on your man boots and go get them."

Robbie smiled. "Yes dear. What do we need?"

Kelly pulled out a list of items she had made of things she felt like they needed for their new home. Robbie looked it over.

"You want me to get all this stuff by myself?" Robbie asked. "Sure you don't want to come with?"

"I think you can manage." Kelly retorted with a smile, "besides, you don't need any distractions out there."

"How about some distractions up here," Robbie leered at her playfully.

"Not until you get back, you naughty boy," she said pulling her robe tightly closed. "No treats until you get your chores done!"

Chapter 17

The next few days Robbie spent accumulating supplies and making sure all the building's exterior doors were closed and locked. He did much of it alone, but it didn't bother him as long as Kelly was waiting for him at the end of the day. She often met him in the doorway wearing just the robe.

Robbie eventually found his way down into the building's underground parking levels and checked that the vehicle entrances were secure. Using a large police style mag light with rechargeable batteries, he had found in a back office, he worked his way around the garage. He found the metal security gates were down and the doors to the street were closed and locked. That was good in his mind as he figured it meant nothing had come in after the outbreak. It didn't mean nothing was down there, just that if there were any zombies inside it meant they had been there a long time.

Exploring the top level of the garage, he found a black BMW and a silver Range Rover parked near each other near the elevators. Several layers of dust covered the two expensive cars but he could still see the glow of fresh paint under the blankets of grey particles. He tried the handles and found both cars were locked. No lights flashed and no chirping sounds came when he pulled at the levers so he presumed the batteries to be long dead. The Rover was for sure a city car, purchased for name and flash rather than its off road abilities. He could tell, in spite of its reputation and heritage, this Rover had never spent any time on any dirt roads.

Walking around admiring the luxury SUV he considered whether it might be worth trying to charge up the battery. If they could get it started, he thought it might make a good escape car if they ever needed to quickly get out of the city. While it looked like it was all for show, the Rover was decked out with all the latest outdoor accessories including a winch, fog lights as well as roof and bike racks.

After inspecting the cars, Robbie found the electrical lines entering along the far wall and was pretty sure these were the same ones running from the solar panels on the roof. The lines went through the floor and down to the next deck. Robbie shined his light down the ramp to the next level. Nothing emerged or growled at the intrusion into the darkness so he began to slowly descend. He checked each level as he went down, to verify that he was alone, but found nothing but dust and empty parking spaces.

It grew darker and colder as he went down. His light beam seemed to narrow the further he went, as if the lower levels had a thicker darkness than those above. The crunch of his footsteps on the pale concrete sounded loud in his ears and frustrated him as he tried to listen for other sounds. Each of his steps echoed off the cold walls and bounced around the cave like structure. He jerked his head back with nearly every step to ensure nothing was creeping up behind him. As he went deeper, every pop, click and drip of the building vibrated around him and added to his jumpiness.

He started to turn back several times. Told himself he should come back with Kelly to watch his back, but he dismissed the notion. If there were any mobile zombies in the car park, they would have emerged already. There was the possibility that some non-ambulatory flesh eaters were in the area but he would see them well before they could get to him. And given that there was nothing on the floors above, he doubted there would be any below. Still, he remained jumpy and alert as he emerged onto the bottom level.

Shining his light around, he could see that the parking area on this floor was half the size of those above. A wall had been built through the middle of the lot, with two large steel doors at one side. The doors were surrounded by 'no parking' and 'safety' signs. He took the "Danger – High Voltage" sign as an indication that he had found the electrical panel room and sighed with relief that his journey into the dank old cave had not been in vain.

Several spaces from the front of the doors, a white Ford Ranger pickup truck was parked. Even from a distance, he could see that it had been well used during its lifetime. It had the scratched and dented look of a utility or construction vehicle. A ladder hung over the back gate and a steel tool box was attached in the bed near the cab. The windows of the truck were dark and dusty so that he couldn't make out anything inside the truck's cab, not from a distance anyway.

Noting the trucks doors were closed and nothing inside had reacted to his light, he decided it was probably safe. He knew better than to focus on something before clearing around it though, so he went about making sure the open area of the level was clear. Walking to each corner, he found only stacks of construction supplies and debris piled about. This area wasn't as neatly maintained as the areas upstairs where customers might wander. Fast food wrappers and cups sat wherever they had been left by the construction workers.

Robbie checked under the truck before making his way closer along the passenger side. Through the back window the light beam revealed a silhouette in the driver's seat slumped against the window. Robbie paused and tried to make it out, but the dust and grime had fogged up the window too badly. He slowly eased around, stepping closer to the passenger window to shine his light in. He readied his hatchet even though he knew, if it was a zombie, it probably couldn't get out of the truck.

The figure didn't move so he stepped up to the window and tapped the glass with the light. Some zombies went into a sort of hibernation if they were trapped and nothing was around to attract their attention. They would just sit there until something came along to wake them up. This was always a danger when walking around old cars as many were still strapped into their seat belts. If the window was down, they could suddenly activate like an animatronic monster in a haunted house and start grabbing. Felicia went that way, he remembered the curly haired woman who had been with them for a short time. While hiding behind a car, its inhabitants suddenly bolted to life and dragged her in. The memory of it made him shiver.

Robbie tried to make out more detail, but through the thick layer of dirt that coated the passenger window, he could only tell it was a human figure slumped behind the wheel. Keeping his flashlight aimed at the cab, he moved around the truck until he stood a few paces from the driver's door. The shadow inside remained motionless, and from his new position, it appeared that the person's face was pressed against the glass of the driver's window. Robbie stepped up, tapped on the glass and quickly jumped back. The figure remained still.

Robbie had never seen one of the things play dead, or remain still, for so long. Especially in the presence of motion, noise and a nearby snack, so he became more confident that whoever it was, they were dead – fully dead. He decided to leave it be and continue on his original mission to check out the electrical room. If it did wake up and start moving, he figured he would hear it banging around in the cab long before it could get out and be a threat to him. He still didn't like the idea of taking his light off it, so slowly backed away towards the steel double doors.

He was disappointed to find that the big doors to the utility room were locked. After making a few cursory pulls and turns on the levers, he began to think about how to get in. Unfortunately, he noted, unlike the rest of the building that was all keyed with digital locks, which disconnected when the power went off, this was a regular old Schlage bolt style that required a key. He tried to remember if he had seen any keys in the security office but didn't recall any. Still, he reasoned, that was the most logical place to keep them and he fretted that he would need to go all the way back up to check it out.

As he turned, his light ran over the truck and thoughts started assembling in his head. 'Whoever was in the truck was probably a Riverside Condo employee. Being down in the basement, parked just a few feet from the doors, means they probably had access to the utility areas. They likely even had the keys on them. Otherwise, why drive all the way down? All I have to do was open the truck and get the key ring. Heck, it was probably in the ignition. Right? That's logical.'

Robbie took a breath of the cold, dank air and shined his light around the large parking chamber. 'Dark and spooky, yes,' he told himself but nothing else was down there. He knew that. And, he reasoned, he'd been in lots of spooky places. Sometimes with actual spooky things. He figured he could handle opening a door with a dead guy and pulling some keys out of the ignition. He walked calmly over to the driver's side door and started to pull the handle.

'Wait. Don't be stupid.' He said to himself. '99% chance it's just a dead guy in there. Dead from what? Old age? How do you just die in a pickup truck at the bottom of a parking garage as the world is ending?'

'Possible,' he thought, 'guy has a heart attack in his truck and there was for damn sure no ambulances around that night, even if he had been able to call 911. And nobody is going to find him here, ever.'

'Or,' he played various scenarios in his head, 'he gets bit. He drives to the bottom of the garage and turns. But, he isn't reacting so he dies somehow after? That makes no sense. Maybe the cold? No.' He had seen the things walking around in colder places than this.

'The answer', he decided, 'is that it doesn't matter.' He walked around to the passenger side and put one hand on the latch while lifting his machete with the other. He lifted the latch and pulled the door open while jumping back several steps. He half expected the thing to come lurching out of the truck after him. But it didn't. It just sat there.

There wasn't even a smell. Robbie figured the cold of the garage had somehow mummified the body. Being in the cab of the truck would have saved it from any large predators. He didn't see any insects either, so figured they must have come, sucked him dry and moved on.

Moving closer into the doorway, he shined his light into the cab and saw what had probably been a man in a blue work shirt. His skin was black and shrunken from decomposition. The cause of death became clear as Robbie noted the silver revolver still in the corpse's shriveled hand. A hole was also visible on the top of his head with another hole neatly punched through the roof of the truck.

'At least I'm pretty sure you won't be coming back,' Robbie decided with relief as he stared at the body. 'Now, the next question is, did you have the keys to the electrical room?'

Robbie moved his light over to the ignition and saw a jumble of keys hanging there. His elation was short lived as he realized he would have to reach into the narrow space between the body and the dash to pull them out. It was a small cab and the man's knees were nearly against the spot where the keys hung. He looked back at the body. Although he knew it was dead, he didn't like the idea of being so close while he fumbled around with the keys.

The thought of opening the driver's side door and simply dumping the man out of the truck occurred to him but didn't seem right. The truck, humble as it was, was the man's tomb and as many times as he might have violated dead bodies over the last few years, he hated doing it. Especially with someone who chose their own out before the zombies could make the decision for them.

Robbie took a breath, reached over and tugged on the keys. To his surprise they pulled right out with the only ill effect being that the back of his hand brushed against the dead man's dark, green work pants. Robbie stood up quickly with the keys in his hand and pointed the light back in at the corpse. The illogical part of his brain was telling him to run in case his touch might have woken the thing. But it remained still, even as Robbie slowly eased back and closed the door.

'If this was a horror movie,' he thought, 'the dead man would now jump out of the truck and start chasing me for stealing his keys.' He knew this was stupid but he kept his light on the cab of the truck anyway as he walked back towards the utility room. After quickly running his light around the parking level again, just to be sure nothing had crawled out of the darkness while he was busy, he began going through the keys. He worked each key into the lock until one fit and turned the latch. Taking a deep breath for courage, he pushed the door open and stepped back, ready to defend against anything that might burst out.

Other than the creak of long unused hinges, nothing frightening came from the doorway. Robbie shined his light around inside before stepping over the threshold. The interior revealed a long, rectangular room with banks of high tech processors and wiring at either end. The floor was concrete and the high ceilings were crisscrossed with hanging steel air conditioning ducts and heavy coils of cable. Between the processors and against the far wall a dozen or so large grey cabinets, Robbie assumed these were fuse boxes, were mounted. Shutting the door behind him, Robbie stepped into the room and began checking that nothing lurked in the shadows. Finding no surprises, he walked over to the largest of the cabinets and popped open it's metal door.

Inside the fuse box, Robbie found several rows of large black switches. Most of them were marked with handwritten labels. Each one identified the area that they controlled. He scanned quickly up the list reading; "HVAC, KITCHEN, LOBBY, ELEVATORS, POOL, EXT LIGHTS," etc. At the top, he found two switches even larger than the others. These looked like the large electrical switches he had seen in monster movies back in the day. They looked like they might even take two hands to throw.

Looking closely, he noted that to the left of each switch was a label marked "OFF" and to the right it was marked "ON." The switches, however, were in the middle position between the two. He had no idea what it meant if a switch was neither off nor on but he decided it probably didn't matter much anymore. He pushed at the switches, first OFF then ON but nothing happened other than the loud click as they turned on their large plastic hinges.

Moving down the row of fuse cabinets he located one labeled "Roof Solar" and popped it open. As with the others, there were several rows of switches. The switches at the top were also in the half way position.

The darkness of the room was getting to him, so he took another look around but saw nothing. "Not sure it could get any spookier down here," Robbie said out loud. Nothing answered but as he turned back to the box, something caught his eye. Before his light returned to the panel, he spotted a tiny green light just below the main switch. He lowered his flashlight and stared.

'Am I losing my mind?' He considered and answered. 'Highly possible,'

When he looked again however, the small circle of green light was still there, glowing in the darkness like a distant star.

"What the…?!" Robbie said out loud. "Light means power right? That means at least some of the solar is still working. Yes? No way." He thought for a moment. "Only one way to find out I suppose…"

He reached up and pushed the lever above the light one way and then the other. Each time a heavy click echoed through the room. He waited a moment and when nothing happened he did the same with the other switch.

There was a loud thump, after which the building seemed to suddenly take a deep breath. Robbie looked up, stunned, as a cacophony of mechanical snaps and pops sounded through the duct work over his head. From further away, fans slowly began whirling to life. The click-click-click of metal chains turned against cogs to move long closed flaps and shutters. Finally, with a rush the room's florescent lights flickered on and Robbie was basked in electric light for the first time in years. He stood stunned, just listening to all the solar powered mechanisms roar back to life.

"Holy fuck!" He blurted, shielding his eyes from the sudden glare. "Gotta tell Kelly! She is going to freak out!"

He turned and walked excitedly from the room, to find the garage was illuminated as well. He was giddy as he made his way back up the ramps towards the main level, not believing their luck in finding the last building in the world with power.

He was half way up the next ramp when something odd came into view. It took him a moment to process what it was and what it meant. "Shit!"

Light spilled in through a wide open gap in the wall. Not electric light. Sunlight from outside. The gate leading to the back entrance to the parking garage was open. The opening was literally wide enough to drive a truck through. Two trucks, since it was an entrance and an exit. The only barriers at the gate were two long yellow barrier arms that stretched across the lanes, requiring guests to enter their key cards before coming and going. Robbie was not worried about cars getting in.

As he was about to sprint up to the gate to see if he could get it closed a figure stumbled up to one of the barriers arms. Robbie froze as he watched it bounce off and continue along the length of the yellow and orange obstruction until it moved around it and into the garage.

'I can take one.' Robbie thought. 'If there is only one.'

Robbie braced for the thing to spot him and come racing down the ramp, but something upstairs caught its attention and it suddenly lurched up the next ramp and out of sight. Robbie ran to the gate and saw several other undead outside making their way up the narrow drive but far enough away that he had time to figure out how to close the gate. He spotted a yellow box with a key hole attached to the wall by the gate and bolted for it, pulling the maintenance keys from his pocket as he ran. He watched the creatures grow closer as he jammed keys into the box trying to make one fit. Finally, with the things just a few yards away, one clicked into place and he turned it. The gate overhead groaned and its chains clattered as it began to lower. Robs eyes were wide as the gate went down just ahead of the lead zombie who began to claw and bite at the narrow bars.

Another sound up the ramp caught his attention. The sound of moaning and trampling feet as a large group of post human figures began heading down, drawn by the sound of the closing gate. He could see at least a dozen, and suspected many others would be behind them, so he turned and sprinted back down. He looked back up as he turned the next corner and saw that some had run straight down into the gate, drawn by the sound of the zombies banging on the other side. Unfortunately, others had spotted him and had begun to lumber after him in pursuit of food.

Robbie ducked out of sight behind a concrete pillar and paused for a moment to consider his options. If he continued down he would just get trapped at the bottom. He could lock himself in the utility room but he would be just as trapped there. He could try to escape in the truck with the maintenance man's body but the battery was most likely long dead, and again he would be trapped. Also, Kelly had no idea where he was so it was unlikely she would show up to attempt a rescue.

Hearing the crowd of undead reach the bottom of the ramp he emerged from hiding and prepared to sprint down to the next level. To his shock, several of the undead had fallen over the railing of the ramp above, slid between the narrow concrete gap and were now climbing to their feet, directly in his path. Knowing he could not turn back, Robbie got their attention by running directly at them, then bolted to his left to dodge around in the outside lane. Two of the creatures fell into each other as their torsos turned but their stiff wooden legs remained in place. The closest one lunged as Robbie passed and managed to grab the shoulder of his jacket. Robbie's momentum threw off the thing's balance and sent it sprawling to the floor with a fleshy slap.

Robbie kept running, knowing that the others would not be far behind. This time he did not pause at the corner. Instead he sped ahead hoping to have a few moments to make a plan for escape before the rest of the things caught up. He knew there weren't many options at the bottom of the garage.

Chapter 18

Kelly squatted on the outside deck inspecting several tomato plants. High above the streets it was a beautiful clear and sunny day. Gulls sailed lazily overhead as they rode the shifting air currents while smaller birds dodged around between the lower buildings below. She picked a caterpillar off one of the plants.

"How did you even get up here?" she asked the colorful little worm. "I bet you'll be a beautiful butterfly someday but, sorry, you can't eat my tomatoes." She flung the wriggling creature over the railing and sent it sailing towards the tops of the palm trees many floors below.

As she began searching through the leaves, for more insects, she heard a muted thump from inside. It sounded like someone had slammed the front door. "Is that you Rob?" She called out without turning from her work.

It was early afternoon and Robbie had been out on one of his explore and scavenge missions in the building for the last few hours. She thought he might have come back up for lunch. "Rob?" She called again. When there was no answer she rose up, brushing the dirt from her hands, she walked back inside the apartment. She crossed through the familiar room as her eyes adjusted from the sunny glare outside to the darker shades of the interior. "Rob?"

It wasn't until she reached the hallway leading to the front door that the silence began to unnerve her. She blinked her eyes to shake off the bright spots from being outside and scanned quickly around her for danger. The room was quiet but something was wrong. Turning, she made her way back to the couch where she kept her bow staff and hefted it up defensively. She felt better with it in her hands. She briefly felt sorry for Robbie if he intended to jump out and scare her. She smiled as she thought of the walloping he would get in response.

Sunlight was streaming in from the balcony throwing off her vision again as she moved through the room checking behind the chairs. "Robbie, you better not try to scare me or I will beat the hell out of you!"

She paused and surveyed the living room expecting to see Robbie emerge from his hiding place. When he did not, she stood still and as quiet as possible, listening. 'What the hell is going on,' she thought.

A flutter outside caught her attention and she looked over to see a pigeon had landed on the balcony railing. "Damn!" She whispered as the glance into the sunlight caused her eyes to contract again. She squeezed them shut to improve her vision in the shadowy interior.

When she opened them again she was quickly drawn to movement across the room. A cloud of dust particles sparkled as they rained down from the ceiling. Following them up she saw they were drifting down from an old air conditioning vent. "Crap," she sighed out loud. "Must be rats in the vents."

She lowered her staff and took a deep breath. She was relieved but still shaken enough that she decided to check out the rest of the apartment before she completely wrote off any danger. She turned to walk towards the bedrooms when something else caught her attention. A small light blinked on the microwave over the stove. This at once seemed totally normal and yet completely impossible. Stepping closer she saw that it was the clock flashing 12:00, 12:00, 12:00 in its boxed numerals. She stared at it for a moment with the implication of what it meant slowly running up her spine. "Electricity?" She asked herself.

"Can't be. I'm going insane." She said, wrinkling her brow at the thought. "Well it's about time I guess." She walked to the microwave and put her fingers against the plastic over the clock. Her fingers glowed red each time the digits flashed. "I think it's real. Can it be real? No. How?"

"Rob!" She blurted and bolted for the front door, grabbing her jacket from their hooks she raced out into the hallway. The normally dark corridor was washed in light. Not all the bulbs were working but enough were on to cast off the usual gloom and illuminate the spider webs and moldy stains that had begun to grow in the corners. She ran for the stairwell.

Robbie was in a race to the bottom of the parking garage. His mind reeled as he ran, hoping to think of a way to escape from the undead slumping down the ramps behind him. He knew he would have less than a minute to figure it out once he hit the dead end at the bottom. The utility room was all he could think of, but he knew that was a death trap. He could go in, lock the door and remain silent so they didn't pursue him, but then what. He would be trapped in the small room… forever.

The undead were lazy as hell and followed the path of least resistance. Once they were at the bottom of the ramp they would remain there unless something loud and tasty beckoned them to trudge back up. Kelly would never come down there looking for him. She would find the garage doors open and even if she were able to shut them, she would never venture down towards hundreds of zombies that will have accumulated by that time. He knew he was fucked.

Kelly bounded down the stairwell and burst into the lobby with a bang. "Rob!" She called out breathlessly to the empty room. Normally she would have crept slowly and quietly through the long corridors of the condominium's common areas but now she jogged through in a panic. The aged carpet squeaked and crunched under her feet as she dashed from room to room. Each of the offices, lounges and meeting rooms were similarly quiet, dusty and empty. Still, she looked briefly into each and stage whispered, "Rob!"

At the end of the main corridor was the door to the parking garage. In her haste she reached for the bar, pushed it open and stepped through without using her usual caution, and stepped into a nightmare. Finding herself walking into a semi-circle of stinking, rotting undead, she froze in shock. Things went into slow motion as she commanded her legs into reverse but the command seemed on a delay. The drooping, sagging faces of the things around her all began to turn their blank undead eyes toward her. They seemed to react slowly as well, as if they didn't fully comprehend this delicious treat that had fallen in among them. Snapping back to reality, she swung her staff at the nearest heads while she retreated back through the closing door. Heads cracked and several stumbled away but more began lurching forward.

She had barely ducked back into the corridor when rotting hands began pounding against the other side of the door. Grey faces with pale, dead eyes appeared in the narrow rectangle of glass. The loose skin of their lips pressed against its surface while their teeth tried to gnash, tap and scratch their way through. Kelly backed away thankful that the door opened outward into the garage. The harder the bodies pressed to get in the more tightly it remained shut.

She breathed with relief as she saw that it was a steel door set into a concrete wall. She hoped this would hold them back while she found Robbie. She prayed he had not already succumbed to the undead horde. She turned and ran back to the main lobby. She wasn't sure where to start but she knew she had to get out of sight of the mob in the garage.

Robbie was out of time. He heard the slapping steps and moans of the crowd following him reach the last landing and knew they would be at the bottom in seconds. With no other choices, he ducked into the utility room and locked the door. He backed away as quietly as possible, taking cautious steps, knowing if they heard the slightest noise, they would easily tear down the flimsy wall between them. The wall was clearly only intended to be a decorative barrier for any guests who wandered down this far. It only had drywall on the outside and was framed up with metal studs. All of it would crumble if the mass of undead pressed their weight against it.

He stood still and controlled his breathing to keep quiet. He hoped they would forget why they came if he stayed silent. He heard the things scuffling into the last parking level and begin to thump against the wall. It rattled each time one bumped against it and soon they seemed to be packed in tight. He only heard moans and the sounds of dead shoulders sliding along its surface. He prayed it would hold.

After a few minutes, the echoes of footsteps and moans of the undead seemed loud enough to cover up his small movements so he began carefully exploring the room. He had looked around some before but hadn't examined it closely since he intended to come back with Kelly. The back wall was concrete and likely part of the foundation of the building. There were some small alcoves but they were too narrow to get through and mostly blocked by metal conduit and fuse boxes.

He walked around the room twice but saw no way out, so he sat down against a row of metal pipes. For a while, he stared at the wall and listened to the shuffling scraping sounds of the creatures in the parking garage. He wasn't sure what to do other than wait.

'Wait for what?' he thought. 'A miracle,' he decided. It seemed better than the alternatives of 'die from dehydration' or 'zombies come crashing through the thin wall and eat him.' Perhaps, his mind kept working, it would be better to fling open the door and try to fight his way out while he was still strong - before he was dehydrated and hungry and weak. But this just seemed like a quicker and more painful way to die.

Kelly stumbled backwards not believing what had just happened. "Dammit Rob!" She cursed angrily under her breath, "what the hell did you do?!"

She ducked into one of the small conference rooms along the hallway to get out of sight of the creatures banging on the garage door and to get her head together. Leaning against the wall, she sank to her knees and put her face in her hands. They had survived this long by sticking together, by acting together and by always being there for each other. Through bad, terrible and worse they had been side by side, but they had literally been living within feet of each other for the last few years.

The short time they had been safely tucked away in the condominium building had been a breath of fresh air. They had been able to be safe and alone, really alone, for the first time in years. Kelly was able to work on the garden, read a book and lay in the sun on the roof without worrying about being eaten alive for the first time in forever. Robbie had been able to get out and explore, go on short scavenging runs and even do some trading with the Baldwin sisters. They slept together at night but she had begun to really enjoy that he wasn't always within arm's length, all day every day, and they weren't living in a perpetual state of fear.

This comfort had made them lazy, she decided, and might get them killed. The thought that Robbie may already be dead raced through her mind and she quickly pushed it away. "He's not dead," she told herself again. "Maybe in trouble, well definitely in trouble when I find him," she let out a nervous giggle, "but not dead. Definitely not dead."

She ran through the list of places he could be in her head, but kept coming back to the garage. She dreaded it but knew that's where he was. Otherwise, why were the garage doors open? How were the lights on? If Robbie were ok, he would have come upstairs as soon as he got the lights on. He would gloat about it. She could imagine his face.

"Ok, he's in the garage," she said to herself, "...need a plan."

Kelly knew she couldn't fight her way through the dozen or so undead banging around the upper level. "And how many were on the lower levels?" She stood and began to pace as she thought it out. "First, I have to stop the leak. I need to figure out a way to close those garage doors. Then I can figure out a way to kill off the ones inside. Robbie will have to hold on until I can get that done. He can do that much at least."

An idea suddenly popped into her head and she bolted back out into the hallway and sprinted towards the main lobby.

The concrete floor was cold and felt moist so Robbie stood again and paced the room. He wasn't looking for anything. Just pacing to keep moving and keep warm. He stopped at the wall he thought must be on the west side facing the river and rubbed his cold bottom. The wall looked to have been freshly painted before the end but cracks and flakes had begun to appear as time, moisture and cold did their work.

Near the corner, he noticed a faint line of shadow at the bottom of the wall. Sliding over, he saw that it was from a thin four foot by four foot shape protruding slightly from the wall and painted over, making it nearly invisible. Wondering if it might be some sort of electrical access, he knelt and began picking at the paint until he was able to pull several strips away. The white latex came away easily revealing a metallic steel plate set into a recessed steel frame. He pulled out his knife and began cutting around the edges of the plate revealing a small dimple on one edge. Digging the paint and gypsum from the dimple he discovered a finger sized key ring attached.

He gently pulled the ring causing it to give slightly before it seized up. Robbie pulled harder. He could feel it flexing but it seemed stuck. Probably rusted over the years, he thought. The ring was only large enough for one finger and the knife was too large to fit in as leverage so he slid one finger in, wrapped his other hand over it to improve his grip and bracing his legs against the wall for leverage began to pull again.

The narrow ring stung his finger as he put his full weight on it. He gritted his teeth and hoped the metal ring would release the catch before his finger broke. It held. A few seconds later the pain in his finger was such that he could no longer bear the weight. He let go with a grunt and crumbled to the ground cradling his reddened digit. He lay curled up for a minute until the white, hot pain began to recede.

As he lay sprawled on the floor massaging the blood back into his hand, the sound of grunting and scraping on the outside wall increased. Something, whether it was his struggles or another stimulus, had stirred up the things in the garage.

"Shit." He whispered knowing they were just as likely to knock down the weak barrier accidentally as they were to do it intentionally. Probably more likely the former. Just get them riled up enough in an enclosed space and they would start crashing into the walls like bulls in a ring. He sat back up and took hold of the tab again.

Before he started, he wondered if this would be a fool's errand. "I'll probably get it open," he thought, "and find it's just an electrical junction box." He looked at it again, not looking forward to the pain of pulling at it any further. "But if I don't, I'll never know and I'll die here."

Using the knife he dug out more of the paint from the small hole where the ring connected to the inner locking mechanism. Then he reached up and grabbed the ring again. He could hear the things outside growing more perturbed as he began to pull. They scraped and thumped loudly along the wall outside as he struggled with the pin.

The ring suddenly jerked back an inch with a grating squeal. The unexpected movement sent Robbie sprawling backwards. His finger remained lodged in the ring and he yowled in pain as it extended before it broke free. Landing with a thump he writhed on the floor, cradling his injured finger, mewling as the blinding pain overwhelmed him. It was a few moments later when he was able to breathe again, and looked up with tears running down his cheeks.

The wall to the garage was vibrating as hundreds of hands pounded against it. The press of bodies caused the hollow drywall and steel structure to groan as their weight began to bend it inward. Robbie knew it wouldn't last long. He cursed himself for yelling, even though his finger still screamed in pain.

Knowing he didn't have long, he scrambled to his knees and crawled back to the small metal door. He prayed it would at least provide a space large enough to hide before the wall caved in.

Robbie saw that the ring had popped back into place when he released it. Cradling his injured right hand, he grabbed it with his left hand and drew it back. It resisted at first, causing terror to bolt through him.

The pounding on the wall turned from the sounds of slapping against a flat surface to crunches as fists and knees started to break through. He pulled again on the pin and it suddenly gave. Hearing the lock click, he quickly pulled the plate open before it could lock again.

Kelly charged through a glass door marked SECURITY. She had been in the office before when they had cleared the building, but with the lights on it was much less intimidating. A salmon colored counter top divided the room in half. The front was likely intended as narrow public waiting area. She imagined people coming in to report lost pets or pay their parking fees. Ignoring the "Employees Only" sign, she circled around behind the desk and through the door. Out of habit, she stood in the dark for a moment before flipping the light switch on.

As she remembered, several rows of security monitors were mounted onto one of the walls but they were all dark causing her to wonder if they were working. On the desk underneath, she tapped on a keyboard and moved a mouse around hoping to bring them to life but nothing happened. Then she spotted a power strip and pushed the power button off, and then back on.

Worse Than Dead

The room came to life. The flat monitors blinked and several hard drives began to growl as they woke from their long sleep. For a long moment, the screens flashed and went on and off as their connected computers cycled through their rebooting processes. Finally, a timer appeared showing a count down. It was a long minute, but finally whatever they needed was complete and most of the monitors lit up.

She sat down in the office chair, pulled up to the desk and went back to work. The mouse and keyboard were familiar and yet, having not used such tools in several years, they also seemed strange and alien. She hoped she could remember how to use computers well enough to navigate through to find what she needed. Her first problem was that the PC had gone to a blue screen and was prompting for a user log in and password.

She jumped up and began searching for something that might help her reset the password. She opened every drawer and looked in every file cabinet. There were stacks of manuals and warranty books but she found nothing. She slammed back down in the chair shouting, "Crap! Crap! Crap!" She spun around scanning the room for something, anything to give her a clue. Finally she turned back to the monitors and figured she would at least try a few passwords.

Robbie looked inside the opening and found a narrow space lined with pipes and large colorful wires. To his surprise a metal ladder was bolted to the inner wall. Glancing in, he saw that the ladder went up the thin shaft into darkness. A crash behind him reminded him that he didn't have extra time to consider his options. He squeezed through the opening, dragged his legs in and flopped upside down into what could barely be considered a crawl space. By the time he righted himself and reached out to close the metal door, he looked over to see there were dozens of holes in the sheetrock wall. Grey arms, legs and even a few putrid heads had punched through and were desperately trying to get passed the dusty gypsum barrier.

Robbie swung the door shut and, with a click, the key locked back into place. The space was completely dark but he felt safe enough for the moment, so he leaned back against the pipes and massaged his still aching finger. It hurt badly enough that he wanted to yell but he bottled it up in deference to the undead, whom he could hear clattering and crashing into the control room.

A few dark minutes later, Robbie decided sitting there wasn't helping so he reached back with his good hand and found the ladder. It took some doing in the small space to quietly get himself untangled and turned around, but he was finally able to orient himself so he was standing facing it. He could hear the things banging around in the utility room as he took hold of it, stepped onto the rungs and began to struggle upward.

He found that the small space worked to his advantage since it was too painful to use his right hand. Bracing his back against the far side he was able to move up slowly just using his left hand and both feet. The metal pipes and fittings were sharp and painful as he climbed through the darkness but he kept moving. He took his time, feeling his way ahead as much as he could and trying not to panic in the total darkness.

He tried not to let his imagination run away with the muted sounds and groans, echoing up the shaft, from the creatures rampaging through the room below. He could only pray that they didn't get through the small door or that something worse wasn't waiting in the inky blackness above him.

A few minutes into the slow climb, he noticed the glow of a green light ahead. He could tell it was small but in the total darkness it shone like a lighthouse. Growing closer, he could see it was a just a tiny LED indicator, still it cast enough light that he could see it was near the top of the shaft. The shape of the shadows revealed something solid a few feet above it. He hoped it was some sort of hatch to get out of the narrow crawl space.

His elation at having escaped the undead faded, as the pain in his finger extended out through his entire hand and spiked with each heartbeat. The shaft, which was warm to begin with, seemed to be getting hotter. He could feel sweat draining down his back and over his face. He wished there was some way to get his heavy jacket off. The sweat slowed him further as he had to stop every few rungs to wipe his eyes and the ladder seemed to become more slippery.

A few times he had to stop, hold himself in place with his legs and back, while he dried his palms on his pants and waited for the pain in his finger to die back. He wasn't sure how far he had come in the darkness but the green glow, still seemed small and far away.

Chapter 19

She pulled the keyboard towards her and her eyes went wide. "No fucking way!" She exclaimed as she snatched up a bright pink sticky note that had been hidden underneath the carriage. On it was written the log in name and password. She quickly keyed in the code and watched as the monitors went from blue to black.

Rows of small rectangular images appeared on the screens. Kelly used the mouse to choose one of the images and it increased in size to show a picture of the lobby. Looking closer she realized it wasn't a picture but a live video feed.

"Yes!" She shouted and, after some experimenting, she figured out how to control the images with the keyboard and mouse. She excitedly began scrolling through the images of various places in and around the condo. Some cameras were either not working or blocked, but some were functional enough that she was soon able to see that the images were grouped by location. She spun through several angles of the front of the building; looking down at the street, the sidewalk in both directions, the front door from the right and left side, and so on. Finally she found an outside view looking down at the front entrance to the garage.

The gate was up as she suspected. She watched as several undead stumbled out of the opening but were replaced by others lurching inside. She suspected the noise of those still banging on the lobby doorway was attracting them. "Ok, what else we got," she said, switching to another image. This one of the inside of the top parking level. A group of a dozen or more creatures were still huddled at the doorway where she had recently left them. A few seemed to have lost interest and were bumbling around the large open area.

"Well, I found your cars ladies," she declared as she spotted the two vehicles matching the brands on the realtors' key fobs. Scrolling to the next camera she saw an image that she guessed was one floor down, since there was a giant sign that read Parking Level 2 painted on the concrete wall. When she saw the next camera showed the garage door at the rear driveway entrance, she exclaimed "Fuck me! Did you have to open all the doors, Rob?!"

She continued flipping between cameras as she descended further into the parking lot. She became more hopeful seeing that each level only had a few undies stumbling around. 'The fewer the better,' she thought, 'it'll make it easier to take them out.' But her heart sank when she reached the bottom floor.

Several hundred of the creatures were crammed into the space. They were shoulder to shoulder like surging music fans in a mosh pit. In the center of the group she saw what looked like the remains of a wall. A few sections of broken drywall, wiring and insulation hung from an incomplete line of twisted metal studs. The creatures were pushing and shoving each other back and forth through the gaps.

Inside the area she could see what looked like banks of electrical panels, but couldn't see past them to determine what might lie beyond. If Robbie was in there, she prayed he had found a way to hide.

Robbie groaned and pushed himself up. At each rung he desperately wanted to stop but determined that he wasn't going to let himself die stuck in an electrical shaft, he willed himself slowly and painfully upward. It seemed an eternity. Rivers of sweat burned his eyes. His right hand was so swollen that it sent excruciating bolts of agony up his arm every time he bumped something. He didn't know how he did it, but he finally found himself at the top, near the green light. He saw the ceiling was concrete, over which ran wrapped cables bolted into metal channels.

He squeezed his eyes closed while he let the pain in his hand ebb and took a moment to wipe away the sweat from his face. For a moment he feared the shaft was a dead end which, with no way to go back, would be literal. He braced himself and reaching out with his good hand, felt the space above the last rung of the ladder. It was set back slightly but then he touched a flat surface that felt like painted metal. He traced around its edges until he found a hinge and his hopes rose. Sliding his hand to the other side, he felt a latch and almost started to cry with relief.

In front of him was a hatch, similar to the one he had come through at the bottom. He gently pulled at the interior pin to see if it would give and was further relieved when it did. As much as he wanted to pull the door open and get out of the sauna, he paused. He realized he had no idea what was on the other side and didn't want to jump out into some zombie infested area. He tried to think of where he was and how far up he might have gone. He imagined the layout of the building. The ladder was on the west wall of the parking garage which meant he was facing the river front and the hatch could possibly lead outside the building.

If it did, he reasoned, he should be somewhere on the same level as the loading dock. 'Has to be some sort of upper electrical room,' he thought. That seemed logical since he doubted they would build an access to the building's utilities that opened directly outside. But, he also told himself, he knew nothing about condominium architecture and it could be a slide into the river for that matter.

Unable to find Robbie in the garage or anywhere else with the security monitors Kelly began thinking about what to do next. "Need a plan," she said out loud as she looked at the feed from the front garage entrance. "What is the first problem that needs to be solved?" She asked herself and immediately answered, "I need to get those garage doors closed to stop any more undead from getting in."

She clicked around with the mouse until one of the monitors showed the front garage entrance from the outside. She clicked on another until she found the view looking out towards the street downtown. She did the same thing with the cameras looking in and out at the lower level entrance. She studied the layout, trying to think of a way to get the gates closed without getting herself killed.

"Wait!" Kelly scrambled up and out to a small bookshelf behind the main desk. The shelf was lined with manuals and operations instructions for various equipment in the building. She scanned over the bindings until she found a two inch thick binder labeled Secur-A-Gate. Pulling it out she saw an engineering drawing of a garage door on a glossy cover. "I guess nobody had time to read the manual," she said as she sat back down at the monitors and started flipping through the stiff pristine pages.

A few minutes later, she found a section on operating the gates. The chapter explained five ways to open and close the doors. One was using a smart phone application that she could conveniently download from the app store. "Not!" She said turning the page.

The second was by using a programmable key card in the access terminal outside in the driveway. She looked around and found the corresponding key card machine and a box with blank plastic Secur-A-Gate cards. But, she would need to find and figure out how to log into the program, create an account, set up the codes, program a card and then hope it would work while she stood exposed in the driveway. "Risky," she said not dismissing it but moving on to check on the other options.

The third method was from a remote terminal. "Promising…" she thought and found a picture of the item. It was just a small rectangular box with several levers like light switches. Up for open and down for closed. Still sitting, she pushed the wheeled office chair back out to the entry area and scanned for a similar box somewhere near the main security desk. "Too easy!" She exclaimed as she spotted the box near the hard wired phone. When she flipped open the cover of the box she exhaled disappointedly. "Yep, too easy," she grumbled and rolled back to the manual. The box was empty as the switches had not yet been installed.

The last method was a key. A mechanical lock control mounted near the gate could be used to raise and lower it. The downside was, it was not automatic. The gate only moved with the key in the lock and held into the up or down position. Which, she realized, meant she had to stand there until the gate was full closed.

She easily found the grey colored key box near the door to the room with the monitors. It was fortunately unlocked, and while there were many glistening multi colored keys hanging on the rings, there was only one with the odd square shape needed to fit the garage door control.

Kelly sat back down and stared at the monitors while nervously rolling the key in her hands. She watched as a few dozen undead still crowded around the lobby door while others seemed to ramble aimlessly around the concrete parking deck. From the street view she could see that there were only a few near the front garage entrance. It looked as if most that were nearby had followed the crowd into the parking deck.

In her head, she worked out a plan. She could probably drop down to ground level from one of the second floor balconies, slip along behind the building's overgrown landscaping, to get to the gate and kill the ones outside. From there she could slip inside, find the control, without being noticed, but the second she turned the key, all bets were off. The noise of the gate closing would get the attention of those inside and anything in earshot on the street. The unknown factor was how long it would take the gate to close. How long would she have to stand there?

Kelly suddenly realized what she needed to do. She stood up and bolted from the security office. The creatures, with their faces pressed to the small window at the end of the hall, noted her return and renewed their slapping and clawing at the garage door. Kelly ignored them and sped away in the other direction, disappearing around the corner into the main lobby.

Robbie heard nothing on the other side of the hatch, a combination of the heat and the strain of holding himself up motivated him to take a chance. He pulled back the latch and pushed the door open a crack. Natural light filtered in from above revealing a small room lined with grey fuse boxes. The walls were unpainted concrete block with two long narrow windows near the ceiling. Robbie pushed the door open wider to see that the room was maybe 20 x 20 and divided in half by electrical cabinets. The side he was on was empty other than the spiders that had taken up residence in the corners.

He could see one closed door on the other side of the room through a gap in the cabinets. There were two blind spots beyond the cabinets but the areas were small. He reasoned if there were any undead there they would have heard the door open and already have shown themselves. He whistled into the space anyway just to be sure and braced himself to shut the panel if anything appeared. When nothing did, he took a deep breath and squirmed out the hatch onto grey concrete floor.

Rolling onto his back, he lay on the cool concrete surface with his eyes squeezed shut until the pain in his hand was tolerable. He then slowly shrugged out of his jacket while he stared up at the ceiling. A moan from below echoed up the open shaft causing him to jerk, sending jolts of pain through his arm and hand. He lay back down and used his leg to shut the hatch which locked in place with a click.

"Damn it!" he winced at the pain in his hand and the dawning realization that he had let a legion of zombies into their previously safe garage. He quickly ran over the access points he remembered, and determined that they probably couldn't get into the main building. The walls were concrete and the doors all opened outward. That is, unless Kelly opened one of the doors and couldn't get it closed again before they got through. "Can't think about that right now," he told himself as he rolled over onto his good arm to assess the room.

Using his knees, he pushed himself forward a few feet to confirm that nothing was lurking behind the cabinets. Seeing only more dust and spider webs, it was apparent that nobody and nothing had been in the room for a long time. The door was steel set into concrete with a big bolt lock making it look very secure. The windows were too high to look through from ground level and he groaned as he realized he was going to have to climb up onto one of the cabinets to see what was outside.

"This is going to suck," he muttered as he struggled up to his knees. He cringed as just shifting his position caused sharp pain to shoot up his arm. After several deep breaths he stood quickly and nearly fell down again as the blood rushed from his head and his internal gyroscope shifted. He grabbed one of the electrical cabinets to steady himself until his head stopped spinning. "Ah, shit," he wheezed, "yep, that sucked."

Kelly crawled to the sliding glass door leading to the balcony overlooking the street. Although she knew she was high enough to be safe she didn't want to attract the attention from anything in the street below. She slowly pulled back the curtain and looked out on downtown. From this angle and through the fogged window, it could almost be a normal apocalyptic day outside. She reached up, clicked the lock and pulled the door open. She slipped outside to a gentle breeze which filtered in to push back the curtains as she eased herself onto the balcony.

Below in the street, the cars were backed up as she remembered. They looked as if they had been parked bumper to bumper and abandoned. Some had open doors, while others were missing windows, from which their occupants had either escaped or been ripped out by a ravenous mob that swarmed though the metallic buffet. Luckily, the blood and gore from that day had been washed away by rain and storms over the last few years.

She looked closely at the cars and the narrow gaps between them. Weeds, bushes and even a few small trees had sprouted from cracks in the road and some even grew from the cars themselves. She knew that some of the cars still retained what was left of their prior owners. Trapped now, until either they or the car deteriorated into dust.

A few animated corpses lumbered along the street but she couldn't see any within the block in front of the condo building. After making sure that those nearest were not looking her way, Kelly dropped her bow staff down and crawled over the balcony railing until she hung on from the bottom bar. This put her toes about seven feet above the ground below. She couldn't tell exactly since the space between the hedge and the wall had grown over with tall grass and weeds. She didn't take much time to think about it. She let go before any of the zombies on the street noticed that lunch was dangling within grabbing distance nearby.

The fall was fast, and although she had bent her knees in preparation for landing, she slapped hard into the ground. She had planned on rolling when she hit, to deflect some of the impact but found herself simply lumped hard into the overgrowth. The wind was knocked from her and she did her best not to gasp and cry out from the impact. She tried to catch her breath while she looked up the side of the building and realized she must have scratched her face on the wall as she fell. Her cheek was stinging and when she touched it, her fingers came away wet with fresh blood.

"Ooow! Dammit." Kelly whispered to herself as she sat up in the tall grass. Stretching her legs, she made sure she was intact and finding only scratches and an aching butt, she slowly stood up. Through a few gaps in the bushes she could see that the situation out on the street had not changed. None of the local undead seemed to have noticed her arrival in their midst. With that confirmed, she picked up her staff and began slowly edging down the wall towards the garage.

About 20 feet before the garage opening, the bushes thinned down to tangles of brown and dead twigs with no leaf cover. The trunk of a dead tree and clumps of expired flowers, looking as if they had once been part of a neatly laid out landscaping plan, marked the end of the hedge row. Kelly peered out from behind the last green bush knowing that once she went any further her cover would be gone. Seeing no immediate danger she lifted her staff into a fighting stance and began easing out of her cover.

When she stepped beyond the dead tree, she froze. Not 10 feet away on the sidewalk, an undead stood completely still as if staring out into traffic. She realized it had been hidden behind the dead tree and was thankful that it was facing away from her. She did a quick scan of the area to ensure nothing else had been lurking out of sight then looked down at the ground between herself and the creature. The distance was mostly dirt and dead grass with no twigs or dead leaves to give away her approach.

After factoring all this in, she bounded quickly into the opening and swung her staff like a baseball bat at the back of the thing's head. The staff crushed into its skull. The zombie crumpled immediately to the ground without ever knowing what hit it. Aside from the echo of her staff striking its head and the body hitting the concrete, the afternoon remained still.

Kelly crouched down to avoid the attention of anything beyond the rusting traffic and made her way towards the open garage door. Peeking in, she saw the crowd of undead still pawing at the door to the lobby and the two SUVs parked near the elevators. The door seemed to have their full attention and the ramp going down into the lower decks was empty so she slipped inside to look for the key box for the gate opener. It only took a few seconds to spot the large silver plate on the wall with the square hole.

She pulled the key from her pocket and pushed it in, ensuring it would fit. Then, she stood up and made herself visible to the hungry creatures at the doorway. "Hey you sons of bitches!" She shouted while jumping up and down waving her arms.

It got their attention.

Robbie stood uneasily and winced as the pain from his throbbing finger ran through his hand and up his arm. The severity of the pain seemed to surge with each heartbeat and explode each time he moved. He could hear the excruciating pulse in his ears as if it were a beat played by some sort of demon DJ at an evil nightclub. He breathed deeply to gather his strength and stepped over to the steel door in the center of the wall.

Pressing his ear to the door, he heard nothing. He looked down at the latch style handle and contemplated opening it but even tired, hot and in pain, he knew he was safe where he was. He couldn't justify taking the risk of opening a door that could lead to an alley full of hungry undead. Still leaning on the door, he looked over the small room and up at the windows near the ceiling. He saw a spot near the wall where he could step up on the lip of one of the electrical cabinets and climb on top of the metal box. From there he could see outside and maybe down into the area behind the door.

He paused. On any other day, he knew he would be nimble and strong enough to climb up the box almost without thinking. In fact he had done similar climbs many times in the last few years. But with his hand in such pain, he worked each step through in his head while he still leaned on the cool metal door. He carefully worked out how to get a grip with his good hand while stepping up onto the lip of the box, then lift up and balance there until he could pull himself up onto the top. With it all worked out in his head, he put the plan in motion.

Several seconds later, he lay back on the ground again cradling his hand. Unwilling to give up, he rose reached again for the heavy pipe and swung his foot back into the lower lip of the box. Taking care this time to get as much of his boot on the narrow shelf as possible, he pushed off and strained to raise himself with one arm.

As he lifted up, he thought he heard a pop, pop, pop sound. He wondered perhaps if the cabinet was coming loose and paused as he balanced himself on the ledge to ensure the whole unit wasn't about to fall on him. He tested the cabinet which felt stable and when he heard nothing else after a few moments, he continued up. As he hefted himself onto the top, he heard the pop, pop again. But, it sounded more like it was outside and further away.

Balancing himself on top of the metal boxes he lay still and looked out the windows. Down below was a narrow alley lined by high concrete walls that he recognized as the loading dock where they had initially entered the building. From this angle he could only see along the dock where delivery trucks used to back in and the far wall which was lined with large metal dumpsters. He lay still and listened for any other indication of where the strange pops had come from.

The pain in his hand pulsed from the climb and it was difficult to discern any sounds with his heart thumping loudly in his ears but he strained to block it out. After waiting a few minutes and hearing nothing, he concluded that it was just another sound in a dead city. Maybe a piece of one of the nearby buildings had broken loose. That type of thing happened all the time, producing all sorts of strange sounds. He began to breathe regularly again and focused on the good news that the loading area only had a few undead stumbling around. He wondered if they had been there since that day he and Kelly had escaped into the condo garage.

They looked like slow ones and he surmised, hoped, that even with his injury, he could take them out and find a way back into the building. He knew the back door they had come in before was locked, but there were several other access points he and Kelly had set up for just such a situation, where they might get locked out. As he was about to climb down he heard another pop, pop, pop from outside. It was still muffled but slightly louder than before. He stopped and stared out into the loading dock wondering what it could be.

Then he heard something else that sounded like shouting. It was too far away and the room was too well insulated to make out individual words but it definitely sounded like several people talking loudly. He stared out the windows and saw the undead in the loading dock had noticed it as well. They were turning and beginning to stumble towards the street.

'Well,' he thought, 'maybe it's our friends in the trucks come to save the day again by leading the zombies away.' He had decided to take advantage of the distraction to get out of the utility room when he heard the pop, pop again. Immediately following the sound, two of the decaying creature's heads exploded.

'Dammit,' he said to himself, realizing whoever it was, they were in the alley and well-armed.

He heard the shouting again, this time closer. He still couldn't tell what they were saying, but there were definitely several distinct voices and by their inflections he guessed they were barking instructions at each other. The shouts while loud, were not those of fear or confusion, rather they seemed to be controlled and calm.

The last undead went down with another head shot. This time the skull didn't explode. A small hole burst from just behind the thing's ear followed by a plume of pink and gray dust. Its knees buckled and it collapsed into a heap near its companions. These guys were not only well armed, they were also very good shots. Robbie began to get worried. The sound of the voices moved closer and he thought he could even hear the crunch of their footsteps. They were definitely coming down the drive into the loading dock.

Chapter 20

Robbie tensed up and waited. He glanced down at the door to the utility room, which he knew to be locked, and he hoped it would be enough of a deterrent to keep out this armed band. Over the years, he and Kelly had encountered a number of groups of living human survivors, armed and otherwise. Only the Baldwin sisters had proven to be altruistic. The rest were bad news and Robbie did not have high hopes for this one.

Just then, a man stepped into Robbie's line of sight in the loading dock and quickly turned facing down the narrow alley leading to the room where he was hiding. He had some sort of small rifle lifted up against his shoulder and he aimed it left and right as he scanned the area. He was dressed in green camouflage and brown leather combat boots. This was the style of dress that had been adopted by many survivors but the way the man moved, with a kind of purpose, made Robbie think he really was, or had been, military.

In addition to the camo and boots, the man was wearing an odd-looking helmet, a green backpack, knee pads, tactical gloves and what looked like a bullet proof vest. All the gear made him look like a character right out of one of the old X-Box combat games. Even the most well equipped of the marauders and survivalists, he had encountered, had abandoned all the extra gear as too cumbersome and heavy. It was great to have a gun, but there was only so much ammo and eventually you were going to have to run, climb or crawl to get away. All that gear would just slow you down and make you lunch. This guy was either bat-shit crazy or part of some militia. Either way, Robbie surmised, not a character he wanted to meet face to face. Robbie remained still on his perch and hoped the man would not be able to see him through the high windows.

The man called out. "Clear!" His voice was muted, but he was close enough now that Robbie understood the words.

Another similarly dressed man stepped out, pointing his rifle in the other direction. He must have been standing a few feet back, out of sight, the whole time. The second man peeled off and went over to check behind the large green dumpsters on the other side of the loading docks. A few moments later, he also shouted out. "Clear!" He then returned to the center of the drive in a running crouch and kneeled facing back towards the street. The first man did another quick scan of the loading docks before also spinning and facing out.

Robbie heard several shouts from down the drive before two more men ran past the two kneeling and spun back facing out almost like it were some sort of dance. There was another few rounds of overlapping pop, pop, pops from down the driveway. Robbie assumed they were gunshots but couldn't see the source. He also thought it was curious that they didn't seem very loud. He didn't know much about guns but had expected the reports to make more noise.

Five more of the military looking figures suddenly raced past the first group. One of the men who trotted into the alley, had a thick black mustache. "Right lads, square up in here, out of sight." He called back over his shoulder, then pointing at Robbie's door added, "Corporal Stewart! Check that door!"

A stocky dark-skinned man broke out from the group now rushing into the alley and sprinted to the door.

Robbie heard the lock jiggle.

"Locked, Sir!" The soldier shouted.

"Well bloody well open it!" The man with the black mustache ordered, from his position at the corner, peering back towards the street. He then added to the group. "Steady lads! They're coming!"

Robbie didn't have to wonder who or what might be coming.

The group of soldiers backed up into a defensive stance about ten feet from the mouth of the alley. They formed up, shoulder to shoulder, facing out with three kneeling in front and three standing behind with the mustached man taking a place in the middle.

Behind the defensive line, Robbie noticed one man not dressed in army gear. He had thinning, sandy blonde hair and a thick brown mustache. He looked more like he was on a safari than a military maneuver, wearing brown boots, tan cargo pants, a thick button-down long sleeve shirt and a vest covered in pockets. Unlike the others, he didn't have a rifle. Instead, wielded a pistol which he likely carried in the black shoulder holster wrapped to his chest.

While the man they called Stewart tried to pick the lock, the others stood their ground as a large group of undead stumbled into the cargo area and seemed to immediately home in on their position. From the size of the group pressing in, Robbie knew the soldiers didn't stand much of a chance unless they had enough ammunition to literally shoot and stack the dead so high that they couldn't get past their own bodies.

"Fire at will!" The man with the black mustache shouted and the pop, pop, popping started up again as the men started shooting. The dead began falling but each one that went down opened a space for two more to step over them towards the group. The entire dock area was quickly filling up from wall to wall and the narrow opening into the alley was starting to look like a meat grinder as gruesome faces crowded into the gap and were quickly blasted back.

To Robbie's surprise the little militia were holding them back, barely, and the fallen twice dead bodies were actually piling up, slowing the preternatural creatures.

One of the men yelled. "Changing mags!" He quickly dropped an empty ammunition cartridge and rammed home another full one. The process took less than a few seconds, but the dead took advantage of the gap in firing by moving up a step closer.

"Watch your lanes!" a large man with a brown beard growled from the back line.

Other men began shouting. "Changing mags!" These lapses in fire were letting the zombies inch slowly closer. Robbie wondered how much ammo these guys had.

"How's that bloody door coming, Corporal!?" The man with the black mustache yelled.

"Working on it, Sir!" came the reply.

"Well, work a little harder if you don't mind!" The man yelled as he changed out his own magazine.

Robbie couldn't see Stewart at the door, but he could hear him cursing while he alternated between working on the lock and kicking and banging on the latch. He began to wonder if he should let these guys inside but continued to hesitate. Every time, in the past, when they had encountered a militia type group, they had ended up getting robbed or threatened or worse. He stared down at the metal latch as it rattled and wondered how much longer it would hold. When Robbie looked up again, the wall of gruesome decaying figures had moved a few steps closer.

The mustachioed soldier shouted, "Two steps back by ranks! Back rank first! March!" On this command, the men standing in back stepped back two paces without letting up their fire. When they were in place the man yelled. "Front rank, march!" Immediately the kneeling group scrambled backwards, careful to stay below the fire of their comrades.

Retreating gave the group some breathing room, but not much, as the undead horde surged, desperate to get to the buffet. In less than a minute, the space between the two groups had shrunk again.

The mustached soldier suddenly grabbed a tall, red bearded man next to him and shoved him back, "Get behind me!" He shouted, "Mr. Clark! Stay with the Leftenant if you please!"

The man in safari gear stepped over and put his hand on the red haired man's shoulder and yelled, "I've got him Major!"

The red bearded Leftenant jerked away and protested, "Bloody hell Major you need my rifle on the line!"

"They are pushing closer," the mustached Major yelled as he fired, "And, I'll be damned if you go down before I do!"

"For fooks sake, Major, if we all die here it won't matter who went last!" the red bearded man screamed.

"You aren't out of the fight, Leftenant," Mr. Clark reassured him pointing at the gap created as the two men left on the back line had tightened up their ranks into the space he had just vacated.

"Progress report, Corporal!" The Major shouted coolly over his shoulder.

Stewart, who was desperately kicking at the metal door with everything he had, screamed, "Fooking can't get it open Sir!"

"Color Sergeant!" The Major bellowed. "Go blow that bloody door!"

Before he even finished giving the command the burly man next to him broke ranks shouting, "I'm on it," and scrambled back towards the door.

His absence was immediately felt as the zombies slumped a step closer. They crawled and stumbled over the growing pile of stinking bodies beneath them. It slowed them a little but the way the uneven tangle caused them to jerk and tumble about, made it harder for the riflemen to hit them in the head, even at close range. And it created a carpet of still animated undead, who had fallen, crawling out from under the feet of those still advancing. Precious seconds were lost as the men had to sweep their aim up and down, acquire targets, fire and eliminate the threats at several angles.

The red bearded 'Leftenant' and sandy haired 'Mr. Clark' quickly positioned themselves a step back from the group and added their guns back to the fight.

Robbie watched the Sergeant disappear under the line of his window and suddenly what the Major said struck him. Had he said "open the door" or "blow the door?" With all the shouting and banging, and the guy had an accent, he wasn't sure. Did they have explosives too? He thought to himself. Then he heard a thumping against the door frame.

"Oh, shit!" Robbie groaned and he scrambled down from the top of the utility cabinet. His hand and arm screamed in pain but he pushed through as he inched closer to the door. From outside he heard voices yelling.

"It's ready to blow, but we're too close!"

"Blow the bloody thing!"

"Were too close, we need to push them back to get some space or we'll blow ourselves up!"

"There's nowhere to push to, Color Sergeant!"

"Everybody get down and cover your ears the best you can!"

"Keep bloody shooting!"

Robbie was terrified about letting them in, but he knew if they blew it open they were getting in anyway and with no door so were the zombies. And there was no place else to go. He decided to take his chances with just the militia guys. He pushed back the lock, turned the latch, swung open the door and shouted, "Come on!"
     The two soldiers near the doorway stared at him in shock for half a second before the brown bearded Color Sergeant grabbed the smaller Corporal next to him and shoved him through the door. "We're in!!" The Sergeant bellowed to the others as he stepped into the threshold to keep it open.
     Beyond the big soldier's broad frame Robbie could see that the riflemen in the alley were engaged in close quarters fighting. The zombies had pushed right up to their front ranks. Some of the men were swinging their rifles madly against the mob while others were still firing as fast as they could. Their calm demeanor had evaporated into a screaming panic while they fought for their lives. It also seemed very loud, and very real, without the dusty window between him and the action.
     "Fall back!" The Major yelled. "Fall back!"
     Mr. Clark grabbed the red bearded Leftenant and was trying to pull him back towards the door shouting. "The door is open! Go Sir! Go!"
     But the much larger man wasn't having it. He stood his ground and continued to provide cover fire for the men attempting to scramble back from the hungry horde. The Major had grabbed the foot of one of the men who couldn't get up as the mob closed in around him and was dragging him back towards the utility room. The man continued to fire round after round as he was pulled along. The last man out separated himself from the grip of one of the things and tumbled back onto his bottom. The Leftenant and Mr. Clark took hold of his collar and pulled him along as he too continued blasting away at their pursuers.

Robbie stepped out of the way as the men began to rush into the small room. The Major was the last inside and the Color Sergeant slammed the door shut behind him, ramming the lock into place as soon as it hit the frame. Robbie noted that the men didn't relax with the door shut. Rather they seemed to immediately begin checking their surroundings for additional threats. There was lots of shouting and he heard voices on the other side of the electrical cabinets shouting, "Clear!" - "Clear!"

Robbie looked back to find the large Color Sergeant glaring at him. 'Oh great,' he thought stepping back. 'Here's where they stab me with a big knife or something.'

The large man pointed his rifle at Robbie and commanded, "Turn around! Get down on your knees!"

It took a moment for Robbie to understand what he was saying, due to his thick English accent, but by the time he had figured it out, the big man already had grabbed him, spun him around to face the far wall and shoved him to his knees. Before Robbie could protest, the man shoved a boot into his back and knocked him to the floor yelling. "Don't bloody move mate!"

Robbie's hand and arm howled in pain and he wanted to cry, but he stayed where he was. The noisy chaos in the small space was instantly magnified by the slapping and pounding of fleshy fingers on the outside of the door. With his face on the dusty concrete floor, Robbie could only see the boots of the men standing on the other side of the wall through the tangle of wires connecting the cabinets to the floor. He could hear the men yelling back and forth but with the Color Sergeant's large boot keeping him firmly in place, he couldn't make out who was saying what. The accents, and the fact that they were all talking over one another, didn't help either as he could only make out every few words.

Finally, the Color Sergeant shouted with a booming voice that sounded like it was right in Robbie's ear, "Right! Shut it you lot! Quiet! What's going on back there?!"

The room went silent, except for efforts of the creatures outside, and after a moment someone said, "Sergeant Patel's been bit!"

"Bloody hell," the Color Sergeant exclaimed, "Mr. Clark, would you mind keeping an eye on this one while I see what can be done?"

"Of course," the man named Clark stepped into a position behind Robbie as the large soldier removed his boot and could be heard quickly walking to the back of the room.

"Don't make any sudden moves now, son," Clark added. "My foot isn't as big as the Color Sergeant's but my pistol is loaded and I will use it. Do you understand?"

Robbie nodded. Over his shoulder, he could see that Clark stood a pace behind with a gun pointed down at him. Everyone else quickly crowded into the back, presumably around the wounded Sergeant Patel.

"Where are you bitten?" he heard the Color Sergeant ask.

"Fucking shoulder and my wrist," came the answer, this time not an English accent but, what Robbie thought sounded Indian. Robbie didn't know much about accents but he had watched enough BBC America with his mom back in the day to recognize a few. "Bastards got me when we started pulling back," Patel went on, "mother fuckers tried to take me and I fucking didn't let them. I fucking KILLED THOSE MOTHER FUCKERS!" He shouted out the last part as if yelling at the things outside.

"You hear me, mother fuckers!" He screamed with a quiver in his voice, "You didn't get me! You're fucking not going to get me! I'm fucking not going with you! You can't follow me to Nibbanah you mother fuckers!!"

There was a moment of quiet inside as everyone let the man say his piece. Finally, the Color Sergeant said, "Simmons, get some bandages on those wounds…"

"No," Patel said, "don't waste the supplies, we all know what is going to happen."

"We can stop the bleeding," the Color Sergeant replied, "give you something for the pain."

"Fuck that," Patel answered, "I can handle it. I'm not fucking waiting for them to take me. Here, take my gear…"

Robbie heard the sounds of metal and heavy fabric clanging and thumping onto the floor as, he guessed, the man was removing and tossing his things towards his comrades.

"Leftenant?" Patel called out.

"Right here, Sergeant," came the answer.
"Will you do me a favor, Sir?"
"Name it," the Leftenant said.
"Will you tell my father," he began, "that I fought these motherfuckers all the way to the end? That I never gave up and I fucking went down fighting? Will you tell him that? That I never gave up and killed every one of the motherfuckers I could?"
"I will tell him," the Leftenant promised. "I will find him and tell him personally."
"YOU HEAR THAT," Patel screamed at the door, "YOU MOTHERFUCKERS! You are not going to get me!"
"Is there anything else I can do?" The Leftenant asked.
"Just find my father and tell him I never gave up," Patel's voice broke as if he were in tears.
"I will," the Leftenant said, "I swear it."
"Good," the Sergeant said calmly. "Now back up please, Sir, I will not be one of those demons and I will not make my friends do my dirty work. Please back up all of you."
"Patel, don't," someone begged.
"It cannot be helped now, I can feel their damned poison in my veins, it's not long now," Patel said, "Look away my friends. I don't want this part to be how you remember me. I will see all of you on the next plane."
There was a shuffling as the soldiers backed away.
"Hear me, motherfuckers!" Patel shouted again at the creatures outside one last time, "You can all go to Naraka!"
The bitten Sergeant then growled like a body builder pushing his last and heaviest repetition, followed by a bright flash and a loud bang. This was not the muffled pop, pop of the rifles from before, but the deep sound like a cannon that seemed to reverberate right through them with an explosive force. The whole room vibrated in its wake. Robbie's ears rang as if sirens were blaring in them and he wondered if the Indian Sergeant had blown himself up.

For a few minutes Robbie could hear nothing but the ringing in his ears. As the noise gradually began to ebb, he started to sense, more than hear, the things banging on the walls outside again. Still desperate to reach the meals that had so narrowly escaped them. The men in the room started to move around again and Robbie began to hear the crunching of their boots on the dry concrete.

"God rest his soul," the Major sighed as he returned to the aisle behind Robbie. He leaned his back against the far wall and slid down until he rested on the cold floor, his legs stretched out in front of him. The Leftenant and Color Sergeant came in slowly behind him. The officer stood, wiping his eyes, while the big enlisted man stared off into the distance. Although he was staring at the far wall, it looked as if his gaze was fixed on something far out on the horizon.

For a long time, the only sound was the ringing in their ears and the scratching on the door.

"Color Sergeant…" the Major finally said after a deep breath.

"Yes, Sir?" The Sergeant replied without moving his eyes.

"Do you think that door will hold?"

He broke his stare and slowly turned to assess the door, "Um, steel door in a concrete frame. Yes Sir. It would take a fork lift to break through that door."

"Well, that's good I suppose," the Major said sadly as he removed his tactical gloves. "Let's keep an eye out in case those blighters get hold of a bloody fork lift."
"Yes, Sir," the Sergeant responded blankly then looked towards the back area. "Bevins," he didn't say it loudly, but his voice projected.

"Yes, Color Sergeant," the voice that answered cracked and was followed by a sniffle.

"We're not out of the woods here." The Sergeant said pointing at the cabinet from which Robbie had watched the group arrive. "I need you on over watch. Crawl up on that electrical cabinet and keep an eye on our friends out there."

The man named Bevins walked over to the cabinet and stepped up just as Robbie had done. Unlike Robbie, he ascended into the perch without falling.

"I don't suppose they might be losing interest?" the Major asked grimly once Bevins was in place.

"Sorry, Sir," Bevins responded. "They're crammed in like sardines. Looks like more pushing in from behind."

"Lovely," the Major said absently slapping his gloves against his knee.

"So, Fortunato," the Major said dryly to the Leftenant, "we find ourselves bound and trapped inside another crypt."

"Perhaps we should not have insulted them so harshly," the Leftenant replied lifting his eyebrows to indicate he meant the hungry things jammed into the alleyway outside.

"Indeed," the senior officer replied looking up. "There doesn't seem to be a back door. Color Sergeant, could we perhaps blow a hole in the roof?"

"Afraid not, Sir," the big Sergeant answered and tapped on the metal door frame, "the last of our C4 is stuck to the outside of this door."

"Excellent," the Major continued. "I hate it when it's too easy. Is there any chance the buggers outside might set off a spark and blow us all up?"

"Unlikely, Sir," the Sergeant shifted and tapped a pocket on his vest. "I still have the detonator."

"Pity," the Major said as he stood back up, took a deep breath and squared his shoulders as if to regroup himself. "That would have been an easy end to this madness."

"We could blast some rounds through roof to break it up, "The Leftenant suggested. "Then take turns hacking at it with our bayonets. It shouldn't take long to get through."

"Yes," the Major agreed turning to the young man lying on the floor. "That may be our best choice. But, I think first we should see if our new friend has any suggestions."

The group all turned their attention to Robbie.

Chapter 21

"So, Mr. Clark." The Major crossed his arms and raised an eyebrow. "Who do we have here?"

"No idea," the man with the thick blonde mustache answered. "I'm afraid I've not had time to question him, just yet."

"Is he armed?" The Major asked.

"You'll have to ask him," Clark motioned toward Robbie.

"Color Sergeant," the Major said. "Would you mind checking our, um, host for weapons?"

"Not at all Sir," the big man agreed as he stepped in and knelt down beside Robbie. He went on, "Listen here young man. I'm going to search you. Have you got anything on you I should know about? Any weapons?"

Robbie nodded at the big flashlight he had dropped on the floor and rasped. "Just that."

"Anything else?" The Sergeant pressed

Robbie winced at the pain in his hand. "There's a pocket knife in my back right pocket."

"Very well, now hold still. Let's not do anything stupid and you'll be on your way soon enough, yes?" The man said it like a question but it clearly was more instruction than inquiry. Robbie remained still as he was patted down. The man pulled the small knife from his pocket and slid it away behind them. "Alright, roll over slowly onto your back."

Robbie twisted around holding his arm to keep his aching hand from accidentally bouncing against the ground. As the Color Sergeant searched, he could see Mr. Clark standing with the gun still pointed in his direction, while the Major and Leftenant stood behind looking down at him.

"He's clean, Major," the Sergeant finally said. Pointing at the knives he added, "Just these blades."

"Travelling light are we?" The Major seemed to be asking a question but Robbie wasn't sure if it was really a question or some sort of British wit. When Robbie didn't answer, he sighed as if annoyed, stepping forward he motioned for Clark to let him through. "I think you can put the gun down, Mr. Clark. I don't believe he's going to be a problem. Are you Lad?"

"No," Robbie answered with a cracking voice. "No problem at all."

"Good," the Major looked Robbie in the eye. "Now, I'm going to ask you some questions and I need you to answer me honestly. If you tell me the truth, and I believe you, everything is going to be fine. Understand?"

"Yes," Robbie agreed wincing at the throbbing pain shooting from his finger.

"Good," the Major continued. "First, what is your name?"

Robbie hadn't expected the question for some reason and he stuttered his response. "Rob…" he finally got out, "Robert."

"Your name is Robbie Robert?" the Major asked unbelievingly.

"No, my first name is Robert." Robbie stammered. "But, everybody calls me Robbie."

"I see," the Major said as he unstrapped his helmet, "and have you got a last name Robert?"

"Yes Sir, it's Bruce," Robbie said.

The Major looked back at the Leftenant and the two shared a mischievous look. "Is your name seriously Robert Bruce?"

"Yes Sir," Robbie said emphatically as if to convince them. "I was named after my grandfather."

"Of course you were," the Major continued with a snicker as he put his gloves in his helmet and handed it to the Sergeant. "Ok, Robert Bruce. What are you doing here?"

"I live here," Robbie replied.

"Not likely." Clark said looking around the room. "There's no food or water. And the dust is still an inch thick. He hasn't been in here long."

"Are you lying to me, Robert?" the Major said with a lifted eyebrow. "I thought we had an arrangement?"

"No," Robbie blurted, "no Sir. I mean I live in the building. I only got in here just before you did."

"So you were in here while we were out fighting those things?" The Major inquired. "You took your bloody time opening the door."

"I'm sorry," Robbie replied. "I heard the commotion but I didn't know what was going on. Our, my, run-ins with armed groups have not been great. There's a lot of bad people out there. You know?"

"Very true," the Major agreed. "Fortunately for you Robert we are not bad people." Scanning around at his colleagues he added, "…not unless we are pushed that is."

"He said 'our'…" Clark noted.

"So he did," the Major nodded and kicked at the floor. "Is it just you Robert, or do you have friends?"

"It's just…" Robbie started to say he was alone but the Major gave him a look that made him think better of telling a lie. "It's just, Kelly and I."

"I see," the Major continued. "So, just the two of you? No others?"

"There were others," Robbie said, "but they're all dead… or gone, now."

"A very common scenario these days," Clark agreed and Robbie thought he even looked sympathetic.

"And you and your friend live in this building is that right?"

"Yes, for now anyway," Robbie told them. "We moved around a lot before that."

"It's a bloody miracle you are still alive." The Color Sergeant said. "The cities are the worst. Jammed with those creatures. Do you have any guns?"

"We have guns," Robbie said cradling his hand. "Just, no bullets. Plus they make a lot of noise. It's better if we don't make a lot of noise."

"How about food?" The Sergeant asked.

"Scavenging mostly," Robbie admitted. "There aren't many people around so there are plenty of stores and houses with canned goods and even bottled water. You just have to, you know, be careful. And we've been growing some vegetables recently."

"Fair enough," the Major seemed content with his answers.

"What's wrong with your hand?" The red bearded Leftenant asked.

"Are you bitten?" The Sergeant blurted.

"No!" Robbie responded quickly, "I think I broke my finger getting in here. Hurts like a bitch."

"Simmons, could take a look at it," The Leftenant suggested to the Major.

"I don't suppose there is any harm in that," the senior officer agreed. "We're all going to be here a while."

"Simmons!" The Color Sergeant called to the squad in the back aisle.

"Yes, Color Sergeant?" came the answer followed a moment later by a dark skinned man stepping in behind them.

The small group parted to let Simmons through. Robbie noticed that he was about average height and like the most of the others had a thick beard. In the center of his chest was a green and tan tab showing three chevrons. On his shoulder, he wore a patch with a white cross on a dark green background.

"Robert," the Leftenant said, "this is Sergeant Simmons, he is our MA, Medical Assistant. Would you like him to take a look at you hand?"

"Yea, sure," Robbie said and held his hand out.

"Would you mind, Sergeant?" The Leftenant asked.

"Not at all, Sir" the man answered and stepped forward to kneel beside Robbie. He took hold of Robbie's wrist and began to look over the blue and swollen finger. "Your name is Robert, yea?"

"Yes," Robbie answered.

"How'd you do this then?" He asked as he continued his exam.

"Got it stuck in a latch trying to get through a door," Robbie said. "There were a bunch of them coming, so I was in a hurry. I guess I pulled a little too hard."

"Quite so," the medic agreed, "bad swelling that. Probably hurts like a bugger too, yea?"

He then turned to speak to the men standing behind him. "I don't think it's broken but he did pull it out of the socket. Do you want I should reset it?"

Robbie thought it odd that he asked them, and not him. It was like being at the doctor with his mom.

"Yes," the Major said, "if that's what young master Robert wishes, of course."

The medic turned back to Robbie. "You want me to fix it, bruv?"

"Can you?" Robbie sputtered. "Yes, please!"

"It's going to hurt like a mother when I do it, but it should feel better in a few minutes," Simmons advised him. "You ready?"

"Yea, go ahead," Robbie agreed.

"Right, I'm going to count to five and then I'm going pull it out and reset it," the medic said. "Ready?"

Robbie closed his eyes, gritted his teeth and nodded. "Just do it."

"All right, count with me bruv," the medic held Robbie's wrist firmly and gently took hold of the finger. "One, Two…."

"Aaaaah!!" Robbie screamed as his finger was jerked back and felt as if it might be pulled completely off. Pain shot through his body, causing his vision to go red and sparks to fly in front of his eyes. When he opened his eyes he was looking up at the ceiling.

Simmons was leaning over him with a concerned look on his face. "You alright, bruv?"

"Oh my Jesus!" Robbie gasped. "That hurt. Hey! You said count to five?!"

"Yea I did," Simmons laughed. "You're alright, mate. Let me wrap that up."

While the medic put a bandage around the finger, which still hurt but not nearly as bad as before, Robbie looked over at the other men standing nearby. He finally said, "I need to get out of here."

"So do we all, mate," the Color Sergeant said empathetically.

"My friend," Robbie explained, "Kelly. She's in the building and doesn't know where I am or what's going on. I'm afraid she might come looking for me and run into one of those mobs.

"Fair enough," the Major agreed, "…but there's a bit of a pile up at the door so it's going to be a while I'm afraid, unless… you have a secret door somewhere?"

"There is…" Robbie started and paused to catch his breath.

"There is, what?" Clark asked.

"Have you got another way out of here, Robert!?" the Major inquired with heightened interest.

"Yes…" Robbie raised his good hand to signal that they shouldn't get overly excited. "But, it's not going to be easy. There are undead…lots of them, and they won't be easy to get through."

"Bevins, you still up there?!" the Major called out without taking his eyes off Robbie. "Could you give us an estimate of how many unholy man eating vermin are outside in the alley?"

"Yes, Sir," Bevins said. "I'd estimate about a thousand of the blighters. Maybe a few more."

The Major continued glaring at Robbie. "Well there you are. It seems there are more than a thousand waiting to greet us on the other side of this door. So, how many do you suppose we might encounter if we go your way?"

"A few hundred, maybe more," Robbie shrugged his shoulders to show he was unsure.

"Well, ok then." The Major rubbed his hands excitedly as if this was good news. "Door number one has thousands of the ferocious bastards. Door number two has a hundred. I think I'll take our chances with door number two. Why don't you fill us in on where we might find door number two Robert?"

"It's over here," Robbie said as he struggled to get to his feet. Simmons helped him stand and they all parted to let Robbie walk through the cabinets. On the other side he found the other soldiers sitting and sprawled out on the floor. They looked up at him with blank stares through exhausted eyes. Robbie pointed at one of the men in camouflage who was leaning against the wall. "There, behind him."

"Lance Corporal McGregor," the Major said somberly. "I'm afraid we need to see what's behind you. Would you mind sliding over a bit?"

McGregor stared up at them as if they had woken him up and then complied by slowly pushing himself further along the wall. This revealed a rectangular hatch that looked like all the other coverings in the room's many electrical boxes. Robbie knelt in front of it then reached out with his bandaged hand, then switched to his good hand, and pulled the small latch. The door swung open to reveal the top of the dark shaft.

The three men standing, shuffled forward to peer into the darkness which did not reveal much other than a sliver of light reflecting from down below. The men who had been sitting around began to take interest, sitting up and leaning in to get a look.

"Is it a way out then?" One of the men asked.

"Yet to be seen," Clark answered.

The Major and Leftenant had squatted in front of the hatch while the Color Sergeant stood behind them. They all seemed to be inspecting the potential escape route.

"You came in this way?" the Major inquired to Robbie.

"Yes," he replied. "About an hour ago."

"What's at the bottom of this shaft?" the Major went on.

"There's an electrical room, like this… but bigger," Robbie explained. "It's attached to the bottom level of the building's parking garage."

"And there are a few hundred undead down there, you say?" the Major continued. "In the room or in the car park?"

"Both," Robbie replied, "I accidentally opened the garage gates to the street. They came in behind me and chased me down into the lower level. I locked myself in the electrical room but they broke through the walls. I was lucky! I found the shaft at the last second and barely made it out in time."

"Indeed?" The Major rubbed his chin as he considered the story. "You say you came up an hour ago? I suppose it's possible that they have all found something better to do by now."

"Possible, but unlikely," the Leftenant countered.

"Yes. Well it can't be helped." The Major decided. He then raised his voice to speak to the group. "Listen up, someone is going to have to go down and assess the situation. It's a narrow shaft so it needs to be someone small. Do we have any volunteers?"

"Crawl down in a dark hole filled wif the undead," a voice mumbled. "Bugger that."

A few others echoed the sentiment.

"Ahl goo." McGregor said in flat brogue. He seemed to still be in a daze.

"You're too big to move around in there, Corporal," the Color Sergeant spoke up to put the group back in order. "O'Reilly! You're our tunnel rat. Shuck your gear and make sure you have a full clip in your rifle."

"Who's got a working flashlight?"

The soldiers all shrugged or shook their heads, no. "Robert?" The Major turned and said. "What is the visibility like down there? Is there a skylight or anything?"

"Oh, sorry, yea," Robbie replied. "The lights are on."

Everyone had been scurrying around getting O'Reilly ready but they all stopped suddenly and stared at him with disbelief. The Major seemed taken aback by the information and cleared his throat. "The lights... how do you mean they are on?"

"The lights are on, in the garage anyway," Robbie answered, "I didn't have time to check anywhere else. I was coming back up when those things came after me."

"And, how is it that the lights are on?" The Major pressed incredulously.

"Solar," Robbie told them proudly, "on the roof. That's why I was in the basement. To see if I could turn on the power."

"I see," the Major said. "How did you get it to work?"

"There's was a big ON - OFF lever in the electrical room." Robbie smiled. "I just threw the switch and bam, the power came on."

"Fair enough," the Major conceded nodding. "O'Reilly are you ready?"

"Yes Sir," the soldier named O'Reilly stepped up still tightening the laces on his boots. He was a short man with wiry muscles and jet black hair, bushy black eyebrows and a beard. He had removed all of his bulky gear, armor and uniform shirt leaving him in a dark brown t-shirt, camouflage pants and boots. His arms were covered in tattoos and he carried a small rifle on a sling. The rifle had a thick protruding barrel that Robbie thought might be a silencer.

"Listen, Corporal," the Major briefed him, "Mr. Bruce here says the lights are on down there so there should be good visibility. No heroics. Just climb down, take a quick look around, come back up and give us a report, yes?"

The Corporal nodded his understanding and grunted, "Aye Sir," as he began to climb in the hole. His small frame allowed him to easily enter the narrow space easily and get his feet on the ladder. Once he was situated he gave a thumbs up and they watched him descend down into the darkness. They sat silently and listened to the muted scrape of his boots as he stepped down onto each of the metal rungs. The sound grew quieter as O'Reilly descended.

Robbie stood there in the middle of the small group as they waited. Looking around he noticed, for the first time, the body of the soldier who was bitten, leaning against the far wall. His legs and boots kicked out in front of him as if he were resting. Someone had thrown a camouflage jacket over his head to cover his face but the spray of blood and brains up the wall behind him told the story. Robbie tried not to stare at the body. He had seen many dead in the last few years but it never seemed to get easy.

Chapter 22

The Color Sergeant broke Robbie's gaze when he leaned forward and looked down into the dark shaft. There was a click from down below and the bottom of the shaft was filled with light. He could see O'Reilly's small shape squatting at the bottom. He had opened a similar hatch to the one he had gone through at the top, but on the other side. He expected O'Reilly to quickly close the hatch but the soldier sat there holding it open as he looked around whatever room it opened into. The Sergeant watched, expecting the undead to lurch into the hole at any second. He wanted to call out and tell the man to close the door, but he dared not make a sound in case he should somehow attract whatever creatures might be down there to O'Reilly's presence.

O'Reilly finally pulled the door shut and the bottom of the shaft was plunged back into darkness. A few seconds later, they heard the echo of the soldier ascending the rungs again until he emerged again, into the light at the top. In his lilting accent O'Reilly began describing his findings. It seemed to Robbie that this was a well-practiced routine for this group, as they all sat quietly listening while he spoke.

"Lights are on." O'Reilly began. "Long, rectangular utility room, maybe, 6 meters wide by 18 meters long. Walls are lined with electrical boxes like these up here, but larger. Main wall to the car park has been breached in several places. Three targets in the room but they aren't moving much, look to have suffered some major injuries, perhaps in getting through the wall. I couldn't see much out into the car park from the hatch but I didn't see any just outside."

The Major seemed to consider this for a moment before turning to Robbie. "You said there were several hundred undead pursuing you in the car park, are you sure it was that many?"

"Yes," Robbie answered confidently, "at least that many."

O'Reilly lifted an eyebrow. "Well I only saw three, but, there could be more outside the room."

"Indeed," the Major concurred as he considered it.

"They might have been distracted and drawn away by something else down there," the red bearded Leftenant offered. "Any loud noise or warm body will catch their attention."

The Major grunted his agreement and stood, then called over his shoulder, "Lance Corporal Bevins are they still queued up out front for tickets?"

"Oh yes, Major," Bevins replied with a laugh, "looks like they are quite prepared to camp out for the good seats. In fact they are starting to pile up at the door. I should think they will be at window level soon."

The Major turned to the big enlisted man beside him, "well, Color Sergeant, it doesn't look like our fans are going to let us out the stage door. Let's get the band moving on a subterranean escape route."

"Roger that, Major," the Sergeant acknowledged, then to everyone, "Alright! You heard the man! Strip out of your bulky gear and get ready to start dropping it down the shaft. O'Reilly, slide back down there and take out those 3 creepers as quietly as you can. Stewart, and MacGregor, you get down there with him and cover our insertion."

The room came alive with movement as the men, who all previously seemed lethargic, quickly scrambled to their feet and began shrugging out of their heavy gear. The big Sergeant continued to give orders and began to grab individual soldiers to help them out of their straps and harnesses. It seemed like organized chaos to Robbie, who suddenly realized he hadn't been consulted about whether he wanted to go back down there. He didn't suppose staying was a good option, and he couldn't think of a better way to face off with a few hundred zombies than with a group of well-armed soldiers.

The Major and the Leftenant stepped over and guided Robbie out of the way as the group began dropping their gear down the shaft. "Well Robert, I suppose it's lucky we ran into you." The Leftenant said when they were clear.

"Don't thank me yet," Robbie answered. "There really were a few hundred undead down there. I hope they all went home, but if they are still in the garage…"

"Let us worry about that, eh?" The Leftenant smiled. "These are some of the best zombie killing bastards you have ever met."

"I hope so," Robbie said and there was a lull in their conversation as they watched the men working to get all their supplies down the shaft. After a moment, "Oh, I'm glad to have run into you too but, who are you? And why is the English Army here in the US?"

The two officers looked at each other and laughed at this question before the Major turned and explained, "Sorry to disappoint, Robert, but we aren't the English Army."

"No?" Robbie said confused.

"Major John Garrett," he said holding out his hand, "His Majesty's Royal Marines four-three Commando out of Argyle, United Kingdom. I'm the acting Commanding Officer of our little band at the moment. Until I die, or they find someone better."

Robbie returned the firm handshake still not completely sure of what that all meant, "Oh, ok?"

"This is Leftenant Arthur Windsor," the Major continued as the red bearded man offered his hand. "He's my… executive officer. The big man over there pushing people down the shaft is Color Sergeant Bradley, our senior enlisted man."

"I apologize for our delayed introductions, but we were a bit preoccupied before. And I'm sorry about the way you were treated when we came in. As you said there are some bad people out there these days and you can't be too careful."

"I understand," Robbie said. "But, how…? Why?"

"Rather a long story I'm afraid," the Major said nodding to his fellow officer. "I'll be happy to tell you the whole thing once we get out of here and somewhere safe. Yes?" Then he added with a smile. "But, I assure you that we are not here to take back the colonies."

Robbie laughed and though his school history classes had been cut short, he knew enough to quip, "Well I don't suppose there are any Minute Men left to stop you if you were."

The Major slapped him on the shoulder encouragingly. "Don't you worry lad. There are still people out there fighting this thing. And we will prevail."

Before he could go on with his pep talk, the Color Sergeant called over, "Gentlemen, whenever you are ready."

"Ah!" The Major said. "That's our train."

Robbie looked over to notice that most of the soldiers and their gear had already disappeared down the hatch. Only he, the officers, the Sergeant and Bevins remained. The big enlisted man shouted for Lance Corporal Bevins to get a move on, prompting to him leap off of his perch and make a bee line to the shaft.

"Just in time," Bevins said as he started to descend into the dark, "bastards are almost piled up to the windows."

"Time's running out gentlemen," Bradley announced, urging them to prepare to enter the shaft. "Mind the gap."

"I suppose we should go," the Major announced as he began walking to the narrow exit, then turned to Robbie, "Oh, I do hope you'll be joining us? We could use a guide once we get down there."

Soon they were all making their way down the ladder. The Color Sergeant was the last to go. He paused to take a last look around making sure they hadn't left any important gear. His eyes landed on Patel's body lying still on the floor and he said a last goodbye to his squad mate. Sorrow filled him that he had to leave him there and he recalled the many others whom they had been forced to leave in worse conditions. As he began to pull the hatch shut, there was a slap on one of the high narrow windows and he saw that it was from a pasty colored hand. He quickly closed the hatch, until the lock clicked into place, then began crawling down the ladder.

Kelly stopped briefly at the intersection to make sure the mob from the garage was still pursuing her. Seeing that the way ahead was clear, except for a few stumbling corpses that hadn't noticed her yet. She took a right turn and ran on. The six lane street was mostly empty of old cars for a few blocks and the only obstacles were clumps of grass that had grown up through the asphalt. The row of trees planted in the center island had prospered without City maintenance crews to keep them cut back. Their long limbs stretched out blocking what would have been the inner lanes of a busy downtown road. Kelly enjoyed their beauty but kept far enough away, so as to not risk any bony hands that might be hidden behind the thick leaves.

Worse Than Dead

She ran for another block and paused again, to look back. Her pursuers were starting to lurch around the corner in their steady pursuit. Behind them, the wide parkway dipped down to the waterfront. In the distance, she could see the river running by without regard for any troubles taking place along its banks.

Across the street, she spotted six of the creatures begin moving briskly towards her. They still wore the tattered business suits of their former lives and came stumbling out of a tall, glass fronted bank building. Overhead, she heard a crash followed a few seconds later by the thump of a body striking the ground. Several others, who had evidently been trapped on the upper floor, came crashing down after.

She took that as her cue to move on and sprinted further up the street. Coming to another wide boulevard running through the once prosperous business district, she turned right again and jogged ahead. She felt lucky that she wasn't seeing many of the things grouped together. They mostly seemed to be the slow, loner types. Individually they were generally easy to avoid or kill, but in a group they were tireless and deadly. What was once a big woman, stepped out from behind a panel truck. Kelly thumped it hard on the skull with a crack and moved on as it fell to the ground. Behind it, she could see the leading edge of the main group turning the corner to continue their pursuit.

The street was long and ran straight through the cavern of buildings downtown. The once busy thoroughfare was gradually returning to nature, with clumps of bushes and grasses sprouting up through its once well maintained structure. Kelly knew if she continued far enough, she would arrive at the exchange of overpasses and tunnels leading out of town. The last time she had been there it was a trash covered marsh, as storms and river flooding over the years had washed the decay from the city down into the low lying area. She did not intend to go that far.

In a few more blocks, Kelly decided she would turn, loop around and quickly dodge through the back streets to shake off the parade of hungry revelers following behind her. She knew this area fairly well from her and Robbie's scavenging, and the days before the end times. While she didn't like running through the city alone, she felt confident she could do it so long as she didn't let herself get cornered by a pack of those things. There were several hours of daylight left so she didn't feel rushed.

If Robbie were still alive, and she told herself he was, he would be hidden away from the things in the garage. He might already be emerging if enough of the undead had followed her outside. Her mind ran over the possibilities as her feet did over the broken asphalt. She would loop around, make sure he was ok and then beat him to death for scaring her and making her run through the city dodging the dead.

She saw her chance ahead as she approached the next wide intersection. A large delivery truck was stopped at the corner. She quickly ducked behind it and headed up the big road a few blocks before cutting across what had been a wide public parking lot. This took her back the way she had come, but several streets up.
'With any luck,' she told herself, 'I'll give them the slip and the front of the group will march on until they end up in the marshy interchange. From there, they can sink into the muck and rot away into the earth for all I care.'

Once she headed back, she slowed to a more careful pace. She hoped not to stir up anything that might be lurking in the hollowed out buildings. Any noise or commotion might attract the big group to move over a few blocks, and she really wanted to get back before too much longer. She had been out in the open, on her own, in the big quiet city long enough to start getting the creeps. Even on this otherwise sunny and beautiful day she knew things could go very bad, very fast.

The street she was on was narrower than the broad avenue she had been on before. It was slightly cooler, being shaded by the silhouettes of the large buildings looming like giants along its length. There were a few more cars here too, but they were wide enough apart that she didn't think she would have a problem getting through. Water and decay had caused the street to collapse in places, leaving holes and inclines that she dodged around. Big clumps of tall grasses and weeds grew through cracks and indentations where the dirt had built up. Kelly took advantage of this as cover and she slipped quietly through the maze of wet smelling weeds and shrubs.

The few undead she passed were trapped in the street level stores. They did not notice as she slipped by. If she had any sympathy, it was for the ones trapped in the little shops. She imagined some part time barista, or florist, now clocked-in forever at their job. Standing there, behind their counters, in their aprons, until the roof crumbled and failed. Crushing them into place for eternity.

As she came to each intersection, she peered around the corners to see the street she had come in on several blocks below. A steady parade of undead shuffled by in the distance but seemed completely focused on staying in their ranks. A few times she came upon, and barely avoided, some hapless corpse as it staggered drunkenly towards the commotion just a few blocks away. She was surprised that she had captured the attention of so many, and at their ability to gather into large herds rampaging through town.

She wondered if "herds" was the right word and went through the list of terms for groups of animals in her head as she walked, 'school, pack, swarm…murder?' She had come to no conclusions by the time she returned to the last road before she would reach the wide thoroughfare running down to the river. Peeking around the corner she could see that the intersections further down, and the road in between, was clear of the undead. It would seem that the "swarm," or whatever it was, had gathered up all the neighborhood ghouls and pulled them along with it.

She decided it was more like an avalanche, destroying everything in front of it while dragging everything it encounters into its growing mass as it crashes down the mountain.

Up the street she noted a few lone figures who had missed the parade slowly bumbling towards the trailing end of the noisy group. They were several blocks back however, and no immediate threat. Further down the street towards the river, she could see the façade of the Riverside Condominiums building. She couldn't tell exactly what part of it, but she was reasonably certain if she moved directly west along this road she would come out within a block of the garage.

Looking again, she confirmed that her route was clear and darted out into the center of the road. Keeping a low profile, she moved briskly down the hill towards the condo. Glancing back, she realized that the creatures behind her had taken note of the live flesh just down the street and had become more animated in their progress.

'Still not a problem,' she decided as she continued on her way. Arriving at the next intersection, she didn't see anything and bolted quickly across. Behind her she heard the crashing glass of something breaking through a window on an upper floor. It made a loud whump when it hit the ground as if it might have been an old couch. She knew anything close enough to hear it would come looking, hoping for an easy meal so she picked up her pace. It was just a little further to the condo.

As she passed a rusted airport shuttle with flat tires, something struck the inside of its mold covered windows, causing her to jump. She skittered away through the clumps of grass growing up from the street and hoped whatever it was couldn't get out of the van. The scare caused her to lose focus for a moment in an effort to quickly get away and she stepped out into the next intersection without her usual diligence. Half way through, motion in the cross street caught her eye.

A mob of undead stretched across from sidewalk to sidewalk only a few dozen yards away. She did the math and figured this to be the tail end of the big group she had been dodging. They may have been trailing the pack, but they didn't hesitate when they saw her and instantly increased their clumsy forward motions. Several fell over as they overreached on brittle and unstable legs.

Kelly bolted towards the condo, knowing they would probably follow her the rest of the way. Disregarding her usual caution, she ran full tilt towards home. At the next intersection a few more stragglers joined the mob hoping to tear her apart. These moved a little faster than the main group, but she felt confident she could stay ahead of them if she didn't pull some stupid horror movie chic move and twist her ankle. With this thought suddenly in her head, she began paying very close attention to where she was putting her feet.

Finally, she burst out onto the street in front of the condo and corrected her direction in a wide arc towards the open garage. In a few seconds, she ducked into the entrance, did a quick scan of the inside to make sure there weren't any waiting for her and spun around to find the door control. Luckily, the key was still in her pocket and she jammed it into the metal plate just as the first of her pursuers emerged from the crosswalk. She paused for a second, wondering if she should just run inside where it was safe, but she knew if she did her whole trip would be wasted and she might not get another chance. She turned the key and prayed for the mechanism to work.

Corporals O'Reilly and DuPree slowly scouted their way up the ramp of the car park with their rifles at the ready. They were grateful for the overhead lights, even though the florescent bulbs flickered and hummed. Without them, they knew they would be in total darkness. Keeping several shoulder lengths apart, they moved in their well-practiced heel toe step that kept the sound of their boots nearly imperceptible, even in the echo chamber of the concrete garage. Each watched their individual "lanes" of fire ready to engage, in an instant, any threat that might come at them. The unmoving corpses of several of the now twice dead creatures lay scattered behind them as proof of their lethality.

At the bottom of the ramp, the rest of the Royal Marines refitted themselves into their personal armor and other gear as they emerged from the shaft. When Robbie crawled out, he noticed the soldiers had set up a kind of assembly line with all the gear they had dropped down lined up neatly against the wall. Robbie watched as the men quickly snapped and secured all the bulky and heavy looking items back onto their bodies. When their preparations were done, they silently stepped over and took positions facing out from the broken interior wall.

The two officers stood nearby, whispering to each other as they pulled on their own gear. The man they called Clark was a few steps away, already outfitted, his pistol held down at his side, he stared out into the vacant garage.
Robbie made his way over to the men. "I swear there were a few hundred down here!" His confused voice broke the near silence.

The Major's eyebrows jumped and he said in a low voice. "Steady lad. Keep your voice down. I believe you. These things can prove quite unpredictable."
"We've sent a team up to recon the car park," the Leftenant added in a whisper. "So far they have only run into a few stragglers, but we will know more when they get back."

"Just the two here though," Clark added quietly as he pointed to the bodies of the things that had been pulled into a corner.

"But..." Robbie said exasperated.

"It's ok, lad," Clark put his hand on Robbie's shoulder and cut a smirk at the officers, "Damn things probably heard the His Majesty's Royal Marines were coming and ran off to cry to their mothers."

"Bloody right," one of the men, kneeling at the wall, within earshot whispered.

The Major glared but the man was looking in the other direction and didn't get the rebuke.

"Well, in any event," Clark continued under his breath, "I usually think - the fewer reanimated corpses around trying to eat me, the better."

"Indeed," the Major agreed pulling at the shoulder straps to adjust his body armor. Then looking past Robbie he nodded and said "Ah, I see the Color Sergeant has decided to join us."

Robbie turned to see the big man ungracefully dragging himself out of the narrow opening in the wall. He realized the man's size must have made getting down the shaft difficult, even without his armor. Regardless, the Sergeant quickly righted himself, grabbed his gear from the row just as if he expected it to be sitting there and made his way over to the group. "What's the story, Sir?" He asked quietly as he began pulling his armor back on.

"Just what you see here," the Major answered, "We've sent O'Reilly and DuPree up the ramp to scout the rest of the car park. No real resistance yet."

"Thank God for that," the big enlisted man said hoarsely as he looked around seeming to assess how his men were positioned.

Chapter 23

The Major turned to Robbie, "Mr. Bruce do mind showing us how you got the power on?"

"Sure," Robbie answered and then hesitated. He considered that he still knew little about this group, and wondered if there might be a danger in showing them anything other than how to escape the building.

"Well?" The Major noticed that he had paused.

Robbie decided a group like this could probably find the big ON and OFF switch without him so he may as well act helpful, at least for now. "Right over here," he walked them over to the big box marked 'DANGER.'

"McGregor, we need you," the Color Sergeant said prompting the tall soldier to rise up from his firing position and join the men at the electrical box. "Can you take a look at this equipment and let us know if you can operate it?"

"Aye, Coohlars," the man said in his thick brogue and he popped open the door.

"Mr. Bruce do you mind showing the Corporal around?" The Major asked. "Since this is your place you may be able to help him find his way."

"Sure, but I don't really know much," Robbie contended.

"Good," the Major ignored Robbie's protest of ignorance and acted as if it was decided. He then turned and he, and the rest of the small group, made their way back to the broken down front wall.

Robbie stood there as McGregor nosed around in the box for a few seconds and then looked up at the big wires running into it. He followed the lines with his eyes and then turned and began walking towards the back of the room. The tall soldier stopped at a bank of computers anchored to metal shelves and began looking closely at each one. Robbie hadn't noticed before but each one had a small monitor on the front displaying green and white graphs.

"Ohh thas na gaod," McGregor said.

"What?" Robbie asked, not sure what he had said.

"Yer baudries narly daed," the man looked at Robbie and pointed at one of the displays.

"The…battery…is… almost…dead?" Robbie slowly translated the heavy accent.

"Oh aye," McGregor answered. "Mebe morean howr, mebe too."

"Ok?" Robbie said as he tried to work out what the man said.

"Coohlars," McGregor directed his voice to the small group of leaders who seemed to be in deep discussion near the wall.

"Yes, Corporal?" the big Sergeant looked up.

Robbie only understood a few words, as the Scottish Corporal explained the situation in his thick brogue. The Sergeant seemed to have no problem translating, however, and afterward turned to the two officers. "Gentlemen, if we are going to stay here I suggest we turn the system off for the night," he advised. "It's been off a long time with no maintenance and it's a miracle that it works at all, but even more miraculous that nothing has exploded or burst into flames yet."

The Major looked at the Leftenant who nodded his agreement. "Right, you'd better turn it off then. But first, I think most of us should get out of this cave or we will have to feel our way up in the dark."

"What's going on?" Robbie asked.

"Oh yes," the Major put his hand on Robbie's shoulder. "Look Robert, I hate to be a bother but it's late in the day and we need a secure place to bunk down for the night. Would you mind if we stay here? We need to keep moving, so we will likely be out again early in the morning."

"Sure, I think that would be ok," Robbie answered. "But what was that about the lights?"

"Yes, about that," the Major continued, "I'm sorry but we need to shut off your power. McGregor there," he pointed, "is an Army Sapper with the Royal Engineers assigned to four-three Commando…"

McGregor's assignment meant nothing to Robbie, though he tried to look like it made perfect sense, but he was still confused as to why they wanted to turn the power off.

"He's a trained electrician among other things," the Major went on. "He says we need to shut it off because it's a fire hazard, this system has been off for years and likely has all sorts of problems. Brittle wiring, water damage, rat's nests in the works, you name it. Sending high voltage electricity through old worn lines is a recipe for disaster I'm afraid."

"Not to mention," Mr. Clark injected waving up as if to imply the sky, "it will be dark in a few hours and if this building is lit up like a Christmas tree it will attract every madman, living and dead, within a hundred miles."

"Oh," Robbie sighed, "I hadn't thought of that."

"Don't blame yourself," the Leftenant said consolingly, "I quite imagine you didn't expect it to work at all. I wouldn't have."

"I really didn't," Robbie agreed. "I was shocked when the lights came on."

"It's settled then," the Major decided, "Color Sergeant please have Corporal McGregor shut off the power but give us a few minutes to get to the top before you throw the switch. We will drop chem sticks along the way so he can find his way out" the Major added. "Fair enough?"

"Roger that, Sir," the Sergeant responded, "I'll stay with McGregor. You take the rest of the squad and we will meet you on the top level. Hopefully, the group Robert told us about has moved their party down the street."

"Indeed," the Major nodded and then turned to the junior officer, "Leftenant, would you mind forming the men up to move out?"

"Not at all, Major," the red bearded man consented. He then turned to the row of Marines kneeling along the wall and said in a low, gruff voice, "Right! You heard the man, form up, let's get moving. Mr. Clark and Mr. Bruce, stay close if you please."

The Marines began moving out of the enclosure in a well-practiced formation and slowly advanced up the ramp in ranks of two. Robbie and Mr. Clark fell in beside the Leftenant when he stepped out into a position near the center of the group. The Leftenant got their attention and used hand signals to point out where he wanted them to be in relation to him. Robbie checked his footing and moved into the spot just behind and to the left of the red bearded officer. Clark seemed to already be familiar with this procedure and slid easily into his position on the right.

The Major was the last to leave the enclosure. Tapping the Sergeant on his shoulder he quipped. "Don't dawdle, Color Sergeant," as he ducked through the broken doorway to follow behind the main group. About half way up the ramp, he pulled a small green stick from his pack, cracked it, shook it and tossed it to the ground.

The line of Marines moved slowly as they worked their way up each ramp. The only sound was the gentle crunch of their boots on the dirty concrete floor and the occasional whisper from the Leftenant giving them orders. "Check your targets," he advised in a soft but clear voice. "Don't forget two of ours are ahead of us."

Robbie watched and tried to mimic the way the men walked in a kind of hyper alert intensity. He could tell these men had been working together for a long time as they moved with little instruction or interaction. They seemed to know what one another was going to do before they did it and instantly took up positions to support one another. Clark, who didn't seem to be a soldier, moved as they did but seemed more focused on watching the blind corners and large columns. He acted as if something might be hiding there, waiting to jump out, even after the other armed men had gone by.

As they walked, Robbie began to notice the details of their uniforms and equipment. The helmets had short sides, reminding him of backwards facing, bicycle helmets. Their rifles were short and black, with fat looking extensions attached to the ends of the barrels. The camouflage of their uniforms had a distinctive black, green, brown and white splotched pattern. Underneath, their boots were brown suede.

They all had narrow patches on their chests that he thought probably was their rank but it made little sense to him. The Leftenant's patch depicted two squares pointed up, over the letters RM. He had noticed the Major's was a small crown over the letters RM, while the Color Sergeant had three chevrons under a small crown. The other men had one, two or three chevrons with no crowns or letters. He had seen enough war movies, before the rise of the undead, to guess that these were the lower ranks but he couldn't be sure it was the same with these Royal Marines.

The gate squealed and Kelly winced at the loud noise. If the hungry creatures in the street didn't know where she was before, the grinding of gears and turning of rusty sprockets certainly gave it away. The rattling metal gate began to slowly roll downward and she prayed it would move fast enough to cut off the things that would now be rushing towards her. She was able to lean back and see through the narrow decorative gap in the concrete wall that the front of the group at the street corner had turned and were leading the others towards the garage.

"Damn it!" She shouted at the gate as it inched towards the ground. "Hurry up you fucker!"

The lattice of steel shuddered down its track while Kelly watched the ravenous creatures drawing ever closer. At the half way point, one of the things had reached the edge of the sidewalk where the driveway began. Kelly estimated it was about 20 feet away. Behind it, another dozen stumbled and lurched forward. Her hand had started to ache from holding the key turned so tightly and accidentally discovered with a fright, that if she let off it turned back to the start position and the gate stopped moving. This cost several seconds and brought the creature close enough to see the gaps in its gray skin.

She breathed a sigh of relief when the thing hit the grates face first. It made a terrible clatter but the gate continued down. Although there was a foot or so still open at the bottom the thing didn't grasp that it could duck under and instead began to thrash desperately against the bars trying to reach Kelly who stood only a few feet away. The gate closed just as the larger group began to arrive.

Kelly pulled out the key and jumped back as the things began to press and hammer against the steel barrier. She shook as the adrenaline and fear of having narrowly escaped them ran through her. Gasping for breath, she remembered she still had to close the lower level. She spun and almost lost her balance as she began running towards the river side entrance.

O'Reilly and Dupree had been moving slowly up the ramps having only a few contacts with hostiles. Fortunately, the ones they had come upon were slow and not very observant. The two soldiers had been able to dispatch them with little effort.

O'Reilly pulled his bayonet from the skull of one of the creatures he had discovered lurking behind one of the support columns. The human like figure slumped to the ground leaving a streak of slime down the grey concrete's facing.

"Not very sporting, mate," Dupree whispered from a few yards away, his rifle at the ready, while he covered his squad mate. "You caught him taking a piss. Doesn't count towards your total, that one."

"The hell it doesn't," O'Reilly responded as he wiped his blade on the jeans of the downed corpse. He slipped the knife back in his sheath, pulled his rifle back up and motioned that they should continue up the next ramp. "You're just jealous I got more kills than you."

"More?!" Dupree questioned, "How do you figure?"

"I took out at least 50 in that supermarket," O'Reilly smiled.

"I told you," Dupree protested, "knocking down the whole bloody building on top of them doesn't count. Besides, it was Bradley pulled the switch on that."

"Aye," O'Reilly grinned, "but who set the charges?"

DuPree snickered, "Fair enough, you get half credit."

"Bollocks!" O'Reilly growled and was about to tell his friend where to put his half credit when a noise above them made them both stop in their tracks.

It sounded like rusty gears grating on metal as if a cart without wheels was being dragged across one of the upper levels. The grinding continued as the two carefully watched the narrow gap between the ramp coming up and the one going down. Nothing seemed to be coming down but they knew the noise would attract any hostiles to whatever was going on up there.

"That's not good," Dupree said.

"No, but we better get up there and see what it is before the Color Sergeant gets here," O'Reilly suggested.

DuPree nodded and they started moving forward again. Half way up the ramp they noticed that there was an entrance to the car park at the top. The gate was up and it looked like there was nothing to keep anything from getting into the garage. They carefully scanned the area as they rose until he saw that the opening was a car access from the river side of the building.

As they neared the top of the ramp, two undead stumbled inside, in pursuit of the source of the rattling sound that echoed from the building. They might have once been clerks, in any of the banks downtown, but after years in the elements their business attire hung tattered and torn, while their skin had turned a pasty grey. One had a dark socket where its left eye had been and the other seemed to have had its lips ripped off, exposing its white skeletal teeth. They instantly spotted the two live men standing in the middle of the down ramp and all but forgot why they had come. Instead, they turned towards the two meals that seemed in easy reach.

These moved more quickly than the ones they had been dealing with on the way up, so without hesitation the two Marines targeted and pulled their triggers. The backs of the things heads exploded and they spun away from the impact. One slammed back into the automated ticket machine and the other flopped across the yellow exit arrow. The shots of the men's rifles had barely registered against the raucous chain rattling going on upstairs.

The two soldiers quickly advanced to the top of the ramp and scanned the area for additional threats.

"Fuck," Dupree said looking down the driveway leading out of the garage. "Three o'clock! Twelve, maybe more, hostiles. One hundred yards out and heading this way."

O'Reilly took in this information as he scanned his sector. Seeing nothing he quickly turned and glanced down the drive to see a mob of undead stumbling up the two lanes towards the car park. "Bollocks!" He cursed noting that the things had probably been chasing the noise but now had seen the two of them standing in the opening.

Suddenly the grinding of gears from above abruptly stopped. The two men quickly scanned around listening as the echo of the loud noise faded from their ears. The momentary quiet was replaced by the slapping sounds of something running somewhere up above. Some were faster than others, but they had never seen the creatures outright run before. Still, they had both seen enough in the last few years to know better than to rule out the possibility of things getting worse.

"Fall back!" O'Reilly ordered when he realized that whatever was running was coming down the ramps above, directly towards them.

The two Marines darted back down the ramp and ducked behind one of the large concrete pillars. They instinctively took up defensive positions knowing they would need to hold the line until the rest of the unit could get there to back them up. DuPree tapped his pockets making sure his extra rifle magazines were still there. They kneeled and listened as the rapid footsteps grew closer.

To their surprise, a woman, a live woman, suddenly darted down the ramp on their left and bolted for the garage entrance. She leaped over one of the dead they had just killed and seemed to hardly notice it. They were relieved that she was alive and not some new kind of living dead but concerned at what she might be running from. They both remained motionless and assumed she was trying to escape the garage. However, they weren't surprised to see her stop at the gate when she noticed what was coming up the drive.

Instead of running away, as they expected, she began frantically searching around the gateway until she found a square metal box mounted to the wall. Pulling something from her pocket, she spent several seconds working it into the box. Her intentions became clear when her hand turned. The sound of grinding pulleys echoed through the garage and the rolling gate began to rattle towards the ground.

DuPree looked at his partner and lifted an eyebrow, silently asking if they shouldn't give her a hand. O'Reilly, having no idea who this person was or what was going on, decided to be cautious and signaled that they should hold their position. Technically they were the same rank, Corporal, but O'Reilly was the lead scout so movements and actions were his call. Dupree nodded and they remained in observation mode as the gate slowly descended. Both glanced at their watches wondering how fast the group outside might be moving and whether she would get it shut before they arrived.

A moment later several shadows appeared as the angle of the sun gave away the arrival of the hungry creatures at the top of the drive. Dupree realized that the things were just a few feet away and it was looking like the gate would not be closed in time to stop them. He looked over at O'Reilly, who seemed engrossed in watching events unfold, and risked a low whistle to get his attention. When O'Reilly glanced over Dupree raised his eyebrows with apprehension and nodded towards the girl signaling that they needed to go back her up.

O'Reilly thought for a second and, though he clearly didn't want to risk it, he saw the logic in stopping the things at the gate. They could deal with this girl and any issues she had after the immediate threat was blocked from entry. He signaled that they should circle around behind the girl who was focused on keeping the key turned in the lock. DuPree immediately broke from the cover of the support and moved quickly into position about 20 feet back and looking out the gate. O'Reilly was right behind him.

They girl's attention was on the key and looking outside at the approaching undead, so she did not notice them move into position. As they kneeled and started picking targets, they saw that the gate had come down far enough to block head shots.

"Knees and hips," O'Reilly said. "Stop them when they hit the ground. Fire at will."

Dupree quickly lined up a shot on the closest creature, which was within arm's reach of the gate, and took it out at the knee. It fell hard on its side giving him a second shot that went through its head and ended it. O'Reilly opened up as well and began taking down the front line of the gnashing mob. The pop, pop of the rifle reports, though diffused by their suppressors, echoed off the walls and this time were not drowned out by the sound of the gate clattering down.

Kelly jumped and screamed when the shots began to wiz by her. She spun around and gasped at the sight of the two armored and camouflage clad soldiers firing in her direction. She slammed back against the wall as her body subconsciously took her into flight mode. She screamed again when she realized there was nowhere to hide from the armed figures. With no other options, she sank down into a ball and pressed back against the concrete in a vain attempt to escape through the solid mass.

Without constant pressure, the key returned to its off position and the gate stopped moving. Its base plate remained several feet from the threshold and the undead were steadily pushing through their downed comrades towards the gap.

"Better get up luv!" O'Reilly yelled as he watched her slide down the wall. "Lets get that gate closed!"

They continued firing as Kelly tried to regain control of herself. Looking outside she saw the undead clawing their way forward through the hail of fire. The closest were only a few feet from the opening. She took a deep breath and decided she would rather be shot than eaten alive. Jumping back up she grabbed the key and turned it, causing the gate to start closing again.

The two men continued to keep the creatures back until the gap was too narrow to fire through. Soon after the gate closed, the things crashed into its metal grates, shaking and thrashing, desperate to get through and tear at the living humans on the other side.

"Bloody hell," O'Reilly blurted. "You gave us quite a scare there."

"I scared you?!" Kelly still shook as her wits came back. "You scared the crap out of me!?"

"Sorry, Luv," O'Reilly said as he and Dupree stood up, lowering their weapons to the ready. "We saw you trying to close the gate and you looked like you wasn't gonna make it. Just trying to help."

"Just trying to help?" Kelly stuttered while she glared at the men. "Who the hell are you!?"

"Kelly!" a familiar voice called from down the ramp.

"Rob!?" Kelly turned to look but all she saw was another group of men dressed like soldiers coming up from the level below.

Then the lights went out. The garage was plunged into darkness. Only a small square remained illuminated. A narrow shaft of afternoon light pressed through the bars of the gate. Its thin shadows falling over the group. The lines rolled up and down as the creatures outside shook the barrier in frustration.

"Rob?!" Kelly shouted into the darkness. "Is that you?"

"Kelly!" the voice came back, "Yes! I'm right here. Don't move I'm coming up."

The sound of Robbie's footsteps echoed through the cavernous garage as he ran towards the small circle of light where Kelly waited. When he emerged from the darkness and met Kelly's gaze he started. "Are you…"

Kelly leaped up onto him, almost knocking him over, and wrapped her arms around him in her elation. "Oh my god," she cried as she squeezed so tightly he could hardly breathe, "I knew you weren't dead I just knew it!! Where have you been? What did you do? What happened with the lights?"

"I…" Robbie tried to answer but he was still trying to keep his balance as she squeezed him, "can't breathe…"

"Ha ha!" Kelly laughed and climbed down but kept him in an embrace. Suddenly her face changed from happiness to anger, "Jesus you scared me! And, where the hell have you been! What the fuck is going on? And who are these people?!"

Robbie looked around to see that the military group had emerged from the darkness and were watching the two curiously.

"Oh yea," Robbie said with a smile, "these are the Royal Marines four-three Commando. Can we keep them?"

Kelly looked at him quizzically and then scanned the shadowed faces of the armed men standing around them. She finally asked. "The what, of the who?"

"Look, they saved me," Robbie explained, holding up his injured hand, "...and fixed my finger."

"What the hell happened to your finger?!" Kelly grabbed his hand to get a closer look at his wrapped digit."

"It's fine," he said.

"I'm sorry to interrupt this reunion," the Major interjected, and pointed at the driveway full of ghouls struggling to get in, "but I don't know how much pressure that gate can withstand and I don't suggest we find out just now. Is there somewhere more secure we can go?"

"Yes," Robbie answered, "we can go up to our place."

"Rob?! We don't know them," Kelly glared and turned to the man with the mustache. "No offense but we can't just bring every survivor home. I'm sorry, Mr...?"

"Major John Garrett," the man answered politely, "and I completely understand your hesitation. These are hard times indeed. Perhaps we could just move away from the gate so that our friends outside are less inclined to test its integrity, eh?"

"Kelly, they are ok," Robbie said. "I promise."

"That's what we thought before," she replied with trepidation.

"This isn't like that," Robbie assured. "It's going to be ok. They just need a place to stay tonight. Right, Major?"

"Quite so," the Major agreed and nodded again towards the unruly crowd outside, "now, I think it's in all our best interests that we should get moving?"

Robbie took Kelly by the arm and began walking with her towards the up ramp. He noticed that most of the Marines had already stepped away from the light and were working their way through the darkness ahead of them. The Major pulled out another of the small sticks, and shook it until it glowed green in the dark and threw it on the ground.

"What, what's that?" Kelly asked.

"Bread crumbs," the Major said from somewhere near her. "A few of our lads remained in the basement to work on the power. This will help them catch up with us."

"Rob?" Kelly asked. She couldn't see him but he still held her arm.

"He's telling the truth," Robbie said from beside her. "Relax, it's going to be ok."

Chapter 24

"This is quite a view," Leftenant Windsor observed as he looked out from Robbie and Kelly's balcony. The sun was setting in the west, sending its last beams of the day skipping down the river. The dark water's waves, rolled and rippled across its surface as it made its way towards the sea. Sea birds swooped and dove overhead on the evening breeze.

"It's my favorite time of day," Kelly said from the doorway.

"Oh?" The red bearded officer inquired.

"The shadows start to cover up the damage in the street and you can almost imagine everything is like it was." She explained as she walked out and leaned on the railing.

"It's good to have a place to come where you can relax and forget about the state of things for a bit," the Leftenant nodded, "recharge the batteries if you will. Too much time in the trenches starts to wear you down. Even if you survive, it eats you up. All the death."

"Yes," Kelly agreed.

"Sorry," he added, "I didn't mean to get all philosophical and depressing."

"It's ok," Kelly smiled. "Just another day in the apocalypse. Can I get you some tea?"

"Tea?!" Windsor looked shocked in delight. "Are you serious?! You have tea?"

"There are advantages to living in a city of the dead," Kelly joked. "You'd be surprised at how little they are interested in the finer things."

"I'd bloody kill for a cuppa," he quipped.

"Coming right up," Kelly turned and lit a small grill. She picked up a tea pot that was sitting nearby and shook it. She seemed content with the sloshing sounds from inside and set it on the low flame. "Do you mind checking if anyone else wants some?"

Windsor stuck his head inside where the Major and Mr. Clark were sitting. "They have tea!" He called excitedly. "Anyone care for a cup?"

Kelly heard the Major laugh and respond, "Oh gracious yes! God be praised!"

"Phillip?" Windsor asked, "Would you like some?"

"I appreciate the offer and I hate to sound high maintenance but," Clark responded calling past the young officer, "Ms. Kelly I don't suppose you have any coffee?"

"As it happens," Kelly answered, "Robbie has a French Press and some coffee in the kitchen. He can find it for you when he gets back."

"Oh, thank you so much," Clark replied, "It's been forever since I've even smelled any coffee. A French Press you say?"

"Don't get too excited," Kelly warned him with a laugh, "The beans come from the back room of a Costco we raided a while back. They were vacuum sealed but, you know, it's been a while."

"That will be just fine, Kelly," Clark said gratefully. "Beggars can't be choosers."

"Excuse me," Kelly slid past the Leftenant in the doorway and went to the kitchen. From the back counter she pulled an ornate shoebox sized wooden container, which she brought out and set on the coffee table between the men. When she opened it up their eyes grew as wide as if she had opened a pot of gold in front of them. She indicated the small packages stacked neatly inside and said, "There are a bunch of different kinds. Pick what you like. Sorry were almost out of the mint. That's my favorite."

"Aaah smell that aroma," the Major said as he breathed in deeply through his nose. "That's the smell of civilization my friends."

The two tea drinkers leaned in and began sifting through the options.

"You heard the lady," Clark advised as they combed through the selection. "Lay off the mint."

"Roger that," Windsor assented.

"I think I shall go with a simple Assam," the Major decided pulling out a pack. "I swear I thought I'd never have tea again."

"Ah! Here we are," the Leftenant pulled out a pack of Twining's Earl Grey. "Just like my great grand ma-ma used to serve."

Kelly brought them some cups from the china cabinet and stepped outside to check on the water. When she returned with the steaming tea pot in hand, their cups were readied and set out on the table. Pouring the boiling water over their tea bags she apologized, "I'm sorry we don't have any creamer but we do have some sugar packets."

"Think nothing of it," Windsor said picking up the steaming mug of Earl Grey, "this is fine. You are too kind sharing your supplies like this. We really appreciate it."

"Major," Kelly inquired, "can I get you some sugar?"

"Ordinarily I take it NATO style," the Major laughed, "but seeing as there seems to be a shortage of cows, I wouldn't turn away a bit of sugar… if it's not too much trouble?"

Kelly giggled at their extreme politeness and enthusiasm over the tea. She hadn't encountered anyone with such manners since long before the fall of humanity. As she handed the sugar packets to the Major, the front door opened and Robbie walked in with the Color Sergeant.

"We got the lads billeted in some of the other flats on this floor," the Sergeant announced as he came through the doorway. He slowed and guffawed with dramatic incredulity as he entered the sitting area and saw the officers sitting in comfort on the sofas, drinking tea. "What's all this, then? Why am I not surprised to find the Officers lounging about drinking tea at the end of the world?"

"There, there, Color Sergeant." The Major laughed. "Who are we to turn down these good people's hospitality?"

"And all the more so, if it includes tea," the Leftenant smiled while holding up his cup.

"And coffee," Clark said as he stood up. "Robert, Kelly said something about you having a French Press?"

Robbie replied, "Yes, but I'm not very good with it. Do you know how to get it to work?"

"Oh, indeed I do," Clark exclaimed, "please lead the way."

"Ok," Robbie motioned for Clark to follow him into the kitchen. "It's over here."

"Color Sergeant, do we have a watch set?" the Major asked while stirring his tea.

The big Sergeant was still standing trying to look upset with his superiors, when Kelly handed him a steaming cup. He took the cup meekly and said. "Thank you, Ma'am."

"It's Earl Grey," Kelly said, "is that ok?"

"Yes Ma'am," he answered, "that'll be just fine."

After taking a sip, he grinned and said to the Major, "Yes, Sir. In the stairwells at either end of the hall. One Section has first watch. Two Section takes over at zero one hundred."

"You have men in the stairwells?" Kelly asked surprised. "It's really safe in here I promise."

"Standard procedure Ma'am," the Sergeant said, "not to worry. Keeps the lads on their toes."

"But we can leave if we need to, right?" Kelly asked looking worried.

"Of course," the Sergeant assured her, "it's not you they are watching out for. You can come and go as you like." He paused and then added, "but, if you need to go out just let them know it's you when you're coming back up. Wouldn't want them to mistake you for something else in the dark."

"For sure, that would be bad." Kelly nodded.

"There's really nothing to worry about Kelly," the Major said seeing the concern on her face. "I'm sorry if we have caused you some distress."

"No," she replied taking a deep breath and exhaling. "It's ok. We were in a situation not long ago. It was bad, and we couldn't leave."

"I see," said the Major. "Well Color Sergeant please give the men clear orders that they are not to interfere with our hosts comings and goings."

"Very good, Sir," The Sergeant replied setting his empty cup on the table. "Any other night orders for the watch?"

"No, set the standard night orders and make sure the men get something to eat," the Major said and then nodded to Kelly. "Be sure to emphasize that the sentries are not to do anything that might cause our hosts to regret their hospitality."

"Right you are, Sir," the Sergeant said, came to attention and marched back out the front door.

"I hope that sets your mind at ease, Kelly?" The Major said after the Sergeant was gone.

"Thank you, Major," Kelly replied, "we don't see many people anymore and most aren't nearly as civilized as you all. It's become a brutal world out there."

"I assure you, we understand," the Leftenant confided motioning with his cup to the men around him. "The last few years have been trying. We've seen some horrible things on our way."

There was a lull in the conversation as everyone recalled their own worst moments since the apocalypse began. Kelly noted that while they were very polite and seemed upbeat, there were dark rings around their eyes and their faces had the hard look of men who had fought and suffered. They each had a thousand yard stare that made them look like lethal statues. They seemed like they had been good men once, but the deep lines and shadows on their faces betrayed the hardness that had fallen over most survivors.

There were also things she recognized, and remembered from her college psychology class, as small expressions of living with stress. The Major's left hand shook almost imperceptibly. He tended to hold it still with his right, while unconsciously turning the silver wedding band on his ring finger. The Leftenant's eye twitched every so often, and the man they called Clark ground his jaw quietly.

All the soldiers had beards but Clark and the Major who, Kelly observed, except for their thick mustaches, were both clean shaven. While all their hair was longer than what she thought was probably military regulation, they had somehow been able to keep it neatly trimmed. The Major and the Color Sergeant wore wedding rings while the Leftenant and Clark did not.

    Kelly broke the silence, bringing everyone back to the moment. "Speaking of that. How did soldiers from the English Army end up here?"

    "Marines actually, well, mostly." Clark corrected her, as he and Robbie returned to the sitting area with piping hot cups of coffee. "Aside from myself and Corporal MacGregor, they are His Majesty's Royal Marines from the four-three Commando."

    "I'm sorry," Kelly said confused. "I don't know what any of that means. What is the difference between the Army and the Marines?"

    "Yes. Well, don't apologize. It's a common mistake for anyone looking on from the outside." The Major explained. "The easiest way to describe it is that, similar to your own US forces, in the UK we have, or had as the case may be, several different branches of the military. Each one has a specific purpose and area of expertise. The Royal Air Force, for example, handles air power.

    "Airplanes?" Kelly asked.

    "Mostly, yes" the Major answered. "Controlling the skies, dropping bombs and what not."

    "I see," Kelly said.

"The British Army are ground fighting forces. Infantry and such. When you need to fight in, or occupy, a large area of land, the Army is your go-to force.

"The Army boys get all the glory in the movies and TV shows," the Leftenant offered.

"Quite so," the Major went on. "Then there is the Royal Navy which projects sea power with…"

    "Boats!" Kelly responded enthusiastically when he cast her a 'fill in the blank' look.

"Ships and boats, actually, but correct," he congratulated. "We Marines work with the Navy. Marines are rather like the Army's infantry, but we specialize in naval landings and fast operations that require a smaller, more intensive focus. There are indeed similarities with the Army, but it's mostly a point of pride for the different branches.

"And there is a bit of a rivalry between the Marines and the Army," the Leftenant chimed in, "so it's something of a sore point when we get called - Army."

"Ok, I think I understand" Kelly nodded. "So, what are a group of British Royal Marines from the, um, four-three Commando doing here in the United States?"

"We were on some joint exercises out west with your American forces," the Major explained. "Then the whole damn world fell apart, we ran for our lives, fought our way across the country, and well, here we are."

"Surely there's more to it than that?" Kelly encouraged.

"Yes, of course," the Major replied. "We lost a lot of good men to get this far. Every one of their stories should be told. One day. When all this is over."

"You think it will be over?" Kelly asked.

"One has to have hope," the Leftenant said.

"With the right leadership, in the right place, at the right time..." Clark suggested with a nod. "Who knows what is possible?"

"I don't think there is any leadership worth a damn left anywhere," Kelly dismissed him. "But, wait, you said you were out west. What happened? How did you get here?"

"Our struggles are surely not any greater than yours," Garret replied.

"Maybe," Kelly said, "but, we'd like to know what's going on out there. We've been here in the city since the beginning with no news of anything out in the world. Tell us how you made it, what else is out there? It could really help if we knew."

"Very well. Perhaps you better tell it, Mr. Clark." The Major motioned to the sandy haired man, "you're better with recounting the details."

"I suppose I can give you the short version," Clark began, "if that's ok with everyone?"

"Yes, please," the Major agreed. "But, give us the Reader's Digest edition. Let's not bore these good people unnecessarily with our trials and tribulations. I'm sure they've had plenty of their own."

"Very good," Clark agreed. "Back just before everything went bad, the brigade was participating in some multi-national training exercises out west. Our boys were working with the American Marines and some Canadian troops on desert operations at..." He paused as he thought, "What was it called? Oh yes, Flashheart Air Base out in New Mexico. You've heard of it?"

Seeing their heads shake no, he continued. "Well, no matter, it's a rather large US Air Force base out in the middle of the desert. Very remote. Nothing for miles except sand, snakes and scorpions. Anyway, we came back in after a few days in the field and it was all over the news that this plague, or whatever, was causing people to go mad. Before we knew it, several big cities were off the radar. The news was reporting that the President was recalling all US military to help with getting a handle on it. The base went into lock down while everyone waited for orders."

Clark took a sip of his coffee. "We got in touch with the Ministry of Defense who gave us the same story. All British military personnel were ordered home as the plague bloody was everywhere. Except, there was no way to get home. All the civilian airlines were grounded and all the military transport planes had been redeployed to support urban operations. So, we were stuck in our barracks for a few weeks trying to figure a way out of there."

"Just when we thought it couldn't get any worse," Clark twitched his thick blonde mustache. "It got worse. The damn things found us. At first it was just small skirmishes down at the main gate. The Air Force security forces were able to stop them. Not long after that, the attacks got more frequent and the groups of crazies got bigger. It was only a few days later when they finally broke through the fence."

"Luckily we had all of our weapons and gear so we holed up in our barracks and did our best to fight them off." The Major injected. "I was on the phone with the Air Force headquarters who kept telling us they were sending re-enforcements to fight them back…. But none ever came. Right after that, there were some big explosions over at the Command Center and the phones went out. Within a day or so we started seeing the barracks around us go down. Men we knew. The damned things kept getting inside. I don't know how, but once they were in… that was it."

"When our ammunition started running low, Major Garrett here," Clark nodded at the officer, "decided we had to get out, so we hatched a plan. There were about 400 troops in our barracks; US Marines, Canadians and us. We loaded up everything we had, formed square, and fought our way over to the armory. I think everyone came with us. Right?"

"God help any who didn't," the Major recalled wincing. "Anyone who stayed didn't have a chance. It was total chaos. I looked back as we ran and the damn things were smashing in through all the windows."

"It was a running fight all the way, but we had one bit of luck," Clark went on. "When we got there, the armory was wide open. I don't know if the guards had escaped or the things got them, but they left the doors wide open and we were grateful for that. The Major sent a group over to the motor pool, which wasn't far thank God, to bring some trucks and Humvees. We loaded up a bunch of trucks with supplies and ammunition and headed out."

"When we got down to the front gate it was madness, a total slaughterhouse," Clark rubbed his chin. "There were thousands of the things running totally amok. It looked like the Air Force had thrown everything they had at them. There were gun trucks, spent brass, impact craters, blood and body parts all over the place…"

"I think we can skip over some of the gruesome details," the Major said.

"Yes, of course," Clark went on, "I don't know how they got all the way out in the desert like that but there was nobody left to fight. We couldn't get through the gate so we turned around and headed east towards where we had been training in the desert. We passed people in buildings and on rooftops, living people, but we couldn't stop. There were just too many of the damn things…"

Clark paused and sipped his coffee again, "I don't know how long we drove. All night, I think. Somehow, we made it to a small town, somewhere in the middle of nowhere. Completely empty. It was the oddest feeling ever. As if everyone just rose up and left. Anyway, we found some diesel for the trucks and kept going east."

"From there it all blurs together really," Clark sighed. "We fought our way along the highway and through small towns until we got into Texas. We lost over a hundred men in that first week on the road. Also, at that point the trucks were starting to break down and run out of gas. We had to start leaving vehicles behind and we were moving very slowly because we had so many men on foot. We couldn't get anyone on the radio and even when we got in range of a cell tower there was no answer anywhere."

Chapter 25

"Those first days were the hardest," Kelly said. "Not knowing anything or being able to get in touch with anyone. Everyone was just running from place to place trying to survive another day."

"Indeed," the Leftenant agreed with a sigh.

"But at least…" Kelly started to speak but stopped herself.

"At least what?" The young officer asked.

"You…" she paused again, thinking of the best way to express her thoughts. "I mean, I'm not being critical. It was very hard for everyone. I'm not saying it was easy for you. But, you had guns. Guns, training, and a sort of order to fall back on. If you, with all that, were practically decimated, it's beyond a miracle that there are any of us left alive out here. Some days we felt like living was worse than being dead. I mean how? Why are we even alive? How is it possible?"

"All I know," the Leftenant answered with conviction, "is that everything happens for a reason. God has a plan for us all. It may seem that we have been abandoned in these dark times but there is a reason and we will persevere."

"God?" Kelly chortled, "I think he's long gone if he was ever there at all. You think God is still out there watching over us?"

"I do," the red haired man replied looking directly into her eyes. "It's in the darkest times that God tests us most. Human-kind has been tested throughout history with great disasters and floods and famines and plagues. Many perish, yes. Millions during the Black Plague. Millions in the world wars and political battles of the 20th century. Millions have likely fallen to this… whatever it is. But, we few will fight on, defeat these demons, and humanity will re-emerge in a new age."

There was a brief pause before Kelly responded with a nod, "I really hope you are right."

"Pardon me for a moment while I get a refill of this delicious coffee," Clark excused himself and returned to the French Press in the kitchen.

"Wait a sec," Robbie said rising to join him, "let me see if I can do it this time!"

"Absolutely," Clark said encouragingly and stepped aside to let Robbie handle the device. "You'll be a barista in no time!"

He gave Robbie a few pointers and then turned back to the group. "So, to wrap things up, it's been a long slow slog. What was left of us started splitting off in different directions as we traveled. Everyone heading their own way, going home, hoping to find family and so forth. Most of the Canadians went north together and the Americans set out in their own ways a few at a time. That left us with, what? 82 Royal Marines? You can see our numbers have continued to dwindle over the miles. Although our losses were mostly from accidents and contact with our friends out there."

As the conversation progressed the room grew darker with the setting sun. Kelly stood and lit a few candles so they could continue their conversation. "Robbie will you light those candles in the kitchen?" She called over to him as she pulled the curtains closed. "I'll leave these cracked a bit for the breeze, but we feel like it's better to close them at night so the candle light doesn't reflect outside."

"Smart," agreed the Major. "If I may ask, what is your threat assessment of the area?"

"Well of course there's the undies," Kelly answered, "there are plenty of them. I don't know why they stick around in the City. Seems like they would wander off when they ran out of things to eat."

"Undies?" Bradley asked confused.

Kelly smiled. "The undead. We had some friends that called them 'undies' and it kind of stuck."

"Clever," the Sergeant laughed.

"What about the living?" The Major inquired. "Are they a concern?"

"Well," Kelly explained, "there aren't many left but almost every one we have met in the last year or so has not been very neighborly. I think people are getting more and more desperate. Going feral almost, as it gets harder and harder to survive. In the early days food was easy to find and the biggest threat was those things, the undies. Now, we know how to avoid the dead but the people are starving. It makes them crazy."

"You seem to be doing alright," the Sergeant said as he took in the well decorated room with a glance.

Kelly laughed. "Yes, this place is amazing but it's a very recent development. Until a few months ago we were living in much more…challenging conditions. Day to day really. This building has given us a safe place to call home. We are very grateful."

"What about food and water?" The Sergeant asked.

"We do ok." Kelly replied. "Better than many I'm sure. Recently we have started to grow some of our own. You saw our tomatoes out on the porch. We are also starting to garden up on the roof and down around the old pool. For a while I think we were the only ones left in the city, so we were able to stock up on bottled water, dry food and cans without any competition."

"For a while?" The Major asked. "Are people starting to come back?"

"We've seen some activity recently," Kelly said. "Most of the time we just notice when people have been through. We don't actually see them very often."

"How do you know it's the living?" The Leftenant asked.

"We aren't always sure," she replied, "but sometimes we find burnt out camp fires and food wrappers. Things like that. So, we know people have been there."

"Mostly small bands of scavengers then?" the Major inquired.

"Mostly," she agreed, "but bigger groups come through now and again; more organized and better equipped. We saw one, a few weeks ago, that had trucks and guns. But they made so much noise the undies ran them off before too long."

"You haven't made contact with any of them?" The Leftenant asked.

"Early on we tried," Kelly said, "but we learned that most of them are living pretty desperate lives. Now, we stay away from them. You are the first people we have spoken to in some time. I suppose I should thank you for not being uncivilized marauders."

"And we, you," the Leftenant added. "It must get quite lonely with just the two of you."

"It does sometimes," Kelly reflected, "but it can also be very peaceful. Especially now that we have this place."

"What about the Baldwin Sisters?" Robbie called over from the kitchen as he poured coffee from the glass and plastic press.

"Mmmm. Delicious." Clark took a sip and praised him, "I do think you're getting the hang of it, Robert."

"The Baldwin Sisters?" The Major looked at Kelly.

"Oh," She laughed, "yes. The Baldwin Sisters. They are a very bright light in this darkness. They are two old ladies we met just recently. They helped us out after Robbie hurt himself falling through their roof."

"You seem quite accident prone, young man," the Major said indicating Robbie's still wrapped finger."

"Yes," Robbie laughed holding up his hand, with the bandage, "but I'm unkillable so far."

"So these Baldwins have proven valuable allies?" The Major encouraged her to continue.

"Yes," Kelly went on, "or, we hope they will. They have a big greenhouse where they grow their own food and raise animals. They taught us a little about farming and shared the seeds we used to start our garden here. We promised to start trading with them as soon as we get more settled."

"Well that does sound promising," the Major agreed.

"So, you've just been wandering around since Texas?" Robbie changed the subject as he and Clark re-entered the living room holding fresh cups of coffee.

"It certainly feels like it sometimes," Clark laughed. "But no, we have a plan. We just need a... well, Major, do you want to fill in the blanks on that?"

"I suppose," the Major answered. "I don't think there's any harm in telling these good folks. We're looking for an airplane. One big enough to cross the Atlantic and get us home."

"But, there have to be plenty of airports between here and New Mexico," Kelly inquired sitting back down. "You haven't found a single airplane?"

"We've found plenty," the Leftenant provided, "unfortunately, every airport we have come across has been overrun or destroyed. We did find a very nice 747 in the middle of your interstate 20 motorway just west of Fort Worth but it had no fuel and the tires were all flat."

"Aye," Clark added, "we spent a few days trying to get that one to work but a horde of zombies came through and ended that effort."

"That sucks," said Robbie.

"I think our biggest problem is that we are simply stabbing about in the dark," the Major said. "We don't know our way around, we're using old motorway maps, hoping to find a needle in a hay stack. We don't know the cities well so it's hard to tell the difference, on these old maps, between a major airport and a small air field. And it has cost us dearly."

"We are in a race against time as well," the Leftenant added, "jet fuel goes bad and can only be stored for so long. Even in optimal conditions. We are already technically over the limit but if we find a good plane and a decent batch of fuel we can probably make it work."

"We heard there were a few air force bases and a naval air station down here along the coast," Major Garrett said. "We thought perhaps our luck might change."

"If you find a plane, and the fuel is good, one of you can fly… right?" Kelly asked.

"The Leftenant and Mr. Clark are our pilots," the Major pointed at the two men. "So, it's important that we keep them alive."

"I'd prefer to be kept alive also," the Color Sergeant commented as he came back through the front door.

"Don't get your hopes up, Bradley," the Major declared, "you and I are expendable."

"Not a bit of it you two," the Leftenant argued, "get that notion out of your head. We are all going home together."

"Color Sergeant, can I get you some more tea, or a coffee?" Kelly asked being the polite hostess.

"No thank you Ma'am," the big Sergeant replied, "the caffeine will just keep me awake all night. I'd miss my bad dreams. Now, I don't suppose you have anything stronger?"

"Sorry, just some warm soda in the fridge," Kelly smiled.

"Wait a sec," Robbie exclaimed. The group turned to watch as he dashed down the hall.

"What's got into him?" The Major asked.

"No idea," Kelly looked confused.

A moment later Robbie came back holding a bottle and held it out to the Sergeant.

"Good lord!" The Sergeant exclaimed excitedly, "Oban Little Bay! Boy, you've got to be joking! Where did you get this?"

"Scavenging in a liquor store a while back. I almost forgot about it. I was saving it for a special occasion" Robbie said, "and how special is it to get a visit from the Royal Marines?"

"It depends on the purpose of the visit, but in this case I'd say it's pretty bloody special," the Sergeant went on. "Can we really open it?"

"Sure, why not?" Robbie assented.

"Major?" The Sergeant asked.

The Major paused for a moment, considering it, then smiled and nodded, "Just a snort to toast our new friends, yes? I don't suppose there is any harm in that."

Robbie broke out glasses from the China cabinet and everyone but Kelly poured themselves a shot.

"None for the lady?" Clark asked.

"Sorry," Kelly made a face, "whiskey is just too strong for me. Please enjoy yourselves though. Nobody has to drive home, right?"

"True." Clark laughed. "We wouldn't want to risk a drink driving charge."

The Major held up his glass and was soon joined by the others. Each glass held about an inch of amber colored Scotch. "To our gracious hosts," he said and they all took a sip.

"Oh, that's good," the Sergeant said with a rasp. "I think we need to toast Sergeant Patel, and the other good men we have lost."

"Indeed," the Leftenant agreed and they drank again.

After several more toasts, the Major called the drinking to a halt. "Alright lads, that's enough. We have work to do in the morning."

"Right you are," the Leftenant agreed sadly, setting his empty glass down.

"Color Sergeant, have you arranged berthing for us?" the Major asked.

"Yes, Sir," he replied, "right across the hall."

"Robert, Kelly," the Major stood and turned to them, "I think we need to retire for the night. We all need our beauty rest. Thank you so much for having us in your lovely home and sharing your evening with us. It has been a rare pleasure. We will see you again in the morning I trust?"

"Oh I don't know, tomorrow I have a yoga class and I was planning on hitting some of the big sales at the mall," Kelly laughed as they walked the group to the door.

"Sounds as if you have quite the busy day scheduled," the Major smiled, "then we hope to see you soon then."

Everyone said their goodnights in turn and headed down the hall towards their own rooms.

When they were gone, Kelly locked and bolted the door. Wandering through the house, she blew out the candles and glanced outside through the curtains. The night was quiet and the sky was filled with stars. By the time she got back to the bedroom, Robbie was already passed out on top of the sheets.

"You're too young to drink," she scolded his sleeping form before lying down and pulling the sheets up over herself. She fell asleep quickly and drifted into uncharacteristically peaceful dreams.

Chapter 26

The next morning Kelly rose early, left Robbie sleeping in the bed and took care of her morning business before cleaning her face and hands with the water from the bucket they kept on the balcony. Pulling on a sweater, sweat pants and boots, she used a tie to pull her hair back into a pony tail and quietly stepped out into the hallway. The passage was empty and quiet but she noted that the stairwell doors at either end had been propped open. At the far end of the hall, she could see the figure of a Marine standing guard dressed in his helmet, body armor and black assault rifle. He had his back to her and seemed to be looking out the small window.

She wasn't sure why, but she didn't feel like interacting with the guard so she turned and walked the other way.

"Oh!" She exclaimed when she nearly bumped into a young Marine standing inside the stairwell, "I didn't see you there. You scared me."

"Sorry mum," the man apologized. He wore his battle gear like the other guard but she noted he had an Asian look, was thin and not much taller than her. He stepped back on the landing, giving her room to pass, "didn't mean to frighten you."

"It's ok, I should have been watching where I was going. We're not used to having other people up here." She looked at the name tape on his uniform, "Mr… Kim, is it?"

"Corporal Kim, yes mum," he corrected.

"Oh? Corporal, ok." She said as she started up the steps, "I'm just going up to check the garden on the roof."

"Roger that," Corporal Kim nodded as he watched her go.

Kelly liked the roof top in the mornings. It was usually cool and quiet before the sun was all the way up. Even though the people were gone, daytime in the city still seemed much more noisy and active than night with the birds squawking and the creatures banging around down on the street. She enjoyed the short respites of quiet time before the day began. It gave her peace of mind to walk around the garden and plan out her day.

When she stepped out of the stairwell onto the rooftop, the sun was not yet over the horizon but the sky was light enough to reflect a glow from the low hanging clouds. A fog had rolled in from the river overnight, covering the streets downtown in a swirling grey blanket. The roof of the building was at just the right height to sit slightly above the fog and just below the clouds in a layer of thin, wet mist.

But Kelly was not alone with her garden as she had hoped. She saw Major Garrett and Leftenant Windsor at the edge looking out over the city. A few of the other soldiers, not on watch, were also on the roof but further away. Their silhouettes blurry as they moved through the moist air. Some stood alone smoking cigarettes or just staring out towards the river. A few huddled near each other and seemed to be chatting in hushed voices.

"Good morning," she breathed in the cool air as she walked over to the two officers.

"Good morning Kelly," they both said cheerfully turning to greet her.

"It's like a lovely, English morning," the Leftenant waved his hand at the thick fog. "Almost feels like home."

"Did you all sleep well?" Kelly asked.

"Wonderful," Windsor laughed.

"I don't think I have slept so well since I left my own home," the Major added.

Kelly observed that neither the officers, nor the other men on the roof, were wearing their battle gear. They were armed, but had traded their helmets and body armor for dark green berets and, in spite of the cool temperature, had rolled up their sleeves into squared off cuffs around their biceps. On their shoulders each of them wore a "Royal Marines Commando" patch along with a British Union Jack and some sort of black dagger.

"Well if you are up here hoping to catch a glimpse of our famous River Ferry, I'm afraid it hasn't been running lately," Kelly informed them as she looked out towards the river.

"I'm sorry to have missed that." The Major replied. "Actually, the Leftenant and I were just taking the lay of the land."

"It's hard to see anything right now, isn't it?" Kelly squinted down at the blanket of grey covering the streets.

"Indeed," the red bearded Leftenant agreed. "What time does this usually dissipate?"

Kelly held up her empty wrist showing that she had no watch, "I don't know the time but as soon as the sun comes up some more, all this in the streets will burn off."

Windsor looked at his large black and silver wristwatch and then to the Major. "So maybe another half hour then?"

"Most likely," the Major agreed looking at his own watch.

Kelly looked at them quizzically. "How do you still have watches that work?"

"G-Shock, MRG," the Leftenant answered proudly, holding out his wrist to show her a large time piece. It was metallic with a matte black finish. "Tough as nails, water proof and solar powered. You should get one."

"How about you, Major?" Kelly said looking it over.

"Oh, I prefer my old Pathfinder," the Major held up his own watch, its grey plastic looked more worn than the junior officer's though it had a similarly bulky bezel covered in dials and buttons. "Not as flashy as the Leftenant's, but it's been with me around the world and through several war zones. Even before the end."

"Nice," Kelly said, "I'll put one on my Christmas list."

"And where is young master Robert this morning?" The Major inquired with a raised eyebrow as he readjusted the watch band on his arm.

"Still sleeping," she explained, "He was still in high school when this whole thing started. I don't think he's ever had whiskey before. It may be a rough morning for him."

They all laughed.

"Well I suppose everyone has to have a first time," the Leftenant said.

They continued their conversation as the sun slowly rose behind them. The clouds overhead gradually lifted and the fog in the streets seemed to drain back down into the river. When the rays of the sun finally found them, Kelly suddenly felt like a wet cat. The heat and humidity sank down onto them like a heavy syrup. Her hair felt frazzled and the sweater, which had previously felt so cozy, began to feel hot, heavy and damp. She instantly felt self-conscious around all these men as she realized she was not wearing a bra and the wet clingy garment was doing its best to show off all the curves of her breasts.

Kelly crossed her arms over her chest and was about to excuse herself when the Leftenant abruptly pointed at an object in the distance, somewhere down on the street.

"There it is!" He exclaimed.

"Where?!" The Major asked excitedly.

"Will you excuse me, gentlemen," Kelly took their distraction as an opportunity to depart and put on some different clothes.

"Yes, of course," the Major said dismissively as he looked through his binoculars at the street below.

"Just there!" The Leftenant said pointing downward. "Between the blue lorry and the white convertible."

They were so immersed in whatever they had discovered that they hardly noticed as she walked away. Kelly was happy to have escaped without embarrassment but conversely, it nagged at her that they hadn't even seemed to notice her form fitting sweater. She couldn't help thinking, 'is something wrong with me that these guys didn't even notice that my boobs were on display?' She chided herself for even thinking of such things as she quickly made her way back downstairs.

She was in such a rush going down the stairs that she forgot about the young sentry at the next landing and nearly crashed into him again. As she apologized and backed away his eyes went to her chest and lingered. She gasped as she realized that he had definitely noticed her clingy sweater.

"Sorry!" She called as she dashed away both embarrassed, and vindicated.

Robbie was sitting on the edge of the bed when she walked in.

"Good morning, sleepy head," Kelly sing-songed as she began pulling at drawers looking for clothes. "Did you sleep well?"

"Like a rock," Robbie said bleary eyed. "I don't think I've slept through the night like that since the old days."

"No headache?" Kelly nudged.

"No." Robbie replied indignantly. "You think I can't handle my liquor?"

"Rob?!" She said as she changed tops. "Have you ever drank whiskey before?"

"Well, no," he answered, "but it's not like I never had a beer. It's been a while, sure, but I'm no lightweight!"

"Sure, sure," Kelly said acting unconvinced. "Ok, whatever. Your friends are all up on the roof."

"What are they doing?" Robbie asked pulling on a t-shirt.

"Just chilling, I think." She replied. "But, something had that Major, and the big red headed guy all excited. I don't know what.

"Weird," Robbie said, rubbing sleep from his eyes. "They didn't say?"

"It was getting hot, so I came down to change. Why don't you go and find out what they are all fired up about?" Kelly suggested. "I'll boil some water for tea."

"Yea, ok." Robbie agreed, pulling on his boots.

As he started out the door Kelly yelled, "…And they can come down here if they want a cup. I'm not a waitress!"

"You got it," Robbie replied as he walked out.

Kelly lit the coals on the grill, filled the tea pot with water and set it on top of the grate to boil. She was tempted to sit down and enjoy the sunny morning but instead went inside and began setting up cups for tea and coffee. 'I'm becoming my mother,' she thought, as she arranged the cups and saucers neatly on the coffee table. She stepped back and looked at the arrangement and realized it didn't look right.

"Well, mother," she said out loud as she began looking through the kitchen drawers. "See what you have done. It's after the apocalypse and you've got me looking for table settings to serve tea."

A few minutes later she had the coffee table set with napkins, silverware and condiments. She set the ornate box of tea in the center and made sure the French Press and coffee were readied on the kitchen counter. Looking over the display again, she made a few adjustments before deciding her mother would approve. As she made the finishing touches the door opened and Robbie returned with the officers, followed by Mr. Clark.

"Ms. Kelly, I hope we aren't imposing," the Major called out from the foyer, "we heard you might be willing to share some more of your delicious tea."

"Come on in guys," Kelly welcomed them. "Please have a seat and I'll check on the water."

"Very kind of you," the Major said, "can we do anything to help?"

"No, no," she replied. "You boys sit down and I'll bring it in."

Out on the balcony she checked the tea pot which wasn't quite ready. 'What am I doing?' She thought as she waited, 'I should tell these guys to get their own damn tea!'

'You'll do no such thing,' she almost could hear her mother say. 'You mind your manners young lady.'

"Yes, Mother," she smiled looking up at the sky. When the pot whistled, she picked it up and walked inside. "Alright, who's ready?"

As she poured the water for the enthusiastic group she asked, "what were you boys so excited about finding this morning?"

"Ah," the Major began. "Well, yesterday when we ran into that mob of… what did you call them? Undies? I rather like that. When we ran into the undies we had to stash a load of supplies we had with us. We were afraid they might have destroyed the cart but it seems to be intact, and just down the street."

"That's the good news," the Leftenant said with a laugh.

"What's the bad news?" Kelly asked.

"The road is still mobbed with the bloody things," the red bearded officer explained, "all the activity and noise seems to have attracted more of them. So we can't get to it at present."

The Major sighed and leaned forward apologetically, "Kelly, Robbie, I hate to ask as we told you we would be moving on today but would it be too much of an imposition if we stayed a bit longer?"

"It's ok with me," Robbie said, "Kelly?"

"Of course, Major," she agreed. "You can stay as long as you need. Those things can be pretty stubborn sometimes."

"Thank you," the Major said, "We really need those supplies and we can't get to them until the crowd thins out some. With any luck it will only be a few days. And I promise we will help out around the place. We will earn our keep. So, if there are any chores you need done don't hesitate to ask."

"We live pretty simply, with just Robbie and me." Kelly told them, "but now that you mention it we could use a hand turning over the landscaping around the pool so we can plant down there."

"Consider it done," the Major nodded.

"We could also use a hand with the electrical," Robbie said, "do you think Corporal MacGregor would mind looking at the system, to see if we could at least get some of it working? There's a giant water tank on the roof that collects rain. It would be great if we could get the pump working again. It's a shame to have all those solar panels, but not be able to use them."

"Indeed," the Major agreed. "I'll talk to the Color Sergeant and get it scheduled."

Over the next few days, the Marines helped shore up weak points in the building's defenses and pull up the landscaping around the pool to get it ready for planting. One Section pulled drywall and metal studs from the construction areas and used them to cover the large windows in the lobby. The windows were up off the street, but if the undead were to get excited they might pile on top of each other until they could smash though to get inside. Two Section dug out decorative ferns and trees, as well as the tall weeds that had sprung up over the years, from the pool patio.

After some effort, Corporal MacGregor was able to get the batteries for the solar panels connected so that they could turn on the power in a few areas. He disconnected the lines leading to the parts of the building they didn't use or weren't crucial. Even with the power on, Major Garrett forbade any lights be turned on in areas that might be seen from outside. They even assigned several of the Marines to walk through the building in the evening, to make sure nothing was shining from the windows.

"The damned undead are trouble enough," the Major insisted. "We don't need to set up a lighthouse for the hungry living. God knows what that might bring."

In the morning, Robbie showed Corporal MacGregor the water tower's mechanical box on the roof. They found, when it was opened up, that small animals had chewed through the wiring and built a nest in the housing. MacGregor scrunched up his face while he used his knife to dig out scraps of fabric and straw from the crevice.

"Can you fix it?" Robbie asked.

"Ahdonoo," MacGregor said, "Cahnactons lahk ok, but e' naeds a' naew waerang."

Corporal Stewart stood nearby, looking on. Robbie turned to him with a confused look.

"He says you need new wires," Stewart interpreted.

"Can we pull them from somewhere else in the building?" Robbie asked.

"Mebee," MacGregor answered. "Ha ye goot an tahls?"

Stewart snorted in laughter at Robbie's confusion, "Don't worry mate. We don't understand him half the time either. He's bloody indecipherable, that one."

MacGregor growled something at Stewart that Robbie thought must have been an insult.

"Yea, yea," Stewart replied, "at least it's good bitter we're drinking in Manchester, though."

Robbie watched the two banter back and forth with little idea what they were talking about.

Finally, Stewart turned to Robbie. "He says we can probably fix it if we can find the right tools. You got tools?"

"This whole place is a construction site," Robbie answered. "I'm sure we can find some tools. And we can pirate some wiring from something we aren't using. Right?"

"Mebee," MacGregor said wiping his hands on his pants.

A few hours later the pumps were finally working. By turning off the valves to the lower floors they were even able to get enough pressure to run water to the units on the top level. Sergeant Simmons, the medic, advised them not to drink it without boiling but said it should be ok for bathing and flushing toilets.

Chapter 27

That evening as the moon rose, Kelly found herself on the roof admiring the clouds, swirling like waves across the distant horizon. The clouds in the higher altitudes created a misty palette smudging the stars into blurry globes against the deep blue sky. Evening light reflected down on the river, silhouetting the ships and shapes protruding from its surface. In her days as an art student, this would have inspired her to grab her paints and try to capture the image. This evening, she just enjoyed the moment and the fact that it was fleeting.

'Nothing lasts,' she thought, staring into the distance, 'enjoy it while you can.'

"Something out there?" a voice with an English accent broke her melancholy.

"Oh!" She spun, to find Leftenant Windsor striding towards her. She answered. "No. Just admiring the sky. It looks like a painting tonight."

Windsor looked out into the distance where she had been staring and surprised her when he asked, "by whom?"

"Sorry?" She cocked her head uncertainly, not understanding the question.

"Who?" Windsor repeated, then clarified. "Which painter?"

She snickered, "I was thinking VanGogh."

"Oh," Windsor nodded, "VanGogh."

He said the painter's name in a way that, to Kelly's American ear, sounded like spitting with a mouth full of marbles.

"Yes." She laughed, and tried to imitate him, "VangHoph!"

"Ah, you speak Dutch!" Windsor teased.

"Dutch waffles!" Kelly parried.

Windsor leaned on the wall as they both looked out over the night sky.

"Which painting?" The red haired officer finally asked.

"Oh, Starry Night of course," she said, as she swept her arm to indicate everything on the horizon.

"Indeed," Windsor agreed. "The Asylum one, or the one on the Rhone?"

Kelly looked at him curiously. She guessed he was about her age, or maybe a little older. He was tall and fit but had the look of a man who was once, much more muscular. His face was tanned from traveling in the sun, but she could see his skin was naturally pale and sprinkled with amber freckles. Under his curly red beard, his neck was thick. His broad shoulders and muscular chest filled out his dark brown t-shirt while his biceps stretched against the fabric of its short sleeves.

Windsor's waist narrowed into the V of an athlete and, though his military style camouflage pants were loose fitting, she could tell his legs would be equally strong. His pants were bloused neatly into the tops of his brown combat boots.

Kelly expected that with his military training he could probably fight the enemy, hunt animals for food, build a shelter with sticks, and start a fire with rocks. But, she did not expect him to know anything about art.

"The Rhone, I think," Kelly said suspiciously.

"Oh?" Windsor answered, looking at the sky, as if conversing about impressionist painters was all in a day's work. "Before he went barking mad?"

"I think he was ill all along," Kelly replied, "in those days I guess you could check yourself in to an asylum when the voices got to be too much."

"I don't think I'd like being locked up in a nineteenth century asylum much, though," Windsor added.

"Surprising," she said.

"What?" He asked. "You prefer to be locked up?"

"No." Kelly giggled, "I wouldn't have pegged you for an art lover."

"I'm not really," he replied. "I had to take some art history classes at university."

"You had to take them?" She asked.

"Well," he explained with a grin. "My uncle insisted I should take them. He said they would make me more refined and worldly wise. He also said, it was a good way to impress the ladies."

"Did it work?" Kelly laughed.

"You tell me," Windsor replied.

The conversation was interrupted by the sound of footsteps crunching over the gravel roof. They turned and saw Corporal Dupree approaching.

"Pardon, Sir!" Dupree stopped a few feet away, came to attention and saluted the Leftenant.

"As you were, Corporal," Windsor returned the salute and the enlisted man relaxed. "Report."

"Sir," Dupree said. "The Major sends his regards and requests your presence in the squad room."

"Very good," Windsor responded. "Please send my compliments to the Major and let him know I am on my way. Carry on."

Dupree saluted again, then turned and marched away towards the stairwell.

"You will have to excuse me, Kelly," Windsor said, "duty calls."

"Of course," Kelly agreed, and joked. "Next time we can discuss Cubism."

The Leftenant was already making his way towards the stairs but turned and made a face. "Ugh. I hate modern art."

Kelly watched him go, thinking how odd it was to meet someone like Windsor in the middle of the hell they found themselves surviving. It was nice to have a conversation about something other than scavenging for food, how to get the critical supplies they needed or how not to be eaten by the undead. The presence of these Marines made her aware of everything they had been missing in life. She missed having friends and meeting new people. Robbie had been a good and faithful companion, but he wasn't someone she could sit up and talk with all night about whatever was on her mind.

As the Leftenant disappeared through the stairwell door something else caught her attention. She recognized Mr. Clark sitting on the wall near the stair. She hadn't noticed him earlier, and wondered how long he had been there. Clark seemed to be staring at her. It wasn't a malicious or creepy stare. He seemed to be scrutinizing her, sizing her up.

"Good evening, Mr. Clark," Kelly called.

"Good evening, Kelly," Clark replied with a wave. He then stood up and followed Windsor down the stairs.

"This has been a weird night," Kelly said as she watched him vanish into the shadows. Then, thinking back to what Corporal Dupree had said she muttered. "Wait. What squad room? Do we have a squad room?"

Down below, Robbie followed MacGregor and Stewart out onto the pool deck. His arms were sore from working all day while his legs ached from going up and down the stairs. If the two Marines hurt as bad as he did, they did not show it. Neither complained, or displayed any indication that the long day of manual labor had affected them.

MacGregor was tall and lanky with a long face and square jar. His brown hair and beard framed a beak like nose and bright blue eyes. The brown t-shirt he wore was sweat stained and untucked from his camouflage trousers. Dust and dirt clung to his uniform from his crawling around during their work to repair the solar panels and water pump. As soon as they were outside, the Scotsman lit up a cigarette and handed the pack to his squad mate.

Stewart pulled out one of the thin white cylinders and held it in his dark fingers. He was a fireplug of a man, standing average height, with a wide torso and thick legs. His hair was black and his beard curled in waves around his jaw line. He had golden brown eyes and the flat nose and thick lips of many of African descent. He held up the box of cigarettes, offering one to Robbie.

"No thanks," Robbie said.

"Suit yourself." Stewart said, shrugging his shoulders, before stopping to light the cigarette he had perched on his lips. He closed his eyes and took a deep drag. A moment later, he expelled a cloud of smoke and smiled. "That's the ticket."

Robbie looked around and noticed that several other enlisted Marines were already in the courtyard. Up on the wall, a Marine wearing body armor sat, with his rifle in his lap. From that height, Robbie could tell he would have a good view of the streets and warehouses along the river. Stewart waved at the man, who returned the gesture then went back to watching the perimeter. Robbie wondered if these guys ever let their guard down.

Stewart and MacGregor led Robbie over to a steel and glass patio table where two Marines sat, cleaning their rifles. Robbie had been introduced to the two before, but didn't recall their names. Standing nearby he recognized Sergeant Simmons, the medic who had set his finger, trimming his beard with a pair of scissors.

Conversations were hushed. The men were relaxed but seemed aware that their proximity to the street created a need to keep the noise down. In the moonlight, Robbie could see they all wore dark brown t-shirts but each had different designs and slogans. He couldn't read the inscriptions, but most seemed to have some sort of skull or sword emblazoned on them.

Simmons nodded at the trio as they approached, "Aright?"

"Aright, Sergeant," Stewart replied. He pronounced the rank as "Sarnt" and it took Robbie a second to translate what he meant. MacGregor greeted Simmons as well but Robbie had given up on understanding what he said.

The two at the table looked up and smiled.

"Ay-up!" The shorter of the two said, looking up from wiping his barrel with a greasy rag, as if surprised to see them. "Wot's the cat dragged in?"

"No bloody bitter, that's for sure," Stewart answered as he pulled a chair over to the table. He pointed a thumb at Robbie. "You know our boy, Rob?"

"Yea, we met in the car park." He extended his hand. "Cheers. Devin O'Reilly."

"Michael Kim," the other man at the table stood to shake Robbie's hand.

"Robert Bruce," Robbie said shaking their hands as he introduced himself again.

"Es he nam tru, Robert Bruce?!" MacGregor exclaimed with surprise.

"Yes…" Robbie answered, unsurely.

"Oy!" MacGregor cracked a huge smile and suddenly swept Robbie into a headlock. "Ya' dinna tael mae yaer a Bruce!" Ferociously grinding Robbie's hair with his fist, he declared. "Yaer aright w me, Laddie."

The Scotsman released Robbie, who scampered back, unsure how to react. The other men laughed while Robbie rubbed his sore head.

"Looks like you've made a friend," Simmons laughed.

"Why is everyone making such a big deal about my name?" Robbie asked. "The Major and the Leftenant said something about it too."

254

"Do ye nae noo yer Scots heestry, lad?!" MacGregor said surprised.

"I was in the tenth grade when this all started," Robbie answered. "We didn't even get through American history."

"Oae yer namesek were Robert ta Bruce," MacGregor said, "Ahnly wun o' the greetest fraedom feaghters ehn Scots heestry."

"Ok," Robbie nodded thinking he might have understood the Scotsman's brogue. "Some sort of Scottish hero?"

"Aye!" MacGregor nodded vigorously. "The greetest after Wallace. Ye've seen Braveheart?"

"Braveheart?" Robbie asked. "What's that?"

"Ahnly the greetest muvie there ever wuz, aboot the Scots!" MacGregor went on.

"Only, it's shite history," Simmons injected. "And, the English win in the end. Sorry to ruin it for you, mate."

"Oh aye!" MacGregor laughed, "boot ets stahl a greet fahlm. Stack w mae Robbie. Ahl learn ya all aboot the Scots."

"Now you're in for it," Kim said sitting back down. "He's going to follow you home."

"Aye," O'Reilly added, "and, he's not proper house broken."

"Oh, ahm fookin' haws broke enof fer yer mahthers, ye bastards." MacGregor spat back at them, as he pulled up a chair to the table.

"Come on over, Robbie," O'Reilly invited. "Move over Michael. Make some room for the new boy."

Kim slid around the table and indicated for Robbie to join them in the open space. Robbie grabbed a chair and hesitantly moved it in between Kim and the Scotsman. MacGregor looked as if he had already forgotten grabbing the younger man and had started a separate conversation with O'Reilly. Robbie sat down and tried to follow for a few seconds, but quickly gave up.

"Don't mind him," Kim said. "He's a bit uncivilized, but he's good to have in a fight."

"I can tell," Robbie laughed rubbing his head. "If you plan to noogie the enemy to death."

"Ha!" Kim replied as he reorganized his rifle parts. "We send him out to talk to them. Bastards get so confused, they usually just give up."

The evening was overcast and most of their light came from the reflection of the little moonlight that made it to the white concrete surrounding the pool. Robbie was amazed that even in the low visibility, Kim and O'Reilly seemed to have no trouble with the collection of small pieces they had laid out on the table. Their hands seemed to work on their own as they twisted and clicked parts into place. Each carried on conversations and reassembled their rifles almost without looking.

He now recognized O'Reilly as the small man who had scampered down the utility tunnel when the Marines first arrived. He remembered the jet black hair, thick beard and sleeve tattoos.

Kim was trim and wiry but slightly taller, even sitting, than O'Reilly. His accent was English but his face and eyes indicated an Asian descent. His hair was black and, like most of the others, he had facial hair. He kept his beard trimmed back so it didn't hang far over his collar. Kim's beard, reminded Robbie of his own. He had very fine hair that didn't fully fill out the space around his chin and lips.

"Why do all you guys have beards except Major Garret, and that guy... Clark?" Robbie asked.

Simmons, who was finishing up his trim, looked over and said jokingly, "beards are manly, don't you know? Besides, none of us are as brave with a straight razor as those two."

"Oh," Robbie said.

"Not cutting my throat for vanity," Stewart injected.

"Baerds keep oos wahrm en a waenter as wael," MacGregor answered. "Ahnd the lasses lohve a bit o scruff."

"What do you know about lasses," Kim needled. "You're still a virgin."

"Oy," MacGregor countered, "Ah knew mahr abut lasses than ye wael en er hale laf!"

Kelly returned to the apartment and was glad to find that Robbie had not come yet in from his work with the soldiers. She sat on the bed in the master bedroom and placed her hand over the hard spot forming in her belly. The earlier melancholy fell back over her as she sat quietly in the shadows. The room was dark except for a little moonlight creeping through a long, narrow gap in the curtain over the window.

Tears welled up in her eyes as she thought about bringing a baby into this crazy, evil world. She didn't have any idea what to do with a baby and knew Robbie would be even more clueless. The thought of aborting it crossed her mind but she realized she didn't know how to do that either. She had read stories of women throwing themselves downstairs or drinking poison concoctions, but doing that was just as likely to lead to her own death, or worse, to some sort of debilitating injury.

They had only survived this long because they were able outpace the damned undead. Even their ability to do that at their physical peak was questionable at times. A broken hip or a burned out stomach would make that a lot harder, but a baby would make it impossible. A crying, screaming little life, in need of constant care and feeding. It would be totally helpless and dependent on them for years and years. Kelly sobbed, unable to imagine how they could do it.

At the same time, something inside her strongly rejected the thought of not having the child, even if it was the sire of the most vile human she had ever encountered. Part of her, she assumed the primal lizard brain instinct to procreate, screamed in her brain when she considered terminating her pregnancy. It also pulled at her emotions. When she even thought of ending it, her heart sank and she felt like she couldn't breathe.

Tears ran down her cheeks. She wondered if she could even survive child birth. From her college history classes she knew that many women died giving birth, in the days before modern medicine. She didn't have a doctor, didn't have a mid-wife, and didn't even have a book to tell them what to do when the time came. Even if there were no complications in the birth, she was afraid she was very likely to bleed to death afterward.

'I'm going to die,' she thought. 'This baby is going to kill me, even if it gets born alive. That's just the reality. I need to accept it.'

She began to consider what she wanted to do, to prepare for her own death and hopefully, the live birth of her child. Robbie would take care of it, she knew. The best he could anyway. Which, she knew, would not be good enough. He might be able to get help from the Baldwins. She would have to talk to them.

'There is one more thing I can do before I'm too far along,' she told herself as she wiped the tears away, 'I need to do something good. One last big thing.'

She had an idea of what she could do. These Marines needed to get home. She had thought of something that might work. If only the others would go along with it.

Chapter 28

In the morning, the small group of leaders convened in Robbie and Kelly's living room. The two officers and Mr. Clark sat on the couches, drinking tea and discussing plans for the day.

"I think we'll need to make a supply run to get more tea soon," Kelly observed as she rifled through their dwindling selection.

"Yes," Clark said with a regretful look. "I'm afraid we've made quite a dent in your coffee supply as well."

"As soon as the crowd outside moves on," the Leftenant offered, "we will figure out a way to refill your supply."

"Are there any market's nearby?" Clark asked. "Where we might find such things?"

"There's a Publix about two miles up Central Boulevard," Robbie offered. "The gates were still down last time we went by there. I bet they still have a good selection. If the rats haven't eaten through all the boxes by now."

"What is a Publix?" The Leftenant inquired.

"It was a supermarket," Robbie answered. "You know. Groceries and stuff."

"Like a Sainbury's," Clark explained.

"Ah." Windsor nodded.

"Yes, well that all depends on whether there is a reliable path between here and there," the Major said.

"What about this mob of undies?" Kelly asked. "They don't look like they are going anywhere anytime soon."

"It's a pickle, that's for sure," the Major said. "I've been thinking about it and I'm beginning to think we may need to create another diversion, not unlike your own efforts last week, but leading the things away from here altogether."

"How?" Asked Robbie.

"Quite simple really," the Major said, "dangerous, but simple. We send a small team out to make as much noise as possible and lead the things away. When they are sufficiently distant, the team doubles back and meets us here, or wherever."

"What do you mean, wherever?" Robbie asked.

"As much as I hate to say it, we can't stay here," the Major explained. "We must continue on until we find an airplane, or maybe a ship, that can get us back to England."

"Why is it you are so set on going back?" Kelly asked. "I mean, England is probably as bad off as the States and there's more room over here."

"True," the Major agreed. "But, its home and our last orders were to get back there. Also, there are some bunkers up in Scotland that we think the Government, and whatever remains of the military, is likely to have fallen back there. They built them back during the cold war in case the Reds decided to start dropping bombs. Nobody expected this of course, but it's a place to start. Even if there is no one at the bunkers they are full of supplies we can use while we plan out our next move."

"Somewhere, there has got to be an airfield that isn't overrun with the dead, or burned to the ground," Clark said.

"I've been thinking about that," Kelly offered, "and I don't know for sure, but I might know of a place you could look."

"Oh?" the Major said with interest.

"I had a friend in high school whose uncle was in this group that restored old military surplus," Kelly recollected. "They would get old uniforms and jeeps and tanks and restore them and drive in parades and display them on the Fourth of July. Stuff like that."

"And?" Clark asked.

"Well part of the group, I thought they must be rich weirdos, was also into airplanes," Kelly replied.

"Oh?" The Leftenant leaned forward, with interest.

"They had this big compound down by Mullet Run, out in the middle of nowhere, where they kept all this stuff. My friend's uncle took us out there a few times and let us run around. It was like at a big museum," she continued, "I think it may have been an old Army base or something. They kept a bunch of old planes in these big hangers on a little airfield."

"The planes? Were they static or could they fly?" Clark inquired

"They flew them," she said. "Not all of them, but some. They took them to air shows. My friend hated it but they would drag her along sometimes."

"Do you recall what kind of planes?" Clark asked. "Were they small, fighter planes or big like bombers?"

"Both," Kelly answered. "They had a couple of really big ones they only took out for special occasions, but, I remember them saying that a couple of them could fly anywhere in the world."

"How far is this Mullet Run?" the Major asked.
 Kelly and Robbie looked at one another.

"It was about two hours in car, I'd say," Kelly guessed and Robbie nodded in agreement. "On foot, I don't know."

"The regional airport is closer," Robbie offered with a shrug. "Just on the other side of the interstate. Maybe 20 miles?"

"Is that Gulf Regional?" Clark asked looking down into his coffee cup.

"Yes," Robbie replied, "It was the main airport for the state capital."

"Yes, thank you but we can strike that one off the list," the Leftenant said.

"Why?" Robbie asked. "It's technically an international airport so there might be some big planes there."

"We went through there on our way here." The Major offered sadly. "Lost some good men."

"Palin and Cleese," the Leftenant added the men's names with a sunken face. "Damn place is crawling with the undead,"

"And, as I recall there is something very large blocking the main runway." Clark reminded them, "Not sure what type of plane it was but it crashed and burned all over the runway."

"Oh, sorry," Robbie said and looked at Kelly again. "The next closest one I can think of is that Air Force base down on the coast. What was it called?"

"Boynton?" Kelly asked.

"Yea, that's it!" Robbie confirmed.

"I read that was damaged during that big hurricane a few years before the fall," Kelly offered. "They moved all the squadrons up north while they did repairs. There was a big fight in Congress over the funding to rebuild it so it was never completed."

"What about that Naval Air Station further down the coast?" Robbie suggested. "My Scout troop did a camp out there for an air show. We saw the Blue Angles."

"Yes, but it's much further away." Kelly agreed. "And, it was right on the water. There's no way to know what the weather has done to the place over the years."

"Salt air is bad for planes," Clark offered.

"It might be worth looking into," the Major said, "but, I think this… surplus museum might be worth investigating first. At least, to check it off the list."

"Can you tell us how to get there," Clark said to Kelly, "draw us map perhaps?"

Kelly thought for a second. "Maybe? I'll try, but to be honest I've always been terrible with directions. That's why I didn't mention it before. Robbie was the Boy Scout. He's like a human GPS."

261

"Do you know how to get there Rob?" the Leftenant asked.

"I know how to get to Mullet Run," Robbie said, "but I've never been to this museum, so I wouldn't know how to get you there. Especially if it's out in the sticks."

"Hmmm." The Major leaned back thinking, "Well, we still have some time to consider it. Maybe it will come to you, eh, Kelly?"

"I've been thinking about this," she said. "I think we should go with you. We could be your guides."

"We couldn't ask you to do that," the Major said dismissively, "it's much too perilous."

"We can handle some peril, Major," Kelly said, promoting the idea.

"We haven't been up in this ivory tower so long that we've forgotten how to survive outside. Besides, we know the area and you don't. On your own, you all could end up wandering around forever looking for this thing. If we go with you we can take you straight to it. Right Rob?"

"Um, sure," Robbie agreed with a raised eyebrow. He liked these Marines, and did want to help, but he hadn't considered leading them out into the forest that had grown up around the city. It would be a feat, he knew, just getting through the city alive. Beyond that, it was like a thick jungle. He imagined it would be difficult, even without the possibility of encountering packs of wandering undies.

"And," Kelly continued before Robbie could raise any concerns. "I really think this might be what you are looking for."

"But, you said you were bad with directions," Clark protested, "it won't be much help if you can't find your way."

"Ok, I'm terrible with maps and stuff," Kelly replied.

"And don't ask her which way is north or south," Robbie rolled his eyes.

"But…" She continued with a glare at Robbie, "I can find my way around on the ground. I know landmarks and how to find things. If Robbie can get us to Mullet Run, then I'm sure I can find the old air field from there!"

"Look," the Major said, "I know you are capable of surviving out there. You've both proven as much, by living this long, but you are also quite aware that, every time you go outside there is a risk. No matter who you are. We've lost a considerable number of good, brave, trained soldiers over these years. You've been very kind, and you're mostly safe up here. I'm quite hesitant to let you to go out and put yourselves in danger on our behalf."

"You're not asking," Kelly insisted. "We are offering, insisting in fact, that you let us take you there."

The Major nodded but didn't seem convinced. He sighed and said "we appreciate the offer and will take it under advisement. At any rate, it doesn't seem that our friends outside are going to let us leave immediately so we have some time to consider it, as well as other options."

"It's settled then," Kelly smiled and held up the tea pot. "We will be your guides. Now, who wants more tea?"

The days were still hot and humid, but summer seemed to be easing as the nights became cooler and longer. Slowly chewing at the manmade things along its banks the sparkling river continued flowing to the sea. Days passed and the throngs of the putrid undead things remained crowded in the streets downtown. The group in the condominium could only watch quietly from the rooftop as the shadows of the city turned in slow circles like a giant sundial.

The Marines kept busy with cleaning their weapons and other chores thought up by the Color Sergeant. Robbie found that they had hung sheets over the gates and started doing exercises and runs through the garage. He was nearly knocked over one morning as a pair of the leathernecks raced each other down the stairwell wearing their back packs as extra weight. Robbie was only a little younger than most of the men and admired their camaraderie and competitive nature. As he watched the racers rattling down the steps, he regretted that he would never have a chance to join or serve in the military.

That afternoon, they held a funeral for Sergeant Patel. The Marines had returned to the small utility room and found that the undead had never broken inside. They recovered Patel's body and buried him in the small garden behind the pool near where they had buried the realtors. There were no tears but Robbie could tell that these stoic and hardened men were deeply moved by their comrade's death.

"Thank you for letting us bury him here," Sergeant Simmons said to Robbie and Kelly afterward. "He would have liked this spot. You couldn't get him away from the hotel pool when we were in Bahrain."

Chapter 29

Later that night, almost everyone made their way to the roof to escape the stuffy interior of the building and to take advantage of the cooler weather outside. A solemn mood had carried over from the funeral and most of the soldiers sat and relaxed quietly. At the far side, Robbie noticed someone had brought up a folding table and some chairs. Several Marines played cards by the light of a small candle.

"You're up late," the Color Sergeant greeted Robbie and Kelly as he joined them near the edge overlooking downtown.

"It's too nice out here to stay inside," Kelly replied.

"You're right about that," the big Sergeant replied looking around to admire the cool clear night. "I passed the officers on the way up. They should be joining us in a few…oh, here they are…"

Major Garrett, LT. Windsor and Mr. Clark walked out onto the deck and after greeting some of the men close by wandered over to the ledge.

"Evening Sir," the Sergeant saluted the Major and recognized the junior officer. "Leftenant."

The Major returned the salute and the Sergeant relaxed his stance.

"It looks like the carnival will go on for another night," Garrett observed looking down at the grey human figures far below.

"Indeed, Sir." The Sergeant agreed. "Pity they don't sleep."

"Perhaps if we played some pastoral music we might lull them into napping," Clark offered in a dry deadpan.

"You might be onto something there, Phillip," the Leftenant laughed. "I could never keep my eyes open through Beethoven's 6th."

"It is almost midnight." The Major said. "Surely they must be tired of tromping around down there. Does anyone have an iPod? A little Brahms might just do the trick."

Everyone jumped when, in the distance, there suddenly began a loud thumping sound. The noise quickly came together into the notes of heavy bass and drums being played over speakers. A moment later the sound of a familiar squealing guitar riffed in.

"Doesn't sound much like Brahms," Clark observed, as they all looked out into the dark for the source of the rhythmic pounding.

"It's Motorhead I think," the Major suggested.

"Who?" Robbie asked, but was cut off.

"Marines!" The Color Sergeant shouted with such volume that Robbie and Kelly jumped again. The big Sergeant began giving hand signals and commands to the men scattered around the rooftop. "One section cover our 6! Two Section on me! O'Reilly and MacGregor take the flanks!"

Men scrambled into position behind the low walls lining the roof. The Sergeant watched them as if to ensure that they all ended up in the right places. When he seemed satisfied, he turned back to his small group. "We should get down, Sir," he suggested to the Major.

"Quite right," the Major agreed as he took a knee while keeping his focus on the lights and music in the distance.

Kelly felt the Leftenant's hand on her shoulder while the Sergeant did the same with Robbie. They pressed down gently but insistently until they were all kneeling behind the wall. Clark shuffled over for a better view from their lower vantage point.

"Why are we hiding?" Robbie protested, "They can't see us up here."

"High points and ridge lines can been seen from long distances." The Sergeant explained. "Your profile can be silhouetted against the sky. Makes you an easy target and reveals your position. That is, if they don't already know we are here."

"It's probably just some crazies who've had too much hooch," Robbie argued.

"Perhaps," the Sergeant nodded, "or it's a distraction to get our attention while they sneak up on us from a different direction."

"Oh," Robbie furrowed his eyebrows, "I hadn't thought of that."

"Whatever their intent," Clark said. "The undies are definitely interested in what they are selling."

"Yes, the dead are streaming towards the noise," the Major agreed. "If they keep it up, it could clear out the streets down there."

"If that happens, we could collect our supplies and make off. It would certainly solve our problem for us," the Leftenant observed.

"Or, create more problems, Sir," the Sergeant warned. "The question is why play 'pied piper' with the dead, unless there is something around here that they want? Clear them out and that's one less problem."

"99 problems but the dead ain't one," Kelly sing songed.

"Precisely," the Sergeant said with a wink at Kelly, "but what is it they want? What is down here that they might be coming for? There are no boats in the harbor, the buildings are mostly banks and insurance companies, so hardly worth the risk. What could they be coming for?"

"Like you said, the area hasn't got much to offer if you think about it," Kelly agreed. "I mean, we are the only thing down here, so why…?"

The Sergeant raised his eyebrows and nodded, encouraging her train of thought.

"Why would they come after us?" Kelly said frustrated.

"If they have been watching you," the Sergeant explained, "they may have decided you might have supplies they want. Or they may have seen the solar panels up here and decided they want them. Lots of reasons for desperate people to do desperate things."

"Or they could just be crazies out on a zombie hunt," Robbie suggested.

"Let's hope that's the case," the Sergeant agreed. "If that is the scenario, then the Leftenant's correct and we may be able to waltz out of here tomorrow. But, rather be safe than sorry, eh?"

A growl of engines and gunfire in the distance got their attention. They all squinted over the wall but the source of whatever was causing the racket was too far away and behind the rows of tall buildings.

"Sounds like the music is getting further away now," Clark reported. "The engines too."

"Definitely leading them away," the Major said. "Look down there, the street is almost clear."

Robbie and Kelly looked over the edge, and even in the moonlight, they could tell that the crowded mass had begun to shrink. Like a tide being pulled back out to sea, the undead were spilling out of downtown. They lurched through the large four lane avenue just a few blocks away, along the same route Kelly had taken on her recent zombie run.

"Major," the Sergeant said, "I would expect them to hit when the numbers get low enough to get a team through. I don't see anyone on the nearby rooftops but we should keep our heads down until we are sure. There could be snipers."

"Indeed," the Major concurred. "Everyone stay down, if you please. Color Sergeant, stand ready to repel any boarders."

"We're ready, Sir," the Sergeant replied, "I'll just check on the men."

The Sergeant scuttled away in a crab crawl towards the Marines posted along the sides of the building. Robbie watched him drop down beside the closest man and leaned in to speak. After a few seconds, the man nodded his understanding. The Sergeant rose up and continued his low run, hurriedly moving to the next position.

Robbie looked up at the sky and strained to determine the direction the music was moving. All he could tell was that it was getting further away. The volume gradually faded until it abruptly stopped, as if someone turned it off. The night grew slowly quiet again, except for the scuffling echoes of the undead lurching out of the city, like hung-over concertgoers departing a week-long pop festival.

The group waited and the minutes ticked by. The Color Sergeant kept in touch with the sentries through hand signals. Each time they responded it was in the negative. Shrugged shoulders indicated nothing out of the ordinary, no threats sighted.

"Curiouser and curiouser," the Major said quietly as he watched the men report to the Sergeant.

"How long do we wait?" Asked Robbie.

"If they are going to make a move," the Major said, "it should be soon. Otherwise, they lose any advantage from the distraction."

"Perhaps they bit off more than they could chew, "the Leftenant offered. "There were a lot of those things down there. They might have run into trouble or just been dissuaded when they saw the numbers."

"Possibly," the Major considered it.

The awkward silence stretched out as they hunkered down and waited in the cooling evening. The moon was bright, but the sky was filled with dark swirling clouds running across its glowing face. Streets were cloaked on one side, while bluish light lit up the other, and then it would shift. The clouds filtered the light like a giant kaleidoscope. The sentries watched the ground and surrounding buildings closely, while the night played tricks on them with shadows down in the streets.

They all looked up when they heard the sound of engines in the distance. It was coming from a different direction than the music had been. At first they couldn't tell where, from the echo bouncing off the canyon of downtown buildings. But as it grew closer they all began to stare north, down the main road that ran in front of the condo.

"Only a few miles out," the Sergeant reported as he listened. "Several vehicles. Seems like they may have given up on the element of surprise."

"They may be trying to frighten us," the Major suggested. "Hoping we will give up without a fight."

"They may not know you are here," Kelly said. "If they were watching before you arrived, they may think it's still just Robbie and I in here."

"Yea," Robbie agreed. "Who would want to take on a group of armed Marines? They'd have to really be crazy."

"Crazy, yes," the Sergeant replied, "or maybe they have the numbers and don't mind losing a few. We've had a few run in's with marauders who thought they could take our kit."

"Oh?" Robbie said.

"Didn't turn out well for them," the Sergeant smiled.

"Well, whatever they are up to," the Major added, "with any luck, they won't figure out that most of our ammunition is down there in the street."

"At the speed they are moving, we should know their intent very soon," the Sergeant replied.

They all stared down the wide road below them waiting for the cars to come flashing through the spots of moonlight. The sound of engines roared nearer and nearer but then abruptly stopped with squealing tires, still out of sight. They began to hear the echoes of shouts and voices in the distance. The sounds bounced around, and found the group more puzzled than before.

"What are they playing at?" Clark asked out loud.

A barrage of distant gunshots, and more shouting followed.

"Watch your lanes!" Bradley shouted loudly the sentries. Then turned back to the officers and said more softly. "If it's a distraction, it's a bad one."

The gunshots in the distance were not suppressed like the Marine's weapons, they were loud. The bang and pop of each round could be heard, often followed by the crack and zing of a bullet striking something solid and ricocheting away.

"Not military," the Sergeant observed. "Hunting rifles and handguns."

"I think they may have the wrong address," the Major said.

A loud boom echoed through the night.

"Shotgun," the Sergeant noted.

"The Baldwins!" Kelly and Robbie said in alarm almost in unison.

Chapter 30

"They are hitting the Baldwin sisters!" Kelly said frantically. "In the warehouse district. We have to help them!"

"The Baldwin sisters?" Sergeant Bradley asked confused. "Who the hell is that?!"

"The two old ladies with the greenhouse?" The Leftenant asked.

"Yes, it's only about a mile from here," Kelly continued. "They have several warehouses full of fresh food."

The shotgun fired again, and again. Each time a cacophony of small arms fire and shouting responded.

"We can't let them do this!" Kelly insisted.

"I'm not sure there is anything we can do," the Major apologized.

"Look, the dead have cleared out and it's a straight shot to their place," Kelly pleaded. "With your help we could save them. I know it."

"Look Kelly," the Major responded, "I'm sorry, but we have no idea how many there are, how well armed they are or even where they are. We can't just go running into a firefight like that. We aren't superheroes."

"It's two little old ladies doing the best they can to survive," Kelly argued, "and they are probably the only good people left in this town. Maybe the whole 'fricken state. I don't know how many of those guys there are but they won't be able to fight them off on their own. We have to save them!"

"I'm sorry, Kelly," Garrett said earnestly, "it's too dangerous. If they hold out tonight, we might be able to get to them in the morning."

"It will be too late by then," Kelly blurted, "you know that! You wouldn't make your grandmother fight bad guys until morning, would you?"

"Kelly…" the Major began.

"Fuck this!" Kelly stood up angrily. She felt a hot rush of anger course through her. "C'mon Robbie we are going to help them."

She began stomping towards the stairwell. Robbie scrambled up and followed close behind with a pleading backwards glance at the Marines. As she was about to enter the doorway the Leftenant stopped her.

"Wait!" the red bearded officer shouted to her. "We're coming with you!"

"Sir!?" Clark protested. "That really is unwise. We have no idea…"

"I don't care, Phillip," the Leftenant retorted. "If we can't do some good now and again, then what's the point, really."

"We can't save everyone, Sir." Clark argued.

"No," Windsor replied firmly. "But we might be able to save those two old ladies."

"Leftenant, you know what's at risk," the Major argued. "We need to get back to England. What's left of us… and especially you!"

"I know that, John," the Leftenant replied sternly as he stood, "and so we shall. But tonight, we will fend off some raiders, stop the murder of some pensioners and save their bloody garden."

The Major looked surprised that the junior officer was standing up to him and had used his first name. In the old world, both would be considered severe breaches of protocol, but the old world was gone. No Prime Minister in London made any laws, no Generals at the Ministry of Defense issued any orders, and no pay clerks in Argyle issued any checks to the men. Holding onto their ranks and the military structure this long had been done by sheer force of will. He was well aware that once they ended their quest, back in England, the remaining Marines would likely abandon their posts and strike out on their own to find family and friends. He had hoped things would hold together longer, at least until they got back.

"Very well," the Major finally conceded with a sigh.

"Major!?" Clark protested. "Do you think that wise?"

"Yes, Mr. Clark," the Major said. "The Leftenant is right. We need to do some good now and again, or our souls will rot. And that will be a fate worse than death, I should think."

"But…" Clark argued. "You know what's at stake."

Worse Than Dead

"Indeed, I do," the Major answered then turned to the red-haired officer. "Leftenant, I should have been mentoring you more on leadership. Giving you more on the job training as it were. Now is your chance. You take charge on this one. Yes?"

"Aye, Sir!" Windsor saluted the Major, then turned. "Sergeant! Rally the men and follow me."

Bradley looked, wide eyed with surprise, at Garrett. The Major nodded his approval.

"Very good, Sir!" The Sergeant turned to the men huddled around the rooftop and shouted, "Marines! Get kitted up and muster in the lobby in 5!"

The men looked at each other confused.

"Right!" Bradley shouted. "Move it you bastards! We're going to save some damsels in distress! You want to live forever?!"

The Sergeant's commanding voice sent them scrambling towards the stairwells.

Kelly and Robbie reached the first floor just ahead of the Marines who burst out of the stairwell in full battle rattle. The berets and rolled up sleeves had been replaced with helmets, body armor and bandoliers with pockets of ammunition. The officers emerged to stand with them, followed by Mr. Clark armed with his pistol.

"Right," the Leftenant said stepping in front of the Marines. "We're going on a rescue mission to save someone's 'nan. We don't know how well this group are led but given our previous encounters with these sorts we're working with the theory that they are well armed but have minimal tactical knowledge. Our best estimate is its a few dozen civilians armed with hunting rifles and pistols. Any questions?"

"Just hardly seems fair, dunnit?" O'Reilly said, "Only a few dozen of them against a squad of Royal Marines. Am I right Marines?!"

"Hoorah!" The group chanted back a war cry they had picked up while on joint exercises with US Marines. Their American counterparts had used the term as a response to just about any question, or interaction. It meant everything, and nothing, but conveyed an aggressive intensity of spirit. The Commandos normally only used it among themselves when making fun of the Yanks. This evening it just burst out of them at the thought of getting to do something other than running and hiding.

"Good," the Leftenant said, "everyone ready?"

"Always ready!" The Color Sergeant led the cheer which was repeated by the men.

"Ok," the red-haired officer continued, "it's about three kilometers from here and we are going to have to move quickly. Kelly and Robbie are going to show us the way, so we stay with them until we get to the fight. Then we break off into our teams to aggress the enemy. Any questions?"

"No, Sir!" They all yelled back.

"Off we go then," the Leftenant turned to Kelly and waived his hand for her to lead the way, "ladies first."

Kelly and Robbie took the group out through a maintenance door leading onto a balcony overlooking the main street. This side of the building was in shadow, but they could see none of the undead milling around below. They all easily slipped over the edge and onto the ground. As each Marine dropped, he turned to assist the next man down.

The group in front knelt in the shadows until everyone was ready. From street level, the sounds of gunfire and shouting were more muted but could still be heard in the distance. The bangs and pops of the marauders' guns were occasionally broken up by the loud boom of the shot gun.

"Move out," the Leftenant ordered in a low voice designed not to carry in the street, "at the double."

A few blocks into their trip, the Leftenant signaled them to a halt near a blue van with the logo of a local dry cleaners printed on the side. The Marines instinctively spread out into defensive positions behind cars and concrete barricades on the sidewalks. Robbie stuck close as the officer approached and inspected what looked like a rickshaw cart with a large blue tarp strapped over it. The Englishman quickly disconnected a tangle of bungee cords and pulled back the tarp. Underneath were stacks of black plastic crates.

"Colors," the officer rasped, snapping his fingers to get the attention of the big Sergeant kneeling in the middle of the street.

"Sir?" The Sergeant said as he approached.

"Load the men up on ammo," the Leftenant instructed. "Then strap this tarp back down on the cart. We'll pick it up on the way back."

"Aye," the Sergeant wheeled and using mostly hand signals quickly had an assembly line handing out rectangular black cartridges to the soldiers. When their pockets were full, they tied the tarp back down and he signaled the officers that they were ready.

The Leftenant nodded his acknowledgement and low whispered, "right, let's move."

The Marines spread out into their swiftly moving column again. Kelly was surprised at how briskly the troops moved, even under the weight of all their gear. She and Robbie lead the way down the main street along the same route they had taken when coming to the condo just a few weeks before. While it looked like all the undead had left the area, they stayed in the middle of the road and gave derelict cars a wide berth just in case.

Several blocks into the march, they encountered a pitiful creature who looked as if most of its body had been crushed into the asphalt by the crowds pressing, until so recently, through the streets. It flailed at them with one shredded grey arm and tried to moan but the only sound it could make was the clicking together of its few remaining teeth. One of the Marines slowed to slide his knife through its pasty head and quickly moved on.

Crossing under the River Bridge, they left the tall buildings of downtown and began passing the squat silhouettes of industrial shops and warehouses. Here, the brick and stonework of an older more industrial age replaced the modern glass and concrete of the business district. The Leftenant signaled the men to split up onto either side of the road as they approached a rise. Shots and shouting could be heard from just beyond the hill, so they slowed their pace to approach with caution.

Garrett caught Kelly's arm and signaled to Robbie that they should let the soldiers go out in front. Although they had moved quickly, it had been nearly 30 minutes since the attack started. Kelly wanted to rush into the fray, but she held back at the Major's urging. They knelt a dozen or so yards from where the street went over the rise and watched the Marines inch up to its crest. Their crawling figures pushed ahead with only the occasional sound of a boot pushing against loose pavement or uniform fabric sliding over the abandoned roadway.

Out of habit, Kelly began scanning the sidewalks and store fronts around them for threats. The oily odor of wet asphalt and molding piles of debris hung thick in the hot night air causing her to wrinkle her nose. She hadn't been down on the street recently and was reminded how much it sometimes looked and smelled like a garbage dump. Covering her mouth with her sleeve she tried to breath without inhaling too much of the foul-smelling mist. The decaying city itself was such an affront to the senses that it could almost be a distraction from the other, deadlier, things lurking in its dark corners. Almost.

Movement in the shadows caught Kelly's attention. A beat later, two creatures lumbered from a nearby alleyway like a couple of drunks casually stumbling between bars. In the slivers of moonlight, she could see gruesome torn flaps of skin that seemed just barely attached to their pale skulls. Their work clothing hung shredded and loose on their emaciated frames. The things came to a staggering halt as they emerged onto the sidewalk as if deciding the next stop in their pub crawl. Another loud boom over the ridge caught their attention and they set out towards the noise with renewed eagerness.

Kelly watched them for another second before she realized that in a few more steps the creatures would emerge from behind the row of cars and notice the living soldiers sprawled out on the little hill ahead of them. She nudged the Major and pointed out tops of their pale heads as they lurched up the sidewalk. The officer nodded, and in a low whistle got the attention of Corporals Kim and Stewart who were hunkered low on that side of street. He pointed, held up two fingers and signaled them to end the things.

The sound of two bodies collapsing to the ground caused the Color Sergeant to look back over his shoulder. He was about to rebuke someone for making the noise when he spotted the undead sprawled on the sidewalk and the two Corporals sliding back into position on the street. He gave a quick scan for more threats behind them and seeing none, he signaled for the rest of the squad to come forward.

Kelly and Robbie stayed low with the others and lay down at the peak of the hill. Just over the ridge to their left, a high chain link fence topped with barbed wire ran in front of rows of warehouses. Several bore the Baldwin Produce logo in faded and flaking paint. At the bottom of the short hill was a wide driveway where the gate looked as if it had been forced open. Even in the dark, they could make out two pickup trucks blocking the driveway, one in the entrance and one just inside the fence.

The Sergeant set down his binoculars and whispered to the Leftenant, "four men I can see. One in each cab and one in the back."

"Any roving?" Windsor asked.

"I don't see any other movement," Bradley responded. "The rest are probably inside. These guys look like a rear lookout, in case the dead come back. They aren't being very vigilant, so it doesn't look like they expect any living company."

"Kelly, Robbie." The Leftenant whispered. "Is there another way in?"

"Yes," Robbie answered. "See the alley over there? We can cut down that way and come in from behind. There's a gap in the fence back by the river."

"Right," Windsor said. "Major, would you, Colors, and Sergeant Simmons secure that gate? Then move in towards the main group. I'll take Two Section and come in from the behind."

The Major nodded his agreement as he continued looking towards the front gate.

"Stewart, Dupree," the Leftenant went on. "You take up a position here. Get into some cover. Watch our backs, yes? It won't be long before all this noise brings our friends back."

"Will do Sir," Corporal Dupree tapped Stewart and pointed towards a rusting flatbed tow truck sitting up on the curb. Its rubber tires had rotted away so that it sunk down onto its rusting rims. Even low as it was, the bed was still high enough to provide a good view up and down the street. The two scrambled up and eased into the shadows until their silhouettes blended in with the other trash and garbage scattered over throughout the area.

"You two should stay here as well," Windsor said pointing at Robbie and Kelly.

"No way," Kelly replied, "besides, the Baldwins might start shooting at you if they don't know you are with us."

"Fair enough," he said. "Well let's get moving then."

The two teams split up. One filing into the narrow alley and the other moving into the dark parking lots across from the warehouses.

The fence ran back to a point where two buildings paralleled one another with their brick walls creating a dark chasm between. Two Section moved single file into the darkness listening to one another's footsteps over the gravel and dirt surface. Visibility gradually improved as their eyes adjusted to the limited moonlight slipping in through the narrow gap above. They moved carefully but the loud gunfire from nearby made total stealth unnecessary.

After passing several intersections where the chain link picked up, revealing the interior of the cluster of warehouses, they came to the last of the aged brick buildings. They could hear the rustling river a few hundred yards away, beyond the cranes and equipment of the wharf. In the moonlight, they could see a triangle opening where the fence had been cut and bent back against itself.

"Here it is," Robbie whispered.

The Leftenant nodded and signaled for the men to follow him through. Kelly, Robbie, and Clark ducked through last. They worked their way through the area behind the warehouses filled with crates and boxes stacked well above their heads. The shouts now were closer, and the gun shots had become less frequent. The Leftenant lined up against the wall of one of the buildings and the others followed his lead.

"Just there, I should think," the officer motioned with his head that he meant around the corner.

"Come on, grandma!" a male voice yelled from nearby. "You got plenty in there! All we want you to do is share!"

The answer came in a loud boom from a shotgun.

"Go on home, Sonny Jim!" Kelly heard a familiar voice yell. "There's nothing in here but some pissed off old ladies!"

"Sounds like they are holding their own," Kelly whispered.

"Shush," the Leftenant warned, "someone's coming."

The sound of footsteps stepping quickly through gravel preceded the appearance of two men around the corner. The men were bent over and moving fast but stood up as soon as they were out of the potential line of fire from the Baldwins. They adopted an easy gate and lowered their rifles not realizing they were walking within a few feet of the Marines, who were lined up in the darkness along the wall.

"Nick said it was over this way," the taller one said pointing at the opposite corner of the building. "Yea, here it is."

The men sauntered over to a steel ladder attached to the far side of the building.

"Get up there," the tall man said. "See what the hell is taking Dale and Earl so damn long."

"Those two are idiots," the shorter one said as he started up the ladder. "Probably fell off."

"You're right about that," the taller one said as he started up behind his friend.

When the men disappeared onto the rooftop, Robbie turned to Windsor and whispered, "We have to stop them! There is a ladder on the roof that goes down into the green house. They are trying to sneak in behind them!"

"O'Reilly, MacGregor," the Leftenant pointed, "go with Robbie and stop them from getting inside."

The three broke off and ran for the ladder. When Robbie peeked over the rooftop, he saw the two men making their way along the spine of the building towards the ladder in the center. "Be careful up here," he whispered back to the two Marines, "stay on the ridges. The flat spots are all glass for the greenhouse."

The three scrambled up just as the two men reached the hatch for the ladder.

"We have to stop them from going down," Robbie said.

O'Reilly lifted his rifle and took several quickly aimed shots at the two silhouettes ahead of them. The bullets hit their marks causing the men to fall over with a thump and clatter as they and their rifles hit the metal and glass roof.

Kelly looked up when she heard the shots but couldn't see beyond the parapet over her head. The noises had instantly led to more shooting and shouting down below as the men behind the trucks tried to figure out what was happening on top of the warehouse. Kelly wanted to rush out into the loading area and start bashing their heads with her heavy bow-staff but realized this wasn't a very sensible plan. She took a deep breath and looked over at the Leftenant, hoping he had something more practical in mind.

Windsor turned back from spying around the corner and signaled for everyone to come closer. He looked over at the two Marines, Kim and Bevins, and focused on them. "We need to get to the other side," he said quietly, pointing to the dark space behind the warehouse directly across from them. "From there we will have them pinned down when One Section moves into position."

He turned to Kelly. "Wait here. We will come back for you, after we clear them out."

"Screw that," Kelly said, "I'm coming with you. I'm going to bash some heads."

Windsor clearly wasn't used to having his orders questioned but he didn't have time to argue. He paused for a beat then glanced over at Clark who just shrugged his shoulders. The young officer turned back to Kelly. "Fair enough. Stay with Mr. Clark in the back of the stack. Listen to him. Stay down and keep quiet until I say otherwise. Understand?"

"Yes, Sir," Kelly said with a mock salute.

Windsor nodded as if he was still unsure about bringing her along, but since time was short, he turned to the others. "Right. On me. Move out."

The small group kept low, running single file through the shadows between the buildings. If any of the attackers noticed the line of figures slipping past them in the darkness, they didn't respond. Once the Marines reached the other side, they stretched out along the warehouse wall there. Clark guided Kelly into position, and they waited for Windsor to give the next order.

"Oh Jesus! Oh Jesus!" an injured man cried as he lay in the darkness of the rooftop, "Bitches shot me! Tok you ok?! Tok?!"

Tok didn't answer and the man continued to moan in pain as Robbie and the Marines crept up along the same path. They kept low to avoid creating any profiles for any shooters down below. As they neared the hatch, they spotted a pair of boots with the toes pointing down into the mud. The body connected to the boots lay motionless. Beyond the boots they spotted another figure writhing on one of the large plate windows.

"Nick!?" the writhing man called as he saw them approach, "is that you? Bitches shot me. Got Tok, and those two idiots too I think!"

Without hesitating O'Reilly snapped off two more rounds at the man at close range. The rounds slammed through his body and the glass underneath causing it to burst, sending him crashing to the garden below in a shower of glass.

"Sir." Corporal Kim got the Leftenant's attention as he hustled back from scouting the other side of the warehouse. "Looks like they have their getaway trucks parked on that side. Up near the gap between the buildings."

"Sentries?" the Leftenant asked.

"Five blokes, I could see, milling around with rifles," Kim went on. "But they aren't looking this way. All the action at the other warehouse has their attention."

"Any cover between here and there?" the Leftenant asked.

"Yes, Sir," Kim said, "a bunch of old Lorries backed up to the loading bays. Pallets and trash cans all over as well."

Windsor hesitated, thinking.

"We could move up behind them on that side," Clark suggested. "It would also get us out of the crossfire, if One Section starts shooting when they move down from the street."

"Indeed," Windsor agreed and looked at Kelly, "I don't suppose I could convince you to wait here?"

"Hell no," Kelly answered.

"Right then," he turned. "Let's move."

Chapter 31

Robbie peeked over the edge of the roof and saw a row of pick-up trucks lined up across from of the Baldwins' main warehouse. Several of the trucks bore the scars of being pelted by buckshot. Their windows were blown out, tires flat and sides pock marked with tiny holes. Men moved carefully in the shadows behind the vehicles. They were only lit up occasionally by the flashes of their muzzle fire.

"How many?" O'Reilly asked as he slid up next to Robbie on the precipice.

"I don't know," Robbie replied. "Maybe ten?"

"MacGregor?" O'Reilly cast the same question to his fellow Marine.

"Oh, aye." The Scotsman answered while he looked down on the attackers through his rifle sites. "Maya teen o' twalve."

Robbie cast a confused look at Corporal O'Reilly.

O'Reilly smiled, "he says you're right. Ten or twelve."

"Is that too many?" Robbie asked.

"Es jos a rdaht nombr," MacGregor said.

Robbie looked back at O'Reilly.

"He says its fine," O'Reilly translated as he sighted in his own rifle.

Windsor wound Two Section through the old vehicles and stacks of rotting pallets. Thirty yards or so ahead of them, several trucks sat idling. Near one of the trucks, a big red Ford F-250, stood two men with hunting rifles. They occasionally swept a glance over the loading areas and driveway, but their attention was mainly on an alley that ran between warehouses. Cigarettes hung from their lips, and they seemed bored, as they waited for their companions to flush out the old ladies. Their casual manner indicated they might have done this sort of thing many times before.

Kelly was surprised to see that they were dressed so casually. Both wore t-shirts and jeans with no external protection against zombies. One wore cowboy boots while the other had on a pair of sneakers. She supposed, driving around in a big truck all the time, you wouldn't have to worry so much about getting bit or scratched by the undead.

Windsor indicated for everyone to get down as three men they hadn't seen previously walked out of one of the warehouses. They said a few words to the men at the truck before turning and starting to walk directly towards the Marines. The small group hunkered behind whatever they could find as the men approached.

"Hey! Who the hell are you!?" a voice called from behind the Marines.

Kelly spun to see a man standing on one of the loading docks. He must have walked through the warehouse and come out through the delivery area, after they had gone by. He seemed as surprised to see them as they were him, but his hesitation proved his undoing. Two pops from Corporal Kim's rifle sent the man stumbling backwards to the ground.

The men who had been walking towards them shouted and ducked behind a row of metal trash bins.

"Who the hell is that?!" One of them shouted.

"I don't know," another responded, "but I think they got Skillet!"

The men began firing their rifles in the direction of the Marines, but it didn't seem they knew where to shoot in the darkness. Their rounds blasted randomly into stacks of crates and rattled through rusting truck bodies.

"Steve! Kurt!" One of the men behind the bins shouted to the two who had scrambled behind the trucks. "We got them pinned down! Go through the warehouse and flank 'em!"

The two men sprinted from behind the trucks and through the open door, vanishing inside the huge brick building.

Windsor, who had previously signaled for the Marines to stay down and hold their fire, now gave the 'go-ahead' sign. Kim and Bevins immediately slid around their cover and began peppering the trash cans with bullets. The small rounds plinked and clicked as they punched holes through the cylinders. The men who had taken cover behind the thin metal, realized their mistake too late.

"Ah, shit!" One of them yelped in pain as a bullet struck him. The other jumped up and began running back towards the trucks. Kim and Bevins had no mercy for the retreating figure. They kept up their fire until he dropped his rifle and crumbled to the ground.

Peeking around from her hiding place, Kelly saw the man collapse face first into the dirt driveway.

With the men in front down, the Leftenant shouted, "Two coming through the warehouse. Cut them off at the loading dock!"

Kim and Bevins jumped up and ran for the plastic covered doors at the back of the building. The once clear plastic curtains were covered in mold making it impossible to see inside. Kim grabbed the heavy partition and pulled it back. When nothing immediately rushed out at them, Bevins burst ahead into the dark warehouse with his weapon raised to his shoulder. Kim followed immediately behind.

The place smelled like old dirt and long dry manure. A few holes in the roof let in enough moonlight that, after their eyes adjusted, they could see they were surrounded by pallets stacked high with something resembling sandbags. Tucking in against the nearest pallet, they waited for the swish of the plastic curtain to quiet behind them. When the clatter had ended, Kim nudged Bevins and they began their steady heel to toe movement towards the front of the dark warehouse.

Robbie heard the rate of gunfire increase. This time from several directions. He recognized the suppressed fire of the Royal Marines' weapons. It was soon joined by the loud bangs of the attackers' hunting rifles.

"What the hell?!" Someone yelled from down below. Men scuttled back and forth behind the trucks as they tried to escape the deadly rounds. Bullets had started coming in from both of their sides.

"Dammit! They got around us," a man yelled, "Nick! They're killing us!"

"Form up behind the trucks on the left and right!" a loud voice yelled. "Blast the hell out of them!"

Robbie saw men moving into position but before they could begin effectively returning fire, they began to fall victim to the Marines' disciplined and accurate shots. Their bodies tumbled and spun as they were filled with lead even as they approached their new lines.

"We gotta move Nick!" Someone yelled. "There's no cover here!"

Windsor rose and advanced in a crouch towards the pock marked trash bins. On the other side, he found a man lying on his back in the dirt. His shirt was ripped with small holes and covered in blood. His rifle lay at his feet where he had dropped it. The Leftenant picked up the rifle and handed it to Clark who had moved up with him. Clark quickly checked the rifle, unloaded the round in the chamber and popped out the magazine with practiced hands.

"We need to move up into position to support One Section," Windsor said. They could all hear the gunshots increasing on the other side of the building. The Leftenant scampered over to the man lying face down in the dirt. He grabbed the man's foot and unceremoniously pulled him off the rifle underneath him.

"Careful, Sir," Clark warned.

"Dead," Windsor said pointing at the man's pale face. Windsor then quickly unloaded the rifle and lay it back down in the dirt.

Whispers and footsteps carried from the far side of the warehouse. It sounded like the men were walking straight down the middle of the room and not doing much to be stealthy. Bevins signaled that he would take a position between the pallets while Kim should remain and cover the main aisle. Kim agreed, and they each drew back into the stacks to let the marauders walk into their ambush.

A few seconds later, Kim saw movement in the darkness and the shapes of two shadowy figures approaching. They were hunched over as if trying to keep low but the crunch of their boots on the dirty floor negated any efforts to be undetected. Kim lined up his rifle on one of the silhouettes and readied his first shot. He took a deep breath and began to let it out as he squeezed the slack out of his trigger.

"Aaaah!" A surprised shout interrupted him. The shout was followed by the sound of something heavy falling and spilling onto the ground.

The two raiders responded by opening fire in the direction of the noise. Their muzzle flashes lit them up, giving Kim a clear shot at his first target. He popped off several rounds dropping one man to the ground. The second man didn't notice his companion go down behind him and kept firing into the darkness. Kim pivoted to line up another shot when an expanding cloud of dust roiled out into the aisle. He fired several rounds into the spot where the man had been standing but had no idea if he had hit anything.

After firing, Kim leapt to his feet and ran back into the maze of pallets calling out to his friend. "Bevins!?"

Scrambling around a corner he ran into the thick dust cloud that was spreading out over the warehouse. Squinting and coughing, he pressed forward. Rubbing his eyes with one hand and leading with his rifle in the other, he moved through the thick sheets of dust. Ahead, the shadows of two figures kneeling on the floor emerged. They seemed to be digging in a pile of dirt where one of the stacks of pallets had collapsed. Coming up behind the first, a man in grimy coveralls came into focus.

"Oy?!" Kim shouted as he got closer.

When the man didn't answer Kim stepped up and shoved his boot hard into his back. The man tumbled over, spun around to face him, and let out a growl. The thing's dead face was covered in fresh blood. As it began struggling to rise up and attack this new living meat Kim took a moment to look at the other one. It seemed to still be focused on whatever was buried in the dirt. It looked up at him and scowled through bloody teeth as if to warn him against trying to take away its meal.

"Got ya some rats their boys!?" Kim said as the one in the coveralls rolled down the pile towards him. He fired two rounds. The first hit center mass, causing Kim to curse, and did nothing to slow the creature. The second shot zipped through the skin just above its ear, causing its already loose scalp to flip up.

"Bloody fuck," he cursed again as he backed away from the thing, frantically blinking to clear the dust from his eyes. It kept coming and he lined up on its head to fire again.

The shot went wide as he was shoved from the side and sent sprawling down an aisle between the pallets.

"You little shit!" An angry figure shouted from the veil of dust and darkness.

Kim spun, struggling to get his rifle turned around as the figure came closer.

"I'm gonna bash your head in!" A large man with a metal bat emerged and drew it back to strike as he came into melee range.

Kim was tangled in his rifle strap, so he fired a shot. He knew it would miss but hoped it would cause the man to react by dodging away and give him time enough to get free. The man jumped aside but only for a second. Not long enough.

He brought the bat down on Kim's chest plate. The body armor protected him, but the force of the blow still knocked the wind from him and sent pain jetting across his ribs. He groaned and struggled to get the rifle strap to give. The second blow hit his helmet from the side, ringing his head like a bell. As the man brought the bat up again Kim realized the rifle wasn't going to help and spun away in a panic. The next blow hit him hard on his back plate as he tried desperately to wriggle out of range.

"Goddamn! I'll teach you to fuck with me!" The man shouted angrily. "Yer gonna die, Army boy!"

Good to his word the man continued swinging the bat as Kim twisted and spun frantically to avoid being hit. Sometimes it worked. Others, he felt the bat's impact. Sometimes it struck his armor and others it slammed into other areas. The bat slammed hard into his arm and the pain was so intense he began to hope the man would finish him soon. He knew he couldn't take much more.

There was a pause in the attack and Kim opened his eyes to see the man had stepped back. He wiped his forehead with a scowl.

"Whew," he panted, "kicking your ass is wearing me out."

The man suddenly screamed and reeled sideways. At his feet knelt the zombie that had been pursuing Kim just moments before. The thing had bitten down on the man's leg, tearing at a chunk of the flesh through his dirty jeans.

"God damn!" The man howled as he tried to hop away from the biting thing. He swung the bat down and impacted with its shoulder, but it held on tight.

While the man fought the zombie, Kim struggled painfully over and propped himself back against a pallet. Rising gingerly to his feet, he was finally able to get the strap untangled and lift up the rifle.

The man saw him standing and screamed with desperation in his eyes, "shoot it! Goddamn! Get it off me! Shoot it!"

Kim fired. He hit the struggling man center mass, sending him careening backwards. The creature held on tight, continuing to rip and pull at the denim as his quarry tumbled to the ground. The man stared up, wide eyed with surprise and fear, as his life drained away through the hole in his chest.

"No, no, no!" He wheezed, ineffectually slapping at the thing. His strength draining into the dark pool spreading from beneath his body. "I don't die! I don't die! Goddamn it!"

Kim limped carefully around the two. Hugging the wall of pallets to keep out of either's reach. The man's wild eyes glanced up, desperately pleading, as he went past but the creature ignored him, seeming entirely focused on keeping a solid grip on the meal he had just found.

When Kim reached the crossing aisle he looked back at the man, now recognizing him as the marauder who had been swallowed up by the dust just a few minutes before. The man writhed and clawed weakly at the dirt around him trying to pull himself from the thing latched onto his leg.

Kim sighed, raised his rifle, and shot both, man and thing, in the head. Bam! Bam! The two figures jerked and slumped to the ground as the bullets passed through their brains. He didn't do it for revenge, or mercy. He didn't blame the man for the injuries he caused. To him, the desperate people out in the wastelands had become animals themselves.

Like the rest of the world, humans were returning to their natural state. Neither animal nor undead could be blamed for doing what was in their nature. He ended them with as much feeling as one might have for killing a poisonous snake that had ventured into his yard. He just didn't want to risk having more zombies in the dark warehouse to worry about later.

Kim watched them for a moment. When he was sure neither was coming back, he turned away and stepped down the aisle into the dusty darkness. He called out quietly. "Bevins?"

He heard the sound before he saw its source, the snarling snapping of lips and teeth. When he got closer, he could see the zombie had dug a hole into the pile of dirt and was clawing out gobs of bloody looking meat. The thing did not notice him approach and continued with its feast.

Kim's heart sank when he realized what was likely under that mound of dirt. He took a deep breath to stave off any emotion that might try to overcome him. But his eyes watered anyway as he withdrew his large knife from its sheath. Stepping up behind the undead thing he shoved the knife into its temple and jerked it out again as the creature fell over and rolled down the pile. He grabbed its dirty boots and pulled it away, so he had better access to the mound, then sank to his knees and started digging.

"Go!" the voice that Robbie assumed was Nick's called. "Get back to the goddam trucks!"

The men who were still hiding behind the trucks turned and began running toward the narrow gap in the warehouses behind them. O'Reilly and MacGregor fired from the roof as the retreating group exposed themselves. One went down and at least two more howled from hits but kept moving. Robbie and the Marines ducked down as the last man into the gap turned and fired up at them before he disappeared into the darkness. The shots went wide but when they looked up again the men had retreated out of sight.

Kelly had followed Clark up to the first body where he had signaled for her to wait until they had disarmed the other man. She crouched in the shadows leaning against the trash cans watching for any approaching threats. She jumped when the "dead man" in front of her gasped and blood gurgled from his mouth. For a moment she thought he might be coming back as an undead, but something made her pause rather than immediately crushing his head.

The man's eyes blinked, and he turned his head to look at her. "Wait…wait." He gurgled. "It was in the other drawer. I told her. Wait." Then the light went out of his eyes completely and his face rolled aside into the grey sand.

Kelly didn't have time to contemplate the man's last words. Several armed men came rushing through the alley between the buildings. She scrambled around to the back side of the flimsy cans and lay prone. Windsor and Clark were caught out in the open and dove quickly to the ground. The only cover they had was the body of the man they had just shot, and they scrambled to get behind him. Luckily, the men were moving fast and didn't slow down to aim as they fired off several rounds.

The lead men jumped into the idling trucks and, with little regard for those behind them, stomped on the accelerators. Those following barely had time to leap into the beds of the moving trucks as they spun out of the parking lot.

One man did yell a belated warning for their companions as they roared away. "Steve! Earl! Run!"

Clark fired several rounds from his pistol at the retreating vehicles. It took Windsor a few seconds to get his rifle back up, but he was able to get off a few shots into their dusty wake. They heard metal ting and glass shatter but weren't able to tell if they hit any more of the assailants. The trucks continued moving away.

Robbie heard the roar of engines as the men started, what must have been, their escape vehicles on the other side of the next warehouse. The sound of squealing tires followed as they ripped through the gravel and asphalt parking lot towards the front gate. A few more pops were heard as the Marines on the ground fired on the retreating vehicles. There was a crash at the front gate which Robbie assumed was them pushing through the two vehicles they had left there, followed by their roaring into the night.

After a minute of silence, Bradley's loud voice broke the quiet. "Friendlies moving up! Hold your fire!"

The group who had come in the front gate moved through the patches of moonlight and swiftly behind the abandoned and battered trucks. They spread out clearing the alley and checking the bodies scattered there.

"Two Section report?!" Colors bellowed into the night.

"Sergeant Bradley?" a female voice replied. "I'm coming through the alley. Don't shoot."

A moment later, Kelly stepped into the moonlight with her hands raised.

Major Garrett was crouched behind one of the disabled trucks and looked back to watch her approach. "Kelly?" He looked worriedly past her. "Where are Windsor and the others?!"

"They chased a couple of guys into that warehouse," Kelly lowered her hands and nodded at the building behind her. "Clark said to come tell you."

"Right," the Major said. "Colors, Simmons. Will you go help cover the doors to that warehouse. Don't let any bad guys in or out."

The two Sergeants nodded and turned towards the alley.

"And Sergeants," the Major added, "don't go in there unless the Leftenant knows. Yes? We don't need friendlies shooting each other in the dark."

"Aye, Sir," one of them said as they stalked away into the shadows.

"Kelly," the Major shifted his gaze, "everyone ok? What happened over there?"

"Our people, your Marines, are all ok I think," she said. "They took down a couple of guys out back of the warehouse. I'm pretty sure they are dead. Two others ran inside. Windsor sent, um, the Asian guy and the kid with the freckles in after them. A bunch of them took off in trucks just now. Not sure if any of them were hit. But I think they got away." She paused and added. "Sorry."

"Not to worry," the Major consoled her. "They are out of our hair for the moment and, with a bit of luck, haven't got any reinforcements nearby."

"Not sure my luck works like that lately," Kelly sat down and leaned on the truck next to the officer.

"Yes, well, we can cross that bridge when - and if - we get to it." He replied. "As for now, perhaps you can signal your friends inside to let them know the bad guys are gone and they can stop shooting?"

"Yea, good idea," Kelly turned around and rose just enough to peer over the hood of the truck.

All the warehouses were similar. The one the Baldwins were using as their home and fortress didn't look any different from the others from out here. Its long brick façade was broken up by several small barred windows, a set of steps and doorway to the office in the middle, and large loading bays at either end. The rolling steel doors covering the loading docks were pocked with small black holes where they had recently been peppered with bullets.

"Beatrice!" Kelly shouted. "Sunshine! Hold your fire! We ran them off! Those guys are gone!"

"Who the hell is out there, man!?" The familiar voice of Sunshine called from inside.

"It's Kelly and Rob!" Kelly shouted back. "We thought you might need some help!"

"You got that right, man!" Sunshine yelled back.

"Kelly is that really you?!" Beatrice shouted.

"Yes, Ma'am," Kelly answered, "Robbie is here too. He's up on your roof!"

There was a long pause.

"You tell Robbie he best gets down from there before he hurts hisself again," Beatrice finally said with genuine concern.

"Yes, Ma'am," Kelly laughed. "That's a good point."

"Who else you got with you?!" Beatrice called.

"It's a long story but they are friends," Kelly shouted. "Can we come in?"

"What happened to those hoodlums?!" Beatrice questioned.

"We ran them all off I think!" Kelly shouted back, "except for a few who are dead."

"Good!" Bea's voice called.

"Ok, just a minute!" Sunshine responded. "I need to unblock the door."

Simmons spotted the bodies of the dead marauders laying in the driveway as he came out of the alley. He marked them but they looked dead enough. He kept his rifle to his shoulder and scanned the area for other threats as Bradley came out behind him, doing the same. The two had worked together long enough that they did it on instinct with little verbal communication required between them. Both were veterans of Afghanistan and Iraq, before the undead had risen, and walked into dangerous situations like this with a practiced intensity that many might call calm.

They spread out several yards apart and took positions that gave them a good view of both the front entrance and the rear loading area. The old front door hung open on its rusty frame giving them a narrow view into the space. The two Marines had just settled into their cover when movement inside caught their attention. Their rifles lined up on a silhouette moving towards the doorway.

A moment later a man stepped carefully into the threshold and paused to look left and right outside. He carried a pistol with a two-handed grip and came out of the building with it pointed down at the low ready. Seeming confident that there were no immediate threats the man turned and began moving towards the alley from which Simmons and Bradley had just emerged.

"Clark," Bradley called out in a low voice.

Mr. Clark seemed startled as he turned to face them but kept the pistol pointed at the ground. "Colors? Is that you?"

Bradley and Simmons emerged from their hiding places and jogged over to where Clark stood.

"What have you got?" Colors said with concern.

"Bit of a situation inside." Clark replied. "Come with me."

Clark lead the two back into the warehouse and, though it was dark, he moved quickly through a maze of offices and storage spaces until he pushed through a door into the main warehouse.

Bradley and Simmons didn't like moving through unknown territory so quickly, but they trusted Clark so did their best to keep up.

"You clear all these rooms, bruv?" Simmons asked as he stepped from the narrow, cluttered offices into the huge room stacked high with pallets teetering with what looked like bags of earth.

"Yes," Clark said off handedly, "the Leftenant and I did."

"Is the Leftenant ok?" Colors asked with concern as Clark led them into the maze.

"Yes, "he's fine." Clark answered striding ahead so fast the more cautious, slower moving Marines were in danger of losing him.

"Blast!" Simmons cursed after bumping into one of the towers of pallets. The slight impact kicked up a cloud of dust and a small avalanche of dirt spilled down from above.

"Watch out!" Clark admonished backtracking to them. "These bloody things aren't stable. Now, come on. We need to hurry."

Bradley and Simmons glanced at each other and, though they couldn't see each other's eyes in the darkness, both knew the other had a face that asked, 'what the hell is going on'?

"Where is Major Garrett?" Clark asked over his shoulder.

"He and Kelly are out front trying to parlay with the old ladies." Bradley answered as they slid through another narrow gap. Dust and dirt rained down while they jostled through.

"Good. Ah! Here we are." Clark said before rushing around a corner. To someone they could not yet see, he said, "Sir, I have Sergeant Simmons and Color Sergeant Bradley!"

The two Marines rounded the corner to find Windsor and Kim on their knees in a huge mound of dirt where it looked like one of the huge stacks of pallets had collapsed.

"Going to need your help, Simmons," Clark pointed down into the pile.

As they drew nearer, they saw the face and shoulders of a figure that had been partially dug out of the earthen pile. It was so covered in dirt that it took them two steps closer before they recognized it.

"Bevins!" Both Sergeants said almost together.

Simmons leaped forward and shouldered in next to Windsor to look the boy in the face. He saw his eyes were open and began scrambling at his pack to pull out his med kit. "Bevins, you with me bruv?!"

Bevins cracked a pained smile. "Sorry Sarge. Made a mess of it. Knocked the bloody pallets over."

"Don' you worry, bruv," Simmons said looking down at him. Even in the dim light the medical sergeant could tell that Bevin's face was pale. Unscrewing his water bottle, he poured some onto his face to clear the dirt from his eyes, nose, and mouth. "That better? Don't worry. We're going to get you out of here."

Simmons looked back at Kim and the Leftenant who sat there motionless. He realized he was going to have to get them moving. "Sir," he put his hand on Windsor's shoulder to get his attention, "I'm going to need some help digging him out so I can see if he has other injuries."

Windsor looked back at him and weakly motioned to a hole in the dirt in the spot where Bevins right leg would likely be. The hole was coated in blood and gore. Simmons squinted inside and thought he could see bone even in the low light.

"What, the…" Simmons' question trailed off as Windsor turned his head and nodded to another body laid out in the aisle nearby. Its drawn features, clawed hands and threadbare clothes made what it was, or had been, almost certain. "Is that a…?

"Yes." Windsor said before he could finish the question.

"And he already…"

"Yes." Windsor answered again, flatly.

"Fuck!" Simmons spit. His head spun through his medical training for something, anything, but he could think of nothing. Finally, unwilling to give up he began digging into the pile. "Let's get him out of this dirt. I need to see the wound."

"What's going on Simmons?" Bradley had taken up a security position and looked back at them from a few steps away.

"Might have a bite," Simmons replied. "Need to get him out to put eyes on it."

"Roger that," Bradley said. "I've got your six."

Windsor and Kim began digging and they soon had Bevins' body uncovered.

"Is it bad?" Bevins winced.

"It's too dark to tell in here," Simmons said, though he could see well enough that the boy's thigh was shredded. "Let's get you outside. Leftenant, Mr. Clark, Corporal Kim give me a hand."

"I'll clear the way," Bradley said, moving ahead to cover their exit.

"One, two, three!" Simmons counted, and they lifted Bevins up. Quickly carrying him back around the maze of pallets, through the dark offices and out into the moonlight. "Right here, right here," the medic announced causing the group to lay the wounded man down gently onto the hard dirt.

The added light of the moon only confirmed what he feared. The undead thing had dug down and clawed out strips of meat from Bevins leg.

"How does it look Doc?" Bevins groaned.

"Not so bad. How does it feel?" Simmons went about cleaning and wrapping the wound even though he knew it wouldn't help. The boy would be dead and reanimated long before there was there was a risk of any normal infection setting in. "Does it hurt?

"No, can't feel it at all." Bevins stared up at the sky. "Can't even feel my legs, I think. Cold. Just feeling a little cold, Sarge."

"You sure," Simmons asked, "I can give you some pain killers."

"Nah," Bevins whispered, "don't waste 'em on me."

Simmons finished wrapping the gauze and sat back on his heels. Looking over at Windsor he shook his head.

"Christ on the Cross," Windsor answered and grabbed the boy's hand. "Bevins you are one hell of a Marine and It's been an honor to serve with you."

"Thank you, Sir," Bevins replied, "sorry I botched it."

"Bollocks!" Windsor said. "You got our asses through so many tight spots. You are one of the bravest bastards I've ever seen. It's not your fault the damn world is falling apart. I sent you in that warehouse. It's my fault…and I'm really, very sorry, you did everything… everything, right."

"Don't blame yourself, Sir," Bevins whispered. "You never know when your number is going to come up. The Lord's got a day and time for all of us. I just wish I could have gotten home with you."

"Ah, bloody fuck" Windsor sighed. "We'll come back for you, I swear it."

"Nah," Bevins tried to smile. His gums had darkened to a deep purple and seemed to shrink away from his teeth. "Don't swear that, Sir. I'll be fine. You get the rest of the lads home, yea? Besides, it's not so bad here."

Bevins face seemed to grow whiter as they watched. Blue arteries were visible through his cheeks. Dark rings circled his eyes.

"Is there anything we can do for you?" Windsor asked.

"No, Sir," Bevins mumbled. "I can feel it inside me. Nothing to be done now. Just let me lay here and look at the moon. Tell the rest of the lads I said goodbye. I'll see them on the other side, and all that rot."

"Of course," Windsor agreed.

"Michael?" Bevins asked.

"I'm right here," Kim leaned in closer.

"Did you kill those bastards?"

"Yea, brother," Kim answered. "I bloody got all of them."

"Good… Will you do me too?" Bevins asked. "When it's time?"

Kim looked at his friend, eyes frightened and his head shaking. "I'm sorry, I don't think I can do that."

"It's ok bruv," Bevins wheezed, "don't sweat it."

"It won't be long," Simmons whispered to the Leftenant.

"You should all go, Sir," Bradley said from where he kneeled watching their surroundings. "I'll do it when the time comes."

"No." Windsor said with a deep breath and patted Bevins on the chest. "I won't put that on anyone else." He tried to sound upbeat. "I'll take care of it, Corporal, and I'll damn sure put you in for a medal when we get home."

Bevins mouth twitched in a smile.

Rob stood at the peak of the roof talking to Kelly and the Major down below. They had moved out from behind the battered trucks and stood in the drive waiting for the Baldwins to get the warehouse door open. When the heavy door finally slid open Kelly looked up and shouted, "Climb down and meet us inside!"

"Will do," he said back. "Tell them not to shoot us."

"I'll try to remember," Kelly winked.

Robbie pointed at the hatch said, "this way, guys."

Kelly waved as she and the Major disappeared under the eave.

Robbie lead O'Reilly and MacGregor down the winding staircase and into the fetid greenhouse. At the bottom they could see the spot where the man they had shot, had landed. The man lay crumpled and still in the flattened corn stalks. Looking up, Robbie could see several dark rectangles, framing the night sky in the greenhouse ceiling. He presumed these marked where the other two men had fallen through.

"See those holes in the roof," Robbie said pointing to the gaps in the ceiling, "I think those men he was talking about may have fallen through as well."

"We'll check it out, bruv," O'Reilly said. "You stay here."

The two Marines vanished into the darkness. Robbie could only tell the direction they went by the swishing sound of the tall corn stalks as they slid between them. When they were further away, even the sound of them moving through the thick undergrowth was imperceptible. A few minutes later from the far side of the large room, Robbie heard what sounded like a small bird calling. Then the room grew very quiet as he sat on the steps staring into the blackness, waiting.

"Clear," a voice whispered almost right next to Robbie's ear causing him to jump.

"Crap!" Robbie stuttered as he spun around to see the two Marines emerge from the foliage right behind him. "Did you find them?"

"Oh aye," MacGregor said in his brogue.

"Alive?" Robbie asked.

"Not anymore," O'Reilly responded holding up a bloody knife.

Robbie stood. "Alrighty then, should we go in and meet the others?"

"Wae she goo bock oop," MacGregor responded, "tak the hae grund."

It sounded like gibberish to Robbie, who asked. "What?"

"He says, we'll go back up and provide over watch," O'Reilly translated. "Make sure those bastards don't come back. Keep an eye out for the dead."

"Oh, yea that's probably a good idea." Robbie agreed.

"You go on inside," O'Reilly nudged him. "Just save us some tea and biscuits, yea?"

Bradley, Simmons, and Kim leaned on the walls of the alley, waiting. Kim fidgeted, shuffling his feet nervously in the soft dirt, and shifted back and forth under the weight of two rifles strapped over his shoulders. Bradley stood motionless, staring back into the open bay where they had left their three companions. Simmons smoked a cigarette that burned an orange dot in the shadows.

Windsor had asked them all to step away, so they didn't have to see Bevins' gruesome final moments. They had all seen friends go in much worse ways, but the officer insisted this memory not be piled onto all the others. Clark had refused to leave the young Leftenant unguarded but finally took a few steps away and turned his back.

Although they thought they were prepared, they jerked, when the bang of two rounds echoed off the brick and mortar walls around them. Bradley recognized the sound of the Leftenant's 9mm pistol. A few seconds later the crunching of heavy footsteps through gravel proceeded Windsor's approach. He marched past his men in the alley without a glance. His shoulders hunched forward and head down as he re-holstered his weapon.

A few steps behind, Clark followed with his own pistol in hand. He looked pensively at the trio as he came up to them. Stepping over to Bradley he held out a familiar green messenger bag. The Color Sergeant took it and looked quizzically at the civilian.

"Personal effects," Clark responded with a sigh, "along with ammunition and a few other items I thought better not to leave behind."

"Right." Bradley accepted the bag, throwing it over his shoulder. He pointed his thumb out into the wide driveway. "You sure it's sorted back there?"

"Indeed," Clark lowered his eyes.

"And what about the Leftenant?"

"He seems pretty shaken up right now," Clark replied."

"Well, we can't have him falling apart now, can we?" Bradley said as Clark started to walk away. "Keep an eye on him, yea?"

"I will," Clark held out his arms. "It's what I do."

He then hurried ahead to catch up with the young officer. The three enlisted Marines somberly fell into step behind, with Kim and Bradley walking backwards to cover their exit.

Kelly and the Major were standing at the warehouse door talking with Baldwins when the Leftenant emerged from the alleyway.

Beatrice saw him first and quickly lifted the big shotgun. "Stop right there!"

Garrett and Kelly spun to see Windsor come to a sudden halt.

"Ah," Garrett said calmly, "I see you have decided to join us Leftenant."

"Friend of yours?" Beatrice asked.

"Indeed," Garrett smiled and waved a hand at the younger officer. "Ladies may I introduce my executive officer, Leftenant Arthur Windsor of His Majesty's Royal Marines 4-3 Commando."

"Hey, he's handsome," Sunshine said.

"Well, let's not flatter the boy, Ms. Sunshine," Garrett said. "It might go to his head."

The Major went to meet Windsor and saw the sunken shoulders and blank look in his eyes as he drew closer. Gripping him by the shoulders he leaned in and whispered, "Steady lad, what's happened?"

"Bevins," Windsor said. "He was bit. I had to shoot him."

Garrett tightened his grip on Windsor's shoulders. His eyes narrowed as the news ran through him like ice water through his veins. Another lost comrade. Another man down. Another loss under his command. One less rifleman, in a campaign where there were already too few. He steeled himself from the loss as he had done many times before.

"Listen to me, Arthur," Garrett said. "You get a grip on yourself. Buck up and put your game face on, yes? Right now, we need to talk to these ladies and find out what they know about the area. There's nothing more we, or anyone, can do for Bevins. He was a good lad, but we must stay focused on the task in front of us. We must stay strong because the rest of the men are counting on us to get them through this. Push your feelings down. Put them in a box for now. Can you do that?"

Windsor shook his head yes, taking several deep breaths to push back the emotions threatening to explode through his chest.

"Command is a bitch, isn't it?" Garrett sighed.

Windsor nodded. "I've seen men die. I didn't think…"

"It's different when they die doing what you ordered them to do," Garrett said. "It rips your guts out, but you've got to post up and carry on. It's one of those things they can't teach you down at Lympstone."

As Windsor was collecting himself, Clark and the others emerged from the alley.

"Hey?!" Beatrice pointed her shotgun at the group. "Who is that?!"

Garrett glanced over the Leftenant's shoulder and raised his hands up. "Hold your fire. They are with us."

Looking back at Windsor. "Are you going to be ok Leftenant?"

"Yes Major," the younger officer gathered himself. "But I don't think I'm up for taking tea with the locals right now."

Color Sergeant Bradley approached the officers and saluted, "Gentlemen. We need to do a patrol of the area to make sure there aren't any stragglers. I'd like to take a few of the lads and sweep the area."

"Good idea, Colors," the Major said. "Leftenant why don't you go with them? I think Kelly and I can handle the formalities here."

"Yes," Windsor said with relief. "We should also see if we can get that front gate closed. With all that noise it won't be long before our hungry friends are back."

"Sir," Clark stepped up and spoke to Windsor, "I think Colors and the men should be able to handle that? Why don't we go inside and take a break?"

"I'm fine, Mr. Clark," the young officer replied, annoyed at his constant mothering. He took a deep breath before turning to the Sergeant and taking charge again, "Colors, get some men on policing up these bodies and stacking them outside the gates. We don't want them stinking up the place."

"Very good, Sir." Bradley replied.

"And Colors," the Major added. "Secure any weapons and ammunition they may have left behind as well."

"Aye Sir," the Sergeant agreed.

"C'mon inside you all," Beatrice said from behind them. "You and your friends better get on in here before they decide to come back."

"Go ahead, Major." Windsor said. "You too, Mr. Clark. The lads and I will wrap things up out here."

Clark gave Colors a questioning look.

"Don't worry, Mr. Clark," he said. "We will take care of him."

"Very well, Color Sergeant," the Major said finally. "Be careful and watch yourselves. We don't want any more casualties tonight."

"Right then," Colors called and began organizing the work, "One Section, Two Section, gather round…"

Robbie emerged from the greenhouse and found everyone in the building's office. Beatrice, Kelly, the Major, and Mr. Clark stood around a wooden chair where Sunshine sat holding a napkin to her forehead. The napkin was red, and a streak of blood ran down her cheek.

"What happened!?" Robbie asked. "Is everyone ok?"

"Just some splinters from the window frame man," Sunshine said.

Mr. Clark stood beside her, dabbing the wound with a sponge dipped in alcohol. "Fortunately, it's only a small cut. Nothing to worry about."

"I've got a really hard head," Sunshine smiled.

"I think the bleeding has stopped, now let's get that bandaged up, eh?" Clark took the napkin and replaced it with a wide bandage. "There you are. It will be right as rain in a few days, ma'am."

"Robbie," Kelly turned to him, "it was the group with the red truck. I saw it as they were leaving."

"From what the Baldwins are able to tell us, it sounds as if this group is making deeper and deeper forays into the city," the Major said.

"But why?" Robbie asked. "Why would anyone be roaming around down here? It's overrun with undead and most of the supplies expired ages ago."

"You don't know how desperate they may be," the Major replied, "and at any rate they have discovered this place now, which is as good as a gold mine for a group of scavengers." Turning to the Baldwins, he went on. "Ladies, I'm afraid they will be back, and most likely more prepared. You aren't safe here and really should find alternate accommodations."

"Fuck that man," Sunshine spat, "I'm staying right here. They ain't taking my farm. You can go if you want Bea, but I'm staying."

"I'll be staying as well," Beatrice squeezed her friend's shoulder. "We're too old to go running around out there. If they come back, they can have some more of our buckshot. They won't run us out."

"Besides," Sunshine said, "we gave 'em what for tonight. They're gonna' think twice before they come back here."

"Indeed," the Major said it as a question, his face showed he wasn't convinced. Before he could argue further the Color Sergeant walked in.

"Good evening, ladies," Colors said to the women. "Sorry to interrupt."

"Oh, you can interrupt any time," Sunshine smiled, "I just love those cute accents."

"Thank you, Ma'am," the Color Sergeant said uncertainly, before turning to the Major. "Sir, we found a few carbines and some ammunition on the raiders. What would you like to do with them?"

"Anything we can use?" the Major asked.

"Not really Sir," Colors replied. "It's all the wrong caliber and the rifles won't do us any better than what we have."

"Perhaps our hosts can use them?" the Major asked looking at Robbie and Kelly.

"I think the Baldwins will need them more than we will," Kelly said.

"Very good," the Major said. "Would you ladies like some rifles and ammunition? I'm afraid we can't vouch for the quality of any of it."

"I suppose it can't hurt," Bea said. You can just put them in the hallway."

Put them in the main hall if you please, Color Sergeant," Garrett said.

"Aye, Sir." Colors agreed.

"You ladies look like you know your way around firearms." The Major said with a nod to the pile of guns and ammunition the Baldwins had strewn out while defending the warehouse. "Do you need any assistance with these rifles?"

"I like my boom-stick, man," Sunshine answered holding up a pump action shotgun. Blows the shit out of everything!"

"Thank you Major," Beatrice said. "We were both raised on farms. I've been shooting coyotes and wild hogs since I could hold a gun. Sunshine there, might look like a hippie, peace freak but she can hit a deer in the eye at 200 yards. I think we can figure the rifles out."

"Is that so?" Garrett said, impressed.

"Damn right, man!" Sunshine responded.

"Very well then." The Major went on. "Colors, what is the situation outside?"

"I think the human threat are likely gone for the time being, but all the shooting is drawing the dead back into the area." The Sergeant answered. "If we are going to pick up our supplies and return to the flats tonight, we need to exfil quickly."

"That's our cue," the Major said turning to the Baldwins. "Ladies, I'm afraid we must be off. I do urge you to move to a different location as soon as possible."

"We appreciate your concern, Major," Bea said. "But we will be fine. Don't you worry about us."

"Color Sergeant, have you policed the area for any stragglers?" The Major asked.

"Yes Sir," Bradley replied. "No contacts, and we were able to get the gate mostly closed. We chained it up and pushed one of the trucks in front of it. It won't stop anyone who is really determined, but it should provide an adequate barrier to the undead wandering by. If nothing inside catches their attention."

"Quite," the Major nodded his appreciation. He turned back to the Baldwins. "Ladies, I suppose this is goodnight then."

"Thanks for rescuing us damsels in distress," Sunshine said with a wave and a hand on her bandaged forehead.

"Goodnight, gentlemen," Bea said and shook their hands as they went. "Thanks, again."

One by one, they stepped through the warehouse door and back onto the gravel driveway. Kelly was the last out and hugged the older ladies before she left.

"We will see you all again very soon," she promised.

She helped the Baldwins close the big door and listened as they relocked themselves inside. Once it sounded like all the latches and bolts had been thrown, she joined the others.

"Very resilient, those two." Clark said.

"They've made it this long," Kelly agreed with admiration for the ladies.

"Leftenant Windsor," the Major summoned the young officer who stood talking with Sergeant Simmons near the pock marked pick-up trucks.

"Major?" the Leftenant walked over to the group.

"This is your operation. Have you given any thought as to how we will get out of here?"

"Um..." Windsor paused.

The Color Sergeant leaned in and whispered. "I suggest we exit through the side gate where Two Section entered, Sir."

"Yes, Major." The Leftenant repeated. "We should depart through the hole in the side gate."

"Capital idea," Garrett approved, with a nod to the Sergeant. "We will follow your lead, Leftenant."

"Right, then," the Leftenant said, moving so he would be in front to lead the way. "Let's get the men moving, if you please, Colors."

"Right!" The Color Sergeant called to the men. "You bastards form up and get frosty! Take your squad positions! Let's move out!"

Kelly and Rob fell into step with the group as everyone spread out into their sections and began moving along the back of the warehouses. Each of them was soon swallowed up in the night, until they were just shadows moving through the morning fog. The chill of the evening still hung in the air as the light of the sun began to glow on the horizon in the east.

THE END

This is the end of book 1 – Worse than Dead. If you enjoyed this book please leave a review and stay tuned as the series continues, in book 2 – Less than Dead.

What people are saying about 'Worse than Dead'

"Worse than Dead" is a taut thriller that proves the undead aren't the only things to fear in the apocalypse. A fast-paced zombie story that explores the dark side of humanity's survival. Brett takes you inside the darkest areas of a zombie plague, where the undead aren't the only things to fear."

Ryan Thomas, author of <u>Hissers</u>, <u>The Summer I Died</u>, <u>Hobbomock</u>, and many others.

"Worse than Dead is an intense ride from start to finish. You can't help but enjoy each character as they show strength and weaknesses throughout an engaging story about surviving after the apocalypse."

Tyler Barrett, author of the <u>What Remains</u> series.

About the Author

Cal Brett is an author of horror and suspense fiction. While this is his first novel, he has previously published short stories (most recently in the 2020 Nano Nightmares compilation) and an independent film, called "Stiffs", is in production based on his story of the same name. He also has extensive experience in the very frightening realm of writing contracts, policy, analysis and training for government and military purposes. He is a retired Navy Chief Petty Officer who enjoys mountain biking, woodworking and bee keeping. He lives in the southeastern United States with his wife, two kids, a bunch of dogs and a fish.

PLEASE POST A REVIEW

Thanks for reading this book! If you enjoyed it, even a little bit, please post a rating and review on Amazon or the site where you purchased it. Reviews and ratings by readers keep our books in the algorithm and on the list of offered products. Without them our books will be lost in the abyss of Amazon's basement of the forgotten. Thanks again!

Made in the USA
Thornton, CO
12/04/23 22:34:39

ac0dd7c5-869f-4b24-904a-7aed2cf7a2fbR01